One Last Farewell

ISABELLE KANE

ONE LAST FAREWELL

ISBN: 978-1-953735-90-4

Published by Satin Romance
An Imprint of Melange Books, LLC
White Bear Lake, MN 55110
www.satinromance.com

Published in the United States of America.

Cover Design by Caroline Andrus

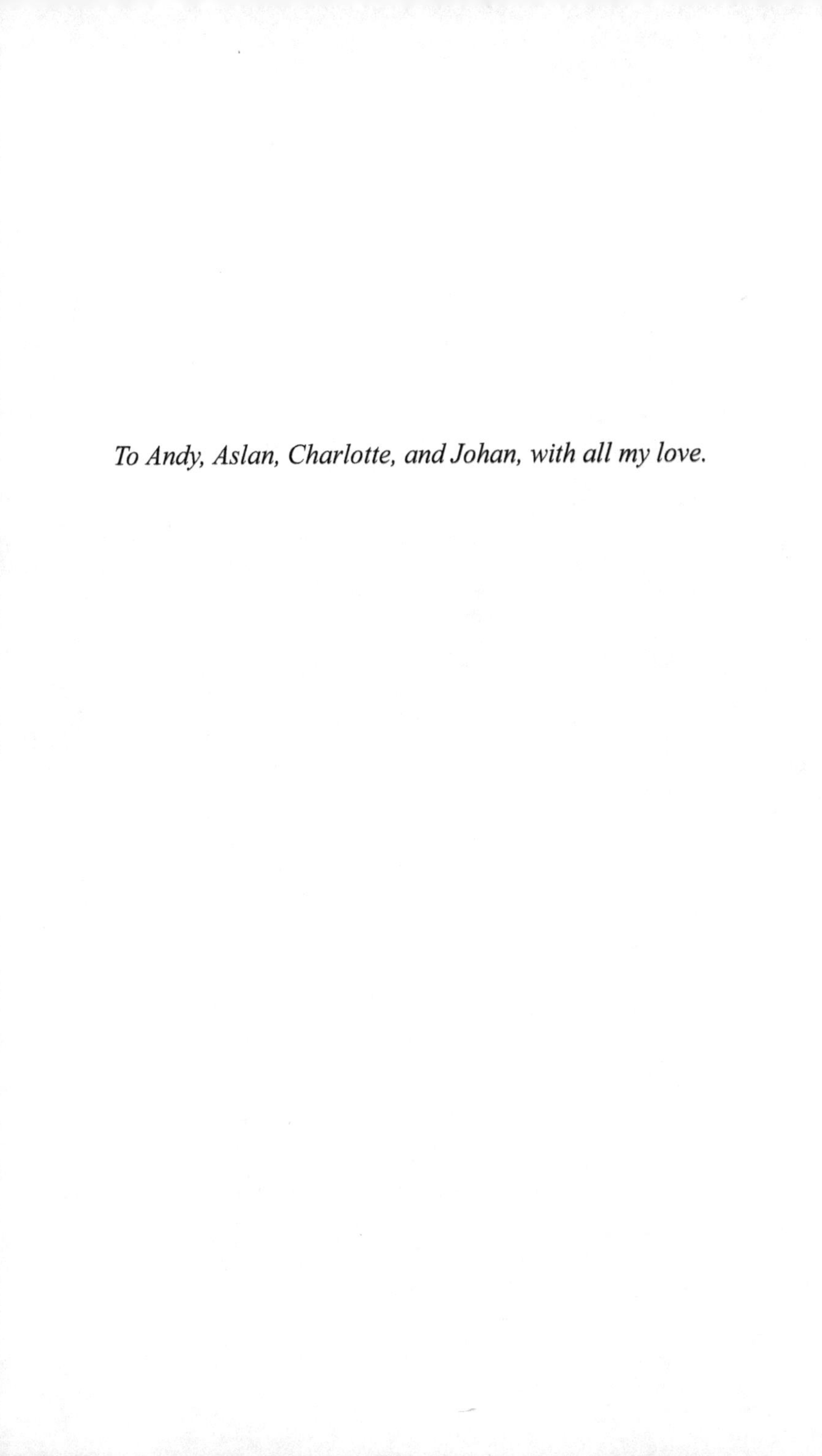

To Andy, Aslan, Charlotte, and Johan, with all my love.

PART I

CHAPTER 1

The scrambling sound of shod hooves striking cobblestones, of a panicking horse, quickened Krystyna's footsteps as she ran into the unlit stable. Her eyes were already accustomed to the darkness, so she could make out the great, muscled mass of her father's red bay breeding stallion, Thor, as he spun in his stall seeking to escape the intruder. There was a loud smack of a leather strap striking flesh. Thor kicked out, striking the wall. His eyes were white-rimmed with fear, and his nostrils flared with panic.

"Who's in there? Get out now! You're going to be hurt!" She hesitated to open the stall door, which, by some miracle, had remained closed despite the chaos within, because she knew a maddened horse would strike at anything and everything indiscriminately.

"I've got you!" The triumphant growl in Russian revealed the identity of the intruder.

"Ivan! Have you gone mad? Get out of there!"

"Yes! I have you now!"

Krystyna watched the darkened figures struggling for mastery over each other in the stall. Thor frantically swung his haunches about, trying to pull away, but Ivan's grip held firm at the rope looped around the horse's neck. He used his weight on the rope to anchor the frantic animal.

"Let go of him, Ivan! You've no right to be here!" Now that Thor was immobilized, Krystyna opened the stall door. Ivan slid the bridle over the trembling horse's head, and the bit into his mouth. "My father told you never to return here!" How she wished her father was here now, but she didn't dare run back to the house for him. Ivan and Thor would assuredly be gone by the time she returned.

Suddenly, perhaps in reaction to her words, Ivan began to jerk mercilessly on the reins, shooting white-hot agony through the bit into Thor's jaws.

"Get back, wench!"

Despite her escalating alarm, Krystyna stood her ground at the front of the stall. What she could see of Ivan was disturbing; his eyes were reddened and his clothing, soiled and rumpled.

"You have no business here! Leave now, and there's no harm done. If you hurt this horse, my father will see to it that you're punished."

"I'm not leaving this place empty-handed!" He tugged on the reins and made to push past her, but Thor lunged back, dragging him back into the stall. Ivan whipped at the stallion's sensitive flanks and belly with the leather reins in his hands. Thor reared up again and struck out with his front hooves. Krystyna raced to where a pitchfork hung on the wall just down from the stall. She grabbed it and hurried back. She held the smooth wooden staff with the sharp prongs aimed at the stall door. "You won't take him. I won't let you!"

"All of this should be mine; this estate, this horse, you. You robbed me! Cast me off, like a worthless serf. I am Ivan Bestuzhev, and I will not be disposed of lightly."

"So you come here drunk to steal my father's horse?" She was incredulous at the inanity of the situation. And she had once

believed herself in love with this fool. Obviously bitter about being cast off by the Sielskis, he had taken to liquid consolation and was much the worse for it. "There's no sense in what you're doing, Ivan. You will be caught. Just leave here now. You'll be glad of it in the morning."

If only someone would come, but it was already well past the dinner hour, and the grooms were sleeping in their cottage.

He dragged on the reins to pull the horse back out. "You are threatening me? You would hurt me? I think not!" With his forearm, he made to push the pitchfork aside.

She feinted at him. "Don't underestimate me."

He grinned, and she marveled that she could ever have found his dark eyes beautiful, those cruelly sensual lips appealing. It sickened her that she'd ever allowed him to touch her.

"Everyone knows this horse! You can't hide him."

"Your father! He should have forced you to marry me when I told him what we'd done together. He didn't believe me. He laughed at me. He threw me out like a dog! Your whole family will pay! All of this should have been mine!" He repeated this last bit with a fanatical edge to his voice, as if it was a lesson he'd learned.

Thor charged out of the stall. His great chest knocked the pitchfork from Krystyna's hands. She fell to the ground and sought to roll away amid the sparks shot out by the deadly shod hooves. She scrambled up and then flattened herself against the wall while man and horse fought to dominate each other.

Screaming, Thor threw his head high, lifting Ivan from his feet. Then, the stallion slipped on the cobblestones and went crashing down, the man disappearing under his bulk.

Suddenly, the barn was eerily silent. Snorting and shaking his head, Thor rose to his feet. Ivan lay like a discarded doll on the ground.

For a moment, Krystyna couldn't move, then she took one hesitant step forward, and then another. Ivan remained limp. To her horror, she saw his eyes were staring blankly up. The prongs of the pitchfork jutted out through his blouse and jacket, and a dark pool of seeping blood was already forming around his body.

There was no doubt. Ivan Bestuzhev was dead.

As the carriage jerked to a halt, Krystyna Sielska awoke abruptly. Out of sorts, she glanced about in a panic. Her breathing was harsh as she took in the darkened interior. She took a slow, deep breath, assessing her situation. It had been only a dream, a haunting memory of that horrible night when her former fiancé had met his tragic end. To diffuse any hint of scandal following the tragedy, her parents had sent her from her family's estate in the Polish countryside to her great-aunt Jadwiga who lived in the glittering capital of the Austrian Empire.

And now, after several weeks of travel, she had finally arrived at her destination, Jadwiga von Gebler's house in Vienna. A servant opened the carriage door wide, and she stepped out. She stared up at the darkened façade of her new home. Despite the recent trials and difficulties of her life, excitement stirred in her. It was time to begin a new period in her life.

CHAPTER 2

1791
Vienna, Austria

A Tartar manservant greeted her at the door and ushered her through the house into a drawing room. A fire roared in the marble fireplace, fending off the damp chill of a Viennese autumn in the air. The room was colorful; the walls were covered in a complex red and gold silk material. A richly hued oriental carpet covered the marble floor. Expensive tallow candles burned in the chandelier as well as in candelabra throughout the chamber, rendering it surprisingly light and welcoming after the darkness through which she had been traveling.

Suddenly a tiny dog darted out from behind an inlaid settee. The stout, little bundle was immediately upon Krystyna barking furiously. It dove for the hem of her traveling skirt. She gently tried to toe the beast away, but it wouldn't be swayed from its intent. She glanced about in consternation, but the Tartar manservant had disappeared.

"Sara… Sara! Behave yourself." A straight-backed figure of medium stature bustled into the room. "Krystyna, dear, I'm so very pleased you have arrived at last." Jadwiga von Gebler was well into her fifth decade of life. She had fine amber-colored eyes, unpowdered gray locks which she wore in a becoming though not elaborate style upon her head, and a disarmingly frank smile. There were deeply drawn lines of obstinacy in her forehead that were countered by an abundance of smile wrinkles at the corners of her mouth. Her lower jaw jutted out belligerently. She was outrageously attired in a daring rose silk that would have better suited a much younger woman. She had a fine shawl tossed over her shoulders, and though she wore no rouge or powder, she had an abundance of ostentatious gold jewelry about her wrists and ears, and a large diamond that dangled between her breasts and peaked out from beneath the shawl as she went after her dog.

"Come, Sara, that's enough. Don't mind her… Sara is convinced she must protect me." She chased the dog behind the settee. "You leave Krystyna alone, Sara," Jadwiga admonished, wagging her finger at the still growling dog. Then, she turned back to her great niece. She kissed her on both cheeks and scrutinized her.

"You have your mother's coloring, her lovely red-gold hair. You're very like her, except taller, of course. Your height comes from your father. Jozef was taller than I before his thirteenth birthday. It always annoyed me that I was the short one in the family. You have lovely eyes, the Sielski eyes, like my own and your father's. Welcome to my home, my dear girl. Please consider it your own."

"Thank you, Aunt Jadwiga, for allowing me to stay with you, especially under the circumstances."

Jadwiga shook her head determinedly. "We'll not discuss that unfortunate matter. It's over and done with. You're going to have a fresh start here. I'm delighted to have a member of my family visit me here, in Vienna, at last… Please, Sara, that is quite enough," she reprimanded her growling dog. "You must know I've been pestering your father for years to visit me. Vienna is my home now, and it's such an exciting place. My only regret is I miss my family. Jozef would so love the music, but he never can get away from his land and his horses. Well, you're here now. It'll be like having a daughter of my own."

"Thank you, Aunt Jadwiga. My parents sent this for you." Krystyna removed a small, silk pouch from her reticule and handed it to her aunt.

"A present." Jadwiga's face lit with child-like enthusiasm. "How dear!"

"It's from Mother and Father."

Jadwiga quickly worked the knots open to reveal a large, ornate amber and gold brooch. "Oh, it's lovely. Your mother knows my fondness for amber. I am pleased. And now, you must be famished. Pavel, have Edda bring us something to eat here. Krystyna, I hope you don't mind the informality, but it seems rather silly to move to the dining room at this hour. We'll be so much more comfortable in here."

The Tartar, who had remained in attendance at the door, inclined his head and soundlessly moved to obey his mistress's directions.

"Please, sit." Jadwiga curled up on the settee, and Krystyna settled opposite her great-aunt in an armchair. "So tell me about your parents."

Krystyna dutifully related all the news of her family and her home, a rural Polish estate called Sea of Grass. About fifteen minutes passed before a servant appeared bearing a tray. Krystyna had thought that she was too tired to be hungry. However, after she had had one taste of the chlodnik, a cold, creamy beetroot soup, she realized she was famished. She devoured the soup and then ate some of the cheese and bread. After she finished her meal, which Jadwiga had interrupted with many questions, the maid servant returned with a smaller silver tray on which sat two diminutive, cut crystal glasses as well as a crystal decanter filled with a clear liquor.

"Bring it here, Edda," Jadwiga ordered. The girl set the tray on the inlaid table beside Jadwiga, whose rings flashed in the firelight as she picked up the decanter. "It's zubrowka, vodka made from bison grass straight from Poland. We'll drink it tonight in honor of your visit." She poured the vodka into the two glasses and passed one to her great niece. Then, she held her own glass up. "To your visit, Krystyna. Na Zdrowie, on health."

"Na Zdrowie, Aunt." Krystyna raised her own glass then tossed the zubrowka back, as her father had taught her. She leaned back in the chair and allowed the warm, heady burn of the vodka to course through her. The two women passed an hour or so more in amiable discussion. Krystyna found herself warm, full and slightly intoxicated. For the first time in weeks, she felt both at peace and optimistic, and she looked forward to the next day.

CHAPTER 3

Jadwiga saw to it that Krystyna settled quickly and smoothly into her new life in Vienna. She introduced her niece to the Baroness von Reigler and her daughter, Marta, who was of Krystyna's age. Marta was warm-hearted and enthusiastic, and the two young women became friends. This was fortunate, as Jadwiga and the Baroness von Reigler were very close and often attended social functions together. On a particularly bright and sunny September afternoon, Krystyna and her Aunt Jadwiga accompanied the von Reiglers on a drive through the Prater, the imperial park in the center of the city, which the Empress Maria Theresa had opened to the public. It was a venue where the social elite of Vienna came to see and be seen by each other. There was just a hint of chill in the air, and so the women had opted to have the top of the landau opened.

Still, Krystyna found it difficult to breathe comfortably with her corset so tucked and tightened. In Poland, she'd worn a much looser, more comfortable style of dress. Nevertheless, it quite amused her to watch the riders and other carriages in the park. If weeks before someone had told her she would enjoy being carted about in a carriage at a parade pace, she would have laughed outright. She had always been more of the type to go for a gallop and savor the wind in her hair. But here, in Vienna, she was discovering new aspects of herself in her role as an eligible, young, Polish noblewoman.

Occasionally, and per the Baroness's instructions, she carefully inclined her head in polite recognition, so as not to disrupt the beribboned hat perched precariously atop her hair. She grinned at her friend, earning a reproving glance from the Baroness. Krystyna could see Marta shared her enjoyment. The younger von Reigler was adorably attired in lime silk, with a cunning matching hat. The ensemble set off her pale blond coloring, and her face was becomingly flushed with warmth and excitement.

The hawk-faced Baroness maintained her straight-backed, military posture and slightly bored expression while offering whispered comments to Jadwiga, who sat beside her and opposite the younger women. All four had opened up their parasols to give them refuge from the bright sun.

Krystyna had originally opposed this outing when the von Reiglers had suggested it: "But Aunt Jadwiga, it seems so silly, just to drive about in the Prater."

"No, dear girl, it's far from pointless. When you decide to buy a horse, what's the first thing you do?"

"You contact the dealers or breeders you know, and then you go and take a look at the animals they have available."

"That's exactly what you and the other young people will be doing. At some point, my child, you will have to consider marriage. Don't groan at me. It's my responsibility while you're here to see you encounter appropriate young men."

And so, the two of them sat, decorously arrayed, in the von Reigler landau, listening to the Baroness's running commentary.

"That's the Countess von Bis. She lives in a new palace her husband built for her on Linden Strasse. Georg von Bis is at least thirty years older than this wife and completely enamored. There! Did you see that? Did you see how she smiled at that cavalry officer? She is completely amoral. I would warrant there's a reason for the twinkle in her eye.

"There's Madame Bessenyi and her two daughters. Look at their ruddy skin. They have nothing to protect them from the sun. Their complexions will be ruined. Their mother should know better. She has a hard enough time getting any young men to dance with them. They're so stout."

"Do you know that man?" Here the Baroness questioned Jadwiga, who shook her head. "That's Seigfried von Saurau, a terrible rake. I heard Amelie von Honniker's hasty marriage to the Bromman boy had something to do with him. Amelie is said to be heavy with child already, and it hasn't been more than four months since the wedding. It will be interesting to see in which month that child is born." The Baroness nodded her head knowingly, her lips thinning with disapproval.

Krystyna peered around, taking it all in. A born and bred horsewoman, an enormous, steel gray hunter headed relentlessly in their direction caught her eye. Despite his size, the animal was beautifully built, and his rider was equally striking, tall, broad, and unfashionably muscled in the arms and the long thighs which gripped his steed. This man who sat his restive mount so easily was attired starkly in his brown coat, buff breeches, and tricorn hat. With a soft touch on the reins, he guided his horse in the direction of von Reigler's landau.

"Oh dear. It's Morzinski again. He simply will not give up."

Krystyna, surprised by her aunt's fond tone, watched as Jadwiga straightened in her seat, smoothed her bodice and touched her hat, as if making sure it was in place. For a moment, Krystyna was almost sure she saw a blush rising in those weathered cheeks. "If he weren't charming or so handsome, I wouldn't give him the time of day."

"Andrzej Morzinski, isn't it? My husband says he's a troublemaker."

"He's a patriot, Ewa. A true Polish patriot. He's sincere and passionate about a cause I'm afraid is nearly lost. He comes from a very fine family. If I were twenty years younger…"

"Jadwiga!" The Baroness wiggled her eyebrows in some alarm and gazed pointedly at her daughter and at Krystyna. "I believe he intends to waylay us." She spoke these words in some alarm. "What can he want?"

"Nothing very interesting, I'm sorry to say. Only my late husband's connections. He's trying to raise awareness for Poland's plight. He knows I still maintain contact with many of the General's old comrades in arms." Jadwiga referred to the third and most recently deceased of her husbands.

"He wouldn't approach you about such matters here?"

"Ewa, you don't know Morzinski."

All four women watched in rapt attention as the tall, handsome Pole rode up to their carriage and then alongside them.

"Greetings, ladies." He doffed his hat and bowed his head in greeting while keeping a light but steady grip on the reins with his other hand. "Baroness von Reigler. Frau von Gebler. Young ladies. You are all looking very well today." He met each of the women's glances in turn. The Baroness eyed him archly, and Jadwiga beamed at him. Marta simpered and looked away. His eyes met Krystyna's last, and awareness shot through her. It was like a chord within her had finally been struck. His reaction to her was equally obvious. He stared back, as if equally surprised. Finally, he recovered and addressed her aunt. "Are you enjoying your drive?"

While her aunt responded appropriately, Krystyna struggled to understand her immediate reaction to this stranger. There was more to it than his rugged good looks or the deep timber of his voice. There was a rightness, a sense of providence to this encounter.

Despite speaking with Jadwiga, he kept looking back at Krystyna.

"Your father, Morzinski?" Jadwiga prodded.

"Excuse me?"

"How is your father? When we last spoke, you informed me he'd been unwell."

"I haven't had any more news."

Krystyna found him mesmerizing. Though not classically handsome, as Ivan, her one-time fiancé, had been, there was a masculine allure to his more roughhewn features. And despite the fact she'd nearly married him, Ivan had never had this instant, overwhelming impact on her, and this man wasn't dancing with her or even speaking to her. He was merely riding alongside her carriage.

"I'll keep him in my prayers."

"Thank you. Ladies, enjoy your day." As he spoke, his gaze settled again upon Krystyna, and she didn't flinch from his regard. The instantaneous attraction between them flared through their mute interaction. Then, after nodding once more to them all and resettling his hat, Andrzej rode away.

"Well, that wasn't so bad," Jadwiga said as she leaned back into the squabs.

"Wasn't so bad," the Baroness muttered. "I was terrified he was going to bring up politics or solicit your aid directly."

"No, he knows his presence is enough to remind me of his interests."

Marta gripped Krystyna's gloved hand. "He was staring at you." Jadwiga watched her niece with a bemused expression.

Suddenly, they heard a disturbance behind them, the rhythmical pounding of frantic hooves, the explosive crack of a driving whip, and shouts and exclamations of encouragement. The women peered back and saw a sweat-slicked team of bays charging along the road. The driver of the curricle goaded his horses to ever greater speed, wreaking havoc on the stately flow of traffic. Riders and carriages pulled off the road to get out of the way.

Meanwhile, the nearly out-of-control curricle bore down on them. A group of young men were in the conveyance, and they cheered and shouted, goading the driver on to greater speed and recklessness.

Jadwiga's driver pulled the landau to one side of the road, and the curricle caught up with them and then sped past. The grinning driver was slender, dark and lean with a lush moustache and wearing a uniform. Suddenly, Marta dug her fingernails into Krystyna's arm. "That's him," she whispered frantically.

"Who?"

"Lukacs. Lukacs Dellos. He's a cavalry officer. Did you see that? He waved to me!"

"You mean the driver?"

"Yes! Yes! The handsome one."

From Krystyna's brief glimpse of the man, she concluded his lean, dark looks weren't particularly to her taste, but saw no point in disagreeing with her friend.

The rowdy group continued to proceed at dangerous speed, frightening and panicking several teams, and nearly un-mounting a heavyset fellow on his horse.

"Impertinence!" The Baroness was outraged. "Young fools will kill themselves, or someone else driving in that reckless manner! It's unforgivable, especially in the Prater. Someone should do something."

Krystyna continued to stare after the curricle. Clearly, disaster loomed. She watched as Dellos bore down on a now familiar gray hunter. The gray reared in alarm, and Morzinski struggled to control him. The horse leaped into the air and then spun about in a circle. Swiftly, Morzinski regained control of his steed. For a moment, the pair stood as still as a statue, then, like a silver shot, they streaked off after the runaway curricle. Krystyna drew a sharp breath as Morzinski grasped the rein of the driver's side horse and checked his speed. Ignoring the vociferous protestations of the driver and his companions, Morzinski led the team off the road and onto a grassy shoulder. There, it appeared that Morzinski and Dellos became involved in a heated exchange. Normal traffic resumed through the park.

"Jadwiga, I've had quite enough for today. Shall we return home?" The Baroness was clearly distraught.

"Actually, I'd like to see what transpires here. This is the most excitement I've had in some time."

"Really, Jadwiga, the entire situation is vulgar in the extreme. Who knows what other mischief those young scoundrels will get up to?"

"What can you see, Krystyna? My eyesight is inadequate at this distance. What's Morzinski doing?" Jadwiga demanded.

"This isn't an appropriate scene for my daughter or your niece."

"I suppose you're right." Jadwiga was clearly disappointed. "But you must promise you will bring me the entire story tomorrow. You know all the truly worthwhile gossips."

"I'll find out what I can. Hans, take us home." This peremptory command was directed to their driver. "That Hungarian Dellos was the driver. He's a worthless scamp of a fellow, wild and poor besides."

"He's not worthless, Mother. You're wrong. You don't know him."

"Nor do you, my dear. I saw how you looked at him. He's not for you. Do I make myself clear?" She dismissed the subject with a wave of her hand, wholly disregarding the fire of rebellion in her daughter's expressive eyes.

Marta lapsed into a brooding, sulky silence.

The landau turned, and Dellos, Morzinski and the curricle were blocked from view.

Jadwiga had been quietly observing Marta. Now, she spoke up. "Lukacs Dellos is very romantic, isn't he? Now I understand why the Countess von Refte is so taken with him. I'd heard she has been showering him with gifts, including that carriage and team. She can undoubtedly afford it, but it's a rather ostentatious gift, particularly with the way he flaunts it. People will talk." No one could miss the innuendo.

The Baroness eyed her friend with narrowed eyes and then followed Jadwiga's lead, "Johanna's almost my age."

"Being pursued by handsome young men is one of the benefits of being a rich widow, not that I've taken advantage of it. I find it hard to take an interest in wet-behind-the-ear boys. They're pleasant to look at, but eventually one must speak, and they can be so tiresome.

"Johanna is a widow, too, not that it excuses such blatant behavior. She was the Count's second wife. They were married for ten years before he became an invalid, and then she nursed him until his death. I don't blame her for wanting to… Ah, what's the phrase? Carpe diem! Seize the moment. In any case, she has no children, and her stepchildren are fully-grown. I wish her all the joy such a young man can provide."

"That's a lie!" Marta fairly shouted.

"Marta, control yourself!" The Baroness intervened. "Don't speak to our guest in that manner."

"But she's lying. I know it. Lukacs would never… How could you even suggest such a thing?"

"Child," Jadwiga's voice was calm and unruffled. "Lukacs Dellos and Johanna von Refte are the subjects of all the current gossip. I am simply surprised I heard about it before your mother. My dressmaker shared it with me just yesterday, when I went in for a final fitting on a ball gown I'd ordered. She had cut it all wrong at my waist. We were lucky that the fabric wasn't ruined. In any case, Dellos has little to recommend him. The only way in which he can maintain himself in the style to which he aspires is by securing the affections of a wealthy 'friend.' There are a thousand others like him in Vienna."

Marta was silent, and Krystyna could tell from the way she breathed that her friend was fighting sobs.

"I see now, Marta, that it was wrong of me to try and hide the sordid nature of some of the goings on of the Imperial Court. I've tried to shelter you. But you insist on harboring romantic notions about this boy. No longer will I dissemble. Lukacs Dellos is a kept man. He will rely on the generosity of wealthy women until he finds an heiress who can maintain him alone. His flirtation with you reflects his interest in your father's finances. You must be realistic. Your inheritance is large though not sufficiently so to hold a man like Dellos."

Marta began to sob openly.

"This display today leads me to conclude you've been encouraging Dellos. It's unacceptable, and it will cease."

They passed the rest of the ride back to the von Reigler mansion in a very tense silence. Marta stifled her sobs, but continued to glare mutinously at her mother, who ignored her daughter but continued to sniff disapprovingly. For their part, Krystyna and Jadwiga found the situation socially awkward and so didn't speak.

Krystyna did reflect on Marta's situation and how it mirrored her own before the accident that had caused Ivan's death. Later that afternoon, when the two young women were alone in Marta's small parlor, Krystyna had an opportunity to speak honestly to her friend of her concerns. She set aside her needlepoint. "I have no talent for needlepoint. Mine's all knots and wrinkles. And look at yours. It's perfect."

"I have a small talent for handwork." Marta smiled her pleasure at the compliment. "It's one of the few things that I do which my mother can find no fault in. Marta, my dear," Marta spoke in a highpitched, nasal voice, clearly imitating her mother, "you've no gift for the pianoforte, merely a passable voice, little proficiency with languages, but you do very fine needlework. In addition, I don't entirely despair of your ability to run a household after you marry. Thanks to my tutelage and the dowry which your father has provided, we should be able to secure an acceptable husband for you."

Krystyna burst out laughing. "You're very good, you know. Has your mother ever heard you mimic her?"

Marta grinned back, revealing an endearing gap between her front teeth. "Of course not. She'd be furious."

"She isn't that... Can't be that."

"Overbearing," Marta provided. "Oh, but she is. Worse, in fact, and quite determined that I marry well. She doesn't seem to care at all about how I feel, whom I love."

Krystyna cleared her throat discreetly. "Marta, we've only known each other for a short while, but I do consider you a dear friend."

"As I do you."

"I want to tell you something in confidence, a story which, if it got out, would ruin me socially. Do you understand? You can tell no one."

Marta nodded solemnly, her eyes, huge.

"I was in love, or thought I was, back in Poland. Ivan was a Russia nobleman but of little or no estate. I didn't care about such matters. He was handsome and charming and seemingly smitten with me. From the first, my father dismissed him as an adventurer seeking his fortune. He was vehemently opposed to a match between us, but I wouldn't listen."

"So your father sent you away to separate you from your Russian." Marta set her own work down, rushed over to Krystyna and grasped her hands. "We are very alike you and I. But you will find a way to be reunited with your Russian, as I will be with Lukacs."

"No, wait. I learned the hard way that my father was right. Men sometimes have insight into other men that women seem to lack. I caught Ivan entangled with a maidservant and realized his claims of love and devotion were false. And there was no possible way I could have misconstrued what happened. Neither wore much in the way of clothing."

Marta's hand covered her opened mouth.

"And that's not the worst of it. All that transpired afterwards revealed him as an opportunistic fortune-hunter."

"Lukacs is nothing like your Russian," Marta broke in heatedly.

"I don't know if he is or isn't, but you have to admit, his reputation is questionable. Your mother and my aunt are not fools. Perhaps you should pay them some heed."

"So you're on their side, then. I'm sorry for your troubles, but they have nothing to do with Lukacs or me."

"Your loyalty is admirable, just be careful."

"You don't know him. You'll see, he does love me."

Krystyna met her friend's glance but didn't respond.

Sensing her friend's disbelief, Marta returned to her own chair. She settled and then spoke again. "What do you think of my new watered silk gown, the striped one with the puffed sleeves?"

Understanding Marta's eagerness to change the subject, Krystyna responded appropriately. When the conversation lagged, the other girl picked up her needlepoint while Krystyna glanced at hers in distaste. Eventually, she picked up a book, but didn't find it engaging. Despite the developments of the afternoon and its theme of reprobate men, her thoughts drifted back to the handsome Pole with the fine, dark eyes who had captured her attention.

CHAPTER 4

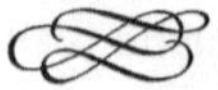

A highlight of the autumn social season was to be a reception in honor of the Tsarina Catherine's birthday at the Russian embassy. The affairs at the embassy were generally extravagant and not to be missed. The cream of Viennese diplomatic society, including the von Reiglers, Jadwiga and her niece, were invited. Both families had accepted their invitations and eagerly anticipated the event.

In the days leading up to the reception, it became clear Marta wasn't the least convinced of Lukacs Dellos's unsuitability. If anything, her mother's and Jadwiga's remarks had hardened her determined devotion to her unworthy suitor. The sweet-faced blond seemed even more obsessed with the man.

Krystyna had tried to reason with her friend. "Marta, your mother's no fool. She knows Viennese society. If there are rumors about Dellos and this Countess..."

"You don't know Lukacs!" Marta protested passionately. "If you did, you would understand. He loves only me. He will only ever love me."

"Have you ever asked him about this Countess?"

"I could never let him think I doubt his honor."

"Just ask him."

"No one understands. No one, not even you." Marta was incapable of critically discussing her suitor.

On the day of the reception, Krystyna arrived at the von Reiglers early in the afternoon. That morning, her Aunt Jadwiga had taken to her bed with a headache, thus Krystyna was to accompany the von Reiglers. Krystyna had offered to pass on the event as well, but her aunt wouldn't hear of it. She had argued, "I'm far too old for that sort of foolishness anyway. No one wishes to see me all done up in lace and silk. No, you go along. Parties like this are meant for the young."

As she dressed in Marta's chambers, Krystyna was aware of butterflies of excitement cavorting in her stomach. Baroness von Reigler sent her French trained lady's maid to prepare their hair. Krystyna's was elaborately arranged atop her head in a style which Marguerite, the lady's maid, informed her was reminiscent of the manner in which the Greek ladies in ancient times had worn their hair. Her strawberry blond tresses were lightly powdered, and she wore delicate gold slippers and a dress of sea foam green. Her corset was very tight about her waist and thrust her ample bosom high into the shockingly low décolletage. When all of the preparations were complete, she turned slowly before Marta's full-length mirror.

"You're so lovely," murmured the other girl, whose blue eyes were bright with excitement. Marta was enchanting in pale pink. "No man there will be able to take his eyes off of you."

Krystyna studied her own reflection critically. She was no sylphlike creature. Despite the abundance of soft white breast that her finery revealed, she was unfashionably firm from the active, outdoorsy life she'd lived in Poland. She would never be described as classically beautiful, but there was a sauciness to her dimpled smile, a sparkle to her great brown eyes, and a jauntiness in the way she held herself that were undeniably attractive.

The Baroness von Reigler watched as the two giggling young women descended the staircase. For a moment, she doubted her wisdom in allowing Krystyna to accompany them to the reception, despite her friendship with Jadwiga. The Baroness was in the market for a husband for her daughter, and when searching for a husband one didn't weaken the effect of the bait, her daughter, by placing her in the company of a more attractive woman. But by encouraging the friendship between the two girls, she'd done just that. While Marta was soft and feminine, a traditionally attractive sort of girl, there was something riveting about Krystyna, an almost peasant-like sensuality. The Baroness knew she'd have her hands full that night.

Upon arrival at the Baroque palace that served as the Russian embassy, liveried servants met the von Reiglers and Krystyna, took the ladies' wraps and directed them through a grand archway that overlooked the packed ballroom.

For a moment, they stood at the top of a grand staircase gazing down upon the glittering assemblage. The cavernous chamber with the molded, golden ceiling had originally been designed in the Baroque style, but had recently been dramatically renovated in the popular Rococo. The combination resulted in an elegant, lush yet frivolous backdrop. Guests from all over Europe attended the celebration. The men wore richly-hued garments, some belonging to nationalities Krystyna couldn't identify, while the women favored the elaborate French fashions.

This was far and away the most formal and intimidating affair she had ever attended. Her heart hammered as she observed the couple ahead of them be announced and then descend the staircase.

Marta babbled as they awaited their turn. "None of the Hapsburgs are here yet. I wonder if they shall come, though Father says they must or it will be a snub to the Empress Catherine… Wait, there's Lukacs." Marta gripped Krystyna's arm delightedly. "He's here! He's here!" She whispered shrilly in her friend's ear, rendering their introductions incoherent to Krystyna.

Aware of the eyes of the assembly upon them, Krystyna nearly held her breath when it was her party's turn to descend into the throng. But she soon discovered her fears were unfounded. Admirers instantly swarmed around both women. A seemingly endless parade of people, mostly young men, whose names she was sure she could never remember surrounded Krystyna. She found she enjoyed flirting lightly and manipulating her fan coquettishly. At home in Poland, on her family's rather remote estate, she'd had neither the time nor the opportunity to engage in such light-hearted pursuits.

More than once, Krystyna glanced up from chatting to find the startlingly blue eyes of a slender, young man upon her. Clearly a dandy, affecting to carry an ornamental cane, he was dressed in a peacock blue silk coat ornately trimmed with braid that matched the adornment on his tricorn hat, which also boasted a jewel on the left cock. His wig was elaborate and in the latest of styles. She found his repeated perusal of her person both disconcerting and uncomfortable. Once, he even had the audacity to raise his wine glass to her in toast. She determinedly looked away, and eventually lost sight of him.

When it was time to go into dinner, she saw Marta escorted on the arm of young Dellos. She also glimpsed the icy look on the Baroness von Reigler's face. But there was nothing to be done about it, and, despite her earlier popularity, no one had yet asked to escort her into the dining room. She felt her heart sink when she saw a hoary, lecherous, Austrian Major General whom she had met earlier heading her way.

Still, she plastered a smile on her face, for it appeared most people had already gravitated to companions.

"How charming of you to wait for me, lovely lady."

She spun about and looked into laughing, bright blue eyes.

She stared in consternation at refined, lovely features as the dandy raised her gloved hand to his lips.

"We haven't been introduced," she pointed out.

"A great tragedy, especially since you already command my heart and my life, but one easily remedied. I am Sebastjan deSzinay, and we are countrymen. My mother was a Pole, though my father was Austrian. And you, you are the toast of the ball, Krystyna Sielska. Frankly, I'm stunned at my good fortune to find you here alone. All of my competition must have assumed you would already have an escort. I would be honored if you would allow me to conduct you into the dining room." He offered his arm.

She inclined her head in acceptance and took the proffered arm. Though he was clearly something of a scoundrel, he didn't strike her as dangerous or unpleasant, like the Major General.

"I saw you once before, you know. You were riding in a carriage in the Prater."

"I saw many people that day."

"You wound me. Apparently, I didn't make an impression on you, but then we did simply pass by your landau, and we were going quickly."

She turned to look at him. "Were you in that curricle with Lukacs Dellos?"

"You know him? How pleasant to have mutual acquaintances. It bodes well for our future encounters."

"I don't know him, but I do know of him, and I thought that he behaved very badly that day."

"You mean you didn't find him dashing?"

"I found him reprehensible. Someone could have been hurt."

"We got carried away. Dellos recently acquired the team, and…"

"What sort of man is Dellos?" She wasn't going to waste this opportunity to learn something of the man who enthralled her friend.

"So, he has caught your eye. That's always the way of it. I meet an enchantress, and she seems equally taken with me, until she encounters Lukacs."

"Is he…" Krystyna hesitated. Already this conversation had gone way beyond what was acceptable for a first meeting between a young lady and a gentleman. Now, they stood at the dining room doors, waiting to be directed to their seats. "Does he have an eye for the ladies?" she whispered, glancing about, hoping not to be overheard.

"You drive a dagger into my breast." He released her hand and dramatically pressed both of his to his heart. "Only you, my lady, have made my heart beat so. Only you. And yet, you wish to speak of another man." He turned away from Krystyna for a moment to give their names to the servant.

"This way, please, my lord. The lady's seat is on the other side of the table."

As they skirted the table, Krystyna noticed that a plump, young matron glanced at Sebastjan, and then glared at her. Krystyna observed her escort looked hurriedly away and pretend not to see the woman in question.

Rather amused, she poked him with her elbow. "Are you quite sure there is no one else here with a prior claim to your attentions? Specifically, that lady in purple whom we just passed?"

"Which lady? Oh, that one." He appeared momentarily chagrined. "She must be jealous of your radiance. Here we are." He seated her. "Until later, my angel." He nodded in greeting to a spectacled, pleasant-faced man of middling years who stood behind the chair to Krystyna's right.

She followed Sebastjan with her eyes as he made his way to his seat, which she noted with righteous satisfaction, was beside the lady in purple silk. He was an amusing rascal.

But she soon forgot about him as she was caught up in the gastronomic event that was dinner. There was so much to observe as they proceeded "from eggs to apples," or, in this case, from Beluga caviar, through borscht, and then venison. Her dinner companions, the spectacled man, a bureaucrat, and a Viennese baroness, were pleasant and undemanding. Krystyna found she was enjoying herself. A toast to the Russian Empress accompanied each course. The room grew warmer, and the people seemed ever more brilliant.

Conversation eventually lulled, no doubt from sheer fatigue after consuming stupendous quantities of food. It was then she overheard Baron von Reigler, who sat farther up the table from her, comment, "We understand the Polish seym is attempting to incorporate the Polish insistence on freedom with the needs of the modern state. It's a fascinating situation which bears watching."

"Poland!" An enormously fat Russian count whose ruddy face glistened with grease erupted into laughter. "Poland is a joke," he scoffed. "The Polish king is one of the Tsarina's discarded toys. Polish freedom is anarchy. It makes the Poles weak. Russia is strong." The man thumped a meaty fist on the table so hard that silver and crystal shook. "Our Tsarina knows how to rule. Poland…she is nothing."

Baron von Reigler didn't respond. Instead, he reached for his wine glass.

"On the contrary," a strong baritone voice arose from somewhere below the salt. All heads turned to the other end of the table. "Poland is the most forward thinking country in Europe. If the precepts that our representatives at the seym are debating are put into effect, Poland will become the most politically advanced country in Europe. If it weren't for the meddling of the Russians and Prussians, Poland could stand strong." His words, in only moderately accented German, rang clear and loud.

"Russia and Prussia occupy so much Polish land because she is such a 'forward thinking' country." The enormous Russian erupted into guffaws, and his end of the table joined in the laughter.

"Since Potsdam, it's been clear Russia and Prussia are seeking to eradicate my homeland from the map of Europe."

"Do you expect me to deny this? Some of your own countrymen have invited us in. They know you Poles aren't competent to rule yourselves. You've no one to blame but yourselves. Do you find fault with the wolf that brings down a cow that has wandered too far from the herd? But this is neither the time nor the place for such talk, boy. I've no wish to ruin my digestion or anyone else's with talk of politics. Tonight, we drink to Catherine. To the Tsarina." He rose heavily to his feet with his glass held aloft in salute. Everyone else at the table followed suit.

After reclaiming her seat, Krystyna tried to unobtrusively peer around the other guests to find out who had spoken in defense of her homeland. The Russian's words had infuriated her as well. Had she been just about anywhere else, she would have spoken up in defense of her country. As a guest and one linked socially to the von Reiglers, she couldn't rail against the Russian count. For an unmarried young woman to do so would be socially disastrous for everyone associated with her. By keeping her silence, she felt not only outraged but also guilty about not coming to Poland's defense. And so, when this other Pole spoke up for their country, her heart soared with pride and relief.

She had a niggling suspicion she knew who the patriot was, but there were simply too many heads between her own and the speaker. The man's German indicated he was well educated. Could it be Morzinski from the park? She was consumed with curiosity.

Unfortunately, it was time for the ladies to retire to another chamber while the men enjoyed after dinner drinks and smokes. The two groups would reconvene later for dancing in the ballroom.

After looking for and failing to locate Marta or the Baroness, Krystyna took a seat alone at the very back of the host of women in the music room. A singer and her accompanist on a harpsichord provided entertainment which most of the guests ignored while engaging in discussions amongst themselves. Not sure where Marta or the Baroness were, and only slightly acquainted with a few of the other women, Krystyna sought to actually listen to the music, which proved difficult with the rise and fall of voices, the rustle of skirts and the occasional outbursts of laughter. Time passed slowly. She looked forward to the dancing, but the warmth of the room, the lilting music, and the heavy meal and alcohol she'd consumed all conspired to make her doze. She caught herself more than once just as her chin drifted down to her chest.

Suddenly, the touch of a hand on her arm startled her. She almost dropped her fan in surprise.

"Easy, sleeping beauty. I've come to rescue you. No one's looking this way." It was Sebastjan deSzinay. He took her hand and drew to her feet before she was quite aware of what was happening.

He led her out of the salon and down the corridor. Krystyna stopped short.

"Don't worry. They didn't see us leave."

"Where are we going?" she asked with a cocked eyebrow. She wasn't about to be cozened by another rake.

"The garden, Panienka." He used the Polish term for Lady or Miss with warmth. "May I presume to call you Krystyna?" Still attempting to propel her forward with his hand in the small of her back, he didn't await her response to his question. "I'm told it's very lovely."

"I would never have guessed you have a passion for flowers."

"Only glorious Polish roses."

"As appealing as fresh air sounds, I'm not going out in the garden with you."

"There's nothing like a discrete flirtation to ease the digestion."

She laughed. "I failed to take that benefit into consideration." She commented wryly as she considered her ardent admirer; there was a disarming boyishness to him that decided her. Sebastjan simply didn't seem dangerous. She had no doubt she could handle him.

"Come walk with me, sleeping beauty," he implored her. "You can't prefer to return to that misery."

She nodded. "All right. Let's go."

His blue eyes went wide with surprise and pleasure. He tucked her arm through his own and led her down the corridor, through one doorway, and then another, and out onto an immense porch. They descended broad steps into a magnificent formal garden that remained lovely despite being past its prime flowering time. In addition, there were some fanciful shrubs and bushes trimmed to resemble animals, both real and imaginary. The dark figures appeared eerily real in the relative darkness of the garden.

Krystyna took a deep breath, savoring the clean, crisp air after the heat and cloying perfumes of the music room. "It's delightful out here. Do you see the unicorn? And me without my golden lasso," she teased.

Sebastjan paused in his strolling and turned Krystyna to face him. "Sweet Krystyna, only a virgin of pure heart can capture a unicorn. I wonder, do you meet the requirements?"

At first, her cheeks flush guiltily, but then, she remembered no one else in Vienna, with the exception of her aunt, knew of her secret shame. The young man who was gazing at her so ardently was trying to seduce her. Instead, he had effectively banished all romance from her mind. He leaned closer perhaps thinking to steal a kiss.

She stepped back from him and deliberately unwound his arm.

"Don't be frightened, darling."

"I'm not frightened in the least, but I'm also not remotely interested in a romantic rendezvous."

"What do you mean?" Sebastjan questioned as he followed her. "Then why did you come out here with me?" He sounded like a boy who had just been told he couldn't have a treat he coveted.

"I came out for the air, and I'm not about to fall swooning into your arms."

Sebastjan reached out and grasped her bare wrists. "You pretend to be so sure of yourself, but I can see the way you tremble when I am near you. You smell so sweet."

Abruptly, she jerked away again. He had gone too far this time. Enough was enough. "You presume too much. If I'm trembling, it's because the air is cool, and my shoulders are bare. I'm returning to the party now." Krystyna dropped all pretense of dainty lady-like steps as she marched through the gardens and then up onto the porch. She castigated herself for going out into the garden with deSzinay. One would have thought Ivan had taught her enough about men's illicit intentions.

Caught up in her fury, she swung the door open and walked face first into a man's chest. Large hands immediately grasped her naked upper arms. Stunned, she stared up a long white cloth shirt and cravat, past broad shoulders covered in rich forest green material to familiar rugged features and dark blond hair tied back with a ribbon and unpowdered. Her countryman, Andrzej Morzinski, stared at her in some consternation. "Excuse me, my lady."

There was a weathered roughness to his touch as he set her away from him. She hadn't realized he was so tall when she'd seen him riding in the park. She actually had to tilt her head back to look him in the eye, which was a most unusual experience for her given her own height. His features were rugged. His nose had obviously been broken a time or two, but his expression appeared friendly and open. He was not a pretty man, rather a handsome one.

A familiar thrilling awareness coursed through Krystyna. “Oh no, it was my own fault. I beg your pardon. I wasn’t paying attention.”

“A fortunate accident then, which brought you to me.” Morzinski’s hands dropped from her arms, which felt scorched by his touch. He stood there, staring at her, taking in all of her. Then, he grinned at her in obvious approval. The smile transformed him from merely impressive and masculine to utterly devastating.

“If you will excuse me,” she began, for once at a loss for words. Both oddly unsettled and intrigued by the man before her, she didn’t want their interlude to end as abruptly as it began but had no idea of how to extend it.

“May I escort you back inside?” He offered his arm, and she was reaching out to rest her hand upon it when Sebastjan appeared.

“I’ll escort the lady, Morzinski,” Sebastjan interrupted before she could respond.

It was all she could do to keep from groaning aloud. Ever since hearing Morzinski speak at dinner, no, since she saw him at the Prater, she’d wanted to encounter him again. And now, Sebastjan had to ruin it all. Morzinski was sure to guess they’d been out in the moonlight together.

Sebastjan offered his arm to Krystyna, who was acutely aware of how Morzinski’s brown eyes narrowed at both the gesture and her dismay at Sebastjan’s proprietary manner.

“I don’t think so, deSzinay. The lady doesn’t wish to go with you.” The words were bland, but they rumbled forth from his chest, ominous and threatening

But Sebastjan, to her amazement, didn’t back down. He

stood toe to toe with Morzinski, though he was a full head shorter. Krystyna couldn't risk another scandal. She could easily imagine her aunt's reaction if she proved the reason for an outbreak of fisticuffs at the Russian Empress's birthday ball.

"Enough. Both of you." As she spoke, she heard her own mother's voice when intervening in a dispute between servants at Morze trawy echoing in her mind. The anger and the authority ringing in her voice felt good. She'd had enough of men causing problems for her. To the best of her ability, she would control her own destiny. "This is neither the time nor the place for such behavior. I will reenter the ballroom alone. Good evening to you both." With a dismissive swirl of skirts, she left them staring after her. Guided by music, she soon found her way to the ballroom.

Andrzej followed Krystyna's progress with his eyes. Awareness of this woman filled his senses. She had backbone, a trait he'd always found admirable. In addition, she possessed the most remarkable coloring. The combination of the red-gold hair and rosy cheeks made her stand out like a flame against the pale Austrian beauties. Her German had been perfect, but he'd detected the accent that revealed she was a countrywoman. He had suspected as much after glimpsing her in the landau with Jadwiga von Gebler. Krystyna Sielska was also tall and firm, which suited his particular taste. He'd never cared for fragile women who felt as if they'd shatter when he put his hands on them.

The sound of deSzinay clearing his throat got his attention. He glanced over at the smaller man. It was unfortunate that such an enchanting creature as that woman should be entangled with such a frivolous person. "Shall we proceed outside to ah…take the air?"

Andrzej caught the look of real dismay on Sebastjan's features and immediately surmised that the other man had no intention of being dragged into a physical altercation when there was no audience around to appreciate his daring or to tend to his injuries.

"The lady has snubbed both of us. So, I see no need to proceed to violence. Therefore, shall we go and have a drink?"

Andrzej relinquished his animosity as swiftly as it had arisen. The boy was right; the Polish beauty had rejected them both.

"Morzinski?" Sebastjan inquired.

"Indeed," Andrzej nodded his head. "Tell me, deSzinay, what's her name? I generally like to know a woman's name before I kill another man over her."

"Krystyna. Her name's Krystyna Sielska." Sebastjan's voice came out rather high and tremulous.

Andrzej laughed and clapped him on the back. "Relax, deSzinay. I'm only joking."

As they meandered over to the refreshment tables, Andrzej reflected on Krystyna. She had struck him the first time he'd seen her. Tonight, her impact on his senses had been devastating. She was lush, as bright, colorful, and as full of life as a sunset over Lake Wiren. Home, it was time to go home. Maybe that was why the girl affected him so much; she reminded him of home, of Slodki powietrze or Sweet Air, his family's estate in eastern Poland.

CHAPTER 5

One afternoon, while Jadwiga and Krystyna enjoyed coffee with an exquisite marzipan torte, Pavel announced the Baroness von Reigler.

The lady charged into the room in a swirl of puce bombazine and silk. The plumes on her hat bobbed wildly with her rapid movement. Her face was pale and anxious. “Jadwiga! Jadwiga! Marta is gone!” Ewa von Reigler collapsed into a chair. She fanned a note wildly before her face.

“Gone? Where?”

Krystyna experienced a sinking in her stomach. “Marta is with Dellos.” It came out as a statement, not a question.

“You knew!” The Baroness rose in righteous fury and bore down on her. “You wicked girl! My only child.”

Jadwiga interrupted her outraged friend authoritatively. “Sit down, Ewa! Calm yourself. We’ll never get to the bottom of this if you insist on behaving impetuously.”

“My sweet girl. She left me this note. She says they’re to be married, though I don’t believe it for a moment.” The Baroness collapsed back into a chair. “What can I do? My baby. She’s throwing everything away!” Her imperious facade had been torn from her. She was wounded and aching, completely beside herself.

"When did you last see her?" Jadwiga stood and paced the floor like a general plotting strategy.

"She left this morning. I found this note less than an hour ago. What shall I do? What can I do?" she wailed.

"Ewa, if we're to do anything, you must first compose yourself." Jadwiga snapped, and it appeared her advice got through to her friend, for the Baroness's sobs diminished. She struggled to get her breathing under control while she dabbed at her ravaged face with a lace-edged handkerchief, never relinquishing her hold on Marta's note. In that moment of vulnerability, Krystyna finally observed a resemblance between the Baroness and her daughter. "Tell me what to do."

"That's my girl," Jadwiga approved. "Now, we need the facts. First of all, does the Count know Marta's missing?"

"No. He isn't even in Vienna. He's off on some business for the emperor. I believe in Budapest. That's how it's been our entire married life. He's always away, and I'm left holding things together."

"Good, Ewa. This is a matter better handled by women. Krystyna," Jadwiga paused before her great niece, fixing her with a piercing glance. "What do you know about all of this? Hold nothing back. Marta's future is at stake."

"In truth, I don't know anything. And if I did, I wouldn't hold back. I'm in complete agreement with you about Dellos. I think he's a scoundrel and an adventurer."

"We must conclude they have gone away together. Now, Ewa, does anyone else know she's missing? Think, woman!"

"No." the Baroness shook her head slowly and thoughtfully. "I left home to come here as soon as I got the note. I didn't discuss the matter with anyone. No, that's not true. Marta's maid knows she's missing. Gretchen's her name. The defiant creature wouldn't tell me a thing when I questioned her. Now I have her locked in her rooms, and I said I wouldn't release her until she told where my daughter has run off to. I intend to fire her from my service without references." The Baroness sniffed with a hint of her former condescension.

"You must keep her away from the other servants at all costs, at least until we can get Marta back. You know how rumors spread in back halls. No, we must keep this discrete. When you return home, release Gretchen from her imprisonment and let it be known that Marta is here. Krystyna, are you quite sure you have no idea where she may have gone?"

"No, I'm sorry, but I don't."

"We must assume she's with young Dellos. They cannot have gotten far in the hour or so since they've been gone. Is that correct, Ewa?"

"Yes, we dined together at midday."

Jadwiga nodded shrewdly. "It's to our advantage Lukacs has little money. He relies on his current paramour to maintain his lifestyle. But he couldn't tap such a source for funds to facilitate an affair with another woman. Do you know if they took Marta's jewelry?"

"I've always kept Marta's jewelry with my own. She's far too careless with such things. I have the only key to the jewelry chest."

"That's a blessing. Does she have any money?"

"I only give her enough for small purchases. But they've been together unchaperoned! She could be ruined."

"Until the situation becomes public knowledge, I believe we can avert tragedy. But we must find Marta. Do you know any of Dellos's companions, Krystyna?"

"I know some of them by sight. I've been introduced to several of them socially."

"I can name every member of the entire worthless bunch," the Baroness interrupted.

"Do be quiet, Ewa. Do you think any of these young rakes

would tell you, Marta's mother, anything? No, I'm afraid we have to rely on Krystyna in this matter. One of them might be compelled to reveal what he knows to her."

"Dellos is very close to Sebastjan deSzinay. They're always in each other's company." The Baroness broke in again. "But going to that young man would be impossible for your reputation." Now she spoke to Krystyna, "I would never allow my daughter to do such a thing."

"I care more for Marta than I do about my reputation. I'm willing to risk it."

"Krystyna, do you know deSzinay?" her great-aunt probed.

"Yes, I met him at the Tsarina's birthday ball. Not to sound conceited, but I believe he was taken with me."

"Those young men are taken with anything in skirts," the Baroness commented disdainfully.

"A truth which makes matters relatively straightforward." Jadwiga spoke through lips thinned with concentration.

"We shall all go to him." Ewa lunged to her feet. She had experienced a dramatic transformation in both bearing and expression now that her old friend had taken control and restored her hope.

"We'll do nothing of the sort, Ewa, and do sit down. This popping up and down of yours is very distracting."

Jadwiga's pacing back and forth was equally so, but Krystyna knew better than to offer this observation.

"You intend to send your niece alone to a bachelor's rooms?" The Baroness was appalled.

"I trust Krystyna's good sense. She can handle herself. Ewa, you will return to your house and behave normally. Again, make sure you let it be known Marta's here. This subterfuge will buy us a little time. You must be a convincing actress for as long as it takes to get your daughter back. We'll handle the rest."

The Baroness nodded her head in agreement to all of

Jadwiga's directives then asked, "You believe this may take some time?"

"I have absolutely no idea, but we must be prepared for any eventuality."

"But that means Marta may spend several nights with this… this seducer!"

"It is a possibility."

"But what if he…he… They"

"Compromises her? Marta won't be the first girl in Vienna to whom it's happened or the last. As long as no one finds out about her escapade, she'll be none the worse for wear, and she'll be wiser. If she's pregnant, yes, you must consider the possibility, Ewa. Then the two of you retire to your country estate for an extended visit. Afterwards, you share the happy tidings that you have produced another child, miraculously and despite your years.

"Regardless, it is a very salvageable situation on all levels, as long as the news doesn't get out. The best thing that you can do right now, Ewa, is return to your house and behave as I have described. Krystyna and I will take it from here and do all that can be done. We will get Marta back if it is at all possible."

The Baroness hugged her friend fiercely. Her rigid aristocratic face blurred with tears and emotion. "I will do exactly as you say. Oh, thank you. Thank you. A thousand blessings on you and on you, Krystyna. I do not know what I would have done without you both!"

Jadwiga hurried the Baroness out as quickly as she could. When the von Reigler carriage had departed, she hastened back into the salon. "Now here is what we must do…"

CHAPTER 6

It was in the evening of that same drizzly gray day when Krystyna, accompanied by Pavel, left Jadwiga's house through the back servants' entrance. They skirted the building, appearing to be day help departing for the night to any suspicious eyes. Pavel swiftly led the way along slick, darkened side streets, and, once they were some distance from Jadwiga's house, out onto a large boulevard. Here, he hailed a public coach and handed Krystyna up. Once she was safely ensconced in the shabby interior, he gave her intended direction to the driver and then faded away into the night.

The driver clucked to his horses, and they started moving.

Krystyna's heart pounded loudly in her ears until the rhythmical clap of the shod hooves on the cobble-stoned street drowned it out. She exhaled shakily and leaned back against the odiferous and meager seat cushions. Everything was going exactly as Jadwiga had planned. Earlier, Krystyna had sent a message to Sebastjan requesting a private meeting in his rooms that same day. Her missive had ended with the line: "I rely on your courtesy as a gentleman not to mention this appointment to anyone."

Apparently, there had been some difficulty locating him, for the messenger bearing Sebastjan's response returned just before the evening meal. Jadwiga had taken the note and read it aloud. In it, Sebastjan remarked that "he was pleasantly surprised" to hear from her and that he "looked forward with the greatest anticipation" to their meeting that evening.

Jadwiga had raised her eyebrows at her niece. "This young man believes you are plotting a romantic rendezvous."

"We did request a discrete meeting."

"Just prepare yourself. You're no fool, girl."

"Don't worry, Aunt," Krystyna stated grimly. "I know what I'm up against. I will succeed. For Marta." And also for herself, because it infuriated her that careless, selfish young men, like Lukacs and Ivan, could so easily wreak havoc in or even destroy a young woman's life.

It had been easy to be so confident while she sat safely at table in Jadwiga's home. But now, traveling in the rain through unfamiliar streets of the darkened city in a hired conveyance, it was an entirely different matter. Krystyna felt both terrified and exhilarated.

Suddenly, the coach stopped moving. She jumped at a thump from the roof above her head. Then she heard muffled mutterings, and the door swung open.

"Here we are, miss." The damp but well-bundled driver offered her a hand down.

She emerged in front of one of those large, somewhat down-at-the-heels townhouses, built in a bygone day, that stood in a now not quite-fashionable section of the city. Jadwiga told her an elderly female relative of deSzinay's owned the house, a maiden cousin who kept to her country estate more often than not. It was a far less impressive edifice than the Wolski palace where Sebastjan's uncle held court. The Baroness had once pointed out this magnificent if rather ostentatious building. Clearly, Sebastjan was not willing to live under his uncle's thumb, for he chose to live in this weathered townhouse over his uncle's glittering establishment.

She squared her shoulders and, raising her skirts up from the wet street, started to step away from the coach.

"You'll not be walking off without paying, miss."

"Yes, yes, of course."

With the transaction completed, her driver asked, "Would you like me to wait for you, miss?"

Krystyna considered for a moment. She had no idea of how long her errand would require, but once it was accomplished, she intended to have Sebastjan convey her a reasonable distance from her aunt's house. She would walk the rest of the way. Even if he did refuse to help, as a gentleman, the very least he could do was ensure she returned safely home. "That will not be necessary."

The driver swung back up to his seat, adjusted his coat and hat, picked up the reins, and clucked to his horses, leaving her standing alone in front of the darkened house. She peered up at it. There were some lit rooms on the second floor.

She took a step and was immediately aware of frigid water penetrating her boot. It was a miserable feeling, compounded by the fact that her hat wasn't doing much good in the now driving rain. Her neck and face were getting soaked. She raised her shoulders against the damp coldness, tucked her chin down, and marched briskly towards the house and up the steps. The entrance was still impressive but had seen better days. Two stout, comically hideous gargoyles grinned malevolently at her from their nooks on either side of the doorframe where the paint pealed in places, and the residue of many nights darkened the glass around the flickering flame of the lamp.

Resolutely, Krystyna pounded the doorknocker. She waited. No answer. She shivered as more icy rain meandered down her neck, under her collar. She knocked again, more loudly. This time, the door abruptly swung open. A white-haired servant of mature years with a severe and disapproving mien stood in the doorway. He perused her up and down.

"The trade entrance is at the back. However, at this hour, I'm quite sure you have nothing of interest to my master." The man sniffed distastefully and attempted to draw the door closed.

Krystyna placed her foot in the doorway, effectively blocking his efforts. "I am expected. Please take me to Sebastjan deSzinay. This is his house, isn't it?"

"Your name, mistress, and I will investigate the matter."

"Perhaps I have not made myself clear." Krystyna's mother had taught her daughter that the key to mastering any situation was to act as if one already had it well in hand. "I'm not willing to stand out here in this foul weather, and I am expected. So, if you would be so kind..." She pushed past the disgruntled man and entered the house. She swung the soaking cape from her shoulders. "Please, hang this somewhere. And my hat." After removing the hatpin and hat, a plain, brown felt affair with a modest brim, no ribbons and a drooping pheasant feather on one side, she handed over both pieces of apparel.

"This way, mistress," he intoned grimly, grudgingly accepting her authority.

He carried no lamp, and so all was shadows and darkness as they passed through a sparsely furnished entrance hall. Krystyna shivered, as the house seemed little warmer than the out of doors. She crossed her arms and hugged them to herself. The servant led her down a corridor to a doorway under which a line of light glowed brightly. He knocked once and, without waiting for an answer, swung the door open. For a moment, Krystyna was taken aback by the radiance.

The darkness of the last hour rendered the spectacle even more remarkable. She now peered into a Rococo pleasure suite, brilliantly lit by a massive fire roaring in the white marble fireplace and candles in candelabra. The chamber was lushly decorated in pastel colors and luxuriant materials. Statues graced elegant pedestals, paintings adorned walls covered in dove gray silk, a golden harpsichord stood to one side, and richly appointed furnishings were arranged to promote both comfort and pleasure to the eye.

The portrait of a lovely, blond woman hung over the fireplace. She was dressed as a shepherdess and posed against a lush meadow in which winged cherubs tended to her flock while the lady gazed out at the viewer with enormous, oddly familiar blue eyes. The shepherdess wore a teasing smile on her pouting lips. Her figure was dainty and neat.

Krystyna caught her reflection in the enormous, gilt-framed mirror that dominated one wall. Her simple brown dress hung limply around her. Her hair was a bedraggled mess, while her cheeks glowed wet and rosy with cold. She was wholly out of place in this extravagant room.

The double doors at the opposite end of the chamber swung wide, and Sebastjan deSzinay entered. He appeared dapper in a burgundy velvet jacket and hose a shade darker. As always, his garments were elegantly cut and detailed, from the gold embroidered cuffs to the matching work on the lapels. His hair was meticulously coiffed and arranged in formal, powdered curls about his face. Krystyna glanced up at the portrait of the shepherdess. Her features were stamped onto Sebastjan's face, from his striking blue eyes to his slightly weak chin.

"Krystyna, welcome." He stepped forward arms extended. He took both of her hands in his, paying no heed to the fact that she dripped water onto the Persian carpet. He leaned forward, and before she could draw back, kissed her lightly on the back of each hand. He beamed at her. "I was very surprised to receive your note."

She deliberately drew her hands away from him. "I would prefer if we could speak privately." She glanced significantly over at the manservant who remained at the ready inside the doorway.

“Tomas, that will be all. Please inform Gretal we will be ready to dine shortly.”

“Dine? Sebastjan, you misunderstand. I didn’t come here to eat… I came to…”

“There will be time enough later, my dove,” he murmured as he took her arm and drew her beside him to a loveseat before the fire. “You are drenched through. Would you care to change your clothes? I’m sure something more comfortable could be found for you.”

“I’m fine.” Krystyna sat poised at the very edge of the diminutive sofa. “Sebastjan, this isn’t a social call.”

“While I have fantasized about your coming here to visit me, I had pictured you in more beguiling attire... Oh, but how foolish of me. This must be your disguise, so you could slip out unnoticed for our rendezvous. Do forgive my ignorance.”

Despite the gravity of the situation, Krystyna was amused. He was incorrigible. She brushed distractedly at her skirts, preparing to broach the reason for her visit.

“You’re nervous.” Sebastjan gloated, his eyes bright with anticipation. “That’s to be expected. Perhaps I could read you some poetry? Some lines from the ‘Pan Thaddeus?’ Or maybe you’d like to hear some of my own work?” He sprang up from the settee and crossed over to a writing desk where he shuffled through papers. He held a thin book aloft triumphantly. “Here it is!”

“Sebastjan, you misunderstand my intentions.”

“The time for maidenly virtue is past, my dear. It is charming affectation, yes, but so unnecessary. You’ve already won me. Tonight is our night.”

Krystyna was hard pressed not to laugh. She couldn’t help herself. He genuinely believed she’d come to make love with him, poor fellow. And she couldn’t be frightened of him. He simply wasn’t a convincing rake. “I’m not here to exchange love sonnets with you. I need your help." She stood up as he neared her.

"Your wish is my command, my angel."

Desirous of maintaining pleasant relations between them, she retreated as he pursued her. She backed into a little round table. A translucent ivory vase crashed to the floor and shattered. She righted the table and hurriedly knelt to pick up the pieces of the vase. "I'm sorry. I didn't see it." As Sebastjan stooped down beside her, Krystyna recoiled. She again collided with the round table. It teetered, on the brink of capsizing. As she reached to steady it, she bumped heads with Sebastjan, who was also grasping for it.

First, both rubbed their foreheads. Then, Sebastjan leaned toward her with the obvious intention of kissing her. She forcefully thrust him away. He fell back onto his haunches with a look of pure chagrin on his face. "You really don't want me to make love to you, do you?"

"Of course not."

"Oh. That's unfortunate. I'd planned everything, down to the minutest detail. No, an apology isn't necessary," he waved his hand dismissively, misinterpreting Krystyna's intention. "Still, this situation is most perplexing. You arrange an assignation, then appear garbed more poorly than most housemaids and dripping wet besides." Sebastjan's impish blue eyes danced with laughter. "I should have known better. I simply don't have that kind of luck. Why did you contact me? All of my friends were most impressed."

"You didn't share my note with them, did you?" She felt ill.

"Of course, we were all out dining together." Sebastjan stood and carefully adjusted his cravat in the mirror. He flicked at some barely visible lint on his left sleeve.

"I simply needed your help," she sputtered. "Do you have any idea what damage you may have done to my reputation?

Your friends will believe that I…and that you… How could you?"

"This assignation has quite made *my* reputation, that a lady would go to such great lengths to secure a rendezvous with me."

"You cad! You've destroyed my reputation to impress a bunch of spoiled ne'er-do-wells. How dare you!"

"Don't worry, Panienka, I didn't reveal your name." Sebastjan slipped easily into Polish. "I even suggested you were a widow, to protect your identity, and widows are considered fair game by my set. Preying on a young maiden, even one as enchanting as you, isn't quite sporting. So, why are you here?"

"I'm here because of Marta von Reigler. We—my aunt, her mother and I—believe she's run off with Lukacs Dellos."

"These ladies know of our meeting?" Dismay clouded the refined features. "That won't do at all. Mothers and guardians should have nightmares about their daughters spending unchaperoned time in my company."

"You are the only one to whom we could turn."

Abruptly, he turned away from her, walked over to the doorway from which he'd entered.

"Where are you going?"

"Just a minute," he responded, opening the doors and stepping through.

"What are you doing? Please, Sebastjan." She started to follow him. "There's not much time."

He ignored her. She paced in front of the fireplace, debating her plan of action. "Sebastjan?" He returned carrying a large, exotic flask from which a silken cord that ended in a mouthpiece dangled. A thin thread of smoke snaked its way out through the mouthpiece.

Krystyna became aware of a cloyingly sweet, herbal aroma.

He bonelessly sank down opposite her on the silk settee. He propped his feet carelessly on the silken cushions of a matching ottoman, and, balancing the flask in the crook of his elbow, inhaled deeply from the mouthpiece. Closing his eyes, he exhaled an undulating stream of smoke. A blissful expression smoothed the elegant lineaments of his face.

"What are you doing?"

"It's opium, Krystyna. Since you don't plan on entertaining me this evening, I shall have to amuse myself."

She didn't like the way Sebastjan's eyes were glazing over. "You'll be of no use at all if you continue to indulge. Enough. Be done with it."

He lazily squinted at her. "Under the circumstances, you can hardly deny me this gentle comfort."

She nearly ground her teeth in frustration. "Stop being such a child. We need your help." He didn't respond.

"Are you hearing me?" Desperation drove Krystyna. She stepped over to him, grasped him by both shoulders and gave him a shake.

Still, he held tightly to his flask and gazed up at her limpidly.

"What would you have me do?"

"Please tell me where Marta is."

"I am no more willing to betray my friend than you are yours. So, we are at an impasse."

Krystyna found the blue eyes focused upon her relatively clear and comprehending despite the light haze cocooning their possessor.

"Why do you assume I'm asking you to betray your friend?"

"You seek Lukacs Dellos, do you not?"

"Listen to me. Concentrate. We need you to be our hero, our knight in shining armor."

He chuckled weakly. "As my uncle tells everyone, I'm no hero. At times, he even questions whether I'm a gentleman. So, attempting to evoke my chivalrous side is doomed to failure. Do you know, you are even more beautiful when you're angry?"

Krystyna considered Sebastjan. She was not handling this well. He comfortably laughed off her orders and commands. She had to be cleverer than he, and, in this, the opium could very well help her. The man might well prove more manageable this way. “Perhaps we can negotiate.” She adjusted her damp skirts to take a seat on the highbacked, embroidered chair opposite his settee.

At this rejoinder, Sebastjan’s eyes opened wide. A smile of appreciation curved his lips. “What do you have in mind?” He made a move to rise.

“No, no. Stay there. Sebastjan. You must win my cooperation. Let’s play a game, a game of chance. You play for your pleasure, and I’ll play for your obedience.”

“You don’t mean for us to play cards now?”

“You are a gaming man, are you not? Consider the prize, a night with me if you win, and if I win, you must take me to Marta, wherever she is. Think of how impressed your friends will be when you regale them with this story, should you prevail.”

“You would make such a gamble?” One blond eyebrow arched in astonishment.

“I gambled by coming here this evening, and I’m willing to play the odds now.”

“You will keep your word should you lose?”

“I assure you I’m a woman of honor.”

He considered her proposal for a long moment. “All right then, it’s a gamble.”

“Shall we seal it with a kiss?”

Krystyna deliberately sought to overwhelm him. After all, though she had no intention of losing, she had to make the game seem real. She moved to him, leaned forward and allowed her lips to gently caress his. His thin, blond moustache tickled her upper lip, and she resisted the unromantic urge to scratch. Though he smelled of exotic herbs, his lips were disappointingly soft and far too passive for her taste. She drew back from Sebastjan’s embrace, but he didn’t relinquish his hold upon her.

"May I kiss you again?"

She pulled away from him. "Consider that an appetizer, but you must still win the prize. Where do you keep your playing cards?"

"Cards be damned! Come, my Belphoebe. Let's lose ourselves in the Garden of Adonis. You'll be amazed at how the opium enhances your senses. Do you know the story of Old Man in the Mountain? He was an Eastern potentate who maintained his power through an army of assassins. He ensured his men's loyalty by admitting them for a few opium-enhanced hours to a paradise filled with the most beautiful of women. There, every possible earthly desire was fulfilled, so that when the assassin returned to the everyday world, the memory of such ecstasy was enough to drive him mad. In the hopes of one day being allowed to return, the assassin did whatever his master desired, even if the ultimate cost was his life. After all, what is life to one who has experienced paradise?"

"An interesting story, but it doesn't sway me, nor does it change the nature of the game. We gamble. Time is of the essence regardless of the outcome."

"Are you quite serious?"

"Like any true Pole, I'm always serious in my gaming."

"Then, what shall we play?" Sebastjan rose and strolled over to a corner desk. He rifled through several drawers and drew forth a small box from which he removed a deck of cards. He handed them to Krystyna.

She took the deck, sat down on the settee and shuffled the cards onto the small table before her. Her fingers moved swiftly and thoughtlessly over the polished edges of the cards. "Let's keep it simple. I suggest we simply draw for the highest card."

"You've handled cards before."

"As a child, I played with my father."

"Are you also a skillful cheat?"

"How can I cheat with your deck? I've not studied these

cards, marked them or ordered them. I am as much fate's fool as are you. But I'm willing to take the risk for Marta's sake." As she spoke, her fingers slipped, and the cards spilt out of her hands and onto the table and the floor. "Forgive me, I'm so clumsy. My nerves are positively frayed."

"Here let me help you." Together they picked up the cards. Krystyna resumed shuffling. Her former dexterity had returned.

She set the deck face down, fanned the cards open and drew one. Not yet looking at her card, she watched Sebastjan.

"You are going to see this through to the end, aren't you?" His tone was both surprised and impressed.

"You have my word." She forced her hands to remain steady as she waited.

He drew a card. He flipped it face up onto the table. Jack of Hearts.

Krystyna turned her own card over. Queen of Spades.

There was a long pause then Sebastjan drew a deep breath. "I'll summon my carriage. Now, if you'll excuse me for a moment, I need to prepare for this change in the evening's plans."

Krystyna collapsed back into the settee as he left. Her father would have been proud of her. The hand had proven quicker than the eye. The only tricky part had been organizing the cards after she'd deliberately dropped them. It had made matters more complicated when Sebastjan tried to help her. Thankfully, he'd not been very observant in his condition.

She returned the cards to their small box decorated with the image of a lady with shockingly low décolletage.

"My carriage will be ready momentarily. The cape is for you." Sebastjan returned followed by his manservant, Tomas, who carried a burgundy bundle draped across his arm. Sebastjan had already donned his own cloak and hat. He grasped an ivory, hawk-headed cane from an urn by the door.

"Yours is still damp," Tomas proffered as he held the warm, heavy folds open for her.

"We go to rescue the fair damsel," Sebastjan bowed mockingly, "whether or not she wishes to be saved."

Outside, it was still raining, a chilling drizzle accompanied by a penetrating wind which stung their faces. Grateful for warmth of the borrowed cape, the hood was more effective in keeping her dry than her own, now ruined, hat had been. The carriage surprised her. It was magnificently appointed, adorned with a coat of arms and hitched to a fine black team. Sebastjan spoke with the driver and then handed her into the plush, well-padded interior.

As she settled in, she couldn't resist commenting: "You are very well prepared."

"This carriage and team are my Uncle Edward's. Tonight, the tiresome old windbag again demanded my presence for one of those interminable sessions in which he reminds me of how worthless I am. On such occasions, he always sends his carriage around to fetch me. His driver is under orders not to return without me, and it amuses me to keep Uncle's carriage out as long as possible. A public coach would have been far less comfortable or convenient."

"But your uncle's sure to be furious with you."

"No doubt he'll threaten to cut off my allowance, but don't worry, he has yet to do so, and I doubt this little adventure will motivate him to finally act."

"I don't mean to cause you…"

"Don't apologize," he interrupted with a casual wave of his hand. "I had no intention of joining him tonight. View it as providential that Uncle Edward's coach was hitched and ready to go."

"You don't care for your uncle," she observed, the intimacy of the situation having removed her reticence about making such a personal observation.

"Probably as much as he cares for me."

"Did he raise you?"

"If you can call it that. He's been my guardian since my mother died."

"Was that her portrait over your fireplace?"

"Yes."

"She was lovely, and you are remarkably like her."

"Mother died when I was fourteen. I've lived with Uncle Edward ever since."

"What was your mother's name?"

"Anzelika, and it suited her. She was like an angel, so golden and beautiful. The thing I remember most about her is the sound of her laughter. It always seemed to echo through the house. My uncle was furious with my mother for marrying my father. Though my father's family is of the Polish nobility, the szlachta, they weren't wealthy enough for Uncle Edward. He'd planned a grand match for her, but Mother and Father eloped. Then, Father further complicated the mess by dying in a hunting accident when I was three."

"How horrible. I'm sorry for your losses."

"No need. I don't remember him. Uncle Edward says he was a wastrel, but I don't believe him. Mother adored Father. He was a dashing cavalry officer. Then Mother became ill. She coughed endlessly. It was a wasting illness. Still, she read to me when she was well enough. Whenever I hear Kochanowski's poetry read aloud, I can close my eyes and imagine I'm curled up on her bed." He paused, his voice, deep with emotion. "When she died, I was sent to Uncle Edward. Now, Krystyna," he summarily dismissed the pain of his adolescence, "my pride is demanding the answer to a question. Were you at least a little nervous about meeting with me in my rooms unchaperoned?"

"I was terrified," Krystyna admitted, though she didn't explain her dread was a result of her fears for Marta, not concern for her own safety.

"That's something then." There was a genuinely pleased note to his voice.

"Where are we going, Sebastjan?"

"To a hunting lodge outside the city that belongs to a friend. We should be there within an hour."

"Who is this friend?"

"You wouldn't know her, but I'm confidant Lukacs would take his paramour there. We should be able to travel there and still get back to the city well before dawn."

"Thank you, Sebastjan. You're a good person, even though you would have me believe otherwise."

"I would never dream of disagreeing with a lovely lady," he teased self-deprecatingly.

CHAPTER 7

They lapsed into a comfortable silence. In a short while, the rocking motion of the coach and her warmth beneath the borrowed cloak eased Krystyna's passage into sleep.

But she awoke abruptly when the carriage hit a particularly large hole in the road. She was immediately fully alert and aware of her surroundings. Though it was very dark in the carriage, by leaning forward and squinting into the darkness, she could see that Sebastjan remained sleeping. His mouth had fallen open and he snored softly.

She flicked a curtain open and peered out into the night. There was as yet no hint of the dawn. She was unsure of how long they'd traveled. She sent up a quick prayer to the Virgin Mother that her arrival would be timely enough to prevent a major scandal for Marta. Everything was taking so much time, time she simply didn't have. It was both frustrating and agonizing. She nibbled at her nails, ignoring her mother's voice in her mind directing her to "Stop biting your nails."

All of a sudden, the rocking motion of the carriage ceased. One of their horses whinnied, and there was an answering call from somewhere out in the darkness. They had arrived at their destination.

Sebastjan awoke, yawned indelicately and stretched out his arms. "Not much of a rake, am I?" His voice was still thick with sleep. "Here I have you at my mercy in an enclosed carriage, and I merely fall asleep. I can imagine what my friends would say." At the mention of his friends, his expression altered from one of lazy good humor to a defensive one. "I'm afraid our reception will not be warm."

Preparing to disembark, Krystyna shifted her legs under her blanket. "Shall we face the lions?"

"There's no point in delaying the inevitable, is there?" Sebastjan put his hat back on, as it had fallen off while he slept.

"You might want to take a moment to fix your queue." Krystyna observed.

"May I be so bold as to suggest some repairs to your own coiffure?"

"Blast," she hissed as she reached up and found her heavy, silky hair had worked its way free. She pulled the long pins out. Then, she grasped the thick mass, twisted it about and drove the pins home again. Finally, she drew the hood back over her head.

"You're a marvel."

A liveried footman opened the carriage door, and Sebastjan disembarked first. He offered Krystyna his hand as she, too, stepped down.

Outside, it was impenetrably dark with a stillness that spoke of the deepest hours of the night. The rain had ceased, though the air remained chilling, damp and penetrating. Newly formed frost crunched under their feet as they stepped toward the hunting lodge. They had arrived at one of those sprawling edifices to which the Viennese aristocracy retreated to escape the Imperial city.

Krystyna fancied there was a sinister air to the building as she pondered what she would find beneath its turreted roofs.

Light flickered in several windows on both the ground and second floors.

"Where are we?"

"This hunting lodge belongs to the Marchioness von Treutter."

"The Widow von Treutter? Why she's scandalous!"

"Delicious is the word I would use."

"I have heard of her… er… appetites."

"Really? I wouldn't have believed them to be a suitable subject for a gently brought up young woman, but they are legendary, though I would contend extremely exaggerated. She's a decent soul, albeit lonely. Occasionally, she does choose a companion, and she has sworn never to remarry. She has no need to marry. Her husband left her as rich as Croesus. That's why the gossipmongers go after her so much. Right now, she's in Italy. She allows her friends to use the lodge in her absence. The place has become like a second home to several of my comrades, Lukacs among them. Well, here we go."

They stood facing a studded, wooden door. Sebastjan drew a breath and knocked using the heavy door knocker. The noise resounded. Immediately, there was an eruption of dogs barking, followed moments later by a crash, and then some cursing and shouting in masculine voices. Sebastjan and Krystyna glanced at each other as the door swung open. A tall, broad man glared out at them. He held a silver candelabra in his left hand, illuminating the chiseled planes of his face, the stubbled cheeks, the nose which had been broken more than once, the full lips, and the dark blond, tousled hair. His eyes were large and dangerously shadowed with fatigue.

Krystyna drew a startled breath and stepped back. This was no servant. Though his current rumpled, disordered appearance was a far cry from how she'd last seen him, she immediately recognized Andrzej Morzinski.

"What do you want? Do you know what time it is?"

Andrzej's glance skewered them both.

"We have come on a mission of mercy," Sebastjan responded gallantly as he tossed his cape back from his shoulders. "We come seeking a lady."

"There are no ladies here." Andrzej attempted to shut the door in their faces.

"Please, Morzinski," Sebastjan poked the tip of his cane between the door and the doorframe, effectively blocking the other man's efforts. Then, emboldened by the need to impress Krystyna, slender Sebastjan stepped straight up to this bear of a man who glared ever more furiously down at him. "I know Lukacs Dellos is here. I… We must see him."

"He probably has no more wish to be disturbed than I do. Now, if you want it in one piece, I would suggest you remove your cane."

"You don't understand," Krystyna spoke in Polish as she stepped forward from behind Sebastjan. "I will see Dellos, and a drunken lout with boorish manners will not stop me." She boldly placed her hand squarely on Andrzej's firm chest and pushed. She might as well have attempted to shove a mountain out of her way. The oaf simply stood there like a massive tree rooted to the spot.

Now that she was so close to him, he examined her face in the candlelight. "You. I remember you. You fled this young rooster's attentions at that reception for the Russian bitch, but you've enlisted his aid for this evening's adventure. What baggage women are. And if my drinking offends you, well, I wasn't planning on entertaining fashionable guests this evening." His tone was mocking.

"Pan Morzinski, if you please." She addressed him formally using the Polish term for sir or lord.

"I do not please." Then, his eyes upon her, he hesitated. Finally, he shrugged and stepped aside. "On the other hand, this may prove amusing." He held the door wide and ushered them in. "As the servants have retired for the evening, allow me to welcome you to the Bear's Den. It is deSzinay, isn't it?"

"Yes, Morzinski."

"Please introduce me to your companion. Though I have not forgotten the lovely face of a countrywoman, we've never been formally introduced."

"This isn't a situation which requires a formal introduction." Krystyna interrupted angrily. "There's no time for this nonsense." She stepped past him into the entrance hall only to abruptly stop before an enormous wolf-like dog. The beast had a narrowed snout, tall, upright ears and a bushy tail. His coat was multicolored, and his head was dark. He stood as tall as her hip, and he didn't growl or bare his teeth, but simply stared at her with great dark eyes which possessed an almost human intelligence.

"Peter, down." Andrzej ordered. The dog whined in protest but sank back into a Sphinx-like position right in front of her. "He won't bite," Andrzej commented. "Go ahead."

Krystyna deliberately glanced away from the dog, and then stepped over the animal's forelegs with a dismissive swish of her full skirts. She paused again at the entrance to the darkened corridor, but then a firm, disturbingly muscled arm captured her own and proceeded to direct her footsteps. Hastily, she glanced up at the substantial man now at her side.

"This way."

"I protest." Sebastjan's voice shrilled fearfully. "Please unhand the lady."

"If I unhand her," the deep voice chuckled, evoking a strange, butterfly-like sensation in Krystyna's stomach, "I fear she may trip and fall. Besides neither of you have any idea where you're going."

She couldn't argue with his point, and she did feel more secure with his solid arm linked through her own. In addition, his candelabra made a world of difference in the unfamiliar passage.

Despite her anxiety, she was aware of his body pressed firmly, almost inappropriately, against her side. Morzinski clearly had no interest in the proprieties. She was immersed in his scent, a heady combination of liquor, the outdoors, a vague hint of tobacco and the decidedly ungentlemanly musk of the man himself. To her dismay, she found it appealing.

"This way, my lady," Andrzej said. "Together we will descend through the various levels of hell."

They continued along the corridor at the end of which more candlelight glowed and flickered. Voices murmured.

They entered upon a scene of debauched chaos. Krystyna counted four young men seated or reclined in various states of disarray about a table covered with playing cards and coin. Two women, both blonds, were draped over two of the men. The women appeared disheveled, with their bodices loosened and their smudged faces as brightly done up as any French courtesan's. The men as a group glanced at the interlopers and then back at their hands. A small fortune lay upon that table.

"Come on, Andrzej. She can wait. It's your turn," a gaunt young man with pitted cheeks and an unruly thatch of dark hair stated.

"That one's a ripe pigeon," a plump, blond fellow cooed as he leered at Krystyna. "You were holding out on us, Morzinski. And here you had us all convinced you planned to spend this night alone. You saved the best one for yourself. Come here, liebchen." He reached out for Krystyna. "Sit on my lap. I need some luck."

"You misunderstand, Franz. This is a lady," Andrzej emphasized the word, "on a mission of mercy."

"One of the of the Marchioness's friends?" The dark haired one darted a disparaging look at Krystyna over his cards.

"Pick me." A pleasant-looking young fellow with wavy hair and a baby face rose to his feet facing her. "Morzinski is so serious minded, and since he finished with the Marchioness, may

God bless our hostess, he has sworn off women. You'll have much more fun with me."

"Calm yourself, Roch. You all misunderstand," Andrzej interrupted with a shake of his head. "This lady is, in fact, a lady, and she has come to rescue a friend from our foul clutches. DeSzinay brought her."

The curious but accommodating glances swiftly changed to hostile.

"What the hell are you thinking about, deSzinay?" The dark-haired fellow of the scarred cheeks demanded, his gaze now on Sebastjan.

"Henryk," Sebastjan implored as he stepped forward. "She needed help. She was worried about her friend."

"Fool," Henryk spat the word back. "This place is to be kept secret. You presume on the Marchioness's generosity."

"Krystyna will never tell anyone, will you?" Sebastjan implored.

"Of course not. I simply wish to collect my friend."

"What is your name, and who is your friend?" the baby-faced one asked. "I'm Roch, and I'm at your service." He reached for her hand, but Andrzej sidestepped in front of him, pushing Krystyna back behind his body and out of the light.

"The lady's name is of no importance. She thinks her friend is with Dellos. Have any of you seen him?"

"Lukacs is here," Franz put in. "But he came alone. I saw no lady with him."

"He still may have one tucked away in his rooms," Andrzej pointed out.

"Andrzej, are you in or out?" Henryk demanded. "I would win my money back."

"I'm out then," Andrzej dismissed the pile of money in the center of the table with a shrug. It would have helped, but he had already won enough to pay for his trip back home. These wealthy sons of Austria were remarkably careless with their money. Besides, the woman whom he now shielded intrigued him, with the way the candlelight played on her thick red gold hair, by her full lips and large eyes, and most of all by her assertiveness and her loyalty. She was a breath of the fresh Polish air, of home, after the stale perfume of the women of the Austrian court.

"Roch, where are Dellos' rooms?"

"He's usually in one of the rooms off the hallway near the portrait salon."

"At the bottom of the stairs?"

"Yes."

"This way." Andrzej turned.

"You forfeit your money," Henryk called after them.

Andrzej didn't bother to respond. This night of gambling and debauchery had proven dissatisfying. The arrival of the Polish valkyrie had definitely improved matters.

He guided Krystyna along another hallway while Sebastjan followed. They went up some stairs, turned once more, then Andrzej paused in front of a closed door. He knocked. There was no answer. He waited and knocked again. Still no response. He tried the knob. Unlocked. He pushed it open and, before she could grasp his intentions, he took Krystyna's hand and drew her to the foot of an enormous bed encircled with velvet drapes. There, he yanked the curtains back to reveal an entangled and very naked couple staring up at them in shock.

"Hey, what's this about? Morzinski? Have you gone mad?" a man who was not Dellos demanded.

A girl with long, tousled dark hair watched them in dismay, unaware that the sheet she defensively clutched left one large nippled, melon-sized breast uncovered.

"Is this your friend?" Andrzej demanded.

"No…No, it's not." Krystyna shot the words back, thoroughly shocked by Andrzej's actions.

He said nothing further. He simply dragged her out of the

room. Sebastjan shut the door on his way out, after offering apologies to the distraught couple.

"Wait," Krystyna spoke up. "Are you sure we should be doing this? I mean, isn't there some other way?"

"Do you want to find your friend? Trust me, this is the only way. Dellos won't willingly reveal that your friend is with him."

Andrzej had said, "Trust me," and, strangely enough, Krystyna did. For now, he seemed as determined as she to search the house until they located Marta.

He banged on another door.

There was an immediate reply. He thrust the door open on a young man reading alone in his bed. He didn't seem disturbed, merely nodded to them and continued to peruse his text.

A third door, on the opposite side of the hallway, was large, ornate and obviously indicated chambers of some importance.

Andrzej proceeded directly past the door.

"Shouldn't we check in there?" Krystyna queried.

"That's the Marchioness's personal suite," Sebastjan explained from behind them. "Morzinski's the only one with access to those rooms."

Andrzej didn't bother to refute or even acknowledge Sebastjan's heavy-handed innuendo. Krystyna was surprised Sebastjan had the courage to make such a suggestive comment. They turned a corner. Morzinski knocked upon another door. This time a muffled voice questioned: "Who is it?"

"Dellos? It's Morzinski. Open the door."

"Why? What is it?"

"Open the door now."

It opened, and Krystyna followed Andrzej inside to find Dellos disappointingly alone. To her great relief, he was still dressed in his blouse and breeches, though his feet were bare.

"What are you doing here?" Dellos inquired with a baffled look at Krystyna.

"Where's Marta? I'm here to take her home. What have you

done with her?" Krystyna snapped, as she jerked back the bed hangings to see the rumpled bed was, indeed, empty.

"Morzinski, I wouldn't have thought this Amazon your type," Dellos jibed. "What would the Marchioness say? And in her own home, too."

"Where is the girl, Dellos?" Morzinski demanded, his tone, ominous and deep. He set his candelabra down on the desk, though two other candles in wall mounted sconces cast a weak glow.

"I fail to see where this is any concern of yours, Morzinski."

Andrzej took several strides across the room, grasped Dellos by the front of his shirt, and dragged him up against the wall. In a quiet voice, he repeated, "Where is the girl?"

"The baggage is in the dressing chamber," Dellos choked out fearfully. "She locked herself in there hours ago. Won't come out. I've been asleep for the past few hours."

"There," Andrzej indicated the adjoining door with a nod of his head. He continued to hold the cringing Dellos up against the wall.

Krystyna rushed over to the dressing chamber door. She banged on it and shouted. "Marta. Marta! Please answer me." No one answered.

"Marta! Open the door."

"Is that you, Krystyna?" Marta spoke in a weakly tremulous voice, the tone, disbelieving.

"Yes, it's me. Open up."

A key scraped in the lock, and the door swung open to reveal a red-eyed, disheveled, pale-faced girl who threw her arms around Krystyna in overwhelming relief and then burst into tears. "You've come. You've come. Thank God!"

Still holding the sobbing girl, Krystyna glowered at Dellos. "What have you done to her?"

"Nothing! Ask her. I swear. The words squeaked out of his compressed throat.

"Did you hurt her?" Andrzej's words came disturbingly calm and soft.

"No! No!" He choked out.

"He did. He did!" At Marta's exclamation, Andrzej's grip tightened on Dellos's neck.

"She's lying. I swear it!"

"Did you compromise her?" Andrzej growled.

"She wanted to run away with me. It was all her idea. But nothing happened. She locked herself in there as soon as we got here."

"We were to be married. Instead, he brought me to this terrible place."

"Listen, Marta. Did Dellos do anything to you?"

"He… He kissed me, quite a lot," she managed to sputter. "Then, he started to paw at me, but I locked myself in there."

"Out. Get out." Andrzej ordered the two women. "I want a few words with Dellos alone."

"Don't hurt him. Please," Marta cried out.

"He's not worth your concern," Krystyna muttered as she half dragged Marta out of the room and down the hall. With the candelabra in his hand, Sebastjan walked directly behind them. As they rounded a corner, they could hear Dellos pleading, but Krystyna didn't allow Marta to turn back or slow. They made their way to the front door. Within minutes, they were back out in the carriage.

Sebastjan gave orders to the driver to "Return to Vienna with all possible speed."

Krystyna was so busy consoling Marta she didn't realize until they were some distance from the hunting lodge that she hadn't thanked Morzinski.

CHAPTER 8

For Krystyna, the weeks following Marta's rescue remained thankfully quiet. Jadwiga was unwell, so they rarely ventured forth into society. As the fall breezes became brisk with the promise of winter, Krystyna daydreamed about home, missing her parents, and thinking a great a deal about Andrzej Morzinski.

"Krystyna, would you serve the coffee?" Jadwiga asked. "At this time of year, I long for Italy. Shall we make a trip to Florence to pass these cold months? It would be so pleasant. I could show you so much. That's it, a little more cream. Good. Do try one of the miniature tortes, they are delicious."

"That sounds very nice, but I'd really like to be here for Marta, until she's more settled." This was true, but there was another reason as well, she didn't want to leave Vienna until she encountered Andrzej again.

"You're a thoughtful friend, my dear."

The two women shared a comfortable silence as they sipped their coffee and nibbled cakes while Jadwiga went through her mail.

"Krystyna, here's a letter for you. And another."

"Anything from Mama and Tata?"

"No, I don't think so."

Krystyna set her cup and saucer down and took the two envelopes her aunt held out. She didn't recognize the penmanship on either. The larger envelope, made of thick, soft vellum, bore an unfamiliar coat of arms on its wax seal. She broke the seal.

Her heart began to pound. The letter was written in Polish, and it was from Andrzej. In it, he related his concern for Marta and informed Krystyna of his desire to call on her. He had taken the step of "securing the assistance of a good friend of my father's, the General Von Zetl" who, he explained, was also an acquaintance of Jadwiga's. He signed the note, "Your servant, Andrzej Morzinski."

Euphoria shooting through her, Krystyna jumped to her feet and hugged Jadwiga. She was going to see him again, and he was taken with her. She fairly burst with excitement.

"It must be from some young scoundrel," her aunt discerned. "Only a young man could inspire such a dreamy look on your face. A young man or a new horse," Jadwiga chuckled.

"How did you…?"

"An old woman's intuition. You may find this hard to believe, but I was young once, too. Oh, this is such fun. My dear, I'm teasing you. Actually, while you were out riding this morning, I entertained a guest on your young man's behalf. General von Zetl called on me before luncheon. I haven't seen the man in years. I wasn't even properly dressed.

"Once I got over my surprise, we had a nice chat about the old days. I met him when I was still a young bride. Hans served with my second husband, Jens. Seeing him brought back those wonderful days. He swore I hadn't changed a bit, the liar, though I loved him for it. Maybe he sees me as I used to be, or else his vision really is failing. I was shocked to see how he's aged. Time hasn't been kind to him. He walks with a cane, and his hair is white as snow, but at least he has all of it. Twenty years ago, he was a handsome devil. He had a way about him that had all of the wives at the fort in Sarajevo swooning." She grinned at the memory, but then, her smile faded. "Hans von Zetl brought me the news of Jens's death. A Croatian separatist murdered him."

"I'm so sorry, Aunt Jadwiga. How horrible."

Jadwiga pursed her lips and sniffed, and Krystyna was sure she saw a suspicious brightness in the older woman's eyes. "It was all a lifetime ago. But some mornings, just as I'm beginning to wake, I feel like a child still or a young woman. And then it hits me, I'm almost seventy years old. Time passes in a blink of an eye. One day you're young and in love, and the next, you wake up old and alone. Treasure each moment, Krystyna, sink your teeth into it, and don't let go."

"You're not alone, Aunt Jadwiga. I'm here, and I love you. So many people love you."

Jadwiga gathered herself. With resolution, she re-fixed the smile on her lips and cast off her despondency. "I know, my girl. I have been blessed in many ways, and you are a very special gift to me. Now back to the business at hand, your young man."

"The General. What did he want? Tell me everything!"

"Young Morzinski apparently desires a formal introduction. I don't know why he didn't come directly to me. It's not as if we aren't acquainted. The boy has been positively hounding me on the Polish issue for months now. This must be serious since he's using Hans as a go-between. The story is that Morzinski saw you at a reception and desires to meet you. Of course, there was no mention of your encounter at the Marchioness von Treutter's."

"What else? What else did the General say?"

"We spoke of the lad and found we share the same opinion. Morzinski has a bit of the devil in him, although he is a clever one. He studied at the same academy as Thaddeus Kosciuszko and has traveled extensively. He is somewhat wild and dangerously liberal, but I could tell the General is quite fond of him, and I trust von Zetl's opinions, particularly when I share them."

Krystyna hungrily absorbed the information. "Did you give him permission to call?"

"For as long as he behaves himself."

"Now tell me the rest. You know more, don't you?"

"I did send a note to the Baroness, to inquire about Marta. The silly chit is doing fine, and suitably penitent. Ewa also filled me in on some other details regarding your young man. He was briefly involved with the Marchioness von Treutter. From what I understand, that affair ended long ago, though the two remain friends." Jadwiga watched the emotions flit across her niece's face. Really, the girl was so transparent. It would be such a pleasure to watch love bloom. All signs indicated it was a worthy match. Krystyna's parents were sure to be pleased. Andrzej was a countryman of similar social standing and estate, and he might periodically return to Vienna with his wife. Thus, if all worked out well, Jadwiga would get to see her beloved great niece. "I indicated to the General I would be agreeable to a visit from him and his young friend some day next week, after luncheon."

"You did!" Krystyna bounced to her feet, rushed to Jadwiga's chair and caught her in an enthusiastic hug.

"Easy child, easy, you'll make me spill my coffee. Now, leave me. I need some rest. All of this excitement is wearing me out."

"I don't believe that for a minute, Aunt Jadwiga. You're having a grand time." Krystyna flashed a brilliant smile, and after grabbing the letters, practically skipped up the stairs.

~

A few hours later, Krystyna lingered in her dressing chamber combing through the tangles in her wet hair. It was already fully dark outside, and the air held a definite chill. But the dressing chamber was small and relatively warm. When she finished, she braided her hair, wrapped her dressing gown more securely, and opened the door to her bedroom.

The fire was well stoked for the night. Still, the room was large and drafty, so she leaped into bed and pulled the blankets up to her neck. She started to pick up a book to read when she noticed an unopened letter on her dressing table.

She'd forgotten about this other letter in her excitement about Andrzej's. Its envelope and seal were both plain and unadorned. She leaned over and grabbed it. Lying back in her bed, she broke the wax seal. As she opened the letter, the distinctive shape of the Cyrillic lettering sent a wave of anxiety sweeping through her. It was in Russian, and it consisted of a litany of threats and accusations all revolving around Ivan's death. It concluded: "I will hunt you to the death, you Polish bitch. You will pay for your crime, as will anyone who aids you. You cannot run from me for long. I have your scent. I am the hunter. There is no escape. You will die slowly and painfully at my hands. I will watch the life fade from your eyes. and Ivan will have justice." The letter was signed "Janus."

Her stomach twisted. Janus? Who was Janus? From her lessons in the schoolroom, she vaguely recalled that Janus was the name of the classical god with two faces, one gazing into the past and one looking into the future. Who could he be? What were his intentions? *Jadwiga!* She had to warn her great-aunt.

She threw back the covers and darted out of the bedroom and down the hall toward her great-aunt's suite of rooms. There, she banged frantically on the door to Jadwiga's chambers. "Aunt Jadwiga. Aunt Jadwiga. I must speak with you!"

There was no answer. Her heart hammered, and she felt ill. Frantically, she jerked and twisted at the knobs to open the two carved doors, but to no avail. They were firmly locked. In addition, there were no sounds coming from the other side. Sara was always sure to announce a visitor to her mistress's boudoir.

Could it be that Krystyna was already too late? When had the note arrived? In desperation, she kicked at the door, shouting "Aunt Jadwiga. Aunt Jadwiga." Still no response. She drove her shoulder into the door, but it didn't budge. Something was definitely amiss.

Pavel! Where was he! She tore back down the hall to the backstairs. Though she was unfamiliar with these regions of the house, she knew most of the domestics were housed along this particular corridor. Krystyna shouted as she ran along, "Pavel. Pavel. Someone. Help!"

"What is it?" Abruptly, the man materialized behind her. He carried an oil lamp in his hand. His dark eyes were steady and unflinching.

She was almost sobbing with terror. "It's Aunt Jadwiga! Her room's locked! I think she may be hurt or even… Hurry!"

Pavel didn't question her further. He simply nodded then ran toward Jadwiga's rooms. Krystyna followed and made it to her aunt's door in time to watch Pavel work a long, wickedly curved blade in the lock. The door swung open. They burst into the spacious sitting room that was shockingly empty and dark. A quick survey revealed the dressing room and the bedchamber were also unoccupied. There was no sign of Jadwiga whatsoever.

"What's all of this commotion about?" Jadwiga demanded as she strode in from the outer hallway. "What's going on?"

"Aunt Jadwiga!" Krystyna ran to her and fiercely embraced her "You're all right."

"Oh my. Yes, I'm fine. But what's going on here? Pavel, what have you done to my door?"

"The young one believed you were in danger."

"Krystyna?" Jadwiga questioned with an elevated eyebrow.

"I got a letter. And then your doors were locked." Krystyna paused for a moment as she drew back from Jadwiga. "Why were your doors locked if you weren't in here?"

"I didn't lock them."

"They were locked. Ask Pavel." Pavel nodded mutely.

Jadwiga eyed the bolt in question.

Krystyna rubbed her shoulders and shivered. Jadwiga was all right. She'd been granted a reprieve.

"Why haven't these rooms been readied for the night? Where's Jutta? Why the fire has died out. I'll have to speak with her. There's no excuse for letting the fire die. Even if she starts it right away, my bedroom will remain miserably cold most of the night. Where is that girl, and where is that cold wind coming from?"

Pavel spoke to Jadwiga in his language of the steppes. He gestured to a sheer floor length curtain that billowed gently. Keeping his knife at the ready, he crossed the room and drew the curtain back to reveal the window was open. He peered down into the darkness at the shrubbery two stories below.

Krystyna questioned, "Do you see anyone?"

"No." Still, he stared out.

"Where's Sara?" Krystyna asked. "The fact that she didn't bark as she usually does when I knocked on your door scared me."

"She was filthy dirty from running through puddles during her walk. One of the stable boys is cleaning her up for me. Pavel, do you think someone came in through that window?"

He nodded. "And left as well." He began to prowl through the room, searching the corners and shadows, checking for an intruder.

Krystyna moved closer to her aunt. In unison, they stepped back toward the bed. Krystyna's leg encountered a solid object, and she fell, barely managing to catch herself on the bed. She stared down at what she stumbled over. At first, she couldn't quite it make out. Pavel moved about the room with his lamp, and it was dark by the floor. Then, she screamed. Jutta lay there, staring up at her, dead.

"Are you all right? What is it? Oh no, no... Not Jutta."

Jadwiga bent down beside the fallen servant woman who lay half shoved under the bed.

Pavel pressed his fingers to Jutta's throat. Then, he met his mistress's glance and shook his head.

"Poor child," Jadwiga stroked the dead woman's hand.

Pavel lowered his lamp to illuminate the body. Jutta's neck was bent at an impossible angle. Her face was twisted in death's agony, and a thin stream of blood had traveled down her lips and over her chin. But it was those staring eyes, so lifeless, so void of feeling and thought which seared into Krystyna's memory.

"Pavel, get her onto the bed." Jadwiga curtly ordered. Despite his diminutive size, Pavel was strong. He hefted the body of the much taller Austrian woman onto the bed. Once there, Jadwiga gently shut her eyes.

"Do you think whoever did…this is still here somewhere?"

Pavel shook his head. "He's gone now. Out the window. But I will check the rest of the house."

Jadwiga nodded her assent. He departed soundlessly, and the two women silently contemplated the still warm body.

At last, Krystyna spoke up. "Shouldn't we say a prayer for her?"

"Quite right. How could I be so thoughtless? Jutta was a dear soul. Shall it be the Our Father then?"

They held hands as they spoke the prayer aloud together.

Afterwards, Krystyna gripped her great-aunt's hand even more tightly. "It should have been me and not Jutta."

"What do you mean, child?"

"He came after me."

"Who? What are you talking about?" Jadwiga stared at her niece perplexedly.

"The murderer. He sent me a letter. I have it here. I just opened it. That's why I came looking for you." Krystyna reached into the pockets of her dressing gown and drew forth the letter.

Jadwiga was perplexed. "What's this? Bother, I don't have my spectacles. Please read it for me."

Krystyna read the chilling missive aloud. With the body of the fallen maid stretched out before them, the words and thoughts were even more horrifying.

"Who could blame you for what happened? This makes no sense. Why didn't you show me this earlier?"

"I came to your room to do just that. If only I'd done so earlier, this," she gestured at Jutta, "might not have happened. Janus blames me for Ivan's death. But then, why did he go to your room and kill Jutta? I don't understand."

"The behavior of a madman is not comprehensible to the rest of us. Perhaps Jutta simply walked in at the wrong time. Who could this person be? Think, girl. Think."

"I have no idea. I really don't."

"What about this Ivan's family? His friends?"

"His parents are dead, I believe, and he had an older brother. I met him. He visited Sea of Grass once with Ivan. But they didn't seem particularly close. As for his friends, I met several of them, but none really stick out in my mind. Besides, it was an accident. I couldn't make a horse kill a man."

"Any reasonable person would see that, but we're clearly not dealing with a reasonable person. Consider his letter… We could leave Vienna and go to Italy. No, no, not now. I'm not thinking clearly. This person will surely follow us. I suppose we must call the police, what with poor Jutta here. Krystyna, when you speak with them, you must make no mention of Bestuzhev, of what occurred at your home, or of this letter. The police won't be able to make heads or tails of the whole matter. They'll write up useless reports and ruin your reputation in the process."

"But what about Jutta? What about justice for her? Without all of the information, how will the police be able to solve the crime?"

"I have no faith in the Viennese police. Even if you tell them everything, they won't be able to handle this matter. They won't bring Jutta justice." Jadwiga paced as she thought aloud. "But there are men one can hire for such delicate tasks who are much more efficient than the police. We will also take steps to protect the safety of all who live and work here. This house will become a fortress. We will catch the man or men who did this."

"I should leave here. I'm the one Janus is after."

"We stand a better chance of catching Jutta's murderer if we all remain in this house."

"But if I leave no one else will get hurt."

"Don't deceive yourself. This animal will kill again. If he is after you, he will hunt you, cutting down anyone who stands in his way. No, I will not have my niece driven to ground like a fox. It must end here, where we have the power. And our opponent has lost the element of surprise."

Krystyna nodded her head slowly. Jadwiga's confidence was contagious. "We'll trap him."

"Yes, my dear, and you'll be the bait. We must create the illusion he can get to you, while, in truth, you are wholly protected."

"I don't want to put you or anyone else at further risk."

"We have Pavel, remember. I trust him implicitly. He will keep us safe. With you out and about in the city, I doubt very much Janus will be able to contain himself. And then, we'll have him. Yes, it is the best and most reasonable way to proceed." Jadwiga agitatedly toyed with the gold and amber medallion she wore on a chain around her neck.

To Krystyna's ears, it sounded like she was trying to convince herself.

CHAPTER 9

As the weather grew colder, many Viennese aristocrats, like exotic birds, began to flee the imperial city for homes in the countryside. For those who remained, society was quieter, less hectic. There was a bit of a scandal at Waldstrasse, the avenue on which Jadwiga Von Gebler lived. Rumor had it a robbery occurred, and a servant was killed. The police came and went for several days.

As Jadwiga predicted, the authorities made no progress in the investigation of Jutta's murder. The strain of maintaining both their guards and their social faces wore on Krystyna and Jadwiga.

Then, two weeks after Jutta's murder, they received an invitation to a dinner party at General von Zetl's home. The von Reigler family were also invited. Both families planned to attend.

Despite the burden of her fears, Krystyna was elated. Andrzej wanted to see her. Obviously, he had orchestrated this dinner, as it was common knowledge the General had not entertained in years.

That night, she dressed with special care. Living in a constant state of anxiety had stripped away some of her reservations. She wanted Andrzej to notice her, to keep his eyes on her constantly. And so, she wore a daring bronze silk, the cut accentuated the lushness of her figure. Her hair, unpowdered and swept up in a Grecian style, revealed the long, elegant line of her neck. As an accent, she chose only a single strand of her great-aunt's pearls and a matching set of ear bobs. The pearls glowed warm and luminous against her creamy skin. Krystyna knew she looked her best, and she almost felt giddy with the prospect of seeing Andrzej again.

Since the Count von Reigler was again out of town on a diplomatic mission, the von Reigler women accompanied Krystyna and Jadwiga in their carriage to the von Zetl house. Jadwiga's old friend lived in an outlying section of the city where private parks surrounded substantial homes. It was already dark when they arrived at a rather austere but impressive house. The warm, golden glow in the windows belied the severe exterior and beckoned to the new arrivals.

A butler took their mantles and then escorted the ladies through the entrance foyer into a hall. Portraits of officers in uniform either standing or mounted adorned the walls. A large fire roared in an enormous, marble fireplace while softly flickering chandeliers constructed of countless deer antlers lit up the chamber. A collection of blades covered an expanse of wall opposite the fireplace; there were Toledo steel rapiers, curved scimitars, enormous great swords and jeweled daggers. The firelight danced on the glistening steel and vivified the precious stones in the hilts and sheaths. It was a disturbing and intriguing array dedicated to the implements of war and death. Just then, General von Zetl, ramrod straight and whitehaired, entered the room followed immediately by Andrzej Morzinski.

Both men were elegantly and similarly attired in dark colored silk jackets and breeches with brilliantly white cravats and only slightly more ostentatious waistcoats. Neither wore powder in his hair. The general stepped forward with alacrity despite the slight hitch to his gait and the cane in his hand. He went directly to Jadwiga. His craggy face lit with a warm welcoming smile, and Krystyna was surprised to observe her great-aunt blush in response.

He bowed to the Baroness, Krystyna and Marta each in turn, but then returned to Jadwiga's side. "I welcome you all to my home. Jadwiga, may I impose on our many years' acquaintance to call you by your given name? 'Jadwiga' you have always been to me in my memories of the blond hellion who stole one of my best friend's heart. Ah, my dear, I would have married you myself, if he had not."

"You are a still a scoundrel, Hans." Jadwiga dimpled as the former soldier raised her hand to his lips. "I wasn't born young enough to be one of your wives."

"In my impetuous youth, I failed to understand that women, like wine, get better with age."

"If I were a wine, Hans, I'd have long since turned to vinegar."

"Ah, you are still a saucy one."

"Where is your current child bride?"

"In the country with our daughters. All that femininity is smothering, and I am too old a man to be worrying about hair ribbons and dresses and such nonsense. When I come to Vienna on business, I come alone."

"So what is the grand total then? Six, isn't it?"

"No, there are seven of the hoydens. Seven girls and not one son. But they are dear creatures, always fussing about my health and my diet. I've managed to find the first three decent husbands, and I'm working on arranging two other matches. It's rather like selecting good junior officers. You must have a good nose for people.

Thankfully, my daughters have been accommodating. All of

the married ones are more than content with their respective spouses."

Jadwiga chuckled. "I never quite envisioned you as a matchmaker, Hans. Doesn't your wife help you?"

"Maria has no head for strategy, but I do. Now," the General turned to Krystyna. "It is a great pleasure to finally meet a young woman about whom I've heard so much. You have the look of your aunt about you, girl."

"Thank you." Krystyna felt the amused, intelligent eyes studying her.

"Krystyna," Jadwiga said. "General Hans von Zetl is one of the finest cavalry officers ever to serve Empress Maria Theresa."

Krystyna nodded and commented appropriately, but her thoughts were on the tall, broad shouldered young man who stood behind the General. Suddenly, Andrzej's amused, dangerously perceptive brown eyes captured hers. Wholly disconcerted and aware of a blush rising in her cheeks, she glanced away, raising her fan to hide her confusion. She found this honorable rogue more exciting than any other man she'd ever met, but she also worried she'd never be able to manage him. Andrzej Morzinski was not a man to be led about by any woman. Still, she wanted him and was determined to have him.

"Ladies, please follow me." Taking Jadwiga's arm, the General led the way. "My other guests await us."

Krystyna was aware of the pounding of her heart as Andrzej offered her his arm. When their hands touched briefly, despite her gloves, awareness shot through her. He tilted his head down to her and whispered so only she could hear: "You look beautiful tonight."

"So do you." She almost choked in mortification at the words that came thoughtlessly to her lips. The arrogant man laughed quietly.

The group proceeded into a smaller chamber where several other guests, mostly of the older couple's vintage, waited. To

Krystyna's surprise, Sebastjan deSzinay was also there, and he grinned a warm welcome at both Krystyna and Marta.

For once, Jadwiga had the social advantage over the Baroness. Exclamations and warm greetings passed between old friends from the days in which Jadwiga and her husband had been stationed at farflung bases throughout the Austrian empire. The guests were a dignified set whose conversation was thoughtful and incisive, not at all the usual social nonsense. The future of the Habsburg Empire came up, as well as how to deal with the unruly minorities, including the Hungarians who viewed Empress Maria Theresa as their personal queen.

Under other circumstances, Krystyna would have been fascinated by the discussion. But the fact that Andrzej assumed a relaxed stance just opposite her, his elbow resting on the mantel, unsettled her.

She struggled to meet his warm gaze. Silently, she berated herself. She was behaving foolishly, like an innocent straight out of the schoolroom. She had no intention of allowing any man to gain the upper hand over her again, no matter how devilishly attractive he was. Taking one slow, deep breath, she raised cool, steady eyes and cheeks that bore only a hint of tell-tale pink. However, Andrzej's eyes were now focused on the speaker, a stout Austrian who gestured enthusiastically with his hands as he spoke.

"I'm most concerned about Russia and the Empress Catherine. The woman knows no bounds. And I don't believe Emperor Joseph of Austria is constructed of the same stuff as his mother. I fear he can be influenced."

"I would argue," von Zetl remarked, "that one of Empress Catherine's most offensive yet effective actions was placing her discarded lover, Poniatowski, on the throne of Poland. He is another weakling whom she can control."

"Poniatowski is a fool, but he is not Poland's real problem," Andrzej entered the fray, his dark eyes blazing.

Though she didn't entirely agree with him, Krystyna admired his passion for his convictions.

"My protégé here is a radical," the General explained with a wry smile. "In his travels, he has absorbed all sorts of nonsense, particularly the French sort. I am afraid the writings of Voltaire and Rousseau have taken root in Andrzej. We've had many a rousing argument over such matters."

The room erupted into conversation and comment. Then, one voice, Jadwiga's, rose above the din. "I, too, have read these philosophers. The freedom of the mind advocated by Voltaire is appealing, but is it appropriate for everyone? There must be an order to life, to society. You would turn it upside down."

"In the words of Monsieur Rousseau," Andrzej responded, "'Man is born free, yet he is everywhere in chains.'"

"Young man," Jadwiga spoke up again. "You are impetuous. Rousseau has addressed the matter of Poland directly. He writes that theories must be grounded in reality, that changes to your country should not be made suddenly."

"We have to start somewhere," Andrzej argued. "And it's not the king but the nobility who are Poland's biggest problem. Some of Poland's greatest families work with Russia, Prussia, and Austria-Hungary to keep our homeland weak and tear her apart."

"You speak as if you were not a member of the szlachta, yourself," the General scoffed. "I've watched you Poles grapple with these issues for years now. But I warn you, Andrzej, Poland is too centrally located to be ignored. Austria-Hungary, Russia, and Prussia are hungry predators eyeing a shepherd less herd. I fear it will not go well for your country."

"Is it not better than that we accept Austrian influence, which is relatively benevolent, than to hope Prussia and Russia chose not to intervene?" Krystyna spoke up daringly. As a young, unmarried woman, she wasn't expected to either have political views or to air them. However, her parents and her Aunt Jadwiga believed in the power of a woman's mind and encouraged Krystyna to use hers.

"I couldn't have said it better myself," the General approved with a nod at her and a sidelong glance at Andrzej "And I appreciate a young woman who has more in her head than dresses and ribbons."

"Yours is exactly the sort of attitude which undermines Poland," Andrzej rebuked Krystyna. But he softened his words with a sly wink that immediately elicited a rosy blush on her face and neck.

"If Poland is too weak to stand alone, we have no choice." Krystyna argued, refusing to be disconcerted. "Wouldn't it be better to choose our masters rather than allow the most vicious scavengers to pick the flesh from our bones?"

"There is some truth to your comment, Panienka," he concurred. "But I hope that our homeland can become strong again, so that we need not fear or rely on others."

"And I pray that she will remain safe and peaceful."

"Well said, my girl," Jadwiga inserted. "You overemphasize the danger, young man. But I applaud your zeal. It is refreshing to hear a young person speak of politics rather than gaming or horse racing. Don't you agree, General?"

"Most definitely. But enough of politics. I'm sure some of the ladies would prefer another subject." The General nodded decorously in the direction of several of them.

The conversation shifted to more conventional matters: the weather, the work still being done on Schonnbrun, the emperor's activities, plans to leave the city for country estates for the Christmas holidays and horse breeding.

Krystyna didn't get to speak with Andrzej again, though she was aware of his eyes upon her, and she met his glances boldly, making her interest in him readily apparent. She had always been a straightforward person, but Jutta's murder and her own continuing anxiety about Janus had stripped pretense from her.

She had the feeling there was no time to waste, not when at any moment something else horrible could happen. She wished she could really talk with him about what was going on, but such a discussion was completely out-of-place while they moved through the elaborately choreographed steps of courtship.

Eventually, dinner was announced. As the group milled about and began to exit the chamber, Sebastjan swiftly approached Krystyna. Not wishing to appear rude, she took his proffered arm, but she caught Andrzej's swift, irritated glance. She was aware of his continued scrutiny as Sebastjan inclined his head towards her: "How is gentle Marta's recovery proceeding?"

"As well as can be expected under the circumstances. She's learned from the situation and is little the worse for it, thanks to you. I'm sure she will appreciate your concern."

"She's a charming creature, quite easy on the eyes. It was an adventure. And I came out well with my friends in the end. All most of them can remember from that night is your great, scowling bear of a champion there. He's absorbed all of the censure, to my great relief, though no one would dare voice them to his face. That Pole has quite a reputation in fisticuffs. I find myself growing fond of him. Though I should watch myself if I were you, Krystyna. He obviously has intentions where you are concerned.

"Did you know the General hasn't entertained in years? My uncle was astonished I received an invitation. It irritated him to no end that he didn't. Clearly, this evening was planned for your benefit."

She felt a warm shiver pass through her at Sebastjan's words.

"I feel I should warn you. Morzinski's no lamb, Krystyna. In fact, his reputation is something to which I can only aspire."

"Is he known as a profligate?" She didn't want to believe he was.

"No, he has too many other interests that take up his time and distract him. But he is passionate and impulsive, a true Polish patriot." Sebastjan cocked an eyebrow at her sardonically. "Am I correct in assuming women find his brand of gallantry appealing?"

"I, ah…" Words abandoned her.

"I see now I've already lost you. Well, he probably is the better man." He shrugged his shoulders. "Why is it women prefer the brooding, intense types?"

"Does he keep a mistress?"

Sebastjan hesitated mid-stride and faced Krystyna in mock horror. "I'm appalled at that sort of question from a lady."

"Tell me," Krystyna demanded, as she pressed her elbow into his side. "Does he?"

"To my knowledge," his words were hurried and whispered as they paused outside the doors to the dining room, "Andrzej doesn't keep a mistress, though he has been known to carry on passing dalliances, usually with older women. You already know of his affair with the Widow von Treutter, though it has been over with for some time."

Once inside, the General directed the seating arrangements. Andrzej sat opposite her. She wondered why they hadn't been placed next to each other, but then reflected doing so may have been too overt. It was impossible to carry on any sort of conversation around the platters overflowing with food that passed between them, but she could see him and feel his eyes upon her. She discovered eyes were remarkably adept communication tools. Later, she heard from Jadwiga that the meal was excellent, but she only vaguely remembered the taste or texture of what she consumed. Indeed, her glass of the potent French red wine was never allowed to go empty. Conscious of Andrzej's attention upon her, Krystyna felt vitally alive, as if she glowed in the candlelight.

Then, it was time for the men to retire to the library for a smoke and a drink. Meanwhile, the ladies refreshed themselves or chatted in a bright chamber with white and gold detailed walls. There, Krystyna and Marta took leave of Jadwiga and the Baroness, citing a desire to walk about.

The two young women wandered back through various rooms; doors opened in invitation.

"I still feel warm from that wine." Krystyna fanned her face. "Do you want to step outside? I'm sure we could find someone to bring our cloaks up," she suggested. She wanted to get outside. She recalled her encounter with Andrzej at the birthday celebration for Catherine of Russia. Would he be there as well?

"I don't think my mother would approve," Marta demurred. "Besides, it's cold tonight." She shivered as she hugged herself.

"It'll be refreshing, and we'll only be gone for a minute."

"Krystyna, you go ahead. I would prefer to stay in."

Knowing how fragile her friend was of late, Krystyna didn't want to desert her. "All right, then. We'll both stay in. I'm sure I can find an open window somewhere."

"You go ahead. I'm fine, truly. I'll tell your aunt you will return shortly."

"Are you sure?" Krystyna squeezed Marta's hand and offered her a quick smile.

Marta nodded.

Minutes later, she emerged from the front door wrapped in her mantle, her fingers, tucked warmly in a muff. As she made her way down the stone steps, she inhaled deeply, savoring the feel of the cool night air on her heated skin.

Countless bright stars punctuated the lush ebony night. The air held a promise of frost. Each breath she took refreshed her after the almost cloying heat of the house. The glow from innumerable windows provided sufficient illumination for her to wander about in front of the house. To her disappointment, she didn't encounter Andrzej. After a short while, she headed back to the house and began to ascend the steps when a familiar, deep voice waylaid her.

"You're not like other women, Krystyna, more wildflower

than cultured rose. Bold and impetuous. I thought you would prefer the out-of-doors to exchanging social niceties in a parlor. Would you walk with me?"

Krystyna paused, torn between what was appropriate and her true desires, which had led her into trouble in the past. But this time, she had the wisdom to hesitate. "I should be heading back in. They're expecting me."

"You haven't even been out here for five minutes yet. I know. I watched you leave. Come with me, Krystyna. You'll be safe. This night is too cold for me to have any illicit intentions. Where is that daring Amazon who braved the lions' den to rescue her friend?" His tone teased.

This blithe and romantic Andrzej charmed and amused her.

"She's on her best behavior."

"That's unfortunate. I found her enchanting."

"I'll walk with you, Andrzej."

Taking her arm, he led her around the house and out into the gardens at the back of the von Zetl mansion. She was acutely aware of the heat and strength of his body and of his arm as they brushed against hers.

"I want to show you a special place."

He led her into a manicured circle of trees at the center of which she saw a white, marble bench. She also glimpsed some statues on pedestals placed between the trees around the entire circumference of the circle.

"I'm sure this is quite a lovely spot, when one can see it," she commented dryly.

"Woman," he countered with a chuckle. "You lack vision. Come stand here in the center. Now, look up."

She gasped as she beheld the full moon surrounded by the starry sky and framed by the crowns of the trees. "Oh, it's wonderful! The moon looks like I could reach out and touch it." She extended her arm out towards it, free of her cloak. Her bare skin was an unearthly white in the moonlight. "At my aunt's house, I can't really see the stars at night. But here, it's like seeing old friends. When I was a little girl, my mother used to take me out on summer nights to look at the stars.

We would lay flat on our backs and simply stare up at them."

Andrzej traced his fingers down the length of her arm and then gripped her hand. Where he had touched her, she tingled in response. "I imagine you were a delightful child, full of curiosity and life, and lovely besides. As a woman, you enchant me." He drew her hand, palm up, to his lips, his eyes upon her. She felt the warmth of his breath on her bare palm then the soft firmness of his lips. As sensation coursed through her, she captured his other hand. He leaned down to her and allowed his lips to brush across hers. His scent was rich, intoxicating and enveloping. Ever so gently, he traced her lips with his tongue. His kiss was light and ever so controlled.

She wanted to shatter his control. Reaching up, she rested her arms around his neck and leaned into the kiss that grew more intimate and erotic. She felt his control slipping.

He reached under her cloak and grasped the silken fabric of her dress at her hips, pulling her fully against him. She was exhilarated by the size of him, by his powerful thighs pressing against her through the layers of cloth between them. His mouth slanted across hers. He deepened the kiss, penetrating her mouth with the brandied heat of his tongue. Krystyna longed for more, more of him and of his touch. She was lost in him.

Unexpectedly, he broke off the kiss. He nuzzled tenderly down the side of her neck. He took the lobe of her ear in his mouth, causing her to shiver in reaction, and ran his tongue along the translucent skin just behind it. Krystyna groaned softly, feeling molten inside. She trembled beneath his subtly torturing tongue. Her legs were willowy under her, and she was both grateful for and tormented by the manner in which he held her firmly against him.

At last, he raised his head, and evening air rudely penetrated the heated skin where his mouth had been seconds before. He studied her, as if memorizing her face. There was no need for words between them. He wore such a grave aspect that Krystyna lifted her hand questioningly to his cheek. He closed his eyes as she ran her fingertips along one high cheekbone and then caressed the fullness of his lips. Opening his eyes, he caught her hand and brought it back to his lips. First, he kissed the back of her hand softly and then turned her palm over. He ran his teeth delicately over the bulb at the base of her thumb then drew his tongue along the length of the inside of her forefinger. All the while, he watched her, his eyes aroused and consuming. She couldn't resist the shiver of excitement that vibrated through her.

She dropped her eyes, severing the hypnotic connection between them. Then, with commitment, she stepped back out of his embrace. She fully sensed her danger. This man was like the most potent of vodkas, coursing through her veins, stealing her resolve. She melted for him in a way that she hadn't when Ivan had touched her. Andrzej left her wanting so much more. But she'd already learned the price of passion, and she couldn't allow her desires to guide her behavior now. She had to think of others, of Jadwiga and her parents.

"Krystyna," his deep voice caressed her name. "It was only a kiss, and it was far too delightful to ruin with regrets." He grinned ruefully. "Forgive me, but I can't resist you." He pulled her back against him ignoring her stiff, defensive posture. "I'd like to steal you back to my room."

"The General might take exception."

"Would you believe me if I swear my intentions are strictly honorable?"

"Andrzej, if this is merely passion you feel, I can't afford to indulge it. Then, you should go back to your Marchioness, and let me be."

"So you've been asking about me." Another grin flashed whitely in the moonlight. "That pleases me. If there's anything you'd like to know about me, I'm willing to answer. I'm no debauchee, though I've not led the life of a monk. I don't regret my history, any more than you should your own. The ladies with whom I've dallied always knew the rules of the game. We afforded each other pleasure and then went our separate ways. There were no regrets.

"But on the subject of passion, it is definitely something I am eager to share with you. Woman, I cannot stop thinking about you, imagining you in my bed. What else would you like to know? My prospects are reasonable. I'm heir to a sizeable estate which I intend to make more profitable. I'm a man of simple tastes. I have been known to drink to excess, but I am no drunkard. I enjoy a good hunter and a well-trained hound. I like to learn new things, so I read and study. I have also enjoyed traveling, but it has awakened a longing in me for my home. And when I find something I want, I go after it. I want you, Krystyna."

Feeling his words echoed in her own body, Krystyna resisted the overwhelming impulse to yield to him. Instead, she pulled away from him. There was too much at stake, her entire future. She could not afford to make another mistake. She spoke slowly and carefully. "What do you want of me?" She didn't know where the words came from, but she needed the answer.

Andrzej was silent. Krystyna cursed herself for being twice a fool. Now he must think her both insecure and desirous of praise. But he'd not yet spoken of love, and these were the words she needed to hear. She had taken a halting step back in the direction from which they came when he spoke.

"What do I want, my flame-haired angel?" He came up behind her but didn't touch her. Only his voice caressed her. "I want you, all of you, for my own. I want to fall asleep beside you. I want to have children with you. I want to grow older with you. I want to laugh with you and argue with you. And, yes, I want to share passion with you. Perhaps you find me impetuous, but ever since I first saw you that day in the Prater, I've been aware of a special affinity between us. We're meant to be together. Each time I see you, I become surer of this. You need time, to get to know me, to trust me. I understand, and I will try to be a patient man, for you are well worth the wait."

Krystyna felt her resistance dissolving. He hadn't used the word love, but it was clearly the emotion he described. She inhaled tremblingly and turned. He enfolded her in his arms and kissed her eyelids and forehead while she held him fiercely.

"We should go back in now, sweetheart. Compose yourself. You're getting cold. Your hands are like ice. When I get back from Warsaw…"

"Warsaw, you're going to Warsaw?" Already, Andrzej was directing her steps back to the house.

"I've remained in Vienna on behalf of several powerful members of the Polish seym. I've made the necessary contacts and collected the required information, and now I must present my report to them. I'll be back as soon as I possibly can."

His resolve was clear, and Krystyna was chilled with a sense of foreboding. With Janus after her, she had no idea what the future might hold. Would she even be in Vienna when he returned? Should she tell him of the danger she faced?

"You are so quiet, Krystyna. Does seeing me again not please you?"

"There is so much you don't know." She wanted to tell him, to shift some of her burden onto those broad shoulders. She knew instinctively he would be capable of bearing the load. Still, it was too soon, and she didn't want to ruin the magic of the evening by sharing the grim details of her recent history. Besides, he was soon leaving.

They arrived back at the front door. Krystyna faced Andrzej with a determined smile. "I will miss you, Andrzej." She was unsure of how to end their interlude. She wanted to throw herself at him and shout, "I'm in love with you." Instead, she said,

"Thank you for sharing that special place with me." With that, she opened the front door and swept in.

Andrzej followed after her more slowly. He watched her lightly step down the hallway, and then disappear behind a door. She never glanced back at him, and he had the feeling he'd been summarily dismissed.

There was something significant bothering her, that much was clear. He looked forward to extracting her secrets, and he cursed the luck that forced him to leave Vienna so soon.

The rest of the evening passed seamlessly and swiftly. As Jadwiga's party took their leave, Andrzej subtly pressed a folded note into Krystyna's hand. She immediately slid the paper into her muff, but her eyes and words were polite and distant as she bid him farewell. Nonetheless, he took her acceptance of it as a good sign.

Krystyna waited to open it until she was alone in her bedroom. It consisted of only two lines written in a bold and dramatic hand. They read: "We are meant for each other. Until I return, think of me, and I will dream of you."

CHAPTER 10

After Jutta's murder, Pavel and the rest of the servants kept Jadwiga's house under constant guard. The distractions of the social scene were minimal as Vienna was quiet with the Christmas holidays fast approaching. Even Marta and her parents had left the city to spend the holidays at their country estate. The restrictions of life at the von Gebler mansion wore on Krystyna, who couldn't repress the feeling she was a prisoner inside the stately house. It seemed as if she spent all of her time sitting and waiting for the madman to strike again.

One morning, at the breakfast table, she vented some of her frustrations. "Perhaps, Jutta's murderer was just a robber. We may very well be overreacting. This plan is just not working. Besides, if Janus was the one who killed Jutta, he's probably out of Austria by now. We are driving ourselves mad in this house for nothing."

"Patience, Krystyna," Jadwiga counseled. "You know that murder was no accident, child. No, we will maintain the security measures. If Janus hasn't resurfaced by the New Year, we'll go to my palazzo in Italy."

Krystyna wasn't at all sure this was what she wanted to hear either. She lapsed into silence while toying with her eggs. If they left Vienna, would she ever see Andrzej again?

"I'm sorry, Aunt Jadwiga. It's just that the inactivity is maddening."

"I know, child. It's the same for me." Jadwiga patted her great niece's hand comfortingly.

"I so enjoy being with you, Aunt, but I miss Mama and Papa and Feliks, too. I've never been away from home for Christmas before."

"Having you with me for the holidays will be my best gift. I've been alone at Christmas time for so many years." She said this last bit matter-of-factly, but Krystyna sensed the pain behind her words.

"It will be lovely, Aunt," she responded with determination. Jadwiga was so kind and generous; she wouldn't deliberately cause her great-aunt pain by revealing the degree of her homesickness and her longing for Andrzej.

The Baroness von Reigler, whose husband was politically well connected, regularly sent Jadwiga letters. Occasionally they contained snippets of information about the turmoil in Warsaw. Therefore, Krystyna was aware some of the wealthiest and most powerful members of the Polish nobility weren't backing the seym. They'd betrayed their country for bribes or promises from Russia, Prussia or Austria. Warsaw was a cauldron, seething and boiling under the watchful eyes of three of the most powerful and greedy nations in Europe. As she lay in bed at night, struggling to fall asleep, Krystyna tossed and turned, her stomach in knots. She prayed for her family, for Andrzej and for Poland.

About a month after the dinner at the von Zetl establishment, Krystyna received the first of several letters from Andrzej. With shaking hands, she broke the large wax seal that bore the cunning imprint of a wolf in profile. In it, he shared his dreams and worries for their country, and he wrote of how he couldn't stop thinking about her, of how he wished she were with him. His style of writing was as idealistic and passionate as the man, and Krystyna reread his missive many times.

Other letters followed, and when reading his thoughts, she felt part of her homeland, as if she was not an outcast in this gray, foreign city. And she wrote him back, telling him her opinions and reactions to his ideas, but nothing of their anxious vigil. In response, his letters grew even warmer, more ardent.

Finally, one evening just a few days before Christmas, Pavel entered the library where the women sat reading. He addressed his mistress, and Krystyna was too engrossed in her book to heed what was said.

"Now? At this hour?" Jadwiga asked. "Impetuous!"

"Yes, my lady."

Her great niece glanced up. She watched as Pavel waited stoically.

"Krystyna, it seems you have a guest," her aunt commented with raised eyebrows. "This young man has apparently traveled quickly and far. Though it is long past the polite time for a visit, I wouldn't take it amiss if you spoke with him briefly."

Krystyna was aware of her heart racing in her chest. "Is it Andrzej? Is he here?"

Smiling fondly, Jadwiga nodded. "Remember, dear, some restraint is becoming."

She was already to the door.

"Krystyna, a man only appreciates that which he must work to obtain. Offer him a challenge, my girl."

Krystyna paused, glancing back at her great-aunt. "Aunt, such games aren't for me."

Jadwiga chuckled. Though she was decades away from those heady days of young love, she could still recall the desperate need to behold the object of one's desire. "Fair enough. Go to him."

On winged feet, she rushed down the hallway and into the

entrance foyer. She moved past the footman keeping watch by the front door and, before he could react, she threw it wide, ignoring the blast of snowy winter air.

In the courtyard, she saw a coach with a blanketed team. Then, a pair of powerful masculine arms came from behind her and gathered her close. She twisted in them and then was staring up into the eyes she'd longed to see. Clasped tightly to him, the scent of him suffused her, the essence of man mingled with a hint of cologne, the saltiness of warm horseflesh and the out-of-doors.

Closing her eyes, she found herself captivated by the feel of him, by the cool, wet, stubbled skin against her cheek, the rough wool of his cloak beneath her hands, and by the hard strength of his muscular length. She had forgotten how very large he was, how delicate she felt in comparison.

"I missed you, Krystyna, more than I believed possible." His voice was deep and rich with feeling, and his dark eyes glowed despite the shadows beneath them and the leanness of his cheeks that bespoke days of hard travel.

"And I, you."

Before she could say anything more, with gentle hands, he drew her face up to his own. He placed whisper-light kisses on each of her eyelids, and a more tender one on her lips. Neither knew quite what to say. So, they simply held each other, gratified with the contact, the miracle of being together.

"You must call tomorrow."

"I intend to, though now I'm considering abducting you. I could bundle you into my coach and spirit you away with me."

The idea thrilled Krystyna as his words rumbled forth from his chest and through her body. She felt more alive than she had in weeks. It was impossible, incredible, but they were together again. Janus hadn't succeeded in stealing all possibility of any happiness from her. There was a definite rightness to being locked in this man's embrace. Still, they were standing outside, in front of an opened door. Krystyna glimpsed the startled face of the footman, then, despite the heat of the large body pressed against hers, she shivered.

"You must be freezing. You aren't even wearing a cloak." Andrzej drew her even more fully against him, shielding her from the wind. "You should go back in. I'll return as soon as it's respectable to call." But he didn't release her.

"Don't go. Not yet. I'm warm enough." He kissed her again, this time allowing his lips to linger on her own. Her lips opened beneath his; she held nothing back, expressing all of her longing and passion for him. And he responded in kind. Krystyna lost all awareness of her surroundings, caught up in the sweet seduction of the kiss. Then, it changed, Andrzej became more hungry and demanding, as if he wanted to somehow brand her as his. She'd been kissed before, but never with this single-minded and mutual intensity which swept away all fears and doubts.

Finally, he drew away from her, his long fingers caressing the back of her neck. "You must know I've no wish to leave you. But I'm scarcely human right now. A bath and a night's sleep are very appealing."

Studying his face, she observed his eyes were bloodshot and his features drawn tight with fatigue. She grinned at him. "I think you look marvelous."

Andrzej offered her a sardonic half-smile. "Tomorrow then?"

"Yes, tomorrow."

He raised her hand to his lips. "Come to me in my dreams, sweet angel." Then, he released her. Still watching her, he strode back to the waiting coach and opened the door.

"Wait," Krystyna ran down the steps and into his arms again. "Hold me for a moment longer!"

And he did, kissing the top of her head. "This is so difficult. Promise me, Krystyna. Promise me we won't drag out the engagement. I can't live like this. These weeks away from you have been hellish. You were all I could think about."

A warm glow suffused her. "Andrzej, you haven't yet asked for my hand."

"An oversight to which I will attend without delay. I should speak with your father, but I want you now. If your aunt could speak for your family, we could marry then perhaps travel to your home so I could meet them. I know the General has exchanged some correspondence with your father. I'll speak with the General in the morning. Then, there's the matter of the swat. But promise me, you won't make us wait."

"I promise! If I could, I'd marry you right now." Then, he was holding her and kissing her again, and words were forgotten.

"Krystyna? Krystyna, are you still out there?" Jadwiga called to her from the front door. "You'll catch your death out there."

The lovers separated reluctantly. "Until tomorrow," he whispered.

"Tomorrow," she squeezed his hand then released it.

CHAPTER 11

That night, Krystyna found it nearly impossible to sleep. Thoughts of Andrzej kept her heart beating quickly, her eyes from growing heavy. She tossed and turned, unable to get comfortable. Eventually, she relit her bedside taper and, picking up a novel that Marta had passed on to her, tried to read herself to sleep. With chagrin, she soon discovered she was rereading the same sentence repeatedly. Then, she heard the crash. She leapt to her feet, in the grip of raw panic. Not now! Nothing could happen now that Andrzej was back.

The noise sounded distant, like it came from the first floor. She dashed down the steps to the entrance foyer. Ominously, there no one was in sight, not even the footman whom Pavel had stationed at the front door. Alarm coursed through her body. Janus! It had to be him. But how had he gotten into the house? Had he killed the guard as he had Jutta? Was he still in the house? Then she heard the soft murmur of voices coming from the library.

She hurried into that room to observe a tableau as horrible as any she could ever have imagined. Pavel lay sprawled across the settee like a discarded rag doll. A young manservant in Jadwiga's employ held a bloodied hunting knife to his throat. Pavel's blouse was already streaked scarlet, and the stain was spreading. Blood dripped from his left fingertips to the floor. The manservant was clearly petrified, as his shaking hands and wild eyes revealed. All color had bleached from Pavel's sallow cheeks. But he was still alive; the black eyes now trained on Krystyna were alert and cognizant.

"I had no choice, can't you see?" The manservant, whose name, Krystyna recalled, was Conrad, sobbed to Jadwiga who stood only an arm's length away. "He threatened to kill my babies, my wife. He killed Jutta, and just because she walked in on him. What do you think he would do to me, to my family?" Conrad spied Krystyna.

"You! You are the one he wants dead. You! This is all your fault!"

"Who is this man?" Jadwiga questioned calmly.

"I don't know, I swear it. He calls himself Janus. He gave me the draught to put in the decanter. I told him the young one didn't indulge as often as you do, but he insisted it didn't matter. That was all I had to do," his voice broke on a sob, "simply put it in the decanter, the one you store the vodka in. He said it was a sleeping potion. I knew he wanted to kill her, but I had no choice. Can't you see? I had no choice! Now it's no good anyway. All would have been well had your Russian not followed me in here," the man blubbered the words furiously at Pavel as his knife-wielding hand shook, and a bead of blood emerged from Pavel's neck. "Janus will know I failed…Oh, my Katerina." He dissolved into heaving sobs.

"Conrad," Jadwiga's tone was soothing despite the gravity of her expression, "even had you succeeded, all would not be well. Krystyna and I would likely be dead, and you'd still be at the mercy of this monster. You do yourself no service in killing Pavel. Should he die and you fail to dispose of me, I will ensure that the police hunt you throughout the rest of your days. To satisfy your master, you must kill both my niece and me. Do you really want the blood of three people on your hands? And do you honestly believe Janus will allow you to live after you've served as his henchman? He'll have to kill you, too, to ensure your silence. You have to trust me if you want to save your family. I can help you."

For a moment, it appeared as if Conrad debated. Then, resolution firmed his tremulous features. "No, you're trying to trick me. There's no end to this unless I do his bidding."

"You say this man is ruthless," Krystyna's voice rang out clearly. "Well then, you should know that he will allow you no peace. He will dispose of you after you've served your purpose. Are you a monster like him?"

"No! I'm a simple man. But my babies, my Katerina."

"The only way that you can protect either Katerina or your babies is by trusting us. We can help you."

"Yes," Jadwiga put in. "We can make it look as if you've succeeded. Then, I can get you and your family out of Vienna. Think, Conrad. Think. We are your only way out."

"No. No. He will come after me. He will know."

"Janus is not as infallible as you imagine. He failed to kill me and alerted us by killing Jutta. Let us help you. What would your Katerina think if she saw you now?"

Conrad's sobs increased in intensity. Then, he seemed to crumple. The knife fell from his slack fingers. He collapsed to the floor. Both Krystyna and Jadwiga rushed to Pavel's side. Jadwiga touched her fingertips to his throat. Pavel weakly raised one hand and covered his mistress's.

"It will be all right, old friend. I'm not going to let you go so easily." Jadwiga's voice was husky. "You think to shirk your duty because of a little scratch, a mere nick. You shall not desert me. I will not allow it. I will send for a physician. For now, we must stop the blood."

Pavel smiled. Then, his eyes went vacant, the reason dissolved from them, and his lids shuttered down.

"Is he?" Krystyna couldn't pronounce the word.

"No, merely unconscious. Bring me some clean sheets. Immediately! Run, girl! Pavel will survive." She uttered the words with determination, as if willing it. "You," she spoke to Conrad. "Pull yourself together. You're no good to me or to your family like this. We need your help. Go and fetch the physician."

Krystyna returned with a stack of snowy sheets. Jadwiga took one and pressed it firmly against Pavel's deep shoulder wound. Almost immediately, the blood began to seep through.

"You sent Conrad after the physician?" She questioned incredulously. "What makes you think he won't just bolt?"

"We're his only hope now," Jadwiga explained through pinched lips. "He'll be back."

Conrad did eventually return with the doctor. The manservant seemed to be bearing up now that the responsibility had been shifted from his shoulders.

Hours later, after the physician had cleaned, stitched and poulticed Pavel's wound, he warned that time would tell whether or not the patient would survive. He advised Jadwiga that Pavel must rest and not be moved. He concluded that there was nothing more to be done, that they must wait and see.

In the wee hours of the morning, when all was still and silent, both women kept vigil by Pavel's bed. They'd put him in a guest bedroom, rather than return him to his tiny bedroom, as it was easier for Jadwiga to attend to him there. Each was lost in thought and reflection. Krystyna wrestled with guilt while Jadwiga, she suspected, dealt with emotions deeper than mere concern and fondness. In the flickering firelight, Jadwiga's face appeared old, the lines firmly drawn, the skin loose, the eyes tired.

"You love him." It was a statement not a question.

Jadwiga didn't answer immediately, but their trials of that

night had, for the time being, lowered all barriers between them. "I can't lose Pavel, too."

Krystyna dropped her gaze. The naked pain in Jadwiga's eyes overwhelmed her. For a moment, she imagined how she would feel if it was Andrzej lying so pale and still in the bed. Anguish swept through her, and she reached out and took her aunt's hand. "He's a strong man. Have faith."

Jadwiga squeezed her back. Her eyes were bright with tears. She didn't speak nor did her great niece, who sought to give her time to regroup.

"He will recover," Jadwiga pronounced. "He's survived much worse. He's a Tartar, you know. I found him wounded and near death on the Russian steppes. After I nursed him back to health, he wouldn't leave my side. He said he owed me a life debt, and there was nothing more for him in Russia. His family was dead or gone. He'd been abandoned. He was a loyal servant to me for many years, through two marriages, and that was all, until… When he's well enough, we'll leave Vienna."

"Aunt, I must leave here now. Jutta and now Pavel have already paid for my selfishness in remaining." Krystyna spoke bleakly, hating the truth of her words. She couldn't return to her parent's home, not with this madman after her. Where would she go?

"Nonsense. Don't be so quick to assume all responsibility. Why was Janus in my room the night Jutta was killed? And why did he instruct Conrad to poison the decanter from which I drink? It's clear he intends to kill me, too."

"Because of your connection to me. It makes no sense… What can this person hope to gain by killing us both?"

"That's the question," Jadwiga sighed. "Unfortunately, Janus holds most of the cards. He's sure to be watching the house. He must have seen the physician arrive, so he'll know Conrad has acted. I warned Dr. Graubohm to say nothing about whom he attended this night. He is discreet. Perhaps, we can lead Janus to believe he achieved some success, that one of us suffered a mortal blow. Such confusion might give us the advantage. As soon as we can, when Pavel is well enough, we must get out of Vienna. But which of my servants are loyal? There's no way of knowing to whom Janus has gotten."

"Aunt, it's me he's after. If I go…"

"Don't speak nonsense. Neither of us will be safe until we are free of this person. No, we must all leave Vienna."

"What will stop him from following us? No, Aunt, you will be safer if I'm not with you. You have to see that. The letter was addressed to me. I must believe I'm his primary target. I will go. Alone."

"Speak sense, Krystyna. Where will you go? You won't elude him for long without any protection."

"But I can't stay with you."

Jadwiga's eyes narrowed. "He would have no reason to come after me if he believed you dead."

"What?"

"It just might work." The age and exhaustion vanished from her features, and the dark eyes twinkled. "We will stage a fraud. I will let it be known that you suffered an attack and are at death's door. Shortly after you 'succumb,' we will depart the city, to transport the body, of course. That will give us a reason for traveling at speed and for leaving without notice. Janus will assume that your demise is a result of Conrad's actions. We can flee the city and travel on to Italy before Janus can figure out what has happened."

Krystyna felt ill as she considered all who would have to be taken in for this ruse to work. Marta and the Baroness would have to believe that she was dead, as would Andrzej. She could never see him again, for his sake as well as for her own. Her voice trembled as she spoke, "I am willing to bet anything that Conrad is not the only servant to whom Janus has spoken. He will find out that I am alive."

"There are some holes to the plan. But one thing is clear. We must get out of this house." Jadwiga rose to her feet stiffly. "We must secure the house immediately and account for everyone. We will allow no one to leave, with the exclusion of those whom I trust. This sort of action will make sense to Janus. He will think that we are taking additional safety measures now that another attack has occurred." Jadwiga paused as she took in the stricken look. She moved over to Krystyna and patted her cheek gently. "Child, try to be more optimistic. My plan could work, it could buy us time."

Krystyna nodded her hesitant acquiescence. She viewed Jadwiga's plan as no more than a short-term solution and a shaky one at that. With a sense of impending doom settling on her shoulders like a heavy and dark mantel, she stared into the flames.

Both women jumped when Pavel's arm suddenly moved across the coverlet. The narrow black eyes, though bright with pain, were opened and fixed on Krystyna's face.

"You…you must go," Pavel's voice was hoarse and throaty but clear.

"We will, soon. That's what we've been planning, Pavel." Jadwiga responded, taking his hand in her own.

"You bring death to this house."

"Pavel," Jadwiga countered gravely. "Krystyna is family. I will not abandon her."

"The girl brings death," Pavel repeated. Briefly, he closed his eyes in apparent resignation. Then, the dark reservoirs of pain opened once more. "Not safe for her with you. She must go. Send for Kotyat."

"Kotyat?" Thoroughly perplexed, Jadwiga repeated the name aloud. "Who… The gypsy horse dealer? What use do we have of him?"

"Kotyat, yes." The words were fainter, but Pavel wouldn't give up. He fought to make his message clear. He pointed a bony finger that shook with the intensity of his effort. "Go to him. He'll get you out of Vienna. Away."

Jadwiga clapped her hands together in delight. "Pavel, what a wonderful idea! It might even work. No one would ever connect Krystyna with that troupe." She leaned toward Pavel. "Tell me, old friend, what to do."

CHAPTER 12

Janus watched as two female servants, covered from head to toe against the morning chill, hurried out the back entrance of the von Gebler house and into the street. They followed their customary route in the direction of the marketplace. The only reason he paid them any heed was that comings and goings to the house had been few and far between these last few days. There had been no word from that fool, Conrad. Dispassionately, Janus wondered if the manservant whom he'd been blackmailing was dead. He knew that the man had acted for two reasons: a surgeon had been summoned to the house two nights ago, and all traffic in and out had been strictly limited since.

But Janus wanted to know what had transpired, which was why he continued to watch the house. His brother's murderess, he hoped she'd suffered. He would have preferred to take her life himself, to gaze into her eyes as the realization of impending death came to her. But the knowledge that Conrad had been a puppet whose strings he controlled provided him some satisfaction.

There was nothing remarkable about these two servant

women. He'd already followed them, on more than one occasion. But on this morning, he was unwilling to leave his position. He wanted to be here when they took her lifeless body out. Krystyna Sielska had finally paid for her crimes. If only he had somehow been able to gain control of her inheritance, then Ivan would be wholly avenged. Janus knew he should feel pleased, or at least satisfied. Instead, he felt empty and vaguely cheated.

"Wilhelm, follow them," Janus ordered, without looking away from the von Gebler house.

Obedient to his master's wishes, the young ruffian discretely trailed the two servants as they wended their way through the still sleeping streets. They didn't speak or interact in any way. They simply hurried along their usual route, their heads tucked down against the freezing morning wind, carrying their empty baskets in gloved hands. In time, they arrived at the marketplace where merchants were just opening up their booths.

Wilhelm rubbed his cold hands together as he observed the two women purchase some eggs and milk. It was all tedious and mundane. He'd expected something far different than watching a house and following servant women when Janus had recruited him. The Russian nobleman was odd; Wilhelm often wondered if he was quite well in the head. Still, he couldn't complain about the pay, and the work was easy, if bone chillingly cold. The two women purchased a beef tongue then some spices.

As they moved deliberately between the stalls, prodding a haunch of mutton at one, examining heads of cabbage at another, Wilhelm considered what he would buy with the money he'd earned when the job was done. Wilhelm was so caught up in his reflections that he didn't observe the taller servant woman look about and then stride briskly away from her companion who continued to browse through a cheese stall. Glancing back up at his quarry, Wilhelm noticed with mild concern that only one of the women was now in his line of vision. There was no sign of the other woman.

He moved through the marketplace, looking about for the missing woman. The other servant was still visible at the cheese counter, haggling with the merchant. Wilhelm's heart began to pound. She couldn't have just disappeared. Janus would be enraged if he lost one of them, and he was not a man to cross. Just then, he glimpsed a familiar figure near the amber stall. He sprinted towards her and deliberately stumbled into her. The woman spun in stunned outrage.

"So sorry. I thought you were someone else," Wilhelm stammered at the woman who was not the missing von Gebler servant. He dashed through the stalls. It was still too early for the marketplace to be busy, so there weren't many people about, only a handful of customers and the merchants. But there was no sign of the servant woman. Now only a candle maker's booth and a farrier's forge stood between him and the street where the public conveyances lined up. Then he saw her, moving purposefully in the direction of the coaches. This jaunt wasn't included in the women's usual itinerary. Wilhelm decided drastic measures were called for. He feared if he failed Janus, his life wouldn't be worth much. Besides, the woman had never seen him before. She would probably imagine him a common thief.

He ran across the area separating them. He darted in front of her. To his immense surprise, he gaped at enormous, brown eyes, at a milky complexion dusted with freckles, and a curl of red-gold hair that had escaped the confines of her hat. "You!" Wilhelm had spent too much time watching the von Gebler house not to recognize Krystyna Sielska. "You!" He repeated incredulously. She was supposed to be mortally wounded or dead.

Krystyna spun desperately away. She ran back through the marketplace, dodging behind basket weavers, by the chicken hawkers, past the sellers of fine lace. She heard footfalls behind her then a crash and curses. Risking a glance back over her shoulder, she saw that her pursuer had knocked over a cart filled with potatoes and onions. The produce farmer was hauling the man out of the vegetables by his collar, shouting all the while about who would pay for damages.

She had only a second or two and stared desperately about her.

"Miss," a high, thin voice called to her. "Come here. You can hide here."

The speaker was a fair girl of about eight or ten who addressed her from the darkened back entrance to a merchant's shack. Her face was wizened, and her pale blue eyes, strangely perceptive. Her straight, flaxen hair hung loose over her shoulders. Her clothing, though threadbare, was tidy and clean.

The girl gestured with her hand. "Come quickly!"

Krystyna didn't hesitate. She followed the girl through the small door into the back of the wooden shack. The air inside the small structure was barely warmer than the out-of-doors and dominated by a rich, earthy odor which was not at all unpleasant, just overwhelming. Thick stacks of dried, bound leaves were stored on racks around the tiny room. She recognized this as a tobacco merchant's booth. Near the doorway, the scent was more pungent and overpowering. Further in, it was gently herbal and more delicate. An assortment of pipes adorned one wall. There were long, Oriental-looking ones, stout farmers' pipes, fanciful flasks attached to silken piping, carved black forest pipes, even a pipe in the shape of a naked woman.

"This way, back here."

Krystyna followed the diminutive girl through a curtain and into an even tinier cubicle that was marginally warmer than the other room, thanks to a small stove situated in one corner.

"Lady," the child whispered. "You hide here. I'll tell you when that man is gone."

"Why are you helping me?"

She shrugged her shoulders. "You can sit in my Poppi's chair. He won't mind."

Krystyna sat down. There was barely room for her legs in front of the desk. "Thank you."

"I did right then. My Poppi will be pleased. He says we should help people whenever we can."

"Where is your father?"

"Poppi is my grandfather. He went to get breakfast. He always brings me milk." The girl made a face. "I give my milk to Solomon," she squatted down to stroke the dog-sized, orange cat that was purring loudly and rubbing against her skirts.

"Will your Poppi be angry that I'm here?"

"No, but I expect he'll have to get more rolls."

Krystyna smiled at her unlikely savior. "I am Krys… Babette and thank you for your kindness."

"I am Heloise Fraessdorf. My Poppi sells tobacco."

"I see that."

"You stay here now. I have work to do. I set up the display," Heloise announced proudly.

Then, the waif was gone, and Krystyna could hear her moving about the stock room. She closed her eyes and exhaled slowly. It was possible that the child could betray her, but there was something she trusted about those soulful blue eyes. The man following her could be going from stall to stall, searching for her, but she doubted the merchants would allow him to do so. Now, all she could do was wait and hope her pursuer thought she'd gotten away.

Time passed slowly. She could hear occasional shouts and comments from the market outside. But the heavy cloth lining the walls muffled sound and kept the heat in. Suddenly, she heard voices from the stock room. She recognized Heloise's high tones and the deep, throaty voice of an older man. The curtain between the cubicle and the stock room drew back to reveal a stout, hawk-nosed, older fellow with Heloise's twinkling eyes lost in a sea of laugh wrinkles.

"My little Heloise told me she'd saved a lady," the kind-looking man smiled, revealing a large gap between his front teeth. "I wasn't quite sure whether we were talking about an imaginary lady or a real one, but you seem real enough. I am Wolfgang Fraessdorf, at your service." The merchant held out a gnarled and scarred hand to Krystyna.

She took it. "I cannot thank you both enough." Krystyna glanced at the petite figure standing so upright and proud beside her grandfather. "Your granddaughter certainly thinks on her feet."

"You are in some sort of trouble?"

"I am no criminal, if that is what you mean, but I am in trouble. I will leave here in a short while, and no one will be the wiser."

"Lady," the incongruously youthful blue eyes in the shriveled apple-skin face were solemn. "I've tried to teach my Heloise that we are all on this journey of life together and that we must do for each other. I am proud of you, liebchen," the tobacco merchant bent and placed a kiss on his granddaughter's forehead. He turned back to Krystyna. "You are welcome here for as long as you need to stay. Heloise and I will watch and tell you when this man is gone. Then, you may proceed on you way. For now, we have some rolls and chocolate. Will you share our breakfast?"

And so it was that Krystyna sipped rich, dark chocolate and ate rolls still warm from the oven in the company of a kindly tobacco merchant's granddaughter. The merchant, himself, was tending to his stall and serving customers. Krystyna couldn't help but reflect on how different her life had been just two days before when all that she could think of was Andrzej's return.

Andrzej. She ached at the thought of him. What had he been told when he'd been turned away from the von Gebler house? She knew he'd called. Jadwiga told her so. But in those last two days since Conrad's attack on Pavel, they'd accepted no callers whatsoever. When would she see him again? If ever. All of a sudden, she knew she couldn't leave Vienna without seeing him one last time.

"Do you care for more chocolate?" Heloise questioned as she precariously held up the battered iron kettle.

"No, thank you."

The child set the kettle down and resumed her seat in the tiny cubicle where they sat knee to knee. She tucked her hands under her thighs and stared at Krystyna. "Are you a princess?"

"A princess?" Krystyna sputtered, almost choking on her chocolate. "Whatever gave you that idea?"

"That man who is chasing you," the child continued confidently, "he must know that you're a princess, and that if he captures you, he can marry you and be a king."

"My little Heloise has quite an imagination." The merchant drew back the curtain.

"Yes, she does."

"Where's your prince?" Heloise asked.

"I don't know any princes."

"But there's always a prince."

Her heart cried out Andrzej is my prince. Then she shook her head. It seemed there was nothing she could do about it now. But how wrong, how unfair to lose him because of a madman's twisted plots. "Not for me," her voice trembled on the words, and she had to rest her shaking hand with the cup of chocolate on her lap.

Then, an idea, an impossible, impetuous idea came to her. It would not be safe for her to travel from Vienna today. Janus and his men would be on the alert. Their eyes would be on the public conveyances. No, it would be much wiser to wait until tomorrow. Yes, with a little bit of luck, it was possible. If she couldn't have him for the rest of her life, was it selfish to seize one day?

In the early afternoon, when few customers remained and the merchants were closing up their booths, a woman and her small daughter emerged from the tobacco stall. They joined a handful of folk making their way to the waiting public conveyances gathered along the road at the north side of the marketplace.

Just before climbing into a coach, Krystyna knelt down by the girl and whispered, "Thank you, Heloise. You saved me. Now I have something for you." She twisted off the gold signet ring she'd worn since her twelfth birthday. Heloise's grandfather had already refused payment from her. But they'd put themselves at great risk for her and had probably saved her life. She pressed the ring into the girl's hand. "This is for you. It's a princess ring for a very special girl."

Heloise took it and slid it onto her finger where it hung loosely until she clenched her fist. She ran her fingertip across the crest of the galloping horse. "It's so pretty." The child smiled beatifically.

Krystyna pressed a kiss to the high, broad forehead. Then she turned, and with a pounding heart, gave the driver her destination. Once she was safely ensconced inside the coach, she drew the threadbare curtain back from the window to wave to Heloise, but her fair angel was already gone.

CHAPTER 13

Andrzej sat hunched over his battered writing desk. The blank paper yawned painfully empty before him. What to write? How to tell his father? He stared across the small parlor, observing that the plaster on the wall opposite him was cracked in a line that almost presented the profile of a stag, if one peered at it in the right way. As he touched quill to paper, he realized that the ink had dried while he sat considering. He shifted in his chair. Roderyk had written him repeatedly in the past few months demanding his son's return to Sweet Air. Andrzej had chosen not to inform his father about his return to Polish soil while in Warsaw. Roderyk was opposed to his son's involvement in the Polish cause and felt his only child and heir had more pressing responsibilities at their estate.

Andrzej had returned to his rented Viennese rooms to be greeted with a stack of correspondence from his father. His sire demanded to know all about Krystyna, which meant he'd been in contact with the General. Roderyk expressed his satisfaction that his son was finally "getting to the important business of selecting a wife." But there was a new, disturbing quality to the letters; Andrzej sensed some desperation in his father's words. It was time to return home, and he was eager to do so, as soon as he had matters suitably resolved with Krystyna.

The thought of her unsettled him. Why had he been turned away at the von Gebler house for the past few days? The butler had taken his card then firmly shut the door in his face. All of the servants were being shockingly tight-lipped, and he knew a physician had been called to the house. Even the General couldn't give him any answers. If he didn't hear from Krystyna within a day or so, he intended to go to there and demand to see her even if she was unwell.

He stared at the blank paper. He knew what his father longed to read and what he wanted to tell him, but he couldn't give him any definitive answers about when he planned to return home until he spoke to Krystyna. It all came back to her, and if she was of a similar mind regarding their relationship.

Dipping his plume in ink again, he glanced about his rooms. He wouldn't be sorry to leave them. They'd never been home to him. Sweet Air was home. The study, like the rest of the flat, was small, shabby and without personality. But Andrzej hadn't taken these rooms for style or luxuriance, and they did serve their purpose as a place to sleep and to study. Whenever he had a taste for greater comfort, he went to the General's.

In the months he'd lived here, he'd never bothered to decorate or personalize the space. In the study, his only valued possessions were the books overflowing from the rickety bookshelf. They were old friends, and he intended to bring them with him. He hadn't meant to accumulate so many, but he'd been in Austria far longer than he'd planned.

The first months of his travels he'd spent hunting, gambling, and chasing women. Then, one evening, he'd accompanied a friend to a salon frequented by intellectuals, men and women of thought and substance who discussed matters like freedom and the rights of man. He'd found the atmosphere intoxicating and returned many times. He began to read and study and to participate in debates and discussions. Politically prominent Poles living abroad recognized him as a vocal and loyal compatriot while something of a political radical. Then the representatives of several powerful Polish families had sought him out to be their eyes and ears in Vienna. For these reasons, he'd stayed on in the cramped, impersonal flat. He was definitely ready to go home, but not alone.

Krystyna was always on his mind. It had been the same in Warsaw. Now, it was even worse knowing that she was so close and that he couldn't just go and see her. He'd been in lust before, more times than he could count, and had even imagined himself in love more than once. He was more than passingly familiar with the urgency of infatuation, but there was something new and unique about his feelings for Krystyna. With her, he had a sense of rightness, an awareness that she was the one meant for him.

But back to his current dilemma, what to tell his father? It was best to be honest. So, he wrote that he still had some matters to resolve in Vienna, but that he hoped to return to Poland before spring.

Andrzej had carried on discrete affairs de couer before. His interlude with the Marchioness had been one of the more extended ones. But this time, his intentions were honorable, as long as "honorable" included the possibility that he would soon have Krystyna's goddess-like figure beneath his, her rosy cheeks flushed with passion. An affair was out of the question. She was unmarried, young and of good family. And strangely enough, the idea of marriage to her was very appealing to Andrzej. Should he share that morsel of information with his father? The old man would be thrilled. He was always nagging Andrzej about his desire for grandchildren.

Just then, there was a knock at his door. In both puzzlement and relief, he rose to his feet. He wasn't expecting anyone. To his knowledge, few of his acquaintances were aware that he was back in Vienna. Nonetheless, anyone would provide him with a respite from the unpleasant business of putting off his father. He swung the door wide and was astonished to see the subject of his musings standing there garbed in dark servant's clothing.

"May I… May I come in?"

"Yes," he stepped back, thoroughly confounded. "Of course." Automatically, he glanced behind her into the hallway. Amazingly enough, she'd come alone, unchaperoned. "Please, come in." She stepped inside, and Andrzej closed the door behind her. "To what do I owe this honor?"

"You aren't pleased to see me?"

"On the contrary, I'm overjoyed to see you. But you must admit this is unusual. That is, unless you're accustomed to visiting men alone in their rooms."

"No, I'm not… I just wanted to see you… I needed to see you… Perhaps I shouldn't have come."

"I'm teasing you," he reassured her with a gentle smile. He glanced about then hastened to pick up a few discarded pieces of clothing that littered the worn settee and the faded armchair. "Please excuse these rooms. They're temporary, and I wasn't expecting a guest. I'm very flattered and pleased you've come here today. I'd just expected to see you in a more traditional setting."

"I had to see you before…"

"Before?" He questioned with one thick, dark blond eyebrow cocked.

She collected herself. She was aware that she had to measure her words. "I'm here now. Isn't that enough?"

"It's more than enough." Not a man to waste an opportunity, he stepped closer to her and ran his fingers delicately down the backs of her arms. He drew her to him and tested the fullness of her lips with his own. As the kiss deepened, Krystyna clung to him, eagerly returning the sensual caress of his mouth and his tongue.

When he drew back to scrutinize her features, she deliberately kept her arms about his neck. "I could stay right here until nightfall."

"You can stay here for as long as you choose, Krystyna, but I don't want to anger your aunt."

"There's no danger of that."

"How very sophisticated of her," he chuckled, completely astounded by this development. "Forgive me for asking, but is she aware of where you currently are?"

"No, of course not. I know it's scandalous that I came here, but… um… this is a unique situation." Not wanting to elaborate on the circumstances of her visit, she deliberately sought to change the subject. "I would guess I'm not the first woman to visit you here. Your landlord's expression when I asked after your rooms made that clear enough."

Andrzej shrugged. "I can assure you no other women have been here since that night you rescued your friend from the Marchioness's hunting lodge. Truth be told, I haven't been interested in any other woman."

A warm blush suffused her cheeks. His words elated her. She would waste no time questioning him about the women he'd known before her. This afternoon would likely be the only time they would ever have together. She was aware that she was reasonably safe from conception as it was the week after her monthly flux. A country girl, she knew far more about such matters than most gently bred young women of her age. Coming here, Krystyna had already irrevocably committed herself to her course of action. If this afternoon were all she could ever have with this man, then she would seize the moment and live for all she was worth.

"Andrzej, I'm not here to chat with you."

He watched her with a bemused expression on his face. "Then, why are you here?"

"You're going to make me say it. I'm not subtle, nor am I

coy." The words rushed out of her. "I'm here to be your lover. Don't just stand there gawking at me, say something."

Instead, he bent, and picked her up in his arms. "I am more used to being the assertive one, although, this change is very refreshing." He carried her into a rather stark bedroom in which the only pieces of furniture were a large bed with a carved, wooden headboard and a matching chest-of-drawers. With no fire in the hearth, the room was bone-chillingly cold. He set Krystyna down at the foot of the bed.

Andrzej was both curious and intrigued. He had many questions coursing through his mind. But now was not the time to ask them. There would be time to talk afterwards. He was delighted she was as eager for their joining as he. With great relief, he realized that she, too, must be eager for their marriage to be celebrated as soon as possible. They would have to marry quickly after this.

He gripped her elbows and drew her closer. First, he teased her lips with his own then he nuzzled from the edge of her jaw to the warm, soft crook of her neck. She exhaled unevenly. He loosened the strings on her bonnet, pushed it back and allowed it to fall to the floor. Moving closer to her, until their bodies were in full contact, he moved his tongue along the delicate, sensitive skin at the inside of the outer edge of her ear. He teased her there and behind her ear with delicate strokes that weakened her knees. Apparently unable to stand much more of his exquisite torment, she grasped his roughened cheeks in her own hands and drew his mouth back to her own.

He groaned deep in his throat. With both hands, he grasped her jutting breasts, gently pinching her hardened nipples, then slid his hands down to encircle her diminutive waist. As they kissed, the passion exploding between them, he began to work on the long row of buttons down her back. His fingers fumbled, a button popped off, and he drew back. He grinned at her seductively. "I can't concentrate on these cursed buttons."

"I'll turn." Pulling away from his heat, she presented her back to him.

His hands were gone from her skin for a few moments as he worked the buttons free. Unexpectedly, she felt his long fingers at the nape of her neck. They began to move inexorably up, slowly, through her hair, working pins free, and massaging deliciously. Krystyna feared that she would dissolve with the lush, consuming pleasure of it. When his hot, wet tongue darted along the chord at the back of her neck, her knees turned to warm wax. His arm was immediately about her waist, supporting her.

"Hurry." She issued an order, not a request.

"These cursed buttons!"

"Please." Her words were cut short as he ripped the coarse material of her dress from the base of her neck to the small of her back. She felt his large hands on her shoulders and then he pushed the dress down, so that it slid free of her body and into a pile at her ankles. Buttons clinked as they struck the hard wood floor. She twisted in his arms, her damaged chemise falling about her shoulders, revealing an expanse of creamy breast and the graceful lines of her collar bones. "You first," she challenged.

"Lady, your wish is my command." His eyes scorched her as he jerked his blouse loose from his trousers.

Krystyna was not an inexperienced virgin. In those foolish days before she'd discovered what a worm Ivan Bestuzhev truly was, they'd often stopped just short of intercourse in their love play. Then, they crossed that line twice, to her regret, until she'd discovered him in flagrente delicto with one of the maids. At the time, her mother had sobbed and wailed that no man would want a "ruined wife." But she didn't feel ruined at all now. No, for once, she was grateful to Ivan. If not for her experience with him, she would probably have been fearful of Andrzej in his passion. Instead, she was exhilarated. She had never felt so savage with Ivan.

He reached to pull his shirt over his head when Krystyna surprised him by grasping a side of his collar in each hand and tearing down with all her strength. Her efforts revealed an expanse of solid, lightly furred chest. Her hands traced over broad pectoral muscles, teasing flat, masculine nipples with the very tips of her nails. She stroked the firm surface of his stomach and allowed her thumbs to teasingly drift below his belly button, ever nearer his waistband.

Andrzej's skin was searing hot and silky. Abruptly, he flinched away from Krystyna's caresses, caught her hands and drew them up to his lips. He kissed the nearly transparent skin on the inside of either wrist, and then placed them against the bare flesh of his muscled sides. When he grasped hold of the neckline of her undergarments, Krystyna stopped his hands. She would need them later, though she could hide the ruin of her dress under her cloak.

"I'll take them off." With tremulous hands, she first undid all the fastenings and then stepped out of the thin, cotton garments.

With reverence, Andrzej reached out to cup the curve of one full breast.

"You're trembling."

She shivered. In response, he gathered her up into the warm, powerfully built circle of his arms. He pressed his own furred, hard chest against her keenly sensitive flesh. Her long, well-formed legs entangled with his. With amusement, she noted he still wore his boots and breeches. He picked her up again.

"Please," Krystyna demurred. "I am so heavy, so big."

He nuzzled her lips. "Woman, you are just right. You suit me perfectly."

She savored his words as, with one hand, he drew the blankets back. He deposited her on the unpleasantly cold sheets. She drew the covers modestly up though they felt even colder than the air. Trying to warm the sheets, she squirmed around beneath them. "Hurry." She smiled up at him. As he swiftly stripped naked with his back to her, Krystyna hungrily eyed the firm, hard curves of his buttocks. Andrzej was truly a well-made man. Then, he was in the bed beside her, immediately warming the space with his large body. She welcomed his heat, but she also wanted to explore his body fully. She rose up, kneeled beside him and placed her hands on his chest. "I want you to be still."

His powerful chest flexed as he immediately disobeyed her request and bent to lick her puckered nipple. "You have magnificent breasts." With his tongue, he lathed each one in turn, sending searing impulses coursing through her. He reached for her in order to draw her closer still to his questing mouth.

"I want to look at you." She had dreamed of and imagined his body for too many long nights not to indulge her curiosity.

He raised a sardonic eyebrow but released her. He lay back. "Do I please you?"

She allowed her eyes to glide up the hirsute, chiseled calves, to the powerful thighs. Andrzej's legs, like his arms and chest, spoke of hard manual labor. His rigid penis stood proudly erect in its nest of dark, curling hair. He was well endowed, every inch a stallion. She reached out to touch him, ran her fingertip around the silken head and down the shaft. Then, she leaned forward and took the very tip of him in her mouth. He groaned as she gripped his penis at its base and moved her warm, moist lips up and down, taking more of him inside her mouth with each stroke.

In ecstasy, Andrzej thrust both hands into her hair and raised his hips. He gently held and massaged her head as he savored her ministrations for a few moments. Then, he growled, "Enough, Krystyna." Grasping her forearms, he drew her up along his body. "Now, it is my turn." Following a twisting kind of motion that included heady body length contact that pressed his turgid cock against the softness of her belly, Krystyna ended up beneath him, staring up into his molten eyes. He grinned lasciviously at her. "I only hope I can wait long enough to drive you as wild as you have me. You're a witch."

She groaned at the sensation of him moving over her. Then, she delighted in the muscled forearms and shoulders above her. Down, down, he moved. Until, at last, his breath stirred her pubic hair, and his tongue danced across her woman's opening. Her hips trembled as he traced delicate patterns over the warm nest of her womanhood, the tip of his tongue occasionally brushing the nub of her pleasure. Now, it was her turn to lock her fingers in his hair and to bite her lips in a silent scream. He brought her quickly to edge of satisfaction and then drew back just as the wave was about to break. As Krystyna's hips implored him, he gently kissed and nuzzled the velvet skin of her inner thigh. When it seemed as if she couldn't bear any more of the exquisite torment, he moved atop her.

She welcomed the rough weight of him, grasping him ferociously, relishing her own taste on his lips. The kiss grew deeper and hotter as she felt his manhood pressing at her core. Her legs opened wider, hungrily welcoming his turgid heat. He explored her wet, swollen flesh with his cock. She opened still further, physically begging him for his thrust into her. Still, he held back, his arms flexing, as his hips moved in a gentle motion, the head of his penis rubbing her clitoris. She whimpered in frustration, begging, demanding more.

Nearly mindless with desire, she reached down between their straining bodies. She ran her fingers along the soft head that was now moist with her juice then slid her hands down still further and cupped his balls. Grasping his shaft, she placed the head just inside her. Unable to control his response, Andrzej thrust forward. This time, it was Krystyna who drew her hips back and away mischievously, maybe a little nervously. He was so large. Then, he grasped her hips firmly and thrust his rigid length slowly and deftly into her. She arched up and almost purred in satisfaction as his cock pushed almost to the mouth of her womb. She felt her body stretch to accommodate his size.

"You feel unbelievable," he muttered.

She tightened her vaginal walls around him. He groaned in response and began to move slowly in rhythm. She drove him faster and faster, meeting his thrusts with her own, stroking and gripping his buttocks, encouraging him to pound into her. Still, he maintained enough control to slow down, grinding against her with a circular motion, stimulating her clitoris with each brush of his groin area against her own. He alternated between the grinding and the thrusting motions, until after just a few moments, Krystyna fell over the precipice, shattering with mind blowing pleasure.

"Yes! Oh, yes!" The words erupted as she fell back against the pillows, straining to keep all of him within her. Andrzej slowed, his jaw clenching with his efforts. Then, Krystyna was stunned to discover that her body wanted still more. She began to move with him, encouraging him. All of her muscles grew rigid as she strained closer to her goal. Even her toes flexed as they moved together. He grew impossibly bigger within her then cried out as he, too, went rigid. Groaning deep in his chest, he released his seed, thrusting ever deeper within her. Then, with a groan, he allowed his weight to collapse down onto her.

Krystyna enjoyed the intimacy of his loose-limbed heaviness. As her breathing became more normal, she continued to hold him, her arms wrapped around the moist small of his back. She felt some of the sweat between their bodies trickle down her side. Both of them remained quiet and still. Then she shifted a cramped leg.

"I'm crushing you." He offered her a rueful, utterly charming smile. Taking hold of her, he rolled them both onto their sides. Then, reaching down, he drew the blankets up and over them. She cuddled against him as he yawned, a relaxed and thoroughly sated man. The heat of his body surrounded her, rendering her even more tranquil. She was so comfortable, she could have fall asleep.

But then the deep rumble of Andrzej's voice brought her to herself. "This has been quite a marvelous surprise. I don't mean to question my luck, but I'm curious, what convinced you to come here today?"

She was silent. He rose up on one elbow so he could see her face. He studied her expression and then asked, "Krystyna, talk to me. What has happened?"

Hesitating briefly, she answered, "I came here today because I wanted to. Let that be enough. Please don't ask me any more questions. For now, can't we just forget about everything else, everyone else and just focus on the present?"

Andrzej scrutinized her. She wouldn't meet his eyes, and she tried to distract him by stroking her hand down his belly. "That's not fair," he touched the tip of her nose with his forefinger. "First, I'm turned away from your house. Then, you appear here, make love with me, and refuse to give me an explanation for your actions. Your silence is intriguing and frustrating."

"You make too much of it." Deliberately seeking to distract him, she ran her hands over the muscled curves of his buttocks.

"Touché. Point well taken. But I'm amazed that," Andrzej's voice was soft as his touch lingered on the delicate, curling, red-gold hairs framing Krystyna's face, "one of the most beautiful, sensual women I've ever met would risk so much by coming to my rooms."

"Perhaps I was simply desperate for your touch."

"I've known more than enough women to recognize a light of love. No, though you weren't a virgin, you're not that sort at all. You're a mystery to me, one that I look forward to exploring." His hand caressed her back. "But, I agree, let's continue this discussion later."

She felt him harden against her stomach and inhaled sharply as he gently manipulated her clitoris. Closing her eyes, she savored the renewed sensations. Then, she relaxed her hips, eased her legs apart and surrendered to the sensations.

Andrzej considered the girl sprawled beside him, her glorious hair, lush curves and milky skin. He took in the full, pouting breasts, whose nipples had gone dark and hard. She intoxicated him. What was she not telling him? As he grew harder still, it didn't matter any more. Krystyna was his; she would know that from this afternoon on. With deliberation, he aroused her until she begged for his sweet invasion. Then, he turned her over and raised her buttocks, so that she was on her knees, facing away from him. Still, he ran his hands between her legs and grasped her aching breasts. Next, he pressed the very tip of his cock against the outer lips of her wet, hot vagina. He clenched his teeth against the nearly insurmountable desire to thrust fully in, and gently stroked his way around her opening, occasionally brushing the nub of her pleasure.

"Oh yes, please!" Krystyna reached back to grasp him, to pull him into her, but he drew away. Her hips followed him. Now, she was crouched before him, her legs wide, her womanhood, decadently open and ready for him.

He grasped the base of his shaft and placed it so that the head barely entered into her pleasure opening. "Tell me you want me," he growled. Though it was nearly painful, he held his own desires in check.

"You know I want you!"

"Tell me… Say that you're mine."

The significance of what he was asking her penetrated her erotic haze. She froze for only a moment. Then the feel of him against her, his hands on her hips, the needs and desires that he alone could satisfy released her inner voice, the one that expressed her true feelings. "Yes, yes… I'm yours!"

At the words, he drove into her, claiming her irrevocably. He thrust into her again and again, nearly coming apart at the incredible sensations. But aware that she wasn't quite with him, he reached down and grasped her hand, drawing it back to nearly where they were joined.

"Touch yourself here. It will increase your pleasure." He placed her fingertips on her clitoris. Then, using his own fingers to guide hers, he traced slow circles on the sensitive organ.

Her reaction was immediate. Waves of pleasure washed over her, promising something greater, more intense.

"Oh, my… Oh, my God." Feeling her spiraling excitement, Andrzej drove into her harder and harder. He achieved a blinding orgasm, and her own fulfillment followed only seconds later and milked the final aftershocks from him.

Afterwards, too exhausted to speak, they simply lay together.

"What a surprise this afternoon has been," Andrzej remarked as he ran lazy fingers along the side of her breast. Then, he rolled over on top of her, resting his weight on his elbows. She was aware of his maleness and, in contrast, of her own femininity. He nuzzled her neck, and she found herself titillated by the roughness of his whiskers, his scent. "I had planned to spend the afternoon on correspondence. I never expected Venus to appear and seduce me." He caressed his way up the side of her neck and then raised his head to gaze her in the eyes. The look in his warm, golden gaze was half serious and half teasing. "Now that you've had your way with me, I suppose I should ask you what your intentions are."

Krystyna ignored a nervous twinge and smiled gamely back at him. "Intentions? Should I expect someone to call me out then, for 'dishonoring' you in this way? I didn't think you had any brothers."

"I don't, and I intend to be the only one who does any 'fencing' with you in the future."

Krystyna couldn't resist giggling. "I must admit, you are quite the swordsman."

"And you, wench, call forth my finest mettle. I believe both of us would benefit greatly from future matches." Now he eased back onto his side and rested his head on his elbow. "It is good to speak in Polish again. Do you ever long for our country?"

"Yes, with all my heart. At night, I dream I'm back home. I miss waking up to the sounds of the country, riding out and hearing nothing but the voices of birds, the cranes and the larks, the music of crickets. Vienna is magnificent, but I'm not a city person."

"It's been too long for me as well, and I know difficult for my father. He has always wanted me to enjoy every opportunity, the best education, the chance to travel, so that I would ultimately be the best possible steward for our estate. Still, I think he has worried that my journeys would lead me permanently away. But the longer I've traveled, the more I've missed my home. So, you, too, plan to return home. Then, you don't seek to marry an Austrian count?"

"Most definitely not."

"But wasn't that what your parents hoped would result from sending you to your great-aunt? Will they be very disappointed?"

"No, they want me to return to Poland."

"Is there some local fellow to whom they wish to see you wed?"

"They just want me to be happy."

"And what would make you happy?"

"I'm happy right now." She sought to sidetrack him by grasping his shaft in her hand.

"You're trying to distract me."

"It appears I'm succeeding."

"I'm very willing and able to accommodate your desires, but first, tell me, what is it you hope for? A life of more travel with a diplomat husband, perhaps?"

"No," now she spoke from the heart. "A home of my own in the country, a good man, children."

"Again, I find we are in accord." His voice rumbled forth from deep in his chest as they began to make love again.

It was only later on in the afternoon, when Andrzej lay asleep beside her, his face softened to the likeness of a boy, that Krystyna paused to reflect on what she'd affirmed during the afternoon. The two of them were supremely well matched. With her body and her soul, Krystyna recognized the man who should be her mate, and he'd forever marked her as his own. But these truths didn't matter, for she would soon disappear from his life. A single tear worked its way down her cheek, but she couldn't cry now, not now. She stared down at him, seeking to memorize his face. Carefully, she shifted his limbs.

He muttered and pulled her close, wrapping his long thigh about her. "Don't move," he ordered sleepily.

"Andrzej, I have to get up. I have to… There's no way to put this delicately. I'm about to burst."

"Hurry back."

As she sat up, Krystyna shivered at the shock of the cold air on her body. She longed to fall back into the cocoon of warm blankets, into his embrace. He rolled over onto his side, facing the wall.

Silently and swiftly, she gathered up her garments and her boots. She hastened from the bedroom. Dressing hurriedly before the still smoldering fire in the study, she managed as well as she could with her torn garments, reassuring herself that her cloak would cover the damage. After braiding her hair back and lacing her boots, she paused. How could she just leave without any sort of explanation? But then, she had no right to impose the burden of her problems onto Andrzej and no willingness to place him in danger, too. There was no time to explain it all to him in a satisfactory manner. She couldn't live with another person suffering because of Janus's vendetta against her, especially not the man she loved. She had to leave, for his sake, and he wasn't the sort of man who would simply let her go. He would want to take charge, to help her, and in doing so, would place his own life in jeopardy. She couldn't allow him to risk playing the hero.

The only way to ensure his safety was to totally abandon him, to leave him with no clue as to her future whereabouts.

But after all they'd shared, how could she do so? A note, she could write him a note. Glancing down at the cluttered desk, she observed a newly started letter addressed to "Dear Father" on top. She set it aside and took another piece of paper from the cubicle above. Grasping the quill, she dipped it into ink then hesitated. A drop of the black liquid splotched down on the paper. She stared at it. Time, there was no time! Her hands trembled. What to say? It was impossible. She couldn't think. "My love, I'll never see you again. I can't tell you why, but I'm leaving to protect you." No, she couldn't write that. If someone ever left her such a note, it would drive her mad. She wanted to tell him that she loved him and would never forget him. But would sharing these truths be hurtful to him when she had to disappear?

In the end, she couldn't decide what to tell the man with whom she'd dreamed of spending the rest of her life. She wanted him to be happy, not haunted by memories of her. Though it nearly killed her to do so, she didn't leave him a note. Her disappearance was the best gift she could give him.

Before departing, she fought the temptation to return to the bedroom door and peek at him for one last time. Too risky. And so, with pounding heart, shaking hands, and teary eyes, she silently exited Andrzej's rooms and his life.

CHAPTER 14

She emerged into the already-darkening world of an early, winter evening. The buildings around her loomed shadowy and forbidding. She hesitated and cast a fleeting glance back up at the one she'd just left. She peered up at Andrzej's rooms. Then, shivering and deliberately ignoring the way her stomach rumbled, she hurried down the street, to that same intersection where she'd disembarked early that afternoon. On one side of the dingy square, several haggard-looking horses rested while hitched to equally sorry conveyances. Krystyna immediately approached the first driver in the short queue.

"Step right in, miss." After tugging on his leather gloves, the driver jerked the carriage door open. "Where would you be going?"

"An inn," Krystyna finally answered. It was too late to go to Kotyat's farm, and she couldn't have stayed at Andrzej's. With the dawn would have come questions she wasn't prepared to answer.

"Which one?"

Though she remained outwardly serene, she was panicking. She didn't want this man to know she had no real destination in mind. “Oh, I can never remember names,” she muttered vaguely, her tone deliberately carefree. “I was supposed to go directly there after work. My husband must have told me the name a half dozen times. It was something like the Wolf’s Layer or Fox something or other,” she paused suggestively. “It was on the outskirts of the city, to the east. Oh, do help me, you must know the place.”

“Do you mean the Fox Hollow?”

“Is that a large place, where many of the coach drivers stop?”

“No, but it’s small and respectable.”

“I don’t think that would be the one.”

“Miss, do you know how many inns are in this city?”

“I’m sorry. It’s just that my husband is waiting for me. We’re to go to his sister’s wedding. He went ahead with our things because I worked today. Oh, he’ll be furious with me. Could you just name a few more inns to the east, where you drivers go? I’m sure I’ll recognize the name.”

The man rolled his eyes and stomped his feet against the cold. “Ah, how about the Bear’s Paw, the Inn at the Well, Tilda’s… Wait a minute, that place is also called the Wolf’s Den.”

“Yes, that’s it! I’m sure of it.”

“All right then, here you go.” He handed her in to the dim interior. “We’ll be there in half an hour or so.”

With relief, Krystyna sank back against the ratty, old squabs. She was going to an inn. God alone knew what sort. She hoped she’d picked a reputable place from which she could travel on with little difficulty. But the driver hadn’t appeared shocked with the one she had chosen. At least this Wolf’s Den was to the east, in the direction of the Kotyat’s farm. In the morning, she would head straight there. But for now, she was exhausted. She needed to eat and sleep. Perhaps, afterwards, she wouldn’t feel so fragile and close to tears. Perhaps then, she could ignore the aching cavern where once her heart had been.

She awoke abruptly when the coach finally lurched to a stop. She had no idea of the time. The carriage door swung open, and she looked out into a dark, starless night.

"Here we are, miss." The driver told her the fare, and she wordlessly paid him. She peered at her destination. The Wolf's Den was a large and rambling inn. The warm glow of a fire in the hearth beckoned through the green glass windows. The glass on the windows reassured Krystyna; they indicated the place was prosperous, one of the better sort of inns. From where she stood, she could just make out the sound of singing voices.

One of the driver's horses snorted. Krystyna jumped.

"That's Tilda's. I mean the Den. Head right in there, Miss. It's not a night to be out-of-doors. I'm headin' home myself. It's been a long day for the girls and me." With a flick of his whip-holding wrist, the driver urged his team to step out.

"Yes, yes… and thank you." Raising her skirts to keep them from dragging along the frozen ground, she advanced to the front door. She knocked and waited. There was no answer. The singing voices continued unabated. She knocked louder. The door swung wide to reveal a round-faced man with ruddy cheeks. He held a mug of beer in one hand.

"Told you I heard a coach out there," the man bellowed to no one in particular. Krystyna stepped back away from the flurry of spittle that exited the man's mouth with each utterance.

"Dropped off this bit of skirt here. Tilda, come here! This one's yours."

"Ach, Klaus. Get back to the bar." A rail thin, hard-faced blond with a no-nonsense look about her appeared.

"The wife will see to ya." Klaus winked at Krystyna, patted Tilda on the rump and strode heavily away.

"Can I be of service, miss?" Tilda questioned with one scrawny eyebrow raised and her arms crossed over her flat chest. She sniffed in disapproval as she took in Krystyna's rumpled and haggard appearance.

"Yes, please. Achoo!"

"God's blessing."

"Thank you. Yes, I need a room for the night."

"Of course. Come this way. Ignore that rowdy bunch over there. We run a decent place, but there's no controlling them. My husband, Klaus, is the problem. He carries on with them. I'll send someone after your things. Dirk!" Tilda shouted peremptorily.

"I have nothing with me."

The other woman was clearly taken aback by this disclosure, so Krystyna plunged on, the words tripping over themselves in her haste to explain. "I sent my luggage on ahead. I'd hoped to be all the way home today, but a wheel broke on the coach. So, here I am."

Tilda pursed her lips but said nothing, clearly not caring about the how or why of her guest's arrival. "Follow me. It's a terrible night for traveling. For dinner, we have pea soup, sausage and bread. You can have whatever you like to drink. Klaus keeps us well stocked. You'll have to sit in the common room with everyone else, and you pay now." Tilda led Krystyna into a quiet hallway where a desk stood. She went behind it and removed a key from where it hung on the wall. "It's a small room, up the stairs, second door to your left. You pay in advance, and then you sign here."

She proudly placed a leather-bound register before Krystyna. "You can write?" She looked somewhat disappointed when she nodded. "I sign for all of our guests who can't write. Here, this is my hand. The nuns taught me how. My Klaus, he can't read or write or do figures, but I can."

"You have a fine hand," Krystyna mumbled as she stared at the book before her. There were two columns, one for dates and the other for names. About halfway down the page, she glimpsed a "Laura." Laura was the name of a peasant girl of her own age who lived at Sea of Grass. The two girls had played together as children, until Laura's family had moved to a larger house in a remote corner of the estate.

Horesko, Laura Horesko. That was it. Decisively, she scrawled the name down.

Tilda turned the register and silently studied the signature. "You'll only be needing the room for this night?" Krystyna nodded. "If you plan on traveling in one of the public coaches, you'll want to speak with the drivers tonight as they leave early in the morning. You're Polish, aren't you?"

Krystyna froze, fear oozed down her spine. "Why… Why do you ask?"

Tilda eyed the young woman before her. She was definitely hiding something. Her transparent reaction, bedraggled appearance and lack of luggage all led the inn keeper's wife to conclude "Laura" was running away from something or someone.

She smiled shrewdly. "I make a game of guessing. Because we're on the outskirts of the city and because so many coaches stop here, we get people from all over the Empire. Just the other night, we had a group of Hungarians. They about drank my cellar dry. You were harder to place. Your accent is not so thick, and your German is very good. But I'm rarely wrong these days. I've been at it for too many years."

Krystyna needed to get away from Tilda's prying eyes and probing mind. "Well, good night and thank you." She turned to go.

"I'll have Klaus light the fire in your room while you're eating. It should be warm enough by the time that you're done."

Gripping her cloak at the neck, Krystyna paused. "Would you happen to have a needle and some thread? I have a loose button."

"You'll have to pay extra for it."

"Of course."

The two women quickly concluded their business. Krystyna removed a larger sum than she considered fair from her purse and handed it over. But there was nothing to be done for it, and she had no idea what was standard or appropriate. The room she'd been given was small with shabby and worn furnishings and cold as a tomb. It was a grim beginning to her new life. She yanked back the blanket on the bed to find that the linens appeared reasonably clean. About a half an hour later, she returned to the common room where she devoured a bowl of thick, salty soup and some sausage with bread, all of which she washed down with a stein of beer. Afterwards, she returned to her now slightly warmer chamber to collapse onto the lumpy mattress.

Despite her fatigue, sleep eluded her. She tossed and turned, unable to get comfortable, plagued with remorse about leaving Andrzej as she had.

"Andrzej… Andrzej, I'm so sorry, my love." No longer able to contain her pain, she muffled her sobs with her blankets.

That one afternoon was likely all she'd ever have of him, a man with whom she'd imagined spending the rest of her life. What would he think of her when he discovered she'd fled not only his bed, but Vienna as well?

Eventually, fatigue quieted the storm of her emotions. As long as he was alive and well, she consoled herself, there was some chance that they could be reunited at a later date. Unless, that is, he married someone else.

Sleep finally dried her tears.

CHAPTER 15

After waking alone in his rooms following that unforgettable afternoon with Krystyna, Andrzej impatiently waited three days before calling at the von Gebler house. Not wanting to seem overeager, he'd deliberately allowed enough time to pass so that whatever occurred there could be resolved. He wondered what might have gone on before she came to him and he berated himself for not probing further. But his attention had been on other, more pleasureful matters.

The days had dragged by agonizingly slow. Krystyna dominated his thoughts. He found it difficult to sleep for thinking of her. Initially, he'd been dismayed and a little hurt that she'd left him without any sort of farewell. But after some reflection, he'd concluded that she probably had to get back to her great-aunt's house. Perhaps, she'd worried he would oppose her leaving him after nightfall, and he would have. After all, the "damage" had already been well and deliciously done, and he intended to see that they were married in the near future. But rather than belaboring the point, Andrzej savored the memories. He was no poet, but he'd scrawled down some lines that night. He'd saved them in his grandfather's Bible, in which he stored several of his most precious papers. They read: "Krystyna, my soul's music, my other half. All pain is washed away, forgotten, when I hold her in my arms. We are both imperfect, but there is a rightness to the two of us together."

The words were foolishly romantic and embarrassingly naïve when read in the unforgiving, skeptical light of day. But the feeling that inspired them was still there, still consuming him. It had taken all of his self-possession to keep from riding straight to the von Gebler house that next day and asking, no, demanding Krystyna's hand in marriage.

Andrzej didn't consider himself an impetuous fool where women were concerned. In Paris and Berlin, he'd danced, dined and even spent the night with some of the most acclaimed beauties of the day. Such evenings had provided diversion, but his heart had yearned to love and be loved.

For the sake of pride, even though she'd come to him first, a man had to wait at least three days. Thank God those endless days finally passed, and he could see her and share his plans with her. He'd already discussed his plans with the General, who approved of the match and agreed to assist. He'd even offered to write to Roderyk Morzinski in support of Andrzej. In his mind, it was all planned out. Once they were engaged, he and Krystyna would return to Poland so that he could personally ask Pan Sielski for his daughter's hand and their engagement could be finalized according to Polish tradition. He imagined they could be married some time in June or July. Perhaps, if his father was well enough, he could join them for the ceremony. Regardless, Andrzej knew the old man would be thrilled and eager for his son and new daughter-in-law to return to Sweet Air and start producing grandchildren.

Six months seemed like a very long time, but it did take a while to plan a wedding, and he wanted everything to be perfect for her. The only problem he could foresee was that she might have become pregnant in their afternoon together. What if there was already a child on the way? He'd not thought to ask whether it was a safe time for her, nor had he withdrawn from her, though he was usually never careless. A child. His child and Krystyna's. Would it be a little girl with coppery locks or a boy with great brown eyes? The possibility of a child would definitely hasten matters, but such a development would be a welcome one to him. His father was right; it was definitely time for him to return to Poland and to marry. He fully intended to do both.

These thoughts occupied his mind as he rode through the streets of Vienna toward the woman of his future. The cobblestones were slick with forming ice. And so, he couldn't, in good conscience, urge his steed to a faster gait. But his heart soared on ahead. At last, he was on her street, and then the house was in view. Andrzej paused, savoring the anticipation. He nudged his steed forward.

When he dismounted, no groom came to take his horse. The house appeared strangely still and quiet. After standing there for some moments, Andrzej, with his horse still in hand, strode around the side of the house to the stables. Impatiently, he jerked the stable door open to reveal a young man cleaning the stalls.

"You there, would you tend to my horse? I'm calling on the ladies of the house."

"Oh, you can't… I mean, they're gone. The mistress left with most of the servants yesterday. Just a handful of us were kept on here to maintain the place. You could speak with Jens if you like. He's in charge out here in the stable. I'll fetch him." The boy leaned his pitchfork up against a wall and scurried away.

"Gone?" Andrzej repeated hollowly. It couldn't be! There had to be some misunderstanding.

"Sir," a lanky, mustachioed fellow materialized from some interior region of the stable. "Klaus said you were looking for Frau von Gebler. She left just yesterday."

"Was this sudden?"

"After..." Jens paused, obviously searching for words. "Yes sir, it was sudden."

"Where did she go?"

"I wouldn't know. Our mistress has houses in so many places," he answered, his eyes shifting about nervously.

"Did Fraulein Krystyna go with her?"

He shrugged his shoulders. "I think so, but there's nothing more I can tell you. It's my job to take care of the stable and horses. I don't know much about the goings on in the house."

Nodding slowly, Andrzej requested, "Would you please see to my horse while I speak with one of the house servants?"

Ten minutes later, he mounted up and exited through the gates of the von Gebler house. The housekeeper with whom he'd spoken had provided no more information on Krystyna and her great-aunt's destination than had Jens. Pausing, he glanced back at the façade.

"Too late," he muttered the words like a curse. If only he'd come a day sooner. Perhaps, Krystyna's great-aunt had found out about their interlude. Maybe that was why they'd fled the city so impetuously. But then, he'd been of the impression that Jadwiga favored his suit. If she'd discovered he and her great niece were lovers, she would have confronted him herself and demanded he marry the girl. No, he was definitely missing a piece of this puzzle. Krystyna was gone, but why? Too distracted by his feelings of abandonment and betrayal, he didn't reflect on the peculiar behavior of the von Gebler servants until he was already home and attempting to ease his pain with a bottle of vodka.

His increasingly alcohol-soaked mind reflected on the day's revelations. It was apparent that the groom Jens had been fearful of something or someone. In addition, Andrzej realized Krystyna must have known she was leaving Vienna when she came to him. She'd not trusted him enough to tell him what was going on.

Then again, he may have been wrong about her all along. Perhaps, she was no different than the other women with whom he had dallied. He downed another glass of the liquid fire and reveled in its scorching path down his throat.

More thoughts and suppositions, like daggers, wounded him. She'd thought little of him, used him. And then, just when he thought that he could hate her, he remembered how she'd trembled when he licked the tender skin behind her ear. He pictured her as she'd been when she had demanded admission into the Marchioness von Treutter's hunting lodge with all of the zeal of an avenging angel.

A few more shots, and a revelation struck him; Krystyna hadn't come to that lodge alone. That peacock of a Hungarian, deSzinay, accompanied her. He might know where she had gone. Perhaps, the two were more than merely friends.

Andrzej calmly contemplated murdering Sebastjan if that, indeed, was the case. He knew where the man lived. One evening, months ago, Andrzej had attended a soiree there.

Driven by anger and desolation, he somehow managed to throw the tack back on his horse. Thankfully, though his steed took one sniff of him and snorted in dismay, the animal was of a kindly and tolerant disposition. He stood still so that Andrzej could drag himself aboard.

The frosty, crisp evening air rendered him more alert, though still hopelessly intoxicated. Regardless of his condition, his impeccable sense of direction didn't fail him. Though the lights swam mercilessly, and his horse moved with a nauseating gait, he managed to find his way to deSzinay's lair. There, he tossed his steed's reins to a terrified stable boy. He drove his stumbling and staggering feet to the front door on which he banged with all of the fury of a bitter and despairing man.

A servant opened the door. "Can I help you, sir?"

Andrzej brushed past him and barged into the entrance foyer. "Where is he?"

"Excuse me, sir, but…"

"DeSzinay," he roared then took off in a maddened rush, so that the doorman was left scurrying after him.

"Sir! Sir, please."

When he encountered the double doors leading into Sebastjan's rooms, his frustrations got the best of him. He drove his shoulder into them. They were locked, and the solid oak splintered and cracked, but didn't budge. Growling in fury, he prepared to make another assault when the door swung wide to reveal a surprised Sebastjan deSzinay. Andrzej, unable to halt his momentum, drove the slighter man to the floor.

"Master Sebastjan, are you all right? You villain. Get off of the young master at once. I've a sword in hand, and I know how to use it!"

Andrzej blearily raised his head to eye first his stunned victim beneath him and then the outraged doorman who was, indeed, wielding a ceremonial sword.

"Morzinski? What's going on?"

"Where is she?" Too far gone to worry about the servant's threats, he gripped Sebastjan by the hair and began to pound his blond head against the floor. An oriental carpet protected him from the worst of it, but the blows remained crushing. "Where is she?"

"Who?" Sebastjan choked the word out.

"Get off of him at once!"

"Krystyna."

"What?"

"I will kill you, sir! I have a sword at your back."

Despite his dulled senses, Andrzej did feel a sharp point thrusting in between his shoulder blades.

"Listen to Tomas," Sebastjan implored. "He means what he says. He does know how to use that sword. He served in the cavalry."

Andrzej rolled off of his victim and lay there supine.

Sebastjan scrambled to his feet. With surprising élan, he

dusted off the embroidered sleeves of his pale blue jacket. Though his hands shook, he carefully adjusted his cravat in the gilt mirror that hung on the wall. Then, he turned to face his assailant.

Andrzej hadn't risen from his position on the floor. The alcohol was pulsing through him, particularly behind his closed eyes. He felt sick, defeated, frustrated, heartbroken and more than a little foolish. Despite the effort involved, he opened his reddened eyes to glare up at Sebastjan's manservant. The man continued to hold the point of his sword to the base of his neck.

"Are you sane now? Ready to behave like a human being?" Sebastjan questioned.

Andrzej gave a curt nod.

"Let him up, Tomas." Sebastjan poured a drink from a crystal decanter on a side table. He thoughtfully swirled the amber liquid in its goblet and queried, "Would you care for one, Morzinski?"

Tomas eyed Andrzej warily as he staggered to his feet.

"I've already had more than enough."

"Well then, one more won't do you any harm." Sebastjan's voice was steady, but the delicate quivering of his drink revealed the true state of his nerves. "That will be all, Tomas. Please return the sword to its usual spot."

"I prefer to remain at hand."

"Morzinski means to be reasonable now, so I have no need of you, Tomas."

"I will be right outside the doors."

"Please shut them behind you."

Andrzej considered the dapper, young man before him. Sebastjan was conducting himself with sangfroid despite being attacked in his own home by a maddened drunk. Apparently, beneath the curls, silk and powder there was some substance.

Sebastjan took a seat in an armchair then he met Andrzej's eyes. "What can I do for you, Morzinski? I am at your service."

For a fleeting moment, Andrzej had been ashamed of his behavior. The thought had crossed his mind that he might have misjudged this man. But, unreasonable as it was, seeing Sebastjan infuriated him. No man had a right to be as pretty as a woman. It was easy to imagine Krystyna preferring Sebastjan's blond loveliness to his own more rough-hewn features and form. "Where is Krystyna Sielska?"

Blue eyes coolly scrutinized Andrzej. "So, she caught your fancy as well. I'm not surprised. She is strong-willed, perhaps too tall, but fabulous coloring. Are you quite sure you wouldn't care for a drink? It seems rather inhospitable to indulge alone."

"No."

Sebastjan never imagined he'd see this sophisticated and worldly man brought so low by a woman, the same woman who, truth be told, held his own heart. Feeling a sense of comradeship with the miserable man, Sebastjan answered: "Krystyna and her great-aunt left Vienna just yesterday."

"Where did they go?"

"I don't know. Perhaps to Italy or home to Poland."

"Christ, man! Do you know anything at all about this matter?" Andrzej shoved his hands through his already tousled locks. "I thought you had more than a passing acquaintance with the family."

"Do you intend her harm?" He spoke the words softly.

"At this moment, I could strangle her with my bare hands."

"Morzinski, you try my patience. Do you… care for Krystyna?"

"She left Vienna without a word to me. Why did she go? If you know something, please tell me!"

"Can I trust you? Or, more importantly, can she trust you?"

Andrzej was silent. Then, he glanced up. "Yes."

Something like resignation flitted across Sebastjan's elegant features. "In that case, I'll tell you what I can. Someone is after Krystyna, followed her from Poland, in fact. She has been receiving threats for some time, and a servant woman was murdered in the von Gebler house. Just recently, there was another attack, which is why they weren't receiving visitors. The women left so abruptly in order to elude Krystyna's pursuer."

"When did all of this happen?"

"You were away for a while, were you not? But even if you were in Vienna, you might not have heard anything. It was all kept very quiet."

"Krystyna never mentioned anything in her letters or when…"

"It should be of some comfort to you to know that she didn't bid farewell even to her closest friend, Marta von Reigler. I spoke with Marta after I visited the von Gebler house and found both women gone. The only reason I know so much is that Marta shared the story with me. She trusts me because I assisted in her rescue that time.

"There is definitely something sinister afoot."

"Do you know if they went to the authorities?"

"The police did investigate the murder of the servant woman, but they never unearthed any suspects to my knowledge. The event was regarded as an attempted robbery gone wrong."

Krystyna was in trouble; that much was clear to Andrzej. Why hadn't she trusted him enough to let him help her? He rose somewhat unsteadily to his feet and paced before the hearth. He paused to glare at Sebastjan. "Why are you telling me this? How do you know that I'm not the one after her?"

"Oh, you are after her," Sebastjan mocked, "of that I am completely convinced. But your motives are entirely different. You are in love with her."

"DeSzinay, you misread me. I am enraged with Krystyna Sielska."

"Yes, yes, of course. You descend upon me like a maddened beast. You have obviously been indulging heavily since you learned of her desertion. All of these clues lead me to conclude that you are a distraught lover. Come, come, Andrzej, don't take me for a fool. I must admit that the girl has gotten under my skin, too. In all likelihood, it's probably some sort of nostalgia for Poland, for she never gave me any indication that her feelings for me were ever more than friendly." A flash of some unhappy emotion crossed those carelessly lovely features before Sebastjan deliberately glanced away. He swirled the amber liquid in his goblet.

"DeSzinay, do you have any idea where she might have gone?"

"No. Honestly, I don't. Morzinski, don't be a fool and go after her. If you do find her, you may lead whoever is chasing her straight to her. Krystyna is neither a fool nor a tease. It's clear to me that she had grave reasons for fleeing Vienna. If you have any feeling for her, you must respect her wishes. You have no choice but to wait."

Leaning against the mantle, Andrzej stared broodingly into the fire. The peacock was right. She was gone, and he couldn't endanger her by following. With a sickening sensation twisting his innards, he considered the destruction of his dreams and plans for the future. It was all over now. He couldn't stay in Vienna and wait for her indefinitely; his father needed him at home. And he had no way of knowing if she would ever return, or if she had any desire to see him again. It was time to go home.

A hand fell lightly onto his shoulder. Sebastjan stood behind him smiling at him in a comradely manner. "She's not dead, you know. All is not lost."

Andrzej shrugged one broad shoulder. "She's lost to me. Excuse my intrusion, deSzinay. My behavior has been inexcusable."

Sebastjan considered the defeated figure of the tall man before him. Krystyna had really touched his heart. He commiserated with Andrzej, but he didn't see the situation as hopeless. Always an optimist, he held fast to the prospect that

Krystyna would return to Vienna one day, and he would be there waiting for her. "Stay here for a while, Morzinski." The man was in no condition to depart. "Dine with me. I've a fine bottle of German wine that I was about to open. We could drink to women and the exquisite misery they cause us."

Andrzej eyed him dispiritedly. "Thank you, but no, it's time for me to go home." He wasn't referring to his rented rooms where her scent still lingered on his bed coverings.

"Morzinski?"

He paused in the now opened doorway. True to his word, Tomas, sword at his side, stood in attendance in the hallway.

"You're not alone," Sebastjan said.

"What?"

"I envy you."

"For what?"

"At least you had something to lose with Krystyna. I wasn't so fortunate."

"If this is good fortune…" Andrzej couldn't finish his thought.

He merely shut the doors.

CHAPTER 16

Tilda, the inn keeper's wife at the Wolf's Den, used her damp cloth to take one last swipe at the bar. Her legs ached from another long day on her feet. She glanced around the common room. It was growing late, and most of the supper crowd had already retired. Two soldiers in the blue and red Austrian uniform lingered over their beers. The only other occupant of the common room was an enigma to her. He, too, had finished eating and drinking hours ago, and yet he remained.

Tilda wished Klaus would hurry back from his chores in the stable. There was something disturbing about this stranger, not that she could explain exactly what. His appearance was unremarkable. His hair and eyes were dark, and his clothes were well made but not extravagant. After more than twenty years running an inn, Tilda had a talent for placing people. Within moments of meeting a guest, she could usually guess their backgrounds with a surprising degree of accuracy. But not this fellow. He didn't have the mien of a merchant, and there was a coarse arrogance to him that bespoke an aristocratic background. But he'd spoken so few words she hadn't even been able to guess his nationality. He knew how to write, but Tilda could make nothing of the name he'd scrawled so carelessly in her register. It read "Janus." What sort of name was that? The man had taken an interest in the register. He had studied it for several long minutes, flipping back through the long pages.

She was glad he was leaving in the morning. Tilda shivered involuntarily.

Just then, he glanced up and caught her in the act of staring at him. Tilda dropped her head immediately and began to wipe industriously at the already clean counter with her rag. Her efforts became more frantic as Janus stood up and approached her.

"Madam, I would like a word with you."

He was Russian, Tilda realized. She straightened and then couldn't resist taking a step back from the bar, away from him. "I'm at your service. Is there something you need?"

"I have need of some information regarding a lady who may have been a guest here."

His wife is cuckolding him, Tilda speculated. That explained his barely veiled hostility. "You've already looked at the register. But you're welcome to do so again." She stepped out from behind the bar to be halted by a vise-like grip on her arm just above her elbow. She froze, willing Klaus to step through the door. Still, there was little Janus could do to her with the two soldiers in attendance, she reassured herself, unless he was wholly mad.

"This lady wouldn't sign her true name. So we'll have to rely on your memory, which I expect is quite dependable. Come sit with me." Keeping his grip upon her arm, he propelled her to a seat on one of the long benches.

Tilda was no fool. Janus had paid in advance for the night, and her husband was nowhere in sight. Humoring the stranger seemed wise.

"This lady is a relative, a cousin. She's in some trouble and has run away from home. We are all gravely concerned about her."

Tilda nodded politely though she didn't believe a word of it.

"She would have stopped here early in December last year."

"December!" Tilda sputtered. "That's more than six months ago." She attempted to rise, but his grip on her arm stopped her. Where was Klaus?

"Do you remember this woman?" The man drew a framed miniature from inside his tunic. Despite her resentment at her ruthless interrogator, Tilda leaned in to get a closer look.

The girl in the well-executed little portrait had lush waves of reddish hair and large brown eyes. Tilda knew in a moment she'd seen these features before; she'd always had a memory for faces. The girl had been striking and out of her element. She'd paid for her room without blinking an eye when Tilda had given her an outrageous price though her clothes had been plain and simple.

"She was here. You recognize her."

"She could have been. I'm not really sure. She's a fine lady, and we don't have many of that class here. This is just a simple inn. Could I see that again?" Tilda considered her course of action. What harm was there in admitting the girl stayed a night? After all, she'd done so more than a half-year before, and the girl could be anywhere now. All that prevented Tilda from coming out and admitting the truth was that she didn't want to help this Russian.

"Where was she going? And was she traveling alone?"

"I don't remember. Now let go of me. Those two soldiers will come to my aid if I call to them."

"Then, you'll have their blood on your hands," he responded so calmly, so coldly that she believed him. "Just give me the information I require."

Tilda felt physically ill. She owed no loyalty to the girl. At that moment, the front door swung open and Klaus's large, round form loomed in the doorway. He paused there, obviously chatting with someone still outside.

Janus recaptured her attention by pulling her hand under the table. He turned it, painfully, twisting her wrist.

She inhaled sharply.

"Enlighten me."

The ice in his voice convinced Tilda. There was definitely something depraved and heartless about those eyes. She had no doubt he was capable of murdering her husband, herself, and the two soldiers if any of them interfered in his plans. "You're right. She was here. The girl was here. She left the next morning. I'll show you where she signed in the register. I know the driver who picked her up from here, too. His name is Heiko Munzman. He comes through regularly on Tuesdays and Thursdays. That's everything, all I know."

He nodded his head, released her and smiled courteously as her husband approached the table. He'd finally recovered Krystyna Sielska's trail. Back in December, his man lost her in the marketplace; a mistake for which he paid with his life. Janus and his followers had spent the last six months speaking with drivers, innkeepers, bar maids, anyone who might have seen her. So many dead ends. But now his luck was changing. The pieces were coming together. Krystyna was clever, and that made the hunt more interesting. But it was only a matter of time now.

PART II

CHAPTER 17

Poland
Two Years Later

Andrzej Morzinski waited for a few seconds. Then, leaning into the dark walls of his father's manor house, he, too, hurried along. He turned one corner and concluded that the boy had cleverly eluded him after all. He sprinted along another wall, turned again and froze. The candlelight leaking through windows on both the first and second floors lent the area an eerie sort of visibility. There, crouched just below one of the tall windows were two figures: the shorter one was clearly the boy, and the other was a tall woman in a riding skirt.

The two conversed briefly, and then the woman rose up and peered through the window into the dining room. She was on her tiptoes peeking in when he made his move.

He ran up behind her, grasped her about the waist and covered her mouth with his hand. "Don't be afraid," he whispered as she went rigid and then began to struggle. "I mean you no harm. Don't scream. Can I trust you to be calm?" Anguish shot up from his left foot, into which she drove her booted heel. His arms loosened reflexively, and she was free and running.

Ignoring the throbbing pain, he chased after her. The girl could run, but the cool night air and his rage leant him wings. In a few strides, he caught up with her and, acting instinctively, he drove her to the ground with a flying leap at her legs. He held tight despite her kicking and flailing, and with his superior strength and greater weight managed to drag himself up along her rebelling body. Inch by inch, he fought his way up, until he lay directly on top of her. He was a large man, solid and strong, but still she bucked and fought against him.

"I only want to talk to you. I swear it. Be still, woman!"

He eventually prevailed, and she lay stiffly beneath him with her face turned away from him. Andrzej guessed she was merely gathering for another offensive, when the boy's shout of "Stop! Don't hurt her" intruded into his consciousness.

A small body hurtled onto his shoulders. Andrzej struggled with both the enraged mite on his back and the powerful woman beneath him.

"Will you both stop it," he roared, squinting defensively against the tiny fingers poking for his eyes. "I mean no harm. You are the trespassers!" He managed to reach around and grab the child with one arm. He pulled him off of his back while pinning the girl's arms with a knee and his other hand. Her powerful legs flailed uselessly away from him.

"Boy, I'm not hurting her." He twisted his weight off the prone girl, and he released the boy. Satisfying his curiosity was really not worth this grief, and he didn't want to unintentionally hurt either of them. He rubbed at his eyes reassuring himself that they remained undamaged, despite the boy's efforts—and recognized the child. He was one of a band of Romany horse traders. Andrzej glanced over to find the woman staring up at him in silence.

It was impossible! It couldn't be!

But somehow, it was. He was staring into the face that had haunted him for more than two years, the face of the woman who had seared her presence into his memory in one unforgettable afternoon. And then had disappeared.

He closed his eyes in disbelief. He was imagining things, must have had too much vodka. He opened his eyes again, and there she was, this girl with Krystyna's face, staring back at him.

She leaped to her feet and dashed off into the darkness.

He didn't give chase. He was utterly stunned. She couldn't be here, at his father's estate, and with a band of horse traders! His heart gave a twist.

He still sat in the same position when two men ran up. "We heard the shouting." Jan Mouceski, the owner of a neighboring estate and a life-long acquaintance, panted, out of breath from his exertion. "What happened?"

As he rose to his feet, Andrzej didn't respond. There couldn't be two women so alike in this world.

"I was fortunate enough to meet your son this evening, Kotyat," Andrzej addressed the whip-thin, gypsy horse dealer with Jan.

"Please forgive his intrusion, Pan Morzinski," Kotyat responded deferentially, "and accept my apologies. The boy meant no harm. I'll deal with him tonight. He will apologize to you and to your father. If you will excuse me…" He bowed his head.

"That's not necessary. He's just a child. This situation is as much my fault as your son's, and there's no need to hurry away, Herr Kotyat. There is much about your traveling troop I wish to understand."

The two men stared at each other: one, wiry and lean, the

other, broad and stalwart. Kotyat looked away first, clearly intimidated and uncomfortable under Andrzej's scrutiny.

"What's going on?" Jan muttered, glancing between the two.

"Let's return inside, Jan. My father will be worried about us." Andrzej clasped his neighbor's shoulder.

As the threesome turned their footsteps back to the great house, Andrzej provided a reasonable, though untrue, explanation for the disturbance.

Upon their return into the main hall, Kotyat turned. "Pan Morzinski, you and your father have been very kind during our stay. I thank you for your hospitality. But the roads are becoming less safe with each passing day. We should be on our way."

"Of course," Andrzej inclined his head. He understood the horse dealer hid something, or someone, in this case. "But I will prevail upon you to return to this house tomorrow, so we may conclude some business with respect to your black mare. I will make it well worth your while."

"And I'm interested in the chestnut stud colt," Jan Mouceski broke in. "I'd like to get another look at him."

"Jan, just come here tomorrow around midmorning. That way, both of us can speak with Kotyat, and then he can be on his way."

"So be it. If you will excuse me." The horse dealer bowed low and hurried out the door.

Andrzej understood the man's eagerness to get away. Specifically, he was harboring the young woman who had ripped his heart out two years before.

CHAPTER 18

On the night of her engagement party, Krystyna Janicka, this being the surname she selected per Andrzej's instructions, smiled though the expression felt stiff and unnatural. She even nodded appropriately and managed to engage in conversations. Fortunately, none of Roderyk's guests seemed to notice her uneasiness, or, perhaps, they attributed her nerves to the occasion. After all, she was to formally accept Andrzej's marriage proposal before them. The entire situation seemed so unreal. She imagined, if she closed her eyes, she would be back in her gypsy wagon staring up at the canvas and longing for her home and family. Instead, she was perfumed and attired as befitted a noblewoman and awaiting her betrothed.

Unconsciously, her fingers went to the emerald necklace she wore. The heavy, worked gold piece was the only evidence that her fiancé was even aware of her presence in his house. That afternoon, Josef, Andrzej's valet, delivered the jewels to her room in a carved wooden box. Andrzej hadn't even delivered his gift of the Morzinski family jewels to her himself. She only knew of the significance of the necklace and ear bobs because Anna Mielak, a charming, matronly widow who visited the house and assisted Krystyna in her transformation back to well born lady, had commented on the set.

As a young girl, she'd daydreamed about her true love coming to ask for her hand and planned how she would answer the ritual questions. None of her imaginings had cast her as the reluctant bride of a dictatorial suitor. Still, for her own sake as well as for her soon-to-be family, she decided make the best of things. But the evening was beginning to wear on her.

She had made it through dinner, barely. And now a small but sociable group consisting of Roderyk and some of his neighbors were gathered in a drawing room awaiting Andrzej's arrival. Tradition dictated he come in darkness, so that no evil spirits would spy him. But it had been dark for some time now, and, to her dismay, there was still no sign of Andrzej. She nearly ground her teeth in frustration. She wanted to get it over with. She was in no mood for idle chit chat. More than once, she found herself staring out the window, hoping to catch sight of Andrzej and his matchmaker.

After observing her for a moment, Jan Mouceski, a large-bodied fellow of florid complexion who wore residue from their recent meal on his cravat, attempted to offer a compliment: "Andrzej has found himself a beauty. She'll breed well with hips like those, Roderyk. Unlike you, Agata." He sneered at his wife who was making her way over to him.

Agata, a pale, thin shadow of a woman, lowered her gaze in embarrassment.

"How's your daughter?" Roderyk asked politely, attempting to smooth over Mouceski's rudeness to his own wife.

"She has a cough, which is why she couldn't join us this evening," Agata answered softly. "She was very disappointed to be unable to accept your kind invitation, Pan Morzinski."

"The girl's as sickly as the mother, wouldn't you know. That's my luck. Haven't been able to get a boy off her yet, and not for lack of trying." Jan leered at Krystyna, who refused to glance demurely away. The man was a complete vulgarian.

"I'll say a prayer for your daughter's speedy recovery, Madam Mouceska. I can imagine how difficult it must be to leave your child at home alone when she's not feeling well. My heart goes out to you, Agata," she remarked with an ironic smile, suggesting she pitied the other woman for more than just her daughter's illness.

Agata blinked in surprise, while Jan studied Krystyna in some confusion, unsure of how to take her remark.

"Brother, please, you're embarrassing our host and this delightful lady." Vincent Mouceski was built far differently from his brother. Where Jan was solid with muscle from rich food, his brother was soft, narrow shouldered and almost feminine in build. On Vincent, Jan's fleshy features narrowed and tightened to an unfortunate degree. But he was dressed in the latest style with an elaborately coiffed wig. He'd eyed Krystyna critically when they were introduced, and she'd sensed a shrewd and calculating mind behind the effete presentation. "I understand you met our Andrzej in Vienna, my lady. How romantic! Vienna is a magnificent city, almost as delightful as Paris. I visited and toured both a few years ago. Vienna was so cosmopolitan, so sophisticated. And the music… It was such a penance to return to our rustic lives here in the countryside."

"I," Krystyna began before Jan cut her off.

"You didn't have to come back," he muttered to his brother before tossing down another shot of vodka. "I was doing fine on my own."

"Were you?" Vincent's tone of voice made it immediately apparent he was not in agreement with his brother on this point. "Jan, we are a team," he countered calmly. "You see, I have a small gift for management, and my brother has talent for animal husbandry."

"That doesn't surprise me," Krystyna returned with a soft smile.

Roderyk glanced at her sharply, one white eyebrow, arched disapprovingly. Krystyna lowered her eyes diffidently, feeling a slight pang of guilt. Her future father-in-law was doing his best to smooth her way back into society. She shouldn't embarrass him by behaving like a harpy. After all, Mouceski was clearly in his cups.

"You're a clever woman, Panienka." Vincent remarked. "Andrzej is a lucky fellow."

"I'll drink to that," Jan remarked. "You should see the black mare he bought off the gypsies. She's a beauty. Andrzej has an eye for a horse as well as a woman. But where is the bridegroom? He can't already be hiding from his bride-to-be. It's well past time for him to be here."

"He'll be here shortly. He went to get Father Ignacy who will be acting as intermediary."

"Now Panienka Janicka, tell me about your time in Vienna. Where did you go? What parties did you attend? Whom did you see?" Vincent prodded.

"I quite enjoyed Vienna. I was staying with my Aunt Jadwiga. She and the Baroness von Reigler, a friend of hers, saw to it that I participated in the usual social rounds. Two years later, it all seems quite a blur."

"Where have you been for these past two years?" Vincent smoothly questioned.

"Krystyna has been studying in a convent near Czestochowa." Anna Mielak, the plump, middle-aged widow with the pleasant countenance, answered for her.

"Yes," Krystyna answered. She, Roderyk and the Widow Mielak had discussed and agreed to this story because it was socially acceptable and very difficult to disprove. "My mother is quite devout and committed to the Virgin Mother. My father also believes in the value of a good education."

"What's the point in educating a woman?" Jan demanded. "Reading just confuses them, fills their heads with thoughts above their station. Anything you put into a woman's head comes out later as an argument or a complaint."

Vincent clucked his tongue disapprovingly.

"There are many ways to quiet a woman," Victor Brasinski, the final member of their party, offered as he stepped back from admiring some ancient weapons that were mounted on one wall. He wasn't a large man but was stocky in frame and proceeding to thickness about the waist. His lips were full, and his face, unremarkable, except for the charismatic blue eyes that dominated it. Beneath projecting brows, they mirrored the sky. He wore his oily, blond hair just past his ears in a style reminiscent of the Teutonic knights, those German warriors who once raided and murdered throughout Eastern Europe in the name of God. "The better ones leave a woman grateful and asking for more."

"Enough," Anna's pursed lips expressed her disapproval. The Widow Mielak had been on her own, raising her children and managing her estate, for going on five years. She wasn't one to sit back and allow the men to dominate a conversation. "You scoundrels must behave yourselves," she remonstrated in the same tone she would have used on her own sons. "Please remember you're in the company of ladies."

Just then, Kaspar, Roderyk's manservant, appeared in the doorway. "My lady," he addressed Krystyna. "There's someone to see you at the door."

Roderyk moved to Krystyna's side. "It's time, my dear."

Finally. As if in a trance, she proceeded slowly through the opened doors, into the corridor and down the hall to the front door.

Roderyk, now standing in for her father, opened the door.

The priest entered first, but Krystyna barely registered him. She had eyes only for Andrzej, who was formally attired in traditional Polish garments including thigh-high leather boots and a sable-lined kontusz or robe. Next to the diminutive and aged priest, he appeared bigger and more vital than she remembered him from their time together in Vienna, and there was a wariness in his amber eyes which she didn't recollect. He couldn't be unsure of her, could he? Perhaps he, too, was nervous. This thought made the situation more palatable to Krystyna. Truly, it wasn't Andrzej whom she feared. In a moment of insight, she realized it was the giving up of control, of making one's self vulnerable that must occur in a meaningful marriage, that terrified her. There was so much at stake for both of them. But she would never be alone again, and that thought was both terrifying and exhilarating Hesitantly, she offered Andrzej a slight smile.

Clearly, he was unsure how to respond. He cocked his eyebrow at her.

A smile on his incongruously cherubic features, Father Ignacy bowed low. "May the Lord bless you all and this house," he declared. "And how are you, Pan Roderyk? I know you have waited a long time for this night."

"Yes, Father, but Krystyna here was well worth it." Roderyk answered, ushering the priest and his son further into the house.

"And you, my lady?" Father Ignacy queried Krystyna gently.

Surprised by the genuine sympathy in the clergyman's eyes, Krystyna stumbled over her answer: "I am… well, well enough." She saw the questions and the concern cloud Ignacy's expression.

"Is there something…?"

"Shall we proceed to the parlor?" Roderyk inserted.

"Father Ignacy, I would like a word with you."

Roderyk and the Widow Mielak spoke up at the same time. Anna took Father Ignacy's arm while Roderyk took Krystyna's. Andrzej and the other guests followed after.

Krystyna overheard Anna Mielak say to the priest: "No.

There's nothing to worry about. Simply a case of the nerves. You know how brides are. I really enjoyed your sermon last Sunday about honoring one's parents. I just hope my youngest son was listening."

"We'll all be much more comfortable in here." Roderyk directed each person into a respective seat in the parlor. Krystyna felt as if she were a player in a theatrical production. There was even an audience to witness the charade. She never thought she'd be engaged before complete strangers, though she understood Roderyk had invited guests to give legitimacy to the proceedings. She was acutely aware of being the object of collective scrutiny. She'd always imagined joyously awaiting her beloved on the night of her engagement with her mother and father beside her. Instead, she was alone and unsure.

After the usual courtesies, Father Ignacy proceeded with his duties as intermediary. "I understand this household has a heifer for sale. We're interested in buying her."

Roderyk answered according to the ancient formula. "Yes, Father. We do have a heifer for sale."

Krystyna flushed at the earthy repartee even though Anna had warned her about it. Andrzej looked somewhat uncomfortable as well. It was all part of the regional tradition, and yet it was strange hearing the phrases applied to the two of them.

Father Ignacy, who had been carrying the gesiorka, a bottle of vodka prepared for this special occasion, placed it upon the table. According to local custom, it was topped with a bouquet of dried flowers tied with a red ribbon.

Krystyna stared mutely at the man who had captured her heart two years ago and then at the bottle of liquid fire. Her heart hammered in her chest.

Father Ignacy addressed her. "My lady, would you have a glass for this vodka?"

By getting the glass, she would be signaling her acceptance

of Andrzej's suit. She didn't rise immediately to her feet. Instead, she took a deep breath and placed her hands on the table, as if to stand. Her eyes met Andrzej's. For an endless moment, they stared at each other.

Father Ignacy cleared his throat, recalling Krystyna to the matter at hand.

On wooden legs, she rose to her feet. But she kept her back straight and her stride steady as she left the room.

She knew exactly where a suitable glass specifically for her sat on the sideboard in the dining room. She went directly to it and stared at it. Seconds passed and then minutes, but still she hesitated. An engagement agreed to in so public a manner, before guests, family, and a representative of the church would be essentially as binding as marriage. She slowly reached out and picked it up. Her hand holding the glass trembled.

She was going to be Andrzej's wife! Just days ago, she would never have believed this possible. Two years ago, she'd felt as if she could die from the pain of leaving him as she had. And now, miraculously, they were to be wed, not as she'd once imagined, joyfully and surrounded by friends and family, but wed, none the less. In her heart, she admitted she'd never stopped loving him.

She took a deep breath and exhaled slowly. Staring down at it, she forced her hand to steady and then to still. Now that she had her chance to make a decent life with someone she truly cared about, she intended to seize it. Theirs could be a true joining together of minds and hearts, and she would accept no less. Since Vienna, she'd lived from day to day, with no real hopes for the future. Now, it seemed Janus was no longer a threat to her, and her horizon was bright with possibilities. Perhaps Andrzej could come to love her as the strong and independent woman she'd discovered she was. She was ready to fight for him, to fight for them.

Back in the parlor, the guests awaited her return. Anna

Mielak glanced anxiously at Roderyk, who raised an eyebrow in response. The others began to shift about in their chairs.

"Do you think she's coming back?" Jan, already well into his cups, voiced the question in everyone's mind. "I thought she was willing, Andrzej."

"Of course, this is a love match." Roderyk answered for his son. "Isn't that correct, my son?"

"Yes," Andrzej ground out between clenched teeth. She wouldn't run away now, would she? She wouldn't shame him so, and she was no coward. But she had left him once before. Then, she'd lacked faith in his ability to keep her safe. What if that remained the case? Where was Krystyna?

He could take it no longer. She'd been gone too long. He was going after her. He rose to his feet. Everyone stared at him. "I…"

"I'm sorry I took so long." Krystyna walked back into the room bearing the glass before her triumphantly. She handed it to Father Ignacy, but her eyes were on Andrzej, and she spoke for him alone. "I'm ready now." Then, she spoke the words that confirmed her fate. "I accept your gift."

Taking a deep breath, Andrzej nodded in acknowledgement. She'd broken with custom in speaking before the vodka was poured. Nevertheless, a pleased smile touched his lips. Perhaps, this marriage wasn't entirely loathsome to her; maybe there was some chance for them.

The tension in the room dissipated into good-humored ribbing and chatting. Only Brasinski remained silent and watchful.

Father Ignacy's wrinkled face beamed. "Let's drink." He opened the gesiorka and filled the glass more than half full. He handed it first to Krystyna. She raised it to Andrzej and swallowed about half. This was no time for dainty sipping. Then, she handed it to him. Their fingers touched around the glass. Awareness of him shot through her body. Boldly, he took her other hand in his, and, keeping the connection between their eyes, he tossed back the rest of the vodka. He was surprised to feel she was trembling.

Still holding her hand, he turned to face his father, whose eyes were suspiciously bright. "It's done. We are betrothed. Kaspar, bring glasses for our guests to toast our future happiness."

The rest of the evening passed swiftly. Father Ignacy concluded the ceremony by binding their hands over an uncut loaf of bread, which represented the hope that they would always have bread together, that their future would be prosperous. Afterwards, they all spoke of the upcoming nuptials. Andrzej stood with Krystyna at his side accepting the good wishes and congratulations with good humor. Eventually, Brasinski and Jan Mouceski adjourned to the game room. Agata, Anna, Vincent and Roderyk faded away one by one, leaving Krystyna and Andrzej alone in the parlor.

Exhausted from the evening, Krystyna was loath to retire. She wanted to take advantage of this chance to speak with Andrzej.

He poured another full glass of vodka. "I must admit, for a little while, I was worried you weren't returning. I was wondering which escape route you'd chosen when you came back in."

She felt as if she had received an unexpected blow. "Do you truly think so little of me? Contrary to what you may believe, I am a woman of honor. Back in Vienna, I made you no promises. I never deceived you. Why can't you put all of that behind us?"

"Woman, I wasn't attacking you. Perhaps you should strive to be less defensive."

At her wit's end and nearing tears, she glared at him. "Why can't you be pleasant? Why must everything you say to me be an insult or criticism? You weren't like this before."

"Before you played me for a fool, you mean."

"No, that's not what I meant, and you know it. Once, we

enjoyed each other's company. There was more than animosity between us."

"Yes, there was desire." The look in his eyes was hotly sensual as he set his glass down and moved closer to her.

She refused to back down from him even when he stood directly before her, his body far too close to hers. Even now, as emotionally spent as she was, her body felt attuned to his. She ached to touch him and be held by him. "Is desire enough?" Her voice was husky.

"There's only one way to answer that question." He reached out and ran one roughened fingertip along the curve of her jaw to her chin. "So beautiful. It's no wonder I've been haunted by your face."

He leaned down and brushed her lips with his own. The kiss was fleeting and delicate. She couldn't resist leaning closer, closing her eyes and following his lips with her own.

In the next moment, his arms were around her, pressing her against him, while his lips danced and teased hers. His mouth opened, and his tongue was wickedly sensual. She uttered a soft groan and opened her mouth. The passion and intensity of the kiss grew, stoked by memories, cloaked emotions, frustrations and the lustful yearnings of healthy, young bodies.

Her nipples peaked and grew acutely sensitive where they pressed against the hard, flat planes of his chest. She lost herself in the kiss, in the feel of this man against her, and was only vaguely aware of the movement of his hands down the small of her back to her hips. With his body, he directed her backwards until her shoulders encountered the wall. She leaned back against the supporting surface, savoring the feel of his wicked, hot mouth on the delicate skin of her throat, working ever closer to her so-sensitive ears. His hands gathered the material of her skirts. The realization that he was rucking them up was like a chill breeze cooling her passions. She pushed his hands away and shoved him back.

He reached for her arms, his eyes, heavy lidded and dark with hunger, for her.

"Andrzej! What are you doing? Here? Against a wall!"

"What we're doing should be rather obvious. Perhaps, afterwards, we can manage a civil conversation. It's driving me mad imagining you like this. You're so sweetly responsive."

His voice was velvety and seductive, richly dark with promised pleasure. He reached for her again. "Shall we proceed with this in my bedroom?"

She wanted to accept what he offered, to take his hand and follow him to his bed. But she knew, in the end, it wouldn't be enough. She wanted more. For the sake of their future, she dug in her heels.

"You've gone from insulting me to seducing me in less than five minutes. No, we should talk first. We shouldn't do this," her hands gestured eloquently, "while you think so little of me."

He cocked one eyebrow at her, clearly not dissuaded in the least. "I've thought of you a great deal, even though I tried to forget you. And anger will make the passion between us burn even hotter. Be assured there are certain things I like very much about you—your shape, your lips…the way I feel inside you."

She swallowed hard as he stepped closer again, like a predator stalking a willing prey. But, for both of their sakes, she couldn't back down. "No. That's not enough."

She watched as a muscle flexed at the corner of his jaw, and the expression in his eyes went from lustful to angry and frustrated. "Woman, if there's one thing you should have learned by now, there's never a 'right time' for anything. We have to make the time we're given right for whatever we need or want."

His words did make sense, and there was no question she wanted him. But she also knew as delicious as making love with him would be, it would not really resolve anything between them. "No. I want to be more to you than a willing paramour."

He shook his head, as if disappointed. "Krystyna Sielska,

you're a fool. You're going to be my wife. It would be simple enough to fill my bed with a warm and accommodating body, but I want you. And, if I remember correctly, the bedroom was the one place where we were in complete accord. But if you already wish to play the wife's game of withholding your favors, then I will bid you a good night and wish you the joy of your cold and lonely bedchamber." With that, he spun on his heel and left the room.

Krystyna was left standing alone in the now dimly lit room, staring at the gesiorka bottle which was as empty and hopeless as her dreams of finding love and understanding with Andrzej.

Krystyna awoke from the dream abruptly. She sat up in bed, feeling both sick and horrified. It was always so real. Shaking her head, she sought to clear it of the image of Ivan's blood, shiny and almost black, spreading across the cobblestones in the darkened barn. Then, she threw her blankets back and set her feet on the floor. Shivering in reaction, she crossed her arms over her chest and walked over to the window. It was partially opened, and though the air was cool and rainy, she stood before it. The damp kiss of the evening breeze on her cheeks cleansed and soothed her.

The memory of that horrible night continued to trouble her. It was like Ivan wouldn't let her go, that he was haunting her from beyond the grave, while Janus pursued her relentlessly. But it was time to move on, to put the misery behind her. She wasn't responsible for Ivan's death, and she imagined it would be nearly impossible for Janus to follow her to Sweet Air, not when the Kotyat caravan had stopped at so many other estates on their journey. Now, she intended to wrest what happiness she could from this new chance.

It was a good resolution, but she struggled to implement it

once she was back in her bed. The only thought which proved capable of banishing her memories was that of the tall, handsome Pole to whom she was engaged. There was no question he desired her, but he certainly didn't understand her. They seemed to be at odds whenever they were together. There would definitely be passion between them, but could there ever be harmony or peace?

For a moment, she considered how different her life might have turned out had she trusted him with her story back in Vienna. But such thoughts were fruitless; she couldn't turn back the clock or change the choices she'd already made. Nor could she help wondering if there was some way to evoke the idealistic rebel buried somewhere inside the dictatorial nobleman that Andrzej had become.

CHAPTER 19

Most of Roderyk's house guests slept in after the festivities of the night before. Andrzej, alone, was up at the crack of dawn. He rode out to attend to some matters on the estate, but he returned shortly before midday to participate in the boar hunt he'd organized for his guests' entertainment.

Despite the advanced hour, Krystyna would have liked nothing more than to have curled back up in her bed. Though she had a passion for riding, she had never particularly cared for the killing aspect of any hunt. Her head pounded from so many vodka toasts to her and Andrzej's happiness the night before. For the moment, she had no stomach for carrying on with the farce of being the happy bride-to-be for the sake of Roderyk's guests. Nor did she have the energy to hash out matters between herself and Andrzej.

The hunt and the house party served to delay an inevitable confrontation between them. For a moment, she wondered whether he had found someone, perhaps a maidservant, to indulge his carnal appetites on the previous night. The thought immediately dismayed her. No, she couldn't and wouldn't think about that awful possibility. Besides, it had been late at night.

And Andrzej was far too honorable a man to seduce another woman while his betrothed slept under the same roof, at least, that was what she hoped. But then again, she had refused him and, for all she knew, he could have a mistress tucked away somewhere. It was all very troubling and not at all pleasant to consider with one's head pounding, and she had to get through the day.

After a light meal in her bedroom, she emerged into the courtyard to find most of the hunting party already waiting for her. The sun was cruelly bright to her eyes, and her deep green riding frock felt leaden and suffocating on the unusually warm, early fall day.

She exchanged the usual pleasantries with the others while a groom led Hector out of the stable block and up to her.

She gathered her skirts in one hand and took hold of the reins. "Thank you," she spoke to the groom. "Would you please bring me a mounting block?"

The boy blushed, clearly not accustomed to the needs of sidesaddle riders.

"I would be honored to help, my lady," Viktor Brasinski spoke up. He stepped over to her side, and offered her his cupped hands to step onto. Even though she found something disquieting about the man, she was grateful for the assistance and offered him a tired smile once she was seated securely in her side saddle. But then, to her surprise and dismay, he allowed his hand to linger on her booted calf in a familiar and completely inappropriate manner.

She was about to ask him to remove it or to turn her horse away when Andrzej rode up on his raw-boned, angular hunter. She immediately registered the murderous look on his face. She was even more uncomfortably aware of Brasinski's hand upon her, but she couldn't steer Hector away, Andrzej blocked her with his own steed.

"Brasinski," her betrothed growled at the other man. "You're here to celebrate my engagement, not to accost my betrothed."

"I'm hardly accosting her," Brasinski countered, refusing to back down from the larger and clearly furious man, though he did remove his hand from Krystyna's leg. "I was merely helping her to mount. Ladies do sometimes require our assistance, as you shall no doubt learn."

Andrzej nearly ground his teeth at Brasinski's effrontery. "I am fully aware of my future wife's needs, and I'll thank you to permit me to attend to them." He'd intended to assist Krystyna himself, but then he'd been caught up attending to some last minute details.

"Did I offend you, Miss Janicka?" Brasinski asked Krystyna.

He had. But she didn't want to be the cause of a fight between Andrzej and his neighbor, particularly in front of Roderyk's other guests. And Andrzej was clearly ready and eager to take on the other man. She was convinced Brasinski deliberately created the situation. In her mind, she cursed the man. But aloud she said, "No, he was merely helping me. It's a lovely day for a hunt," she stated loudly and with forced gaiety.

Andrzej's hunter tossed his head and snorted, clearly picking up on his master's volatile emotions, but the moment passed.

"Your greyhounds are looking better, Morzinski," Jan stated, oblivious to the tension between Andrzej and Brasinski. Jan eyed the Morzinski pack as it emerged from their kennels. "You can tell the offspring of that bitch I sold you. They're built better than the rest. You should see my new stud dog. He would really improve your lines."

Andrzej glanced over at Jan. "Yes, I would like to see him. I hope we have a good run today. We should. I know where some of our peasants have seen boar recently."

"Good." Jan turned away to berate a groom for some miniscule error in the preparation of his steed.

It was time. Horses and riders milled about in the courtyard.

All of the riders in the small hunting party, Andrzej, Krystyna, Jan, Vincent, Agata Mouceska and Brasinski were now ready to go. Andrzej sought to catch Krystyna's eye once more, but her chin was up, and she determinedly kept her gaze fixed elsewhere. Andrzej sighed. He just wished all of this was over, so that he and Krystyna could be alone, to get to know each other again. Truth be told, he was somewhat ashamed of his behavior of the night before. He shouldn't have lost his temper as he had and said unkind things. It was no way to start a marriage. Cold sober in the light of day, he, too, recognized that they needed time, even though it seemed absurd that he couldn't make love with a woman who'd been his lover and whom he was about to marry. But none of those matters could be addressed or resolved now with this group about them. Instead, the misunderstandings and the icy reserve between them continued to grow.

Andrzej worked his way across the courtyard to face the front porch where his father sat in state with Anna Mielak beside him.

"Is that wolf of yours securely tied?" Roderyk asked of Andrzej. "The greyhounds are terrified of the beast."

"Peter is tied in the barn. There, you can hear him howling."

"Well, good luck to you then," Roderyk offered gruffly, clearly frustrated he couldn't participate in the hunt as well. "See to it our guests enjoy themselves."

"Of course, Father. Until later." Andrzej doffed his hat to the Widow Mielak.

In short order, the small hunt party exited the courtyard and rode out into the surrounding fields. Two of the Morzinski serfs on horseback accompanied the little party to act as huntsmen and tend to the dogs. Brasinski rode alone at the head of the group, the brothers Mouceski fell in beside each other, and Agata followed a little way behind them. Andrzej and Krystyna ended up trailing.

Unlike Andrzej, Krystyna clearly wasn't pleased with this

development, as evidenced by the height of her chin and her absolute avoidance of eye contact with him. She simply didn't feel up to engaging him, and she was worried that he was still angry with her for her rejection of him. But she didn't want to ride with Brasinski or Agata Mouceska.

Krystyna soon found she couldn't maintain the darkness of her mood. After all, the sun warmed her face, and the land was brilliant with end-of-summer exuberance. The horses strolled easily along, waiting for the hounds to get a scent.

"How could you tolerate his hands on you?" Andrzej muttered so only she could hear.

She felt as well as heard his words, and her budding joy in the day instantly evaporated. "I didn't 'welcome' him in any way. He was merely assisting me in mounting."

"Yes, I could tell he was interested in mounting."

"Don't be vulgar."

"That's how such things start, you know, a look, a touch, an understanding. Let me make myself clear, I won't tolerate such an entanglement."

"You sound almost jealous."

He snorted. "Merely possessive, my dear. I intend that my heir will be my own, not some other man's by blow."

"How dare you!"

"I will not tolerate infidelity from you."

"I never intended to be unfaithful. But what is good for the goose is also good for the gander. If you demand fidelity of me then I expect the same of you."

"You're in no position to negotiate. But, I must admit, I'm flattered you want my attentions all for yourself."

"Hush! You're getting too loud," Krystyna intercepted a puzzled glance back from Agata. She smiled cheerfully at the other woman, though the expression felt stiff and pained. "It's not that I... It's just that I think," she hesitated, unsure of how to continue.

"You were never at a loss for words in Vienna," he commented.

"In Vienna, you courted me."

"Then, I trusted you." The words were out before he could stop them.

Stunned into silence, she stared at him.

He reached out to her. "You misunderstand me. There were no secrets between us then, or none that I knew of. I had—"

"There are no secrets now, Andrzej," she cut him off. "I may not live up to the idealized version of me you remember from Vienna, but I am trustworthy. Don't dare you impugn my honor!"

"If you would allow me to finish my…" he began.

"You're a different man, too," she inserted. "You're practically the king of all of this." Her arm swung wide to encompass their surroundings. "You try to dictate to me as you do to your serfs."

"I am responsible for them, for my father and for you, too. Things can be good between us if you will only listen to me."

"And obey. You can't remake me, Andrzej. I am not an addle-patted fool who will mindlessly do as she is told. If you seek that kind of woman, you should have selected a convent raised virgin instead of me." Aware of the emotions welling up inside her and the suspicious moisture in her eyes, she pulled back on her reins so that Andrzej passed her by. Now, she followed him a horse's distance back. She'd no intention of dropping the subject. The stubborn man would have to come to accept her, to care for her as she was. But, on this day, she was in no condition for further battle. Her head was pounding, and she was hot and uncomfortable.

Thankfully, Andrzej, perhaps aware of suspicious glances from the other members of the party, didn't press his case.

The afternoon wore on. The hounds did pick up a few scents, but with little success. The heat and humidity dampened everyone's enthusiasm. Agata had already been escorted back to the main house by one of the servants.

Then, Krystyna heard the hounds ululating yet again. This time, she didn't put her heels to Hector in order to chase after the others. Instead, she drew him back. She had had enough, of the hunt, of Andrzej, of the entire miserable day. She decided to ride back to the house. She was reasonably sure she could find the way.

Giving Hector long rein, she rode through golden fields where the wheat brushed her horse's belly. The tree branches waved with a cooling afternoon breeze, and she hoped it would pick up. She rode for half an hour, but still hadn't glimpsed the great house or any familiar landscape. She was experiencing some misgivings about her decision to set out on her own when she heard frantic barking ahead of her. She touched Hector with her crop and cantered towards the sound. Suddenly, a wildly flapping pheasant launched upwards right under Hector's nose, spooking the horse, which leapt sideways, nearly unseating her. A large, gray dog burst onto the scene, barking furiously, further upsetting her horse. Leaning back, she pulled strongly on both reins, particularly the right one, and turned Hector into a tight circle. Soon, he came to a trembling standstill.

"Cursed side saddle," she muttered. "Easy, Hector. You're okay. It's just Peter. Hello there, Peter." She recognized Andrzej's pet from a certain memorable afternoon in Vienna. Peter seemed pleased to see her. His tongue lolled out from his exertion in the heat, but he wagged his tail enthusiastically. "Do you know the way home? It seems I'm lost. Go home, Peter. We'll follow you."

The dog cocked his head at her then sniffed around the ground, attempting to pick up the pheasant's scent.

"Peter, go home." Of course, the dog had no idea what she was saying. Krystyna nearly groaned in frustration. She'd no intention of following Peter on his adventures through the countryside in the hopes he would eventually tire and return home. Perhaps, she could find a serf's cottage. Yes, she would ride until she found someone to help her.

Just then, Peter bounded back toward her then galloped off in the direction from which he had come. Krystyna touched Hector on the shoulder with her crop. Maybe he was going back to the main house. She decided to follow him.

It was easy to see the path made by the dog through the wheat. Periodically, he paused and glanced back at her, as if to make sure she was coming after him. Raised on an estate not unlike Sweet Air, she knew it was poor form to ride straight through the field, trampling the ripening wheat under hoof. But Hector was only one horse, he wouldn't do much harm, and she intended to make sure Andrzej paid the owner for the damage, unless, as she suspected, these fields were all part of his estate. Besides, she was well and truly lost, and there were no houses in sight. She was tired, hungry, extremely thirsty and frustrated. To make matters worse, Andrzej was sure to be furious with her because she'd left the hunting party. It seemed she had a genuine talent for enraging him.

CHAPTER 20

Following Andrzej's dog, Krystyna wondered if the rest of the hunting party was already back at the house. She was riding along the edge of a wooded area when Hector's head suddenly went up. He issued a clarion call, thoroughly shaking her from her worried thoughts. He snorted, and his ears pricked forward, and Krystyna concluded another horse must be nearby. As for Peter, he was out of sight somewhere among the trees.

She cautiously steered her horse into the woods, not wanting to intrude on a peasant family. However she consoled herself that she had no choice; she would merely ask for directions and then be on her way. The trees thinned, and she emerged into a clearing in which stood a charming cottage and a small barn that opened into a fenced pasture. Four horses had gathered at the end of the pasture nearest them and were excitedly eyeing Krystyna and Hector.

She rode directly over to the stable, expecting to encounter someone. But though everything was neat and tidy, and the horses were fat and well-tended, no one came out to meet her. She dismounted slowly, stiff with fatigue and too many hours in the saddle. Peter suddenly reappeared and frisked around her legs. She patted him lightly on the head. "I'm parched. Let's get a drink, shall we?"

She secured Hector to a tethering post in the barnyard and then wandered about the small homestead. There was a well near the house. She sent the bucket down, drew it up and drank eagerly from her cupped palms. The water was ice cold, fresh and sweet, and she patted it on her face and neck. She set the bucket down for Peter as well, but he must have found his own water earlier for he ignored it and continued to offer her his canine grin.

She reflected it was most unusual for an isolated, little farm like this one to have its own well. And there were no fields at all for growing crops, only pasture for horses. She wondered who lived in the little house, and where they were now, for it was obvious that no one was at home. It was too silent.

She walked over to the pasture to look at the small group of horses. All were mares and fine animals, clearly well bred. What were they doing out here? And to whom did they belong?

The entire arrangement was a conundrum. These horses were finer than any she'd yet seen at Sweet Air. And they were definitely not work horses, of the type a serf would possess. They were fine riding animals, and each of them must have cost a small fortune.

Intent on getting a closer look at the mares, she grasped the material of her skirt in one hand, the top of the split rail fence in the other, then climbed over. Once she was on the other side, the horses crowded about her, each striving to get closer.

"Hello, sweet ladies. My, aren't you pretty." She crooned, stepping away from the fence.

A bay mare nipped at a brown one, driving her away.

Just then, Krystyna heard a man shout and then a loud whistle. Andrzej appeared, recklessly charging his hunter through the trees. Peter shot under the fence, responding to his master's call, spooking the mares directly toward Krystyna. One broad chestnut shoulder knocked her to the ground. Krystyna immediately tucked into a defensive ball, but was struck more than once by the shifting limbs and deadly hooves. Then, the horses were gone, and she opened her eyes, wondering if she was badly hurt, if she dared move. In the next instant, she became aware of hoofbeats pounding the ground, coming closer.

Suddenly Andrzej was beside her. He drew her trembling body against him. "Take slow breaths," he advised in a gentle voice. He stroked her hair and her back, rocking her gently, as she slowly began to move, to test each body part. She relaxed into his embrace, savoring the feeling of being cherished and cared for. She'd been alone for so long; it felt wonderful to allow someone else to be strong for once.

Unexpectedly, a very large, very wet, canine tongue vigorously licked her cheek. She got the benefit of a couple of rough tongued swipes before Andrzej pushed Peter back. Curious about this new form of play, the massive dog loomed over them.

"Peter, sit!" Immediately, the dog no longer blocked the sunlight. Now Krystyna found both master and dog staring at her with concern.

There was no question she was going to be sore, but she didn't think she was seriously hurt, and she began to laugh in genuine amusement and relief. "I have to get trampled by horses for you to be kind to me."

"You're laughing!" He stared at her incredulously. "Are you quite mad?" Then, he rose to his feet, bent down and prepared to pick her up.

Guessing his intent, she pushed his hands away. "Please. I'm fine."

"I don't understand you."

"Nor I you! It's clear you hate me, and yet you say we must marry. I try to be hospitable to your guests, and you accuse me of being flirtatious. And now, you nearly get me trampled. Finally, you allow your dog to slobber all over me. Still, I have survived it all and am well enough." She rose up on her elbows, smiling at him and at the absurdity of the situation. "I know you don't think highly of me, but please don't set your beasts upon me."

He watched her with a bemused expression on his face then extended a hand down to her. "I don't hate you, not at all. I came after you because I was concerned about you."

"Or you were worried about what I might be up to." She took his hand and was startled by the thrilling awareness that shot up her arm on contact. She allowed him to draw her to her feet. Once there, she released his hand, and dusted her skirts off. "I'm all right, honestly. How did you find me?"

"It wasn't easy. I've been searching for you for more than an hour, but some peasants who were working in the fields saw you ride in this direction." There was a new and not unfamiliar heat in his gaze. He had looked at her in much the same way when she'd appeared on his doorstep long ago in Vienna.

"Pan Andrezj!" A servant on horseback burst through the trees and galloped up to them. Vaulting from his steed's back, he questioned: "Pan Andrezj, do you need assistance?"

"No. Everything's all right, Jozef. Please tend to Vita and the others. I will see to the young lady," he responded, never taking his eyes off the woman beside him.

Jozef nodded understanding, secured his own horse and then headed off after Andrezj's still saddled mare that was sniffing noses with the horses in the pasture.

"Are you quite sure you can walk?"

"Honestly, I'm little the worse for nearly being trampled."

"Don't be foolish, woman. Should I send for the physician? Were you stepped on?"

"No, miraculously, I wasn't. I'm fine. Now, if you'll give me directions on how to get back to the house," she stated, hoping to hear him say, "No, we'll ride back together." She didn't want to be left alone. Night was fast approaching, and there was something solid and comforting about Andrzej's presence. He was comfortable in his own skin and moved with a careless swagger that projected confidence in his own ability to handle any situation he should encounter.

He took her arm. "You're not going anywhere right now. First, I need to determine if you are well enough to ride. If you're not, I'll send Jozef to bring the carriage."

"I tell you, I'm fine." Turning away from him, she began to stride toward the barn. She was no longer laughing. There was a definite pain in her side, and his high handedness annoyed her.

"Krystyna!" The sound of her name roared commandingly drew her up short. "You will come with me."

"Have you ever considered asking me rather than ordering me about? You speak so eloquently for Poland's rights, serfs' rights, but what about my rights? I'm not your chattel," she retorted angrily.

He advanced toward her, and before she was aware of his intent, swung her up into his arms. "Not yet, but you soon will be."

"How dare you!" She struggled.

"Calm yourself, Krystyna. You're frightening the horses. Who do you think will come to your assistance here, on my land? As you pointed out earlier, I am the absolute master here."

"Jozef can hear me."

"But he would never disobey me. He's absolutely loyal. All you're doing is embarrassing yourself. Be still. Let me be certain that you are unharmed. Then, we'll be on our way."

His words were reasonable, but she resented his domineering attitude. In defiance, Krystyna remained rigid, unsuccessfully trying to ignore the bold heat of his body where it made contact with her own and the way he carried her with such ease. With a booted kick, he thrust the door to the little cottage open. He stepped inside.

"Enough of this. Put me down!"

"It amazes me you passed yourself off as a peasant these past two years. How did you hold your tongue?"

"I wasn't pretending to be a peasant. The Kotyats are free people."

"Yes, but they're commoners. Your manners, Krystyna, are those of a spoiled, aristocratic brat."

She began to twist about in earnest, ignoring the pain in her side "Yours also leave more than a little to be desired. I loathe overbearing men."

"But you do find us dangerously exciting, don't you?" One of his eyebrows arched as he dared to tease her.

Ignoring the heat in his gaze, she deliberately closed her eyes. "You're impossible. Now please put me down."

Turning her squirming form in his arms, he allowed her to slide down his body until her feet were on the ground. They stared at each other in silence, the air between them charged with sexual intensity. She was keenly aware of him, the feel of his large hands spanning her waist, the heat and hardness of him against her. His lips were mere inches from hers. It would be so simple to just stand up on her toes and kiss him. But then, to her dismay and surprise, he released her and walked over to the fireplace. There, he reached for a bottle of vodka then picked up some pottery cups from a shelf behind the rough-hewn table.

"I assume you know whose house this is?"

"Actually, it's mine." He uncorked the vodka and poured it into the cups.

"But you don't live here," she commented, glancing around. The cottage was clean and neat and furnished with plain but comfortable furnishings. There was even a bookcase filled with books and glass in the windows, both of which were rarely seen in a peasant's home. But there was no evidence of anyone currently residing there, none of the usual signs of life. The fireplace was thoroughly swept and empty, and the table was bare.

"My father built this cottage for his nurse, Dorothea, who also helped to raise me. She was like a mother to me. My own mother died birthing me. When I became a young man, Dorothea wanted a place of her own near the main house. She died several years ago, and this place has become a retreat for me. I built the barn and paddock this past spring for my project."

"What sort of project?"

"With your eye for a fine horse, I am surprised you haven't guessed, or didn't you get a good look at the mares outside? I want this estate to become known for the high-quality horses we produce. Those mares will be the foundation of my stock. Once I have established the herd, I plan to sell a few each year, the way I understand your father does."

"That's why you bought the black mare. It makes sense. But why keep them here? Why aren't they in the main barns?"

"I didn't want my father to know about this until I'd produced some foals. I want to surprise him. We have land, a great deal of it. But my father hasn't been well for some time, and some matters… got out of hand. Not that I blame him. He simply wasn't able to manage things as he once had. In my studies, I learned a great deal about new agricultural methods. Since my return two years ago, I've sought to put Sweet Air in a better financial condition. I've made changes in how we plant and harvest, and our yield is increasing every year. I believe these horses will prove a successful venture. But, as you've probably heard from Mouceski, I'm not viewed as an expert on horseflesh. I didn't want my plans known until I could let the results speak for themselves. Jozef and his sons tend to the horses each day."

Andrzej had impressed her once more. Here was a man who put aside his own interests and pursuits to help his ailing father and restore the family estate to financial health. Indeed, there was much that was admirable about him. Back in Vienna, he'd once spoken of politics with this same enthusiasm in his eyes.

"At home, I helped my father with planning some of the crosses. He is a true student of bloodlines, but he always said I had a talent for it. Some of my happiest hours as a young girl I spent with him talking about horses or in the stables with them. I miss both of my parents so much. I can't believe it's been years since I've seen them. I always thought… dreamed that when I married and had my own home, my husband and I could carry on in my father's tradition."

"And so, this one dream of yours will come true. I would appreciate any guidance or assistance from you."

For a moment, she mulled this over. "Andrzej, if it's money you need, I'm sure my father will settle my dowry upon you once we're married."

"I'm not interested in your dowry."

"My father always intended… It would help you."

"We will do well enough on our own. I'm not marrying you for your dowry. You've shared your dreams. Now let me tell you mine. This estate has so much potential, and I've long wished to institute some reforms here. For this reason, I need to achieve a measure of financial success." Watching her carefully, he continued, "I intend to pay our serfs a fair wage."

"You intend to free them?" She was astounded. This was a seriously radical move that was sure to be viewed as a direct attack on their entire way of life by most other members of the nobility. "You do realize how it will be taken."

"I'm well aware of the ramifications, and it's good to speak with someone about my plans. But I would be a fool to waste this time alone with you." He took a seat at the table, looking up at her, studying her. "For so long, I was sure I'd never see you again. Sometimes I even wondered if you were real or just a dream that became a nightmare. And now you're here, sweetheart, to marry me and make me happy." He offered her a boyish grin. "Are you hungry? Would you like some bread and cheese? I have some in my saddlebag. You probably haven't eaten in hours."

"Shouldn't we be getting back? Won't they be looking for us?"

"Please stay." The soft entreaty in his words held her. "No one will take it amiss if we take our time. After all, we're betrothed, Krystyna, and we need to get reacquainted." His voice took on a deep, seductive edge.

"Yes, that would be wise," she responded. Impulsively, she took the first step. "I think it's commendable that you intend to implement your beliefs and theories here. Back in Vienna, I knew you were intelligent and committed to your causes, but now I am seeing a whole new side of you."

He stood up slowly. "And how do you feel about me now? You said you disliked how dictatorial I've become." He took a step closer.

Her heart began to beat more quickly. She felt warm and too aware of him, but then this was one thing that hadn't changed since Vienna, her overwhelming physical response to him.

"That's true," she admitted, nervously darting her tongue out to moisten her lip. He devoured her with his eyes. He mesmerized her. With each passing moment, she became more sure that he was going to touch her, to kiss her. "I suppose you're not that very different from how you were then, but your attitude toward me has changed. I know you want me, and I'll admit, I want you, too." He moved closer still. "Wait," she held up her hand, staying him. "It's just that I wish you trusted me as you did then."

"What does trust have to do with passion…or loving?" He reached for her.

"A great deal. I don't believe there can be love without trust. Why is it so difficult to have faith in me?"

He snorted rather ungraciously.

"Can you not believe in your own wife? Your father already treats me like a daughter, he trusts me."

"He doesn't know you as well as I do." Immediately, Andrzej was aware that he had said the wrong thing. He sank back down on the wooden bench by the table. "Truthfully, I don't know what to believe about you, and I'm going about this all wrong." He sighed and ran his fingers through his thick, tousled hair. "You want me to trust you, and I was hurt when you did not trust me. We go in endless circles. Why are we arguing? We're alone, for once, by God's grace. Let's not waste this time. Once I enjoyed your company, and I believe you enjoyed mine."

"We argued a great deal even then."

"Discussions or arguments, call them what you will, but they were exciting. These past two years have been hard on both of us. We've lost our joy. So come," he filled both mugs with vodka and passed one to her. "Drink with me to Polish bravery, Krystyna."

"You mean foolishness." She picked up her cup and tossed back her vodka. Her nostrils flared with the potency of the alcohol, but she didn't flinch. She boldly met his gaze.

"I've always been one to fight for seemingly hopeless causes. Perhaps that's why I never really gave up on you."

Hope stirred in her breast. She, too, sat down, opposite him. "So I'm just one of your hopeless causes?"

He grinned at her. "I'll miss you. You, my lady, make a man's heart beat faster, his mind, work. And those are just the beginning of your charms."

"I am glad I prove amusing… You're going somewhere?"

He ignored her question. "You are far more than amusing, Krystyna." He refilled both of their cups. He stared at her hungrily, and she shifted uneasily on her bench beneath the molten softness of his gaze. No man had a right to be so handsome or so appealing.

Two could play at the same game. She smiled, too, slowly

and deliberately. Reaching out across the coarse surface of the table, she took one broad, thick-fingered hand in her own. His palm was callused and hardened, not at all that of a pampered member of the aristocracy. She stroked the long fingers with her own fingertips. She ran her nails along the ridge between the thumb and forefinger. Then, raising his hand to her lips, she darted the tip of her tongue between his index and middle finger.

In response, Andrzej stood up, drawing her up with him and around the table, so that they stood face-to-face, hands intertwined. He drew her arms up around his neck and her body closer to his. She could feel the heat radiating from him, could smell his maleness, warm, honest sweat mingling with hints of cologne. Rising up on her toes, she nuzzled the sensitive skin below his ear. He groaned in response, gripped then kneaded her bottom through the heavy layers of her riding skirt. When their lips met, there was no slow build up of passion. Rather, it exploded between them. They couldn't get enough of each other.

Resting his forehead against hers, Andrzej muttered, "Understand, I won't let you leave me again. Say you're mine."

The raw possessiveness of his plea moved her. She leaned closer and allowed her breath to feather against his neck.

"I need to hear you say it, and there's not much time."

Wanting to purr and arch into his touch, she answered, "But you said they wouldn't be looking for us."

"It's not that," he hesitated, took a deep breath then continued, "I'll be leaving soon. But I'll be careful, so I don't get you with child. I will speak to my father about arranging our marriage for this week. Then you will have the protection of my name even if I don't return."

"No." Dread twisting her stomach, she stepped back. "You can't mean..."

"I'll be joining Prince Poniatowski and our forces at Lubar."

"But you can't win! The Polish forces will be crushed. Everyone knows that. And you're needed here! You can't do this." She could see him visibly withdraw from her. His face hardened, his jaw tightened.

"You've always known I'm a patriot. I'll willingly do my part to defend my country."

"This country will soon cease to exist! You know what's going to happen. I've even heard you speak of it, and now you wish to play the sacrificial lamb. What purpose will your death serve? Andrzej, it's a lost cause. Think about what matters most to you. Is Poland more important than your father, your home, your people, even me?"

His arms dropped to his sides. "You can't ask this of me. I have my duty."

"No, it's about your pride. You owe a greater duty to those you would leave behind."

"I see there's no point in continuing this conversation. You can't sway me from this course. I have to do what I know is right."

"How is riding to your death right? I can't lose you now. Not again." Her voice trembled, and her eyes filled with tears.

"Don't ask me to be less than a man."

Closing her eyes, she shook her head.

"Krystyna, I would have thought you could understand. I've always admired your courage and resolution. You went after your friend in Vienna, even though you knew you were putting yourself at considerable risk by doing so. You left Vienna in the company of gypsies in order to protect others. You know sometimes we have to place ourselves at risk because it is the right thing to do."

"Don't do this, Andrzej. I beg you." She wouldn't consider the veracity of his claims. Doing so might very well mean she would lose him, and she couldn't face that now, not so soon after being reunited with him.

"I see we are at an impasse. There's no reason to continue this conversation." He walked to the cottage door and stared out.

Not looking back at her, he spoke, "Compose yourself. I'll await you in the barn. For the sake of appearances, we should ride back together."

"Please Andrzej, listen to me."

"Enough. In the event that I am killed, you may remain here for as long as you choose or return to your own family. You will still have the protection of my name." With that, he left.

She collapsed onto the table sobbing. It had all gone so wrong! How could she convince him to stay? There was no way she could meekly accept his decision, not when doing so jeopardized his life. She stayed in the cottage until the storm of her emotions subsided. Then she dried her reddened face on her sleeve, gathered herself and went forth to face Andrzej.

He stood with his back to the cottage, one foot on a fence rail staring out at his horses.

"Andrzej," she called out to him then hesitated, not knowing what to say.

He waited for her to continue. When she didn't proceed, he did. "We should be getting back. Jozef," he called. "We're ready for the horses now."

They rode in silence, neither willing to bridge the chasm between them.

CHAPTER 21

Later that afternoon, when Krystyna and Andrzej returned from their interlude at the cottage, they learned that Roderyk's guests were already departing Sweet Air. It was unusual for an engagement party to end so perfunctorily, but these were troubled times. Armies were on the move, and rebellion was in the air. Messengers had arrived for the Mouceskis and Brasinski, calling them back to their estates. Furthermore, in two days' time, Andrzej was to leave Sweet Air to join Tadeusz Kosciuszko's Polish forces.

It proved impossible to arrange Krystyna's and Andrzej's wedding at such short notice. Jozef had been the bearer of the disappointing tidings.

"Father Ignacy is unavailable!" Andrzej raged. "The man hasn't gone anywhere in ten years. Where is he?"

"Monsignor Herburt fell from his horse and was seriously injured. Father Ignacy was called to tend to Monsignor Herburt's flock."

"What about Father Ignacy's flock? Curse it! We'll have to get another priest."

"Calm down, Andrzej," Roderyk consoled. "You're simply

not meant to be married in this rushed fashion, for which I must admit to some relief. You are my only child, and I would like to see you married properly, as your mother would have wanted. It's more seemly that your engagement last more than a few days."

"Father, war is about to break out, and there are far more important issues than what is seemly. I wanted to have everything settled, so you and Krystyna will have each other if I…" His voice trailed off.

Roderyk cleared his throat; his eyes were suspiciously bright. "Krystyna and I will be fine. Don't worry about us. Do what you have to do and come back to us as soon as you can."

In the hectic rush to prepare for Andrzej's departure, there was no time for Krystyna and Andrzej to work through their differences. Even at his leave taking, they remained polite, distant and cool, neither yet prepared to span the distance between them.

"You're both fools," Roderyk muttered in disgust at their stiff and awkward behavior. He turned his back to them and walked back toward the house, seeking to give them some privacy.

"He's right, you know." Andrzej commented, staring at her. His eyes were dark and fathomless with intense emotion, and his jaw was set in determination. "I don't want to leave you this way. If this is to be the very last time I look upon you."

"No, it won't be. It can't be!" She rushed into his arms and embraced him with all of the emotions roiling through her. Tears coursed their way down her cheeks as he held her. "I love you," she confessed through her sobs. "I never stopped loving you these two years. And I've been so dreadful to you. I'm so sorry. I just wanted you to admit that you cared about me as well. But it doesn't matter if you don't. I'll be a good wife. I'll…"

"Sweetheart… Sweetheart." He soothed her by gently kissing her forehead. "Of course, I care. You're the woman I intend to marry."

"But that's just because you want to save me, and you're noble by nature."

"Let me make one thing clear. I'm not marrying you out of pity or nobility, but because you are the woman for me, the woman I've waited for and dreamed of. There may be other men who can offer you prettier verses, a life of style and ease, or greater wealth, but no one will ever, can ever love you more than I do." Then, he gently took her face in his hands. He kissed her softly, lingering, as if memorizing the shape and texture of her lips. And she kissed him back with longing and desperation, not wanting the moment to end. When he raised his head, his dark eyes were molten with emotion. "I will be back, make no mistake. I'll not let you out of our agreement so easily."

She clung to him, and he to her. She could feel his heart pounding in his chest. He held her tightly with rock solid arms. He was too vitally alive for anything to happen, right? He had to come back. It couldn't end this way.

Not long after, Krystyna and Roderyk watched Andrzej ride away. Just before he disappeared at a bend in the road, he turned back to them and waved. From the stable, they heard a frantic howling and scratching. Peter, the wolfhound, vocally expressed Krystyna's own feelings of loss and despair.

After the leave taking, she retired to her chambers. Once the storm of tears passed, she went over to her writing desk, opened a narrow drawer and removed a small stack of old letters tied together with a faded ribbon. They were all from Andrzej and she'd received most of them while he was in Warsaw and she in Vienna. Her great aunt had sent them on to the Kotyats with some other personal items of hers. She'd kept them with her through all her travels and knew most of them by heart. Untying the ribbon, she sorted through them quickly until she found what she was looking for, a small, folded square. It was the note Andrzej had surreptitiously pressed into her hand after their dinner at General von Zetl's. Hungrily, she read: "We are meant for each other. Until I return, think of me, and I will dream of you." These words, written two years before, soothed and reassured her, but her fears for his safety consumed her. She prayed desperately to God to keep Andrzej well and to bring him back alive.

CHAPTER 22

In the weeks that followed, Krystyna had endless time to reflect on what she wished she'd done with or said to Andrzej in the short time that they'd been reunited. She thought about him, worried about him, and even day-dreamed about him. At night, as she lay in her bed, she tried to visualize his face, his smile and recall the sound of his voice. Many nights, she cried herself to sleep. She felt oddly disconnected to life, as if part of her was missing.

That's not to say that she passed her days in aimless melancholy. She was busy from the break of dawn until well after nightfall. Much of the actual running of the estate had fallen onto her shoulders. Thankfully, Roderyk was reasonably well and was able to advise and direct her. Krystyna was glad to be of use, to be needed, to finally put the skills her mother taught her to good use. As the months passed and fall turned to winter, she grew fonder of Andrzej's home. Indeed, that it was his was part of its charm. So much of him surrounded her. She could easily imagine him examining his livestock or tending to the needs of a serf. While dealing with accounts in his study, his presence enveloped her.

The holidays passed and then the endless months of late winter. News concerning the war was generally bleak. It was a fretful time.

Roderyk, who had come to care for and appreciate his future daughter-in-law, could see that the anxious vigil was wearing on her. He wanted to do something for her, to cheer her up and return a smile to her lips. Then, he received a letter from Jadwiga von Gebler.

The two of them had struck up a correspondence shortly after Krystyna's arrival in the household. After some reflection and discussions with Krystyna, Roderyk concluded that it would be reasonably safe for him to establish contact with Krystyna's great aunt. According to Krystyna, Jadwiga corresponded with many people in far flung regions. Jadwiga was delighted to hear that Miss Janicka, the granddaughter of a dear friend from her childhood days, was soon to marry Roderyk's son. Both Roderyk and Jadwiga were careful to make no direct mention of Krystyna for fear their letters might be intercepted by Janus or his spies. In her most recent letter, Jadwiga mentioned Sebastjan deSzinay, a young man in whom she had taken an interest and whom she viewed as completely honest and trustworthy. Apparently, young deSzinay had inherited some lands in eastern Poland from his mother. Thus, despite the war and the difficult traveling conditions, Jadwiga asked Roderyk whether Sebastjan might call upon him at Sweet Air.

Reading between the lines, Roderyk understood that Jadwiga was asking that a trusted friend of Krystyna's be permitted to visit her. Initially, Roderyk hadn't wanted to be bothered with a house guest, especially given the unrest in the land and Andrzej's absence. But then he decided a familiar face would probably be a welcome sight for Krystyna. In his opinion, she had been deprived of her friends and family for far too long. As for this Janus who had driven her into exile, nothing had been heard from him since she arrived at Sweet Air. It seemed quite possible that he had given up his pursuit of her or had somehow been driven from it. It was even possible that he was dead. Roderyk firmly believed that Krystyna was safe at Sweet Air. It was then that he'd been struck by an inspiration; he would host a house party! *Every young lady enjoys a party, pretty clothes, music and dancing.* It was a marvelous idea! He'd plan it for when her friend visited. The rest of the party would consist only of local people he'd known their entire lives, people whom he knew could have no connection to the mysterious Janus.

But on the bitterly cold, April night of the party, a lone rider who knew nothing of the festivities was following the treacherously slippery path that led east to Sweet Air. Despite his fatigue, Andrzej was anxious and tense as he finally drew closer to his home. It had rained throughout the entire miserable day, and his garments were soaked through, as was the heavy winter coat his horse still wore. The roads were mucky and heavy and made for slow traveling. He itched to push his mare into her ground eating canter stride, but it wasn't safe to do so in the dark and uneven footing. The past months had been endless. He'd thought about Krystyna incessantly. It had proven even more difficult, if possible, for him being gone this time than when he thought he'd lost her. Now, he knew that she was promised to him, that she awaited his return, and that Russian troops were on the move all over the eastern regions of Poland, where Sweet Air was located. At times when he should have been focused on life or death matters like impending battles and how to maintain the food supply for his men, his reflections turned to her, wondering if she was well and if she thought of him.

Finally, Kosciuszko had granted him several weeks of leave, to see to his family. The sorry condition of the roads and his necessary avoidance of enemy forces ensured that he would have a little more than a week at home. But to see Krystyna again would be well worth the days and nights of travel.

He wondered if a marriage could be arranged for that very

night. Even though she deserved the wedding that every girl dreamed of, at least as close an approximation as could be managed given the war, he was no longer willing to wait to be with her, ceremony or not. Life was too fleeting and unpredictable. He'd seen too many men die. Now, he fully intended to celebrate life with the woman he loved for as long as they had together.

The great house was sure to be still and quiet. Having imagined their reunion many times, he tantalized himself with the possibility that she would greet him with a kiss.

As long as she was still there. As long as Sweet Air still stood. At these thoughts, an abyss yawned impenetrably dark and dim before him. There was no way of knowing in these troubled days. The Russian invasion had effectively ended any correspondence. If she'd left his home, whether for need or want, there was no way he could go after her. He had to return to his men.

Through the trees, he caught a glimpse of golden, welcoming light. His heart soared, and his pulse quickened. Almost there. As he wove through them, ducking branches, he savored these final moments of anticipation. He would soon see her. Then, the woods opened up before him and he was on the road that led to the main house. He pressed his heels to his mare's sides, but she was exhausted and barely responded.

The distant light beckoned him. Briefly, he considered his appearance. He hadn't shaved or bathed in weeks and was covered with the grime of several days' hard riding. Thankfully, Krystyna wasn't one of those frivolous, powdered court ladies who cared about the cut of a man's coat or the way his cravat was knotted.

Then, he was in the courtyard, staring up into the warm eyes of his home in which an extravagant number of rooms glowed, and he was aware of a sense of readiness for whatever awaited him there. He had no plan, except that he would see Krystyna and make things right between them. As he'd ridden across Poland, dodging Prussian and Russian patrols, it had been the thought of her and of marriage to her that drove him on.

Noe, who was finishing evening chores, glanced up as the barn door swung open. An immense black figure loomed there with a wild-eyed gray horse whose body steamed in the relative warmth of the barn.

"Don't stand there gawking, Noe," the giant shouted in familiar tones. "Take this horse."

The doomsday figure passed beneath a lantern that hung from a beam. Enough of the dark and heavily whiskered face was visible that Noe could recognize the lineaments of the young master. "Yes, Pan Morzinski. I'll take extra care with him, sir."

Andrzej tossed over the reins, gave the horse a quick pat and was gone.

His long-legged steps devoured the distance through the darkness and the rain, and then he was at the door. He heard some music and an echo of feminine laughter, but his travel-fogged senses didn't recognize them. Thrusting the door wide, he stormed into the entrance foyer. *What was going on?* To his consternation, the interior of the house blazed like midday. To a man used to no more than the ruddy glow of a campfire, it was shocking and unexpected, like entering another world. He followed the sound of music. Formally attired servants stopped and stared at him in dismay and alarm. *Why was everyone dressed so?*

He thrust wide the massive, carved doors leading into the ballroom.

CHAPTER 23

Krystyna savored the swell of the music as she moved with practiced gracefulness through the steps of the dance.

"You're lovely tonight," Sebastjan whispered, his blue eyes, sincere and shining with admiration. He was light on his feet, a talented dancer.

"Sebastjan, you are a flatterer. I can always count on you to make an evening delightful."

"I'm glad I'm of some use to you. Having traveled across a war-torn country to see you, at least I can leave with that knowledge." There was an edge of cruel self-mockery to his usual easy banter, and his expression was serious.

She glanced sharply at him. "Sebastjan, we're friends, and that's all. It would be in poor taste to try and seduce me while we're guests in my fiancé's house. And don't blame me for your decision to come here, it was your own choice."

"I had hopes."

She drew back from him. "Don't ruin this evening for both of us."

His impossibly long lashes dropped down, shielding his eyes.

"I understand, but please grant me one boon. Would you walk with me so we can speak privately?"

"What do you have to say to me that can't be said here?" She suspected it was something she definitely didn't want to hear.

"Humor me in this, Krystyna. I'll be leaving soon, and the Lord alone knows when, if ever, we'll meet again. You rejected my proposal and me. Couldn't you at least grant me this?"

She studied him and judged his expression to be open and honest. "Come with me." Arm in arm, the two strolled through the ballroom past the musicians Roderyk had hired so there could be dancing. Fortunately, the other guests didn't pay them any heed. Vincent Mouceski continued to dance with his brother's wife. Krystyna proceeded to a billiard room not far from the ballroom. None of the gentlemen had yet retired there. She'd chosen it specifically because it lacked intimacy.

"What is it that you wish to say to me?"

"May I," he glanced over his shoulder. "Would you mind if I closed the doors?"

"Yes, I would. It isn't appropriate for us to be here alone, doing so could cause Pan Roderyk some embarrassment. I find myself losing patience with you, Sebastjan. There's nothing so secret between us that should warrant us seeking seclusion to discuss it. I'm returning to the party."

He laid his hand on her forearm. "Wait, Krystyna. I've no right to importune you. I know that, but there is something important I wanted to share with you. When I return to Vienna, I'm going to tell Uncle Edward that I intend to join the Polish forces."

His words stopped her in the act of pulling away. She'd never expected to hear this from him. "What? But why? I mean… I didn't realize Poland was so important to you."

They faced each other now, and he took her hands in his own. "Poland wasn't, at least not until I met you. I want you to know that I'll be doing it for you."

"Sebastjan," she exhaled slowly. "That's not fair or reasonable. Don't do this. Don't make some grand sacrifice for me. We're speaking of war. Men are wounded, even killed. If you choose to enter this fray, do it for your own reasons, not to please me. I don't want your blood on my hands."

He laughed softly, but she glimpsed hurt in his eyes. "You don't have much faith in my abilities, yet you're convinced Morzinski is coming back to you. And how long has it been since you last heard from him?"

"It has been far too long," she admitted gravely. "But I try to have faith that he will return… It's difficult sometimes. But don't do this just to compete with Andrzej. Sebastjan, I value our friendship, but I…"

"I'm doing this," he cut her off, "because it's the right thing to do. I don't mean that if I'm killed it should be on your conscience. I just wanted you to know you inspired me. Back in Vienna, I was barely a man. All of my thoughts and energies were spent entertaining myself. I made no major decisions without my uncle's approval because he controlled the purse strings. Uncle Edward will oppose to my plan. He'll probably disown me. Now I want to become someone whom you can admire. I came to Poland to look after the lands my mother left me. For the first time in my life, I'm assuming responsibilities. This is the next step for me. And I wanted to thank you. Now, when I look at my face in the mirror, I feel a sense of pride."

"That's wonderful, but—"

"You can't talk me out of it, but I asked you in here for another reason as well." Releasing her hand, he reached into his jacket and pulled out a small, silken pouch. "This is for you."

"I can't accept a gift from you. I'm engaged to Andrzej. You know that."

"Please," he held it out to her. "It's nothing extravagant. But it would mean a great deal to me if you would keep this and think of me sometimes."

Sensing the importance of this moment to him, she silently took the pouch. Opening the drawstring, she spilled a golden chain with a pendant into her hand. It was heart shaped and filigreed and detailed in amethyst. A small amethyst teardrop hung from the point of the heart. "It's lovely."

"It was my mother's favorite piece of jewelry. My father wasn't a wealthy man. He was a landless noble. It was his only gift of jewelry to her. He gave it to her when I was born."

"I can't accept this." She held it out to him on her opened palm. "You should give this to your future bride."

He closed her fingers over it. "I want you to keep it."

"Sebastjan, you will meet someone special one day."

"Krystyna, don't patronize me."

"You know I can't accept this."

"Why not? No one need ever know about it." His blue eyes were angry now. "It seems little enough to ask, particularly when a man may be going off to his death."

"No. It wouldn't be right. Give it to your bride on your wedding day."

Reluctantly, he took it back. He was about to speak again when they heard a loud commotion in the hallway. Hand in hand, they hurried back into the ballroom.

CHAPTER 24

Pushing the ballroom doors wide, Andrzej was stunned by the extravagant brightness of countless expensive candles reflected in the wall-sized mirrors on opposite sides of the room. The colors, music and warmth physically assaulted him. He'd feared his father and fiancée had suffered deprivation and possibly worse. Instead, they were having a grand party.

Hungrily, his gaze slid past a number of people to freeze upon Krystyna, who was a vision of coiffured loveliness. Her glorious red gold mane was upswept with a few delicate curls artistically arranged over her creamy shoulders. She stood draped in smoky blue silk which was cut indecently low over her lush bosom. Wide, flowing skirts billowed out from a diminutive waist. There was a delicate blush along her regal cheekbones. And, to his outrage, her hand was linked with another man's, and the couple's posture clearly bespoke some intimacy. In the next moment, he recognized his rival was none other than Sebastjan deSzinay. Rage and jealousy coursed through him.

At first, his eyes devoured her. Then, they condemned her. He'd risked his life riding through a perilous, war-torn countryside to be with this woman. He'd dreamed of her, prayed for her, worried about her endlessly through long months of separation. These last days that he'd spent riding to her side had been almost unbearable. Now, it appeared she had not suffered at all in his absence. In fact, she looked shocked and dismayed by his appearance.

Finally, he glanced away from her, taking in the scene into which he'd intruded. As he became oriented to his surroundings, he realized this was not a grand ball, but merely a gathering of friends and neighbors, including the Mouceskis and Brasinski. He also realized that not all of the chandeliers were lit, merely those closest to the mirrors and thus capable of throwing off the most light. In addition, the musicians were just a quartet from the village. But he'd emerged from months in a gray, frozen world of war and wintry deprivation into a bright, colorful artificial spring. His eyes flashed back to the woman about whom he'd been so pointlessly concerned.

Leaning heavily on his cane but moving as quickly as he could, Roderyk called out to his son. "Andrzej! You are here! My son… My son!"

Their guests moved out of their way, and then they were face-to-face.

"Father, you're walking again." He went to kneel down before his father, but Roderyk wouldn't allow it. He drew his son up, and the two embraced with unabashed enthusiasm and affection.

"This is a blessing," Roderyk announced, his eyes, suspiciously bright. "Everyone, my son has come home from the war. This is, indeed, a special occasion."

There was a polite round of applause. With the exception of Roderyk, none of those present seemed to know quite what to make of him. It was clear to Andrzej that the war hadn't yet penetrated into this corner of Poland, or maybe, the loyalties of his father's guests were in question.

Still, he was very pleased to see his father. He observed an improvement in Roderyk's appearance. Though still frail, there was now some substance to his form.

With his arm still about his son's shoulders, Roderyk addressed him more quietly. "How is it that you're here? No, wait. We should discuss this in a more private setting. Are you well? You look thin."

"I'm well enough, Father, and you, you look hale and hearty again. How did this come about?"

"Krystyna has done more for me than any of those butchers who call themselves physicians. She got me back upon a horse, old Anka, your old pony. Kaspar had to lift me up onto her back the first time, and we walked slowly. But with that little bit of riding each day, my legs got stronger. My appetite improved. Krystyna also made them stop with the bloodletting. I feel better than I've felt in years. I must tell you I am pleased with her. She has been a most welcome addition to our family.

"Now, perhaps you would like to wash up, to change your garments? We won't be eating for a while yet."

Andrzej glared at his fiancée. Despite her fairy princess trappings, her large, expressive brown eyes resembled those of a cornered doe. DeSzinay had yet to release her hand. One of Andrzej's dark brows rose ominously. He hadn't anticipated this sensual, silk clad goddess. Nonsensically, her beauty and her pleasure in his absence irritated him. He nearly ground his teeth in frustration and anger. "She's not yet a member of our family."

"A matter I hope you will remedy shortly."

Andrzej shook his head. Tonight was not the night to deal with Krystyna. He knew his own mood was closer to that of a rabid dog than a reasonable man. Tomorrow was another day. "Father, the road here was long and difficult. I won't be rejoining your party tonight. Please understand. I am tired." The last words carried connotations far beyond physical fatigue.

Roderyk nodded, wondering how much the past months had

changed his son. He saw deprivation, suffering and even death in his son's sunken eyes. "I understand. Most of the guest will be departing tonight. They haven't traveled far. I'll hurry them on their way. In the morning, we'll talk."

Andrzej knew his father would want to discuss the subjects he most hoped to avoid, but he was saved from having to answer by the approach of Krystyna and deSzinay. Unable to contain his jealousy, the first words he spoke to his beloved, he'd recognized that truth in the bitterly cold months of encampment broken up by terrifying bursts of fighting, were, "Woman, you're making a spectacle of yourself."

"Andrzej!" his father rebuked.

Krystyna was completely taken aback. She was appalled by the changes in him but ecstatic to see him. The heat and passion in his eyes when he gazed upon her were familiar, but his clothes were ragged, his bearded face gaunt. He resembled a lean, hungry and dangerous wolf.

"Morzinski," Sebastjan performed an elegant bow. "How goes the war? You must tell me all about it later. I'm thinking of joining up. How fortuitous that you should return tonight. This little gathering is in honor of your betrothed. But, though I hate to be a nuisance, would you please step off the dance floor. Krystyna promised me this one. Pan Morzinski, I must commend you, your musicians are quite excellent. I hadn't expected to be so pleasantly entertained so far out in the countryside." Though his words were polite, and his request seemingly benign, there was an unmistakable challenge in the way Sebastjan held himself.

"Krystyna is quite finished dancing." Andrzej growled. He stepped closer to the pair, grasped Krystyna by the waist and pulled her to him, handling her like a doxy in a tap room.

"Andrzej, have you lost all sense of couth?" He barely registered his father's outraged tones. "For God's sake, release her. People are staring."

"I wish to speak to my betrothed now."

She pushed away from him, and he didn't hold her against her will. "You can't just drag me away. Don't bring shame on us all." Resuming her place at deSzinay's side, she took his arm.

Andrzej stared at the couple blankly. This was his home! Krystyna was his fiancée. "I must speak with you."

"You storm in here, interrupting your father's party. You rudely demand I leave with you immediately. You've no right to order me around, as if I were your handmaiden. This is your father's home. I'm here at his invitation." She wanted to run into his arms and hold onto him fiercely, but she couldn't allow him to dominate her.

"Welcome home, Morzinski," Sebastjan imprudently added with one blond eyebrow quirked wryly.

"Why are you here?" Andrzej challenged.

"I'm in Poland to check on the status of some lands I inherited from my mother, and I decided if I was going to risk my neck entering this country, I might as well come all the way. After all, what are a few more days of travel for a dear friend?" Sebastjan offered Krystyna a warmly exclusive smile that outraged Andrzej. "Morzinski, we would like to proceed." He glanced significantly at the quartet of musicians.

"Indeed," Andrzej growled.

"Yes, finish your dance," Roderyk spoke for his son. "I would have some words with my boy."

Andrzej's fists flexed as he watched Sebastjan take Krystyna into his arms. In his opinion, the man held her too close, but she made no protest.

As the music swelled up around him, he wrestled with crushing disappointment. He was a fool. He'd imagined himself a hero riding to the succor of his lady. Instead, he'd been an uncouth barbarian who'd embarrassed his father as well as his fiancée, who even now smiled enchantingly at another man. It was just that he'd anticipated, dreamed of his reunion with

Krystyna for so long, that the reality was like bitter ashes in his mouth. It was time to retreat and regroup. Spinning on his heel, he exited the ballroom.

"Andrzej!" His father followed in his oddly graceful, limping gait. "I wish to speak with you."

He paused outside the ballroom doors. "What is it, Father?"

Roderyk drew the doors closed behind him and accompanied his son in the direction of the staircase. "You were completely inappropriate back there. The girl is a jewel and has behaved impeccably in your absence."

"I can see that everyone finds her charming."

"You see nothing, you arrogant fool! Listen to me. I will be proud to have Krystyna as my daughter-in-law."

"At least one of us will be happy."

"The girl loves you. She has been pining for you. DeSzinay's arrival three days ago cheered her. I arranged this party in the hope that it would distract her from her melancholy."

"It appears you have succeeded admirably."

"She has done nothing to earn your disfavor."

His father was correct, but he remained savagely disappointed in how things had gone between them. "Father, I'm weary." He ran one hand through his filthy, tangled mane, his callused fingers catching in the knots and snarls. "Tomorrow we can talk."

"You don't intend to back out of the marriage now, do you?" Roderyk's voice was shrill. "The bans have been read every week since you left. You need only select a date."

"This marriage is the least of my concerns," he lied.

"My son, my son, you have become so bitter. That is exactly why this marriage must proceed. Nothing is guaranteed in this life, except that we shall all one day die. You must make the most of the days you've been granted. Don't allow jealousy, despair and fear consume all that remains."

He let out a slow breath and confessed, “Father, I came back because I had to see Krystyna.”

Brown eyes so similar to Andrzej’s own became ominously full and bright. “Then don’t waste time.” Roderyk patted him on the shoulder, turned and leaning heavily on his cane walked slowly back to the ballroom.

CHAPTER 25

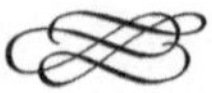

All through the dignified steps of the minuet, Krystyna's thoughts centered on the broad-shouldered figure who had blown into the soiree like a gale force wind. Why had he returned now, and what did he want from her? When did he have to leave again? She prayed it wouldn't be for a while. Aware she was wasting valuable time that could be spent with Andrzej, she wanted to rush off the dance floor and go after him. But what would Roderyk and the others think if she followed him right away? Life had been much less complicated living with the Kotyats. The rules of the society she moved in now dictated she had to display some restraint and finish the dance.

"Krystyna, it is customary to maintain some pretense of interest in your dance partner."

"I'm sorry, Sebastjan."

"Don't apologize. I must admit my thoughts were on your barbarian also. I cannot imagine why you find him so irresistible."

"I don't find him irresistible at all. He is aggravating, rude, arrogant and impossible."

"But he does bring out your fire, doesn't he? While I have failed to evoke even a spark."

"You are my dear friend, Sebastjan. I trust you."

"Ah, and there is the kiss of death. You trust me! How unfortunate. We would have done well together. We understand each other and make each other laugh. I even risked life and limb to come here when I heard of your betrothal. I worried you were being coerced. But now, seeing the two of you together, I know my cause is lost. He has your heart, doesn't he?"

As the piece of music finally came to an end, she met his eyes and answered. "Yes, he does."

Sebastjan closed his eyes in acknowledgement then escorted her from the floor.

"Thank you for the dance. Now, if you will excuse me, I want to freshen up."

"Of course. As always, your wish is my command." He bowed low before her before moving away.

"My lady?"

She pivoted with some impatience towards the voice. "Yes, Pan Brasinski?"

The stocky, blond man with large, pale blue eyes and fleshy features held out his arm to her, clearly expecting her to take it. "May I have this dance?" The quartet was proceeding with the sweeping strains of a polonaise.

"I'm sorry, but I find I'm overheated. I'd planned to sit this one out."

"Then, allow me to accompany you. We should get to know each other better as we are to be neighbors."

"No, I really do need to go and refresh myself. You are too kind. Perhaps another time?"

"So be it."

With relief, she turned from him and hastened out of the ballroom. Once she had secured the doors behind her, she raised her skirts and took off at a run. She fairly flew up the staircase and down the long hall towards Andrzej's rooms. With her heart racing, she knocked on his door. In the quiet of the darkened hallway, her knock sounded obscenely loud. She waited. Where was he? An endless moment passed. She raised her hand to knock again.

"It's open. Come in."

She twisted the knob, pushed open the door and froze. A bare-chested Andrzej was kneeling in just his breeches before the hearth, encouraging the fire. Peter, his dog, stood beside his master. The room was frigid, goose bumps rose on the naked flesh of her arms. In response to the cold, she reminded herself, not to the display of the muscular planes of his broad back.

"Please set the tub in front of the fire. I need to get this chill out of my bones, and this filth from my body." Orange-red sparks flew up as he manipulated a burning log with the poker. Well defined biceps flexed. Krystyna's breath caught in her throat.

"Don't dawdle, Lukasz. I feel stiff and old tonight." He turned her way. Making no effort to cover himself, he went still.

Her memories of that long ago afternoon they'd spent in his bed hadn't done him justice. He was very large and blatantly male with broad, square pectoral muscles, small dusky nipples and a dusting of golden brown hair that darkened as it descended into the snug top of his unlaced breeches. He was also very thin. His ribs stood out on his sides, and his stomach was gaunt, as were the hollows of his face. Unable to resist the impulse, her eyes skimmed over the well-muscled thighs, down the hairy, chiseled calves.

"My lady?" He arched an eyebrow at her quizzically while his eyes grew dark and unfathomable. "I thought you found my presence objectionable. As I haven't bathed in weeks, I can assure you I haven't yet improved." Rudely, he turned away from her and moved to a table on which was set a decanter and one glass. He poured several fingers of the syrupy, slow moving liquor and swallowed it. His eyes scorched her as he said, "I'm in need of liquid comfort tonight."

"Andrzej." She took a step closer. "I—"

"You should return to your guests, pretty lady. DeSzinay is sure to be missing you. I'm not fit company for anyone tonight." His fatigue and disappointment at their reunion had blackened his mood.

"Why are you here? What's happened?"

"You refer to my bedchamber?" He deliberately misinterpreted her question. "I imagine my reasons must be apparent. A more interesting question is why are you here? How does it come to pass that you, a woman who pretended to be gypsy for two years to avoid notice from society, should appear as the central attraction at a party with all of our neighbors?"

"Your father invited only people whom he has known well for years. That Sebastjan came to visit was as much a surprise to me as it is to you."

Andrzej swore softly. "My father is a reckless man."

"He's a kind and generous man who has done everything he could think of to ensure that I am happy and comfortable here. He even wrote to my parents, and he was careful about it. He sent his letter to my aunt Jadwiga, who then sent it on. You can't imagine how wonderful it was to read my mother's hand, to have my parents' good wishes, to know they still love me and think of me."

Not responding, he took another long and reckless swallow.

"Why have you come home so suddenly, Andrzej? Tell me the truth, please." She needed to hear him say that he cared about her.

He shrugged dismissively. "What does it matter?"

"In the middle of a war, you decided to ride home for what is it? A few weeks? Knowing you, I'm sure you haven't deserted."

"Kosciuszko granted me leave. A few weeks," he grudgingly admitted. "I foolishly thought I might be needed here."

Carefully but very deliberately, she continued, "I hope you didn't travel all this way to see me? After all, ours is not a love match, merely one of convenience." Her salvo was bold and intentionally cruel. She wanted desperately for him to contradict her.

He stiffened, but didn't speak, merely stared into the fire.

"Your reasons must have been compelling to travel in such circumstances." Stepping directly up to him, so near she could feel the heat radiating from his body, she boldly met his eyes. "It had to have been more than longing for a clean bed and a warm meal that brought you home. Perhaps, it was concern for your father's well being?" Andrzej was undeniably rank from many days and nights of living in filth, but she wasn't put off by his stench. This was the man she loved, and even as he was, she preferred him to the powdered dandies downstairs. Nervously, she wet her lips with the tip of her tongue.

Still, he said nothing. His expression was unreadable and strangely intent.

"But as long as you're here," she said and ran her fingertips along the hard curve of his upper arm and over his shoulder. She felt as well as heard his sharp inhalation. "We could amuse each other."

Gasping as she was dragged up against the solid wall of his chest, she gazed up into furious and despairing eyes.

"Don't play the whore with me, Krystyna! What has happened to make you so? Has life hardened you so much?"

"Tell me," she persisted. "Did you come back to see me?"

"Yes! Damn you!" Then, his mouth was upon hers and she welcomed his savage possession. A wild and desperate passion flared between them fanned by need, despair and longing.

"You're crying," he murmured wonderingly, his lips, never far from her own.

"I had to press you so you would tell me how you feel. Otherwise, would you have simply left without telling me?"

"You drive me to distraction, woman." The anger and the pain began to recede from his features. "Witch! My witch. I came near to killing poor deSzinay tonight because of you." His voice was a sensual whisper. "This is much more the sort of welcome that I was hoping for."

He kissed her again, and she answered in kind, feeling his arousal pressing at her stomach through her skirts. She savored the warm sweep of his breath against the delicate skin at the nape of her neck. Her hands adored the hard planes of his shoulders and the heat of his skin. He pressed her ever closer, beginning to bunch her skirts up around her waist.

They both froze when they heard a knock at the door. "Master, I have the water for your bath."

"Kaspar, set it down there," Andrzej ordered through the closed door.

"Right here in the hallway?"

"Yes, Kaspar. Lukasz hasn't brought the tub up yet, but please bring me some more hot water. My bones need to thaw out." Krystyna heard the buckets hit the floor with a thump.

"But the buckets, I'll need them to get more water."

"I'm sure you'll be able to find others."

Kaspar muttered something incomprehensible and moved down the hall.

Andrzej chuckled. "He'll be telling the other servants that I've gone mad. But it's good that he interrupted us when he did. Otherwise, we may not have stopped. You should return downstairs for a little while. For my father's sake."

"I think he'll understand," she murmured throatily.

"No, you have to go."

"You've come all of this way to see me, and now you send me away."

"I'm delighted to see you. The evidence is clear."

Comprehending his reference, Krystyna's eyes dropped

down. She reached for him, slid her palm across the arousal that thrust out blatantly against his loosened breeches.

With a groan, he caught her hand and drew it to his lips. “It’s just that I’m aware of how long it’s been since my last bath as well as my last meal. Return to the party. Stay for a half hour or so. Then, plead a headache. I’ll be waiting for you. I’ll take care of everything. Meet me in the stable.” He pulled her close for one more long, soul-draining kiss. “Now hurry, my enchantress.” With that, he spun her about, patted her on the rump and sent her forth from his room.

Feeling his eyes following her, Krystyna repressed the urge to skip her way back down to the hall.

CHAPTER 26

A slow hour passed before she finally broke free from the festivities. The usual social courtesies grated on her. She dutifully danced with Jan Mouceski and others. She chatted with the wives and daughters of local magnates. Though she knew Brasinski's eyes followed her, he didn't approach her again for his promised dance. Finally, it seemed that enough time had passed so that she could make a graceful exit. While chatting with Anna Mielak, she deliberately swayed slightly and raised a hand to her forehead.

"Are you feeling poorly, child?"

"My head. Perhaps I should sit down."

"A few too many toasts tonight, my dear. No, the best thing for you would be to go directly to bed and sleep this off. You'll be a different person in the morning."

"But I don't want to abandon Pan Morzinski."

"He'll understand. You've had quite enough to deal with tonight, particularly with your young man returning so unexpectedly. Besides, as I'm sure I've mentioned to you, I don't hold with these late evenings. They render you worthless the following day. My late husband was a carouser, just like Mouceski there. It used to make me so angry. But he was a good man, God rest his soul."

As a matter of fact, Krystyna did remember how Anna felt about late nights. It was specifically for this reason that she had "been taken with the vapors" in the lady's vicinity.

"Would you like me to accompany you to your room?"

"Oh, that won't be necessary, but thank you. It's just so warm in here. I'm sure I'll be much better as soon as I'm in a cooler place."

"If you're certain, my dear."

"Yes, thank you."

She was giddy, almost breathless as she made her way out of the ballroom. She moved slowly. After all, she was supposed to be feeling poorly.

"Krystyna." Sebastjan stopped her. His fine features were animated and pleasantly flushed. "You must come. Vincent and I…"

"Please, Sebastjan, I need to sit down."

"Don't be an old woman. We are having the most delightful time."

"I'm retiring now."

"Oh," he relinquished his hold on her forearm. All frivolity left from his tone. "I see. Not that I blame you, of course. I hope he realizes how very fortunate he is."

"Thank you, Sebastjan. Again, you have proven to be a true friend."

"Yes," he smiled thinly. "A true friend…Well, the others are waiting for me. Good night, fair Krystyna."

Her thoughts were on Andrzej as she exited the room. So, she didn't see Sebastjan pause and watch her. His expression was bleak and pained, wholly at odds with his usual pleasant if facile demeanor.

Only when she stood with the ballroom doors drawn closed behind her was she at a loss. She was to rendezvous with Andrzej in the stable? For the first time, the peculiarity of his request struck her. She could think of so many more romantic places. But then again, it was likely to be the one place where they wouldn't be disturbed until morning. And, at least, they would be together. At long last.

She made her way to the great sweep of the main stairs and dashed up the steps to her room. Once there, she wiggled her way out of her evening finery and threw the dress and undergarments onto the down turned bed. After a moment's consideration, she picked it all back up again and tossed it across a chaise. Then, she rumpled up the bed coverings, so that any servant coming in the morning would conclude she'd slept there. Next, she dressed rapidly in a simple day gown, boots and a long, hooded cloak. Pulling the hood up about her face, she tiptoed down the hallway to the servants' staircase. To her relief, no one appeared as she dashed down the precipitous steps, along darkened corridors and then out into the chilly night.

The rain had stopped, and the moon had finally emerged from behind the clouds. And so, she could see her way, though she clung to the shadows to avoid discovery. As she tugged open the stable door, sweet smelling hay and the warm, rich bouquet of horse greeted her. Feeling her way, she worked her way down the aisle to where her horse, Hector, was stabled. She was almost abreast of the stall, could make out the shape of the horse's head when strong arms seized her from behind. Closing her eyes, she relaxed into that so longed for embrace.

"Thank God you're here at last." The words were nuzzled into her neck. She reveled in the feel of him against her. Just a few hours ago, it had seemed impossible that he would ever hold her again. And yet, here he was, embracing her as if he wished to absorb her into himself.

“Come,” he drew away only to pull her gently along in his wake. Once they were back outside in the frigid air, he led her around behind the barn to that section of the house that adjoined the hedge maze. He paused before a window-less foundation wall and stood peering at the vine-covered structure. “If I can just find it again…” He let go of her hand and probed with his fingers under the vines.

Krystyna shivered, drawing her hands under her cloak.

There was a barely audible grinding sound, and the wall moved suddenly, receding away from them. A splash of light from somewhere within gilded his features.

She followed him into a narrow, down slanting passage. Torches in sconces mounted on the walls illuminated their way. Andrzej gestured at one. “I lit them before I went to wait for you.”

“Where are we going?”

“We are almost there. It’s a secret place where no one will disturb us.”

As the passage twisted around, they passed several closed doors. Then, to her surprise, he pushed one open to reveal a presentable bedchamber with a hearth in one corner. A fire had been started but had yet to dispel the damp in the air. Andrzej immediately set to work encouraging the flames.

“What is this place?”

“My father’s more of a patriot than he would have anyone know. For years now, he’s been aiding our side against the Russians and the Austrians. Under the guise that he was having damaged foundation walls restored, he had this room, which was once just a storage room, secretly expanded and made livable. Even the chimney was cleverly routed so it blends with the others and isn’t apparent from the outside. Many couriers have spent a night in this chamber before proceeding on to their destinations. Only Kaspar and Matylda know about this room, but no one will bother us tonight. It would be too risky for a messenger to come here with so many guests in the house, and I've spoken with Kaspar. We are ensured of privacy."

"Your father is working for Kosciuszko?" she questioned, feeling awkward as she stood behind him. She had come to this place with the intention of making love with him, but now felt insecure and self-conscious.

"My father explains his behavior as working against Russia, not for Poland. But, yes, Kosciuszko does benefit from his efforts. Father doesn't want his loyalties well known, for that would end his effectiveness and possibly his life, particularly since Brasinski is owned by the Russians."

"I never even suspected."

"He's an effective actor. Don't be angry with him for not telling you. He was only trying to protect you. That should do it." Rising up, he stepped closer. He placed his hands gently on the tops of her arms, and his touch seared her through her garments. "Let's not speak of politics tonight. Forget about everything else in the world. Pretend that we are all there is, only you and I. The rest of it can be hanged for just this one night. Pretend with me that this is our wedding night."

Her discomfort dissolved miraculously under the heat of his gaze. Indeed, she soon could think of nothing else but the man touching her, of the heat of his body, of her own hunger for him. There was desperation to their first lovemaking, a frantic assertion of life and love. Still, he was careful to withdraw from her as he achieved his own release. After their first satiation, both found that they could savor and rediscover the magic of each other. They made love again and again.

Afterwards, reclining in the rosy glow of the firelight, he held her spooned against him. Abruptly, he stirred. "I want to show you something."

"No, please don't move. This feels too delicious."

"I'll be right back," he nuzzled the promise into the sensitive curve between her neck and ear.

"All right." She shifted, allowing him to stand up.

He rifled through his discarded pile of clothing, coming up finally with a leather pouch on a cord. Then sitting on the edge of the bed, he opened the drawstring and carefully pulled out a worn and weathered scrap of vellum.

"What's that?" she asked sitting up, sweeping her hair back over her shoulder.

"It's something I wrote that morning in Vienna after I awoke to find you gone. We've had too many misunderstandings, you and I. I would like you to read this."

He handed her the scrap. She took it carefully. Though the words were faint, she could them make out:

"Could it be You? We search endlessly for 'the one.' And then, encounter her suddenly when we have given up the search. She is my soul's music. All pain is washed away, forgotten, when I hold her in my arms. We are both imperfect, but there is a rightness to the two of us together."

"You love me," she stroked the stubbled side of his cheek wonderingly. "I have always loved you."

The paper drifted forgotten to the ground as he took her in his arms again.

Half awake, half asleep, lulled by the beating of her lover's heart, Krystyna ran her nail lightly around his aureole. He didn't open his eyes, just pulled her closer with one long arm. The subterranean chamber was windowless, so the light of the dawn couldn't give away the hour. But both possessed that awareness of time country-raised people tend to have. Though she couldn't see it, Krystyna knew the sky was beginning to lighten.

"My love," Andrzej's voice was thick and gravelly. "It's time."

Fearing to speak because of the lump lodged high in her throat and the tears that threatened to escape her eyes, she got up from the cradle of his arms and dressed. Without the heat of his body to warm her, the room felt uncomfortably chilly.

He lay still, memorizing the long perfection of her thigh, the sweet curve of her belly. Then, he, too, arose.

The fire had died down to smoldering embers. Shivering, she stared at him. One thought troubled her, "Why did you withdraw from me? I would welcome our child."

"As would I. But I don't want to leave you pregnant now. If I don't return—"

"Oh, don't say that!"

He pulled her to him and held her. "My angel, I will come back. I'm too wicked and stubborn to die. You've said so yourself."

"You tempt fate."

He chuckled. "I'd never have guessed that you're superstitious. Don't cry and make this even harder. You have to be brave, as you always are, so that I won't worry about you. I need to believe you can and will take care of yourself and my father, too. I pray that this war will end soon."

"I'll pray, too. I'll pray that you stay safe and come back to me."

"Will you still have me if I'm a poor, landless man?" He cocked one eyebrow sardonically, and a gentle half smile played on his lips.

"Of course. But what do you mean? You think that the Polish forces will be defeated, don't you? Why do you return then?"

"I must go. It's my duty. I'm a Pole, and I must fight for my country."

Krystyna understood; she could never ask him to be less than he was.

"If only there was more time, I would send you and my father away, maybe to England or even to America."

"You think that I would go, that I would leave you? Don't shame me. I know my own duty, as well."

There was nothing more to be said. They embraced again. Then, he led her out of their sanctuary, up the passageway, and out into the overcast dawn.

CHAPTER 27

Krystyna and Andrzej married in the chapel at Sweet Air. Father Ignacy presided over the rather humble wedding mass, attended only by the Widow Mielak, Sebastjan deSzinay, Pan Roderyk, the members of his household, and a handful of peasants from the estate. Still, all who were there remarked on how in love and happy the young couple looked. Indeed, they had eyes only for each other. They spent many hours of the succeeding days in the old nurse's cottage, truly together without any distractions.

Andrzej's leave passed seemingly in a blink of an eye, and then it was time for him to rejoin the Polish forces. He bid Krystyna farewell early one morning in the courtyard.

"If something does happen to me," he hesitated.

"Don't speak that way. Ever!" She hugged him fiercely. "You promised that you'd come back."

"I will. As long as there's life in me, nothing will keep me from you."

"I won't say goodbye. Hold me!"

He complied, and when he finally drew back, there was a suspicious brightness to his eyes. "No matter what happens to either of us, you have my heart. I'll always be with you. But now you have to be brave for me."

Still sobbing, she buried her face in the crook of his neck. Inhaling deeply, she sought to imprint his very scent into her memory.

"Being left behind is so horrible. I can't stand here and watch you ride away from me again."

"There's no easy way to do this," he groaned. "Just go now and don't look back."

"One moment more…" Sobbing, she finally broke away from him and ran into the house. She dashed up the stairs and down the length of the hallway to her bedroom. Muffling her sobs by biting on her finger, she peered out through her window into the gray misery of the morning. Ten minutes then fifteen minutes passed. Where was he? Finally, a heartbreakingly familiar tall figure mounted on a leggy steed emerged from the courtyard below her window onto the path leading west and away from Sweet Air. Andrzej's features weren't visible; he and his mount were little more than slightly darker shadows against a gray haze. When he was about to make the turn that would take him out of sight, he faced his horse back in the direction of the great house. There he paused. Krystyna felt as if he was looking directly at her. Suddenly, a dog began to bark wildly. A smaller shadow leapt up around Andrzej, spooking his horse. It was Peter. Clearly, this time, he refused to be separated from his master.

Krystyna envied the dog his freedom to follow the person he loved. She wanted nothing more than to fly after Andrzej. But she had obligations, too. Her husband needed her to stay behind to see to his father and the estate. Though she felt as if her heart was shattering, or being wrenched from her body, for his sake as well as her own, she had to remain at Sweet Air.

~

More departures followed Andrzej's. Erna Kotyat, who'd remained on at Sweet Air as Krystyna's companion, joined Sebastjan's entourage for its return to Austria. The departure of her two friends was difficult and painful for Krystyna.

But most troubling of all was not knowing how Andrzej fared and imagining the worst. At night, she lay warm and dry beneath her blankets and imagined his misery, his loneliness and the sheer physical hardship of the life he was enduring. Still, she went about her duties, and there were many. Roderyk's health was again questionable, and he rarely left his rooms. Many of Sweet Air's peasants had heeded Kosciuszko's call to arms. Mounted on horses given them by their former master, they, too, had gone off to defend their homeland.

The only bright spot in this otherwise bleak time for Krystyna was her friendship with Roderyk. She assisted in his care and looked forward to the evenings they spent together. Then, they spoke of politics, of Sweet Air, of Ewa, Roderyk's deceased wife, and of Andrzej.

April drizzled into May. Then, all of a sudden, it was June. One lovely afternoon, Roderyk and Krystyna sat out on the porch playing a game of chess. Roderyk was having a good day; he breathed easily and clearly, and he was enjoying the out-of-doors. On the other hand, she was having difficulty focusing on the game.

"It's your move."

"Oh, I'm sorry." She forced herself to study the board.

"My dear, your mind is elsewhere. Would you prefer to stop playing? There's not much of a challenge in defeating the inattentive. We could discuss whatever is bothering you."

She sighed. She wrote to Andrzej almost every day, but she wasn't sure her missives were getting to him. The country was in chaos. His responses had long since ceased, and she didn't even know if he was alive. But she didn't want to relate her fears to Roderyk.

"You're thinking about that report that Jan Mouceski brought over earlier, aren't you? Have faith in our Polish heroes. And since Kosciuszko promised liberation and land to the peasants, volunteers are rushing to him."

"You're patronizing me, Pan Roderyk. I heard what you said to Mouceski, that the peasants are untrained and have no weapons other than the scythes they brought with them from their fields. How can they defeat well drilled, professional soldiers?"

He shrugged eloquently. "We can only hope and pray, and be grateful that the matter hasn't deteriorated to the point that it did during the Confederation of the Bar uprising. Back then, the Cossacks went berserk. They attacked and killed everyone and anyone, landlords and peasants alike. The Confederates retaliated with equally savage slaughter. All of Poland was on fire."

"My great-aunt told me about her experiences during that revolt. A Cossack rescued her and her husband from a troop of them. The man is still with her." Thoughts of Pavel, whose great moustache and fierce expression masked a true and generous heart, brought a slight smile to Krystyna's lips.

"This time, matters are not entirely without hope. Our forces held at Zielence and were victorious. If that coward Prince Ludwig of Wurtemberg hadn't deserted his post, the Russians might have been driven from Poland."

"Yes, Pan Roderyk, but now the Russians hold Wilno, and you told me just last night that Prince Jozef, our best and bravest commander, has returned to his home in Vienna in despair."

"The loss of the prince is a great tragedy. Hopefully, France will send the help Kosciuszko has requested."

"Is there nothing we can do?" She rose to her feet impatiently. "I don't want to just sit here and wait for the end."

"If I were your age, I wouldn't want to be playing nursemaid to an old man either."

"No, sir." She dropped down on her knees beside him. "That's not what I meant. I don't think I could make it through this horrible vigil without you. It's just I wish I could do something, anything, to help the cause, to help Andrzej."

He gripped her hands in his own gnarled ones and met her intent gaze with one equally so. "As you know, I was a soldier in my youth. These past months, I have found it harder to await the return of a loved one from a war than to fight in one. But now I fear the conflict may be coming to us. Krystyna, you know most of our neighbors are sympathetic with the Russians. Brasinski, in particular, has regular dealings with them. I'm not considered a friend to them, and so we must prepare for the worst."

"But Brasinski's frequently been your guest here. Would he turn on you?"

"That man is concerned only with promoting his own interests. He would betray me in a heartbeat. But, in the event matters deteriorate, I've made some contingency plans that I would share with you."

"You mean if we lose, don't you?"

"Child, we must prepare for any and every eventuality. With this in mind, I have told Prym to take the three remaining horses of good quality, including your Hector, and place them in the pasture by the nurse's cottage. That place is well hidden by trees and far from the road. It's less likely they'll be stolen from there."

"I know the place."

"I'm not surprised." The brown eyes, so like his son's, twinkled. "It's a good place for a rendezvous. I know the boy has the servants keep it up. No need to blush, child. I was young once, too. I am glad you know the way there. The trees will provide the horses with ample cover, and there's plenty of grazing and a stream. We need to keep these three out of sight, so that we can leave this place if we have to. Your horse will be far safer there than in the main stable, which is the first place anyone would look for a mount to steal."

"Of course. Then I shouldn't ride anymore."

"At least, not far from this house. We will not live as prisoners, but these are perilous times. Now, I do not believe you have any interest in proceeding with our game, do you? Very well then. I shall read for a while. Would you be so kind as to bring me the book from the top of my desk in the library? Oh, and my dear, there's a letter for you there as well. Look by my correspondence. Please forgive me for my forgetfulness."

"Is it from Andrzej?" she asked, her heart in her throat.

"No, it isn't. I recall it being from Vienna."

Krystyna dashed back into the house, to the library where she soon found a stained and worn missive addressed to her lying atop a pile of other papers. She recognized her great-aunt's handwriting. She located Roderyk's book and returned outside.

"Thank you, my dear." Roderyk took it. "How is your aunt?"

After breaking the wax seal with the distinctive von Gebler seal, she was thrilled to recognize Marta von Reigler's elegant penmanship. "Actually, it's from a friend of mine."

Marta wrote that after swearing her to secrecy about Krystyna's location and condition, Jadwiga had offered to send a letter to Krystyna for her. Marta's writing style was as warm and excitable as the girl herself, whom Krystyna was pleased to discover hadn't changed at all. Marta also explained that Jadwiga had told her of Krystyna's marriage, expressed her warm and constant regard for her friend, and related the gossip concerning shared acquaintances in Vienna. Krystyna laughed aloud at Marta's cunning descriptions. She also shared the exciting news that she was now engaged to a "thoroughly charming and handsome" young Austrian lord of whom her mother "thoroughly approved." Marta assured her she was much in love with her young man. But Marta's last tidbit of news disturbed Krystyna. "I almost forgot, and mother insisted I inform you.

Several months after you left, there was a Russian count asking after you at several of the parties. For the life of me, I can't remember his name. It has been more than two years now. He tried to be discreet, but you know Mother's network. She found out, of course. He claimed that he knew you in Poland, was an old friend of your family's. He had dark eyes and hair and seemed quite taken with you. I am sure he will be heartbroken when he learns of your marriage. To be honest, I found him rather boorish." Marta ended her letter with assurances of her continued affection, good wishes and her hopes that they would be reunited in the near future.

Krystyna stared blindly out of the window. She hadn't thought much about Janus in recent months; there had been so much else going on. It seemed he had finally lost her trail or interest in pursuing her. Besides, how could he follow her here, almost to the Russian border and in the middle of a war?

But now, could her friend have unwittingly provided her with a clue to Janus' identity? Now, when the name Morzinski and her recent marriage provided her with some protection, when she once more had contact with her family, was Janus finally to be unmasked?

A Russian count. Who could he be? Ivan had been the sort to have made everyone aware of any connection he had to a count.

"Is it glad tidings or," Roderyk broke off abruptly and began to cough. Krystyna hurried to his side and held up her handkerchief to him. Straining and hacking, he pressed it to his mouth. He leaned over at the waist, shaking with the intensity of his coughs and struggling to breath. She held his shoulders. When he drew the handkerchief away from his lips, she saw it was scarlet with blood.

"Kaspar! Kaspar, please come here now!"

Later, when she and Kaspar had Roderyk settled in his rooms resting fitfully, she reread Marta's letter and resolved to address her concerns with her father-in-law when he was feeling better.

CHAPTER 28

In the middle of the night, a crash of thunder awakened Krystyna. A brilliant flash of lightning lit up her chamber. She arose from her bed, drew on a wrapper and moved to stand before her opened window in the gusting wind. Holding back the curtain, she savored the sensation of rain droplets on her face. The feeling was revitalizing after the mounting heat of recent days.

Another dazzling flash and the courtyard below was exposed to her gaze. She glimpsed the untamed ferocity of wind and rain whipped branches. One more blaze of white light accompanied by the boom of a celestial cannon revealed figures moving below her. Kaspar and a mounted man circled about. The major domo struggled to keep his hold on the horse's bridle while also supporting the rider, who was in danger of sliding off the other side. In another instant of brilliance, Krystyna saw Kaspar shouldered the rider's body weight while the man's horse shied away from them. She knotted her wrapper more securely about her waist, shoved her feet into her boots, and raced out of her bedchamber.

Moments later, she was down in the courtyard. As she peered

through the driving rain, there was a simultaneous explosion of sound and brightness, and she saw that Kaspar still struggled with the man and his horse. She rushed out into the storm and grasped the horse's reins away from the servant. Jerking sharply, she sought to get the terrified animal's attention while also taking great care to keep her feet away from the sharp hooves.

"Panienka? You… ou shouldn't be out here." Kaspar was breathing heavily from his efforts.

"I'm here to help. Listen to me. Bring him over here." She indicated the modest shelter offered by an overhanging corner of roof. "I'll stay with him. You get the horse into the stable. It's causing too much commotion."

He nodded and moved to obey her directives. First, he leaned the unconscious man against her below the fairly minimal protection offered by the overhang. Then, he took hold of the horse and led it away.

By gripping fiercely, Krystyna managed to hold the limp body half upright, though soon the weight sent painful pins and needles coursing through her arms. Staring down into the man's face, she realized that the stranger wasn't a man at all, but a boy in his late teens. His skin was a ghastly pale shade, his cheeks thin and pinched. His clothes, which were thoroughly soaked, were plain and coarse, those of a peasant, and his skin burned hot to the touch. Suddenly, he shook his head from side to side and moaned. "Mama… Mama." He thrust out his hand and began to struggle, nearly sending them both to the ground. His eyes were opened but unaware with fever.

"I'm here with you." Seeking to comfort him, Krystyna moved her hand into contact with his questing one. He gripped her fiercely and his body movements stilled. *Where is Kaspar? What is taking so long?* Another bright flash of lightning revealed the servant's stocky figure running toward them.

"Thank God!"

"Panienka, thank you for your help. I've got him now." With

a grunt, Kaspar hefted the dead weight of the unconscious boy. "Please go back to your room."

"No, Kaspar, I'm coming with you, to help you with the boy."

"But the master—"

"Are you going to Pan Roderyk now?"

He nodded.

"Then, we'll go together."

She met his troubled glance with flinty determination in her own. Abruptly, he nodded. Without a word, he led her around the house to that familiar hidden door through which she and Andrzej had passed on that unforgettable night several months before.

With one arm, Kaspar sought to push the vines aside and press the release while also maintaining control of the boy's body.

"Here, let me."

"Press right there." He indicated the spot by inclining his head.

She triggered the release, and the door glided silently open. Once again, the torches in the wall sconces were already lit. Soon, they arrived at the chamber she remembered so well. The room was unchanged except for one critical feature: Roderyk sat in a chair by the hearth. His dark eyes riveted on Krystyna as she stepped into the room after Kaspar.

Leaning heavily on his cane, he came half out of his seat in surprise. "Krystyna! Kaspar, what is the meaning of this?"

"I was awakened by the storm, and I saw Kaspar and this boy out in the courtyard."

Not yet meeting his master's eyes, Kaspar carried the boy to the bed and laid him down. "This young one is sick. He was out of his senses, and the Panienka helped me. Afterwards, I thought it best she speak with you."

"By the cross, I wonder how many other people saw this one

arrive! What are they thinking sending one so young? He didn't follow any of the instructions about where to leave his horse, or how to enter the house. Just rode straight up, as bold as day, like a neighbor come to visit. Those fools risk exposing us all. Krystyna, I had no wish to draw you into this, but it seems I have no choice."

"The boy is a courier, isn't he?"

"Yes."

"Andrzej already told me about your um…activities. I want to help."

"He did? Well, there's nothing to be done for it now. I'll explain all you need to know later. Kaspar, did he have the letters?"

The boy shifted and moaned as Kaspar's big hands felt carefully about his chest and shoulders. "Here it is." He removed a stained leather case from under the boy's vest.

Roderyk leaned back in his chair, his eyes bright with satisfaction. "Now, go and fetch Matylda. The boy needs her care."

Once he was gone, Krystyna moved to the foot of the bed. She pulled off the boy's sodden boots then removed his thick, wet, homespun socks as well. His skin was clammy to the touch.

Roderyk rose to his feet and stepped over to the side of the bed.

He considered the boy. "So young. So very young."

"Do you think he'll recover?"

"He needs rest and food, and I am no healer, but he is young. Matylda can work miracles with her herbs and poultices. We'll get him well enough."

"So he can return to the fighting," she remarked grimly. "I don't understand, Pan Roderyk. Why, if you are involved in all of this, have you pretended to be disinterested in the Polish cause?"

"The fewer people who suspect my true inclinations, the more effective I can be."

"But you always seemed furious with Andrzej for his dedication."

"I am an old fool who loves his only child and who worries about him. It nearly killed me losing his mother. I would rather have him safe here with us. But Andrzej has completely disregarded my advice in this matter. My son is a true patriot." Roderyk uttered the words with heartfelt pride.

"He is proud of what you are doing as well. May I ask you what sort of information these couriers carry?"

"I have friends, loyal Poles, in St. Petersburg and in other Russian cities. They send me whatever news they think may be of use to Kosciuszko, information about troop movements and details of diplomatic scheming. I am but one link in a chain that extends across this country. This business is the one small thing I can still do for Poland."

"Your confidence means a great deal to me, sir."

He patted her hand reassuringly. "Every day, you become more like a daughter to me. But we have a predicament here. This boy is in no condition to proceed." He paused at the sound of footsteps in the corridor.

Kaspar reappeared, accompanied by Matylda, who also wore a wrapper and had her hair pulled back in a thick, gray-black braid. Though it was obvious she'd been roused from her bed, her expression was alert and thoughtful as she took in the unconscious boy.

"Kaspar, I'll need a clean nightshirt, a pail of warm water and my herb kit."

"Come, Krystyna," Roderyk directed as he picked up the messenger's leather case. "We will leave Matylda to work her magic."

"I'll do my best, of course, Pan Morzinski. But this one's just a boy, and he's been ill for some time. He shouldn't have been on his feet, much less on a horse," the housekeeper remarked with some heat.

"These are trying times for all of us, Matylda." Krystyna followed him out into the corridor. "This way."

To her surprise, they proceeded down the hallway in the direction opposite from the one in which she'd entered. The passage seemed to descend deeper beneath the great house. In this section, the torches were fewer, and there was more space between them. But Roderyk hobbled gamely along, seemingly unaffected by the near darkness. Krystyna stumbled more than once. Then, the passageway began to slant upwards again. Abruptly, Roderyk paused, his hand extended to a section of wall. It swept back on well-oiled hinges. On the other side of it was a bookshelf. To Krystyna's amazement, they emerged in the library.

"It's a clever mechanism, really very simple," Roderyk explained with some pride. "All depends on this lever here." He indicated a panel of wood that blended convincingly with the bookcase. "You just pull. On the other side, there is a similar device."

"Did you build this passage?"

"Oh no, I believe my grandfather is responsible. He designed and built this house. I have no idea as to his original intent with regard to the passages. But according to family lore, his was not a happy marriage. I think he used that hidden entrance to sneak out and meet with paramours. The old scoundrel showed me the entire business himself. In his dotage, when his mind was failing, we used to play down there. Still, we have managed to keep the passages a family secret." He lowered himself onto the faded tapestry of his favorite armchair and shifted about uncomfortably. "This hip of mine will be a misery tomorrow. Would you be so kind as to pour me some vodka? It does ease the pain."

She dutifully went to the side board on which sat a silver

tray. On it were a crystal decanter filled with clear, viscous vodka and a glass. She poured two fingers of spirit into the glass.

Meanwhile, Roderyk opened the messenger's case. He glanced through the materials. "These are reports about the layout of Russian troops near Cracow. This information must get to Kosciuszko! But Kaspar is not much of a horseman, and he has never been far from Sweet Air. He would be overwhelmed by the task."

Handing him the glass, she took a deep breath. "I've been to Cracow, and the Kotyats taught me a great deal about traveling. I wouldn't get lost. I could deliver it."

"No, that would simply not do. You are a woman! It's inconceivable, far too dangerous. Krystyna, the country is at war!"

"No one need know that I'm a woman. I could ride at night, dressed as a gypsy boy."

"No. No. My son would never forgive me, and I would never forgive myself. No, there must be another solution. I don't have to get the message all the way to Cracow. I simply have to get it into the hands of an old comrade, a retired soldier named Kasimierz Dabbinski, who runs an inn called the Beautiful Boar. It is a little more than a half day's ride west from here. He is the next link in our chain. He will see to it that the message makes it to Kosciuszko. But the messenger must be able to evade Russian patrols as well as Polish."

"Pan Roderyk, the courier need not be unseen if he or she has a reason to be traveling. We could do it! We could be in plain sight. If we are stopped, we have a ready and plausible explanation. Perhaps say we are going to visit my family. It makes sense. It's believable!

"We could carry the message on."

"But the carriage ride. My hip."

"Oh, I didn't think. I'm sorry. It would be too much. Forgive me."

All at once, the bushy, white brows became firm and resolute. “I am not an old woman to die in my bed. This hip has trapped me in this house for too long. We will do it.”

“Please, sir, I was wrong. Don’t make an impetuous decision. Don’t jeopardize your health.”

“We can do this, and we will… Won’t Kasimierz be surprised to see me! The more I think about it, the more I like this idea. As for my hip, the laudanum and the vodka will have to suffice. You, my daughter, you will be my crutch. Together, we will do this work for Poland!”

CHAPTER 29

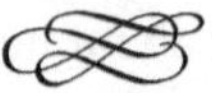

Though it was not yet dawn, the Morzinski carriage stood hitched and waiting. Krystyna was already dressed and ready to travel. She walked up to where her Hector stood harnessed in front of the other two horses. As she stroked his neck, her friend eyed her skeptically.

"I know, my pet. It has been quite a while since you pulled anything. But the day's jaunt will be good for you, stretch your legs. Besides, it's not like you will be doing much of the pulling. I'll let you in on a secret; the two closer to the carriage do the majority of the work. You will just be going along for a pleasant stroll through the countryside. You wouldn't rather be left here alone, would you?" The animal snorted as if in agreement.

"I would be worried about you if we left you behind." She enjoyed the texture of his silken coat. Though her horse had lost some weight, and his dark mane and tail were sun bleached from living in a pasture, he looked well. She was grateful they were still together. Roderyk had suggested they bring Hector along for the trip, just in case they did not or could not return to Sweet Air.

The clamor of raised voices caused her to turn back to the house. Matylda and Kaspar had been arguing since Roderyk had described his plan to them. Their alarm was understandable as it had been more than three years since the master had journeyed from Sweet Air for any reason. Eventually, though Krystyna chafed at the delay, they were loaded. By the time Kaspar took his position in the driver's seat, brilliant scarlet and orange streaks of the dawn had appeared in the sky.

Inside the carriage, the curtains were drawn against the dampness of the morning air, so Krystyna couldn't peer out of the window. She kept a close watch on Roderyk, who was energetic and alert despite the early hour. The carriage proved surprisingly comfortable; it was superbly sprung, and, initially, the road was smooth and well traveled. The gentle, rocking motion proved an irresistible soporific, and her head began to bob. She had just shaken off another such lapse when she found Roderyk's amused gaze upon her.

"My dear, you need not stay awake on my account. I am doing quite well. I wish I could sleep as easily. It does help the time to pass more quickly. But I find our mission stirs my blood. I haven't felt so alive in years."

"I intended to keep you company."

"Sleep, child. Sleep."

She dozed for about an hour. After she awoke, she and Roderyk chatted about nothing consequential until they stopped at midday to dine at an inn. As they disembarked, she was delighted to see that Roderyk, though admittedly stiff, was able to walk and didn't appear to be suffering unduly. After their repast of kielbasa sausage, potato soup and bread, they were back on the road.

A few more hours passed, then Roderyk remarked, "We should be there shortly." But by now, the trip was beginning to wear on him, and his face had grown increasingly drawn. He also started taking occasional nips from his silver flask.

Sensing his pain, Krystyna was greatly relieved when the carriage finally stopped. Peering out the window, she saw that the Beautiful Boar was a traditional Polish long building. Intricate woodwork covered the exterior, and a steep roof topped the building. Over the front door hung the Dabbinski coat of arms, which depicted a fierce boar on a white field. A few smaller outbuildings clustered about the main structure.

Suddenly, the carriage door burst open, and Krystyna fell back. A fierce, deeply lined face topped by a shiny and wholly bald scalp thrust in.

"Hey there! What do you think you're doing?" Kaspar shouted.

"Liuz, is this how you greet your master's old companion in arms?" Roderyk reprimanded in mock irritation.

"Pan Morzinski!" Liuz, the bald servant, stared in stunned amazement at Roderyk. Recovering, he stumbled back and pulled out the carriage step before Kaspar could intervene. Then, still ignoring the irate driver, he assisted both passengers out.

Standing felt wonderful, and Krystyna longed to stretch her arms up over her head. But her heart went out to Roderyk who now looked unwell. Liuz had practically lifted him from the conveyance.

"Please inform your master of my arrival," Roderyk directed from between pinched lips.

Krystyna took his arm on one side, and Kaspar took the other, disengaging Liuz, who darted inside. Together, they moved slowly toward the inn. It was real work steadying the older man's weight as his weakened hip had completely given out. Krystyna saw the sweat forming on Roderyk's upper lip. The three steps up to the door proved another challenge. Once inside, they paused for a moment. They entered a great room dominated by a massive earthenware stove on one side while the wall opposite it was covered with hunting trophies.

"Pan Morzinski!" A substantial man with a full beard and a head of white hair marched forward. He grasped Roderyk at the shoulders and kissed him on both cheeks. “What act of God brings you to my inn?”

Krystyna didn’t hear the rest of their exchange. Her attention was riveted upon a small group of men assembled at one table, on one man, in particular. Those cold blue eyes and fleshy features were unpleasantly familiar. It was Viktor Brasinski, of all the unfortunate luck, and he was staring directly at them. In a panic, like a rabbit caught in a snare, she glanced about the room for an escape route.

Roderyk squeezed her forearm. “I am not getting any younger, and it was time to see an old friend. Besides, I had to travel this way in order to take my daughter-in-law to visit her family.”

“Daughter-in-law! So, your son finally decided to marry. It’s about time. I’m a grandfather eight times over. But none of my daughter-in-laws look like this one. Andrzej has chosen well. At your service, my lady.” He bowed low before her.

“My lord brother.” Brasinski appeared at Krystyna’s side and greeted Pan Roderyk.

“Brasinski, what a surprise,” Roderyk remarked mildly.

“What brings you to the Beautiful Boor, Pan Morzinski?” Brasinski questioned.

“I was just telling my old comrade-in-arms, Kasimierz here, that I intended to take my new daughter-in-law to visit her parents. But I did not anticipate how difficult travel would be. I am afraid I allowed my new daughter’s tears and cries of homesickness to affect my judgment. Andrzej will be furious with me. We will be turning back to Sweet Air as soon as we’ve rested and refreshed ourselves. Krystyna,” Roderyk raised his hand, “I’m sorry to disappoint you, but we will not proceed any farther. It’s simply too dangerous.”

Krystyna sighed on cue. “Yes, I understand. But why don’t you wait to make your decision until you’ve rested and eaten.”

“No, my girl, my decision is final, and your tears won’t alter it. I would be remiss in my duty to Andrzej if I did not stand firm on this."

"Who could resist the entreaties of such a lovely lady?" Krystyna swallowed her revulsion as Brasinski raised her hand to his lips. "When did Andrzej make you his bride? Your nuptials had not yet been accomplished when last we met at Sweet Air. But then, I have been traveling for some time. I may have missed the blessed event."

"It was a small affair," Roderyk answered for Krystyna. "Father Ignacy presided over the service. I would have preferred a more elaborate ceremony, but times being what they are, we chose not to delay. We intend to have a suitable reception, to which you will be invited, when Andrzej returns home again."

"Dabbinski sets a splendid table," Brasinski abruptly changed the subject. "Would you and Krystyna care to join me for dinner this evening?"

"You needn't feel obligated to entertain us," Roderyk responded smoothly. "You already have companions."

"They are my personal guards. These are dangerous times, as you say. Which is why I am so surprised to see you, Pan Roderyk, away from your home."

"I am an old fool when it comes to the tears of a pretty girl."

"Aren't we all? I would welcome new faces at my table."

"Then, we accept your generous offer."

"I leave you in the capable hands of our host." He started to turn away then paused. "It has been quite a while since you last journeyed forth from Sweet Air, has it not, Pan Roderyk?"

"Yes, it has been. But my health is much improved of late."

"I am very pleased to hear it. I would be honored if, on your way back, you stopped at my home."

"Perhaps. Now, if you will excuse us… Kasimierz, will you show us to our rooms."

"Yes, Pan Roderyk. Follow me."

"Dabbinski?" Brasinski halted their progress.

"Yes, my lord?"

"We will require your finest dining chamber this evening."

"Of course. I will instruct my wife."

As they left the great room, Krystyna and Roderyk exchanged glances. Brasinski was suspicious of them.

Krystyna maintained her vigil sitting on the wooden chair in Roderyk's bedchamber. A massive bed hung with green drapings dominated the room. Idly, she wondered whether mites and lice infested the heavy cloth. Then, she dismissed the thought. Kasimierz's wife maintained an immaculate inn. Roderyk reclined on top of the bed coverings, his bad leg propped up on pillows. A gentle breeze came in through the opened window.

She was concerned about Andrzej's father. His complexion was waxy and pale. The day of traveling had worn him out far more than she had originally suspected. But he had persevered through to the conclusion of his task. Once they were alone with Kasimierz, he had explained the true reason for his visit and passed on the boy messenger's leather case.

Kasimierz clearly knew how to proceed. Since the innkeeper had departed with the leather purse secreted on his person, Roderyk diligently applied himself to his flask. By late afternoon, he was sleeping, albeit fitfully. Krystyna didn't blame him for his indulgence. He was obviously in extreme pain. And as the afternoon sunlight faded into a golden twilight, she stayed with him.

She started at a knock on the door. A robust woman with blond hair gone gray popped her head in. She smiled pleasantly, revealing a gap between her front teeth. "Here you are. Panienka, I am Gertruda Dabbinska. Your supper will soon be ready. If you'd like, I can help you dress."

"Thank you. That won't be necessary." Roderyk had proven

wise in his insistence that she bring along some gowns. At the time, it had seemed rather silly, as they'd planned on being gone only one day and returning home on the next. Now, she was grateful for his counsel. It would have looked suspicious if she'd had no garments with her after they informed Brasinski that their intention was to visit her family.

Gertruda took a step into the room, her eyes upon Roderyk. "The trip here was too much for him," she observed.

"I don't want to wake him, even to eat."

"I wouldn't. He needs his rest. I'll send a meal up to him later. Let him sleep for as long as he can."

"But we are to dine with Brasinski."

"Don't worry about Pan Morzinski. I'll tend to him myself. It's an old injury that bothers him, correct?"

"His hip, yes, and a cough. I hope he doesn't worsen because of this trip. It was wrong of me to ask this of him, but he has been so much better lately. And he was so determined to come."

"Don't blame yourself, Panienka. You couldn't have dissuaded him from this mission. From what Kasimierz told me, Pan Morzinski was pleased and proud to have helped the Polish cause. He needs a good rest, and he'll be himself again tomorrow. My Kasimierz swears by a salve I make. It works wonders on stiff muscles. While you're at supper, I'll attend to his leg. Afterwards, I'll sit here, right beside him, and work on my embroidery."

"I don't know if I should leave him." In addition to her worry about her father-in-law, Krystyna was deeply troubled about dining alone with Brasinski. There was something disquieting about him, and he obviously had more than a polite interest in their activities. But declining his invitation at this late hour could prove damning.

"Pan Brasinski is expecting you, what shall I tell him?"

"Tell him… Tell him I'll be down shortly."

~

Half an hour later, a servant girl showed Krystyna into a private dining chamber where Brasinski already awaited her. The room was well appointed, and the table was formally set, adorned with silver candelabra and a damask tablecloth. The cutlery was also fine silver, and the place settings were of porcelain.

Krystyna took a deep breath when Brasinski's oddly opaque eyes rested upon her. She forced herself not to cringe when he took her hand and pressed an almost indecently intimate kiss onto the back of it. Resisting the urge to jerk away from him, she allowed him to take her arm and guide her to a chair.

As he seated her, he whispered, "You are a vision, my lady. How I envy Andrzej."

"You are too kind. Were you informed that my father-in-law will not be joining us?"

"It is unfortunate but completely understandable. Pan Roderyk shouldn't have stressed himself so. And while I do enjoy his company, the idea of dining alone with a beautiful woman is immensely more appealing."

Determinedly, she plastered a smile on her face. "Again, you are too considerate."

"It gives me pleasure to hear you say that." Brasinski took the seat opposite her. "This wine is quite delightful. Would you care for some?"

"Yes, thank you."

Servants began entering the dining room, filling the center of the table with an assortment of hot and cold dishes.

Despite her distaste for her dining companion, Krystyna was hungry. She consumed the delicious food with real enthusiasm. Brasinski also applyed himself diligently to the meal. And so, for a while, conversation was sparse and relatively mundane. When she'd eaten her full, she sat back in her chair. "What business brings you to the Beautiful Boar, Pan Brasinski?" she asked. "I understand most of your lands are south and east of here."

"That's true, but I do have some dower property two day's ride north of my estate. On trips there, I always make a point of stopping here since the food is exceptional. I have attempted to entice Dabbinski and his wife into my service. But he is one of those proud and foolish souls who would rather serve many masters than just one."

"I can understand why he wouldn't want to leave this place. His inn is quite splendid."

"Yes, Dabbinski does ensure his guests a certain level of comfort, and the inn seems prosperous enough. But frankly, I worry for him."

"Why?"

"In times such as these, it's not wise to stand alone. At any moment, a band of unruly ruffians or soldiers, for that matter, could descend upon this place and destroy or carry away all he possesses."

She met his glance. "Such a tragic occurrence could befall any of us."

"True." He raised his wine glass and contemplatively studied her. "Which is why it is even more critical that one associate with the right people. So, let us love one another." The true meaning of this traditional Polish toast was lost in the suggestive manner with which he spoke the words.

Thinking of Andrzej and Roderyk, Krystyna raised her glass and took a sip, though she longed to throw its contents in his face. "In your opinion, who are the right people?"

"You are direct. I admire that in a woman. It is so rare. Very well, I shall speak frankly. The Russians are our natural allies."

"But what do such matters have to do with Dabbinski and his inn?"

"I suspect his loyalties lie elsewhere. He is a patriotic fool. It will not go well for him in the future when Russia and her allies determine the fate of Poland."

"But you are Polish. Doesn't it anger you that the Russians, Prussians and Austrians are like wild dogs waiting to tear apart our homeland?"

"You have spent too much time listening to old Roderyk. Polish days of glory are a distant memory. Russian forces led by that genius Suvorv stand poised to crush what's left of the Polish armies. Soon, this whole episode will be at an end, and the proper order will be established. We Poles have made a terrible mess of ruling ourselves. But I'm not willing to waste an evening alone with an enchantress discussing politics. That is more Andrzej's style, is it not?"

She didn't respond to the barb. Instead, she nodded to the servant who had come to take more plates away.

"So tell me now, what is the true reason my esteemed neighbor has taken to the roads? And without protection."

As she'd suspected, the purpose of the meal was to elicit information from her. "It was a completely impulsive decision. I begged to visit my family. It's been so long since I've seen them. I'm afraid I grew quite tiresome about it, until Pan Morzinski agreed. We thought that by traveling lighter, we would attract less attention. We clearly misjudged the safety of the undertaking."

"I recall you met young Andrzej in Vienna. And yet, it took more than two years for you to accomplish your marriage."

"Yes, but it all turned out well in the end. I couldn't be happier."

"A love match. How unusual. But clearly, Pan Roderyk is well pleased with his son's choice. It must have been difficult for your mother to miss her only daughter's wedding."

"She couldn't travel. My father was unwell."

Ignoring her words, Brasinski continued on: "After our first meeting, I puzzled over you. You were an enigma to me. You're not at all the typical virgin bride, and your sudden appearance at Sweet Air was surprising and unexpected."

Krystyna fought the waves of panic that rose within her. She forced herself to stay seated.

"You must try the venison," Brasinski suggested calmly as he stabbed a sizeable piece with his fork and added it to the remains of pierogi and cabbage already on his own plate. "The sauce is exceptional. In time, I discovered we shared a mutual acquaintance." He took another forkful of food and chewed it slowly, enjoying her discomfort.

"And who would that be?" Krystyna raised her wine glass and took a sip. Her hand trembled slightly, so she set it down.

"This acquaintance of mine told an interesting story. You were engaged once before, were you not?"

"Just what are you asking, Pan Brasinski? What is the point of all of this?" She waved her hand to encompass the meal and the rich dining accoutrements. "What game are we playing?"

Brasinski laughed. "You are a bold one. I admire that about you. I will be equally candid. I know you murdered your former lover. That you, Pani Morzinska were formerly known as Krystyna Sielska."

Her stomach sank. She hadn't anticipated this. Brasinski had expressed an inappropriate interest in her in the past, but never would she have guessed that he would assemble the full story of the past two years of her life. "My maiden name was Janicka. Who told you this nonsense?"

He laughed softly. "The game is up. I know everything. You have no secrets from me. I'm telling you this now because it will be up to you to share it with Morzinski, so that you both can make decisions that are in your best interests. I've had Sweet Air under observation for months now. I've long suspected Pan Morzinski was involved in intelligence communications. This sudden trip only confirmed my suspicions. As for you, my dear, I had you thoroughly checked as well. It was a relatively simple matter collecting information on your life in Vienna. My encounter with my Russian friend was sheer luck or, perhaps, fate. After all, we were both on the trail of the same woman, you. The name, Janicka or Sielska, mattered little. Your appearance is striking, and the time of your visit to Vienna corresponded exactly with that of the woman he sought. It didn't take much in the way of deduction to ascertain that you are, in fact, Krystyna Sielska. Once we realized our common interest, my friend was more than eager to share his story."

"What is his name?"

"I believe you know of him as Janus."

She felt physically ill.

"Now, you must see you are completely at my mercy."

"What is it you want?"

"I want what every man wants. Power, wealth, status." He extended his hands out before him, palms up, as if waiting for them to be filled. Then, he clenched one into a fist. "Poland will soon cease to exist, and I will be on the winning side. I stand to gain a great deal. I intend Sweet Air to be among my rewards."

"Sweet Air belongs to Pan Roderyk and to Andrzej after him."

"The Czarina will have little time for them when all of this is over. Your father-in-law and your husband will lose everything."

"You're supposed to be their friend!"

"To the victor go the spoils."

"Why are you telling me all of this?"

"Why you can assist me, my sweet. If I were to marry the widow of the heir to Sweet Air, it would lend my claim legitimacy."

Krystyna rose to her feet so abruptly her chair fell backwards and crashed to the floor. "I will not sit here and listen to this. Andrzej is alive!"

"A minor detail to which I doubt I shall even have to attend. Remember there is a war going on, and the rebels are greatly outnumbered. Your Andrzej is the heroic sort—he is not likely to survive." Brasinski sipped his wine, a smug expression on his face. "Consider the matter, my dear. Without my protection, you will never be safe at Sweet Air. I need only contact our mutual friend, and your days will be numbered. I would even consider allowing the old man to live out his days there. It would be such a tidy conclusion."

"I will not betray my husband. You sicken me. Pan Roderyk will never allow Sweet Air to fall into your hands." Throwing her napkin to the table, she exited the room and rushed back up the stairs to Pan Roderyk's chamber. She nodded abruptly to Gertruda, who rose from her seat with some needlework in her hands.

"Are you finished already? Was there something wrong with the meal, my lady?"

"No, it was fine. It was the company that was lacking. I'll stay with him now."

Gertruda nodded and, after gathering up her things, left the room.

Krystyna was enraged. She wanted to do something, pace the room, shout her frustration, anything. But most of all, she wanted to speak with Roderyk. She stood at the foot of the bed studying his drawn and pale face. He snored lightly. But he needed his rest, particularly in light of all that she had to tell him during their trip home.

CHAPTER 30

As they prepared for their return to Sweet Air, Krystyna was irritable and nervous. Roderyk, though stiff, was much improved after his full night's sleep. Kasimierz and his wife were both on hand to bid them farewell. Viktor Brasinski also made an appearance. He was courteous as they took their leave, but Krystyna despised and feared his air of arrogant self-satisfaction.

Once safely ensconced in the privacy of the carriage, she found she had no idea how to tell this man who had welcomed her into his home and his family that both were in peril. Finally, she could procrastinate no longer.

"Pan Roderyk, during my dinner with Brasinski…"

"I must apologize for being indisposed last night," Roderyk inserted. "It can't have been a pleasant evening for you in Viktor's company. The man is insufferable."

"I concur, but I also learned that… I have to warn you," she hesitated again.

"Proceed."

She related all that had come out the previous night, holding nothing back even to protect herself. When she started to recount what exactly had precipitated her flight from Vienna, he stopped her. "Krystyna, there's no need to explain. I already know the story in its entirety." He reached over and patted her hand. "I made a point of looking closely into your past when my son rather forcefully explained his intentions with respect to you. I have corresponded with several people about you, including your parents, your great-aunt and General von Zetl. Their information only enhanced the impression I had already formed that you are a passionate young woman of strong character. I am proud you are Andrzej's wife. Indeed, I could not have chosen better for him, myself. As far as this business with Brasinski, I believe he is being overly optimistic. We are not without recourse." Reflecting on the matter, Roderyk held his hands fingertip to fingertip, so that his signet ring occasionally flashed in the light admitted by the moving curtain. For a few minutes, he didn't speak. Finally, he announced, "We shall do nothing."

"What? But we must do something!"

"No, right now there is nothing to be done. This is a time of war. Anything could happen, even to Brasinski or this Janus. We must await Andrzej's return. I'm not yet willing to abandon Sweet Air, nor do I imagine you would consider simply leaving and risk the possibility of extending your separation from my son. We are in God's hands."

"But I can't place you or Sweet Air at further risk."

"Don't assume responsibility for the rest of us. Brasinski has long coveted my land. Sweet Air may or may not remain my own. I love my people, but the time may come when I can no longer guide and protect them. What matters to me most in the world is my son and you, my new daughter. I am an old man who would die happy even if everything else were lost to me as long as you two were safe and together. Land and wealth can only be held in this life. Love and family are what matters. Trust me. This is the only way. We must wait."

Krystyna nodded slowly, the sense of his words gradually becoming clear. “So it will be then, dear sir.”

~

For Krystyna, the days and weeks that followed their trip to the Beautiful Boar were nerve wracking. The estate was very quiet now that only women, children and old men remained. Thankfully, her days were busy with keeping the household going and representing Roderyk about the estate.

Occasionally, they did get news, little of which was promising. Reports came of a great battle near the town of Szczekociny. Kosciuszko and the Polish forces were decisively beaten. The situation was becoming progressively more hopeless. The Prussians took Cracow. The Russians captured Wilno. Defeat followed defeat for the Poles. When Kosciuszko was wounded and taken prisoner, it was clear that the Polish defense was effectively over.

Still, no word came from Andrzej. Krystyna worried about him, dreamed of him, prayed ceaselessly to the Virgin Mother to keep him alive and well. As for Brasinski and Janus, she put them out of her mind. There were too many other, more immediate matters about which to agonize. Battle-crazed Russians roamed a countryside bereft of men to defend it. They heard news that Suvorov, a Russian commander, felt no compulsion to protect the civilian population from his men. More than once, Krystyna, Roderyk and Matylda hid in the secret room, waiting for Russian troops to pass by. Hours later, they would emerge, often to find the house in chaos, many priceless items stolen or smashed. But they dared not leave the comparative safety of the manor. They would be easy targets on the road, and the hardships of traveling would likely be the death of Roderyk, whose health was again in decline.

One evening, Krystyna was in her bedroom reading when she

heard shouting from somewhere downstairs. She rushed out to the top of the stairs. "What is it, Matylda?"

"The Russians! They're coming! We must hide! Hurry, my lady!"

"Pan Roderyk? Where is he?"

"He's safe. Kaspar has already taken him through the library."

Krystyna flew down the stairs. Then, the two women ran to the library, through the hidden doorway in the bookshelf, and down into the subterranean passages. As always, these corridors remained cool, dark and unnervingly quiet. Both were out of breath by the time they arrived at the dimly lit chamber where the master of Sweet Air awaited them. He greeted them with a nod.

"Kaspar?" Krystyna asked.

"Gone to his family."

The two women settled in quickly. Over the past few weeks, during which time they'd had several such scares, they'd stocked their hiding place with a few days' worth of food, candles, furniture and an abundance of blankets. The October nights were already quite chilly, and they dared not light a fire.

They were also fearful of speaking. All of them listened carefully, trying to hear any evidence that their worst fears had been realized or that Kaspar had returned and they could now go back into the house. They passed the time as best they could with card games and chess. Matylda knitted by the barely sufficient candlelight. In order to conserve their candle supply, they often sat in complete darkness. During those times, Krystyna sought to sleep, but remained restive. Her mind spun in endless, anxiety-filled circles. *Are the Russians in the house? And if so, what are they doing? How long will we have to stay hidden this time? Will the Russians set fire to the house?* This thought caused her the most concern. For how would she know before it was too late? And how could she get

Roderyk safely out? Terror smelled like a tangible essence in the air.

Eventually, she managed to doze off. When she awoke hours later, the light of a single candle still penetrated the enveloping darkness. Roderyk remained asleep while Matylda was awake and munching on some bread and cheese. Mutely, Matylda tore a hunk from her loaf and held it out to her. Nodding her thanks, Krystyna consumed several mouthfuls though she wasn't hungry.

"How long have we been down here?" Krystyna whispered.

"What?"

"How long?"

The older woman shrugged. "Hours." Then, she pointed to the table opposite her.

Krystyna glanced at the indicated spot and was horrified to see only one of the four bottles in which they stored drinking water had any left in it, and it was less than half filled. They'd obviously forgotten to refill them. For a moment, she fought a surge of nausea. None of them could survive without water for even a short period of time. Pan Roderyk, in particular, wasn't in any condition to cope with deprivation.

"I'll go," Matylda stated flatly.

Krystyna understood immediately what she meant. Someone had to go for water. "I will."

Matylda shook her head. "No, you stay with Pan Morzinski. I know the way better."

"Perhaps we should wait a while longer."

"I don't think anyone's up there. I haven't heard a sound." Then, taking a bottle in each hand, she disappeared down the darkened corridor.

In her mind's eye, Krystyna followed Matylda down the passage, out the maze door and into the crisp freshness of the out-of-doors.

Endless minutes passed, then half an hour. Finally, when she believed that she couldn't bear it any longer, she heard footsteps coming down the hall. A quick peek reassured her Matylda had returned. Krystyna grasped the filled bottles from her.

Matylda was flushed and out of breath. "The Russians," she panted. "They're everywhere."

They remained concealed for the next two days. On the third day, they again ran low on water. They waited until nightfall, and then Matylda headed out once more. Krystyna wanted to go in her place, but Roderyk had developed a hacking cough and a high fever, and she was loath to leave him even for a short while. In addition, Matylda was eager to leave their sanctuary that was beginning to feel more like a prison.

Together, Roderyk and Krystyna awaited the housekeeper's return. Unmindful of the hour, or perhaps because the unrelenting darkness in which they hid permitted no sense of time, they played three games of chess all the way through. And still, Matylda didn't return. While both of them stared at the game board, they strained to hear the expected footsteps. Then, they tried unsuccessfully to sleep. By the morning, Krystyna feared the worst. *Has Matylda been captured? Or has she deserted us to rejoin her own family?* She hoped the second was the case.

Again, they waited for nightfall. Now Krystyna would have to get water for the two of them. There was no way around it. So, despite her father-in-law's anguished protests, she pulled on a cloak, gripped the two remaining empty bottles by their necks and made her way down the long, pitch black corridor.

She hadn't dared take one from their rapidly dwindling supply of candles as she worried that even a flicker of light moving through the forest might betray her. Her footsteps echoed loudly, and she fancied she could hear her own heart pounding in her chest. Resolutely, she quelled her fears. She had to bring back water, or Roderyk would likely die.

She felt her way along chilly, damp walls to where that familiar door led out into the hedge maze. There was a sliver of light down along the bottom edge of the door. Cautiously, she opened it and stepped out. Despite her apprehensions, she thrilled with the freedom and freshness of the out-of-doors. The frost tipped hedges glistened where moonbeams touched them. Clinging to the shadows, she made her way through the maze then studied the large, silver-bright, open area which lay between where she stood and the woods. Glancing back at the manor house behind her, she saw to her horror that several windows glowed golden with light. But there was nothing that could be done for it. Firming her grip on the bottles, she dashed for the safety of the trees. After endless terrifying moments, she made it. Now, she slowed to a walk, her heart still hammering wildly. Here, she hesitated, struggling to recall where exactly she was and how far from the brook. Her memory proved faithful, and it was only a short while before she heard the babbling of water over rocks. With great relief, she kneeled down, and icy water slid over the top of one boot as she filled first one and then the other bottle.

As she made her way back, the chill night air punished her cold, wet hands, but she trudged forward with determination. One more step than another. She repeated the litany in her mind. Finally, she again stood on the edge of the clearing. Her earlier exultation on being outside had transformed into an anxious desire to return to the secret room and Pan Roderyk.

Again, and despite her burden, she made it safely across the open area. She was on one side of the hedge, about to make the turn that would bring her to the vine covered door in the wall, when she heard the low murmur of male voices. Cowering in the shadows cast by the hedge, she set the bottles on the ground. Despite the panic surging through her, she listened. Two men spoke in Russian, and they were only one section of hedge further in from where she stood. Krystyna hadn't heard Russian in several years, but she'd been fluent once, so she understood what was being said.

"The woman is gone. It makes no sense to stay out here in this cold."

"I agree. The old man swore he's been alone for days. It's obvious why he didn't leave, he's too sick."

"There's no point in freezing our asses off out here."

"I would rather be out here than in there. The count was furious when we found the old man alone."

She swallowed a sob. Roderyk had lied to protect her, and in doing so had given her the possibility of escape. Though the thought of leaving him devastated her, she knew remaining would render his efforts meaningless.

Nudging the bottles under the hedge, she picked up her skirts and ran as silently as she could. To her amazement, she again made it into the woods.

This time, her destination was a good distance away. And so, she alternated between jogging and briskly walking along the shadowed paths. Her footsteps sounded loud. She vigilantly scanned the ground ahead, terrified of treading on a branch that might snap and reveal her. There was time enough, she reassured herself. The Russians had no idea she was out here. Roderyk would never reveal the truth. She sent up a heart-felt prayer that they wouldn't torture the elderly gentleman. Despite his frailty and his current illness, he would revel in defying his captors.

Following a narrow deer trail, which Kaspar had shown her weeks ago, after half an hour of steady quick striding, she arrived at the isolated barn and pasture where they'd hidden the three remaining horses. In the brightness of the moonlight, the small clearing was nearly as bright as day. She inhaled a slow and shaky breath as she looked at the cottage where she and Andrzej had passed blissful hours in their brief time together as husband and wife.

But where were the horses? All of the doors on the small

barn were open, and they let out into the large field whose fence posts meandered through the trees. Whistling low, she peered about and listened closely, but there was no sign of the horses. She fought the surge of panic that coursed through her. What if someone had discovered them? What if Hector had been stolen? These were desperate times, and people were on the move. Had some passersby stumbled upon the animals?

She weighed her options; it was unlikely she could escape on foot. If the Russians didn't capture her, she stood little chance against any cutthroat she encountered on the road. She whistled again. The silence was deafening. Then, a shrill whinny obliterated it. Added to the sound of pounding hooves, she caught the flash of a white star and stockings moving among the trees. Hector snorted as he cantered straight up to her, his head and tail held proudly aloft. He arched his neck as he blew into her outstretched palm. As tears of relief slid down her cheeks, she rumpled his long mane affectionately. He nosed in her skirts, looking for a treat.

"You scared me, old man. Sorry, no treats today," she mumbled hoarsely.

At that moment, the other two horses charged up. There was no need to chase them away, as Hector immediately swung his haunches in their direction. His pinned back ears gave a clear warning. Krystyna grasped a handful of his mane and led her horse to the small barn. The other two animals tagged along behind.

"We're going on a trip, Hector."

The familiar horsy smells and sounds soothed her. Her plight wasn't impossible. She might be able to get away. Then, she would find Andrzej and, together, they could come back for Pan Roderyk.

She resisted the urge to swing up onto Hector's wide, bare back. She was a more than competent saddle-less rider, but she feared that a bareback-riding woman would draw too much attention. Besides, after a few hours of riding, she would be grateful for the comfort and support offered by a saddle.

Hector obediently followed his mistress into the darkness of the barn. The place smelt of mice, musty wood shavings, dried urine and horse manure. Clearly, the horses had been taking cover under its roof. She glanced into each of the opened stalls. In the third stall, the one with a closed door, she could make out a covered mound in the far corner. There, she flipped back a dusty horse blanket to reveal saddles, her own and two others, and bridles as well. The leather was stiff from lack of care, but she made quick work of throwing it onto her waiting horse.

Then, she led him out of the barn and out through the gate. The other two animals milled about anxiously as she drew it closed in front of them. One of them whinnied. Immediately, Hector added his call. Krystyna whispered gently to her horse, “Shh. You’re safe. I’ll be with you.”

But herd instinct proved too powerful to ignore. Hector trumpeted loudly to his field mates. Muttering under her breath, she mounted up. She tucked her skirts securely about each thigh and nudged her gelding into a walk. The other horses continued to call, but now Hector was all business. As they wove their way through the trees, she began to feel better. She’d just lost sight of the barn through the trees when she heard a snort from somewhere ahead. A tall, dark mounted figure suddenly emerged in front of her. She spun Hector about, looking desperately for an escape route. But she was already surrounded; she caught flashing glimpses of more horses and riders moving through the trees. She was trapped.

One rider rode directly up to her. To her amazement, it was Victor Brasinski. His grin was a sinisterly bright rictus in the moonlight. “My dear Krystyna, how convenient to find you already mounted. We’ve been looking for you.”

Another rider plunged toward them in a reckless gallop. He sawed his horse back to a rearing and plunging stand still.

Krystyna couldn't repress her shudder when she recognized the sallow, pitted skin and the livid, dark eyes. "You are Janus." It was a statement, not a question. Why hadn't she thought of him? It was so obvious, and yet she'd never even suspected. The two half-brothers hadn't seemed close during Grigori Bestuzhev's short visit to her parent's estate, and he hadn't presented himself as a count then.

"You've not forgotten me nor I you," Grigori, Ivan's older brother, spoke to her in Russian. "You led me on quite a chase, but the game is up. I've won at last."

Paralyzed, she watched as he pointed his pistol directly at her heart.

CHAPTER 31

She braced for the impact of the bullet, having recognized the savage resolution on the fleshy, bearded face.

"Grigori," Brasinski shouted. "Stop! Remember the plan." Bestuzhev didn't lower his arm.

"We need her alive, Grigori," Brasinski coaxed. "At least for the time being. She will be yours to do with as you choose once we get to Moscow."

"Three years," the Russian growled. "For three years, I've been searching for this whore. She must pay."

"And she will, my friend. But remember how much more you stand to gain if we keep her alive for a short while longer. Think of your brother. Let's keep to our plan."

Slowly, ever so reluctantly, the rigid arm began to lower, though Bestuzhev's eyes remained fixed on his prey.

Brasinski dismounted, disrupting the profound tension of the moment. "Your hands, Krystyna." He spoke to her in Polish as he withdrew rope from his saddlebag, and, tossing the reins of his horse to one of his men, approached her.

"How did you find me?" She ignored his deliberate and disrespectful use of her first name.

"Your housekeeper, Matylda. At first, she wasn't cooperative at all. It took some time and effort to convince her, but she finally broke down."

Her stomach tightened at the thought of Matylda being tortured. "Is she alive?"

"I left her so," Brasinski responded casually as he drew the ropes tight about her wrists. She refused to flinch. "But then again," he continued, "I gave her over into the care of some mercenaries. I cannot speak for their handling of her. Draw your skirts up on this side. I intend to secure your leg."

"Did you… Is Pan Morzinski…"

"Are you asking me if I killed him?" Brasinski's tone was conversational. "No, I saw no need for that unpleasantness. Roderyk is not long for this world."

Though she feared he was correct in his assessment of the older man's health, at least he hadn't been murdered. Then, despair swept through her. Would she ever see him or Andrzej again? "So now you've come to kill me."

He laughed. "We shall see. However, it is my desire that you accompany me on a trip to Russia."

She ignored the familiar way in which he rested one hand on her thigh after tying her calf to the girth. "Why do you want to take me to Russia?"

"I was under the impression that you enjoyed traveling. After all, you spent two years with those gypsies."

"I'm a married woman. I must await my husband's return here."

"You are referring to your union with the reckless, young Morzinski? In all likelihood, the happy bridegroom is dead. So many braves Poles have died in these final days of the uprising. You might be interested in knowing that our king, Poniatowski, has preceded us to Moscow in order to surrender." He finished working on her bonds. Then, holding fast to Hector's reins and to the rope binding her hands, he remounted.

"Andrzej is alive."

"Don't be tiresome. I would also advise you to keep a civil tongue. Unless you would prefer that I give you over to Bestuzhev's tender mercies? I thought not." With that, Brasinski nudged his own horse forward, leading Hector behind him. As they wove through the trees, Bestuzhev took a position at her side. She refused to look his way.

But the Russian count wouldn't allow her to ignore him. He spoke to her in his deep, gravelly voice: "For years now, I have dreamed of this day. I have tried to imagine your face, but often could not, even though I had your image. You are still beautiful, as you were when you seduced Ivan. I will destroy your witch's face, your siren's body then you will die painfully, punished for your crimes."

In astonishment at his words and tone, she glanced over and met his eyes. As she stared into them, she realized that he was mad, completely and irrevocably so.

"Through you, I will acquire all that my brother was cheated of."

"How was Ivan cheated?" She hadn't meant to speak.

"Your inheritance. With the death of Ivan's widow, everything that is yours will come to me." Oddly, it seemed as if he was repeating a lesson he'd been taught.

"But I am not Ivan's widow. I'm married to Andrzej Morzinski." He didn't seem to hear her.

For a moment, Krystyna considered what she'd heard. Then, the plot became clear to her. Brasinski and Bestuzhev were seeking to steal her parents' and the Morzinskis' land by using her as a pawn. Now that Poland was to be divided among the conquering nations, there was sure to be far less circumspection with respect to land ownership. She imagined Empress Catherine would be more than willing to reward those loyal to her with

Polish land, particularly land to which they could already lay claim. "If you want my inheritance, I could disappear. You can have everything you want without having my blood on your hands."

He shook his head slowly, never looking away from her. "You will not rob me of what I've waited for these years."

"Andrzej will come after me."

"You dare to threaten me?"

"He will, of that I'm sure, and then there will be no escape for you or Brasinski. Give me my freedom now and keep your life."

"Bitch, you will not trick me as you did Ivan!" he exploded. Before Krystyna could duck out of the way or even guess his intent, he backhanded her savagely across the mouth. She tasted warm, salty blood, and her head rang with the blow.

"Grigori!" Brasinski's shout pierced the gray mist that suffused her vision. "You must wait. Remember, we spoke of this. We need her in decent condition when we get to Moscow. Afterwards, she's yours to do with as you please. Krystyna, I would suggest that you stop antagonizing him. As you can see, he bears some hostility toward you."

Ignoring the other man, Bestuzhev thrust his hand into her hair then brutally jerked her head back. Tears filled her eyes.

"Enough, Grigori!" Brasinski ordered.

Bestuzhev slowly released his excruciating grip on her then glared at his Polish associate. "Understand, Brasinski, you are not my master. I will not kill her now, because I choose not to. I want her to anticipate how I shall do it, how she will suffer."

"Yes, Grigori. All in good time. You are being wise in this." Brasinski appeared flustered even as he sought to soothe his comrade. Bestuzhev kicked his spurs into his steed's sides and rode to the front of the troop, leaving Krystyna trailing Brasinski.

As they moved through the trees, she pressed her sleeve to her lips to stop the bleeding. Soon, she caught the rich, fragrant aroma of burning wood. Then, great gray phantasms of smoke danced through the trees, lending the woods an unearthly quality. Each breath she took grew more acrid, and when they emerged from the forest, she could not hold back her visceral cry of pain and horror at the scene before her. "No-o!" Roderyk's magnificent wooden manor house was on fire. Without a thought, she kicked at her horse's sides to go to the house.

Brasinski jerked the reins, holding her back. "I've no use for the house, just the land."

"Is Roderyk still in there? Did you leave him in there? My God." She could barely speak so overwhelmed was she by the tragedy before her. Pure rage rose up within her. "You think you've won today, Brasinski. But it's not over yet. You will reap what you've sown here. Maybe not in this life, but you will burn in hell in the next."

The expression in those pale blue eyes shifted from sardonic and satisfied to dangerously cold and shuttered. "Hold your tongue, woman! Remember, I'm all that stands between you and Bestuzhev."

They rode on. Until it was hidden from view, Krystyna stared back at the pyre where once Andrzej's home stood. Before her eyes, Sweet Air, like her dreams for their life together, was disappearing into ash and soot.

CHAPTER 32

After leaving Sweet Air, they rode east. The long, miserable day finally ended long after nightfall when they stopped at a derelict, out of-the-way inn where Krystyna forced some stale bread and greasy stew down her throat. Though physically and emotionally drained, she knew it was up to her to survive. And she intended to live. Afterwards, Brasinski brought her up the stairs into a small, dingy chamber where a puny fire struggled in the hearth.

She glanced about looking for a weapon.

Brasinski laughed, clearly guessing her intent. "You will sleep undisturbed until we reach Russia. I don't believe you would survive a night with Grigori, and he would take it amiss were I to sample you first. He's not a man whom I wish to cross…yet. Lock you door, for your own protection, and don't even think of trying to escape. A guard will be posted outside your room throughout the night."

This proved the pattern for the following days, each of which took her farther away from Andrzej and brought her death sentence ever closer. She was always alert for the opportunity to flee, but there never was one. Brasinski and his men ensured she was never allowed real privacy, even for a moment. As for Bestuzhev, he didn't speak directly to her again, but she was always aware of his malevolent presence, of the way he watched her, with a bestial intensity. Brasinski, on the other hand, spoke with her regularly. One morning, as Krystyna broke her fast with rye bread and cheese, he sat down on the bench next to her.

"You should be pleased to learn that tonight we will stop at a town of some size. It offers much more civilized accommodations than those in which we have lodged of late. We are near Russia now, but I will rely on you to maintain your current level of exemplary behavior." He looked her over, taking in her ragged and soiled dress. She hadn't bathed or changed her garments since that long ago day when she'd first gone into hiding with Matylda and Roderyk. "Perhaps I could be prevailed upon to secure more becoming apparel for you."

"Don't go to any trouble on my behalf. My appearance is of little interest to me."

"But it is of interest to me. I would have my future wife appear at her greatest advantage."

"Your wife!" Krystyna choked and sputtered on the water she was drinking.

"Did I fail to mention it before? We are to be married as soon as we arrive in Moscow. As Andrzej's widow, you are also Roderyk's heir. In this way, I will obtain Sweet Air."

She swallowed hard. "And what of Bestuzhev? Is he agreeable to these plans? You know he intends to kill me."

Brasinski glanced around, as if to make sure neither Bestuzhev nor his men could overhear their conversation. "Krystyna, this need not end as Grigori desires. Perhaps I could be coerced into…"

She cut him off. "You won't get away with this."

"I assure you we will. The difficult part, capturing you and spiriting you to the border, is almost accomplished."

"But you don't need me to achieve your ends. Documents

can be forged. Witnesses bribed. You'll already be doing both. Just let me go."

"No, I'm afraid that is not a possibility. My advice to you is to make to make the best of your situation."

She was uncomfortably aware of the heat of his gaze. He took her hand and raised it to his lips. "Perhaps this evening, after you've bathed and changed, you will be more receptive to this discussion."

"I'm already married," she muttered through clenched teeth. "Andrzej will come after me."

"Your current husband is either dead or imprisoned. Prepare yourself, woman. Soon we will be in Russia, where you will become my wife."

CHAPTER 33

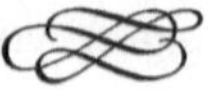

The solitary man mounted his exhausted steed. As he settled stiffly in the saddle, his horse turned its head around to sniff at his boot.

"Only a little way farther, Leo. We should get there before dark."

Suddenly, the gelding raised his head high, his ears pricked forward.

"Easy. What is it? What's wrong?"

There was a bark, followed by a long, keening howl. The rider knew there were wolves in the region. The recent chaos ensured that, of late, the wolves rarely went hungry. Apprehensively, he drew his pistol. He had no intention of being brought down in this deserted clearing. He pressed his heels into his horse's sides, and they advanced cautiously through the trees. There was another ululating howl. Strange, it was still daylight, though evening approached. He suspected that the times had liberated the wolves from their customary nocturnal schedule. In these days, there was no reason for any predator to be surreptitious.

His horse jigged nervously beneath him. There was a distinct rustling in the trees ahead. His pulse quickened. How many of them could there be? He cocked his pistol. He'd not come this far to die less than a two hours' ride from his destination.

A brown and gray shape exploded through the trees. It seemed to leap straight at him, a flying nightmare of long limbs, teeth and a wide grinning red mouth. He tried to take aim at the beast but couldn't manage to do so. Leo leapt about, kicking frantically. All the while, the wolf continued to jump up and bark. As he struggled to get his horse back under control, the rider saw that this was no ordinary wolf, but one that was half dog and, thankfully, familiar.

"Peter? Is that you, Peter?" At the sound of his name, the dog wagged his tail enthusiastically and sank down on his haunches before leaping up again.

Dragging back on the reins, Sebastjan managed to muscle his horse to a standstill. He slid from the saddle. Peter, Andrzej's pet, jumped up and thrust his paws straight at his chest, nearly knocking him down. Laughing and smiling, he hugged the great dog to him.

With his tail wagging, Peter licked his face. Finally, perceiving that the dog was no threat, the horse began to calm.

"You recognize me, Peter. I know, I know. I'm happy to see you, too. You're so thin! What are you doing out here in the middle of nowhere? Gone wild have you? I took you for a wolf." His fingers grew still as he stroked through the thick fur at the dog's neck. Peter would never desert his master. Was Andrzej dead? In the next instant, an unworthy thought entered his mind; if his rival was gone then Krystyna was free, free to be with him. Immediately, horribly ashamed of himself, he cast the notion from his mind.

"What shall we do now, Peter? I was heading to Sweet Air… Peter, come back here. Peter. Peter!" Suddenly, the dog charged off into the foliage. Hurriedly, trying to keep his eyes fixed on the gray-brown shape, Sebastjan remounted. Accommodatingly,

Peter paused, wagged his tail and loped off once more. Sebastjan urged his resistant steed into a trot. He ducked branches and tried not to worry about his horse stepping into a pothole. The dog glanced back at him again. Sebastjan kicked Leo into a canter as the trees began to thin. If Peter would just slow down…

He was jerked from his saddle and thrown to the ground. Wholly unprepared and gasping for air, he fought wildly against the giant, bearded ruffian who attacked him. As he grappled with the much stronger man, his spirit cried out against this twist of fate. He'd ridden so far, through more horrible conditions than he could ever have imagined, to lose his life now to some common cutthroat.

"DeSzinay! Is that you? What the hell are you doing here? Sebastjan? Be still! It is I, Morzinski!"

Sebastjan went limp. He stared at the man straddling him. Could it be? This creature from some child's nightmare was gaunt and dressed in rags. A thick, dark beard obscured his facial features. But the eyes were familiar, definitely Morzinski's. "It's really you, Morzinski?"

"In the flesh." Andrzej offered him a hand, and Sebastjan took it.

Once back on his feet, he brushed himself off. "You have an unfortunate habit of knocking me down. What are you doing here?"

"I should ask you the same question. Recall, my family home is not a day's ride from here." There was a recognizable twinkle to the sunken eyes.

"Why did you attack me?"

"I heard some fool crashing wildly through the woods. I didn't know if you were friend or foe, so I waited for you and checked."

"You sent your dog to lure me to you so you could attack me?"

"Did Peter find you then? I thought he was just off hunting."

Sebastjan discovered his backside was wet from his fall, but the moisture wasn't yet seeping through his outer garments. "I would have preferred a more gracious greeting, but I'm glad to see you." He studied the other man. "You really should take greater care with your appearance, Morzinski. I'm still not sure I recognize you."

"I didn't have a great deal of time for grooming with a war going on," he remarked dryly.

"Oh." Sebastjan appeared chagrined. "I intended to join the Polish forces myself, but my Uncle Edward wouldn't hear of it. In the end, I decided to disobey him. But by the time I got back to Poland, it was all over. King Stanislas had abdicated."

"But what are you doing so far east?" Andrzej got straight to the point.

"I do have lands south of here."

"Significantly south, if they are still your lands. That might have changed."

"To be honest, I had hoped to visit… er, that is, I wanted to make sure all was well at Sweet Air. Have you had any news?"

"From home? No, not in some time. The couriers stopped transporting messages months ago."

"So you haven't heard from either your father or Krystyna in quite a while?"

"I have not. Come, daylight is wasting. Tonight, we will dine at my father's table." Andrzej limped to where his lean steed was tethered.

"What about my horse?"

"He won't have gone far. There's nothing around here for miles. I'll bring him back, and we can proceed on together."

In no time at all, Andrzej located the missing animal and returned him to his rider. Once both men were mounted, they kept a steady pace through the familiar countryside. They rode silently, wrapped up in their respective thoughts. These past months, Andrzej had wrestled with his fears for Krystyna and for his father. Now that he was close to home, he was tightly coiled. What if they were gone, or worse dead? The possibilities were too horrible to contemplate. Memories of his home, his father, and his beloved were what had sustained him through the endless months of warfare. Now, his country was no more. If they were gone, too, what then was left for him? His horse stumbled but caught himself. The motion jarred Andrzej's thigh. He rubbed at where the puckered, healing skin itched mercilessly.

It was twilight when they crested the ridge from which one could see Sweet Air. He pulled harshly back on the reins. "My God!"

"What?" Sebastjan questioned as he came up behind him. "What's wrong?"

Andrzej didn't answer. Instead, he kicked his tired horse into a gallop. Sebastjan followed only slightly more cautiously.

Andrzej charged his blowing and lathered horse directly into what had once been the courtyard of his home. There, he dismounted and took in the devastation around him. The main house was utterly gone; all that remained was a great pile of burnt beams and scorched sections of walls. Most of the outbuildings were also complete losses.

"Hold the horses," he ordered in a choked voice as he began to wander through the rubble of his home.

Sebastjan scrambled to obey. "What happened?"

Andrzej spun about. "Are you blind, man? They burned it."

"But who, and why?"

He didn't respond. Instead, he fell to his knees, covering his face with his hands. "God, why did you preserve me?" The question burst forth from him.

Sebastjan, still not comprehending the devastation, asked. "But what about your father and Krystyna?"

Andrzej looked up at him. To his dismay, Sebastjan saw tears on the other man's face and glimpsed unspeakable pain and loss in his eyes.

"Krystyna's dead. So is my father."

"But you can't be sure. You don't know."

"Look around you." He swept his arm to encompass the scene of devastation. "Now leave me!"

Sebastjan jumped. Then, he moved to obey. He led the horses back to what remained of the stable, to secure them for the night. For, it appeared they would be spending it in the ruins. He had no intention of abandoning Andrzej. Krystyna would have wanted him to stay with him, to help her beloved. And he intended to do both, at least until he had made certain of her fate.

Several hours later, Sebastjan sat by their fire, nibbling stale bread. His eyes kept darting around their makeshift campsite. It was like sleeping in a graveyard. They had settled for the night just outside the ruins of the great house, and he kept imagining that he saw things, heard noises. In addition, he felt exposed and vulnerable in their present location. Many lawless men wandered the countryside who would feel no qualms about slitting their throats for their horses or supplies or for no reason at all.

For a moment, he thought back to that troop of Hessians who'd escorted him back to Austria after his last trip into Poland. This time, his uncle hadn't approved of his venture. In fact, he'd berated and even mocked him. In the end, he'd washed his hands of Sebastjan. "You're just like your mother. You won't listen to reason. When you find out how difficult it is to be on your own, you'll come crawling back to me, unless you're killed by some highwayman first." Sebastjan had managed to survive, but just barely. The further east he'd traveled, the more dangerous it had become. It was one reason he'd been glad to encounter Andrzej, despite the fact that he was married to the woman Sebastjan loved. He'd never wished the other man ill. He genuinely liked and admired him. But it had been a bloody war, and if Krystyna had been left widowed… Admittedly, he'd enjoyed some daydreams about comforting her.

But such thoughts didn't do him credit. They were unworthy of a gentleman, and for the first time in as long as he could remember, he wanted to live up to the full meaning of that word. His new plan was to help Krystyna and Andrzej to the best of his ability, and he couldn't accept that it should all end like this. He wasn't ready to turn his horse around and ride back in the same direction he'd come. Krystyna couldn't be dead.

He glanced over at his silent companion who continued to stare blankly into the fire with his hand on Peter's ruff. Andrzej hadn't spoken in hours except to refuse when Sebastjan tried to talk him into riding on.

After his initial display of pain and anguish, Andrzej had retreated into this silent shell. He automatically assisted with preparations for the night, but his expression was distant and shuttered.

"So where are we going tomorrow?" Sebastjan asked.

"I'm going after whoever did this, and then I'm going to kill them." His tone was flat, emotionless.

"How do you even know where to start looking?"

"Someone will have seen something. To achieve this end," he swung his arm wide to encompass the devastation around them, "a sizeable troop of men was involved. They will have left a trail."

"We should set out early in the morning."

Andrzej turned his dark and soulless eyes upon him. "I'm going alone."

"We can't lose hope that we may find Krystyna," Sebastjan spoke quietly, poking at the fire, "not when there's still a chance."

"What? What did you say?"

"She may still be alive."

Andrzej shook his head slowly, never looking away from

Sebastjan's eyes. "You love her, too, don't you? Look around you. There were no survivors. We both have to accept that she is gone. There is no use in pretending otherwise. But I cannot help but wonder what she must have suffered, what they all must have suffered before their ends. I must know."

Sebastjan leapt to his feet. "I just saw someone back there! By the barn!"

"Where?" Andrzej was on his feet instantly. He drew a wicked, long knife from its sheath.

"There. See! That's a man running."

Both of them took off after the intruder, but Sebastjan was the quicker. He brought him to ground with a flying leap at his shoulders. They grappled about, but Andrzej grasped the man by his hair and placed his blade to his neck.

"Don't kill me please. By the Virgin, I beg you."

"Kaspar? Kaspar!" Andrzej dropped his knife and pushed Sebastjan off.

CHAPTER 34

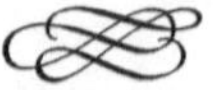

"Pan Morzinski?" Kaspar sounded equally stunned.

"Yes. It's me, Kaspar."

"You're alive! What a blessing. Your father will be so happy!"

"My father is alive?"

"Yes! We've been living in the nurse's cottage. I've been watching this place, and I saw your fire. I came to see who was here."

"They didn't kill Father?" Andrzej was incredulous.

"No, but they left him to die. He's not been well, Pan Morzinski," Kaspar's voice trailed off. "I was gone for a few days. Your father permitted me to go and help my brother and his family. Everything was fine when I left. Then, when I came back," he shook his head. "If I'd known, I never would have left. I swear it."

Andrzej reached out and gripped the other man's shoulder. "You did nothing wrong, my friend. You saved my father's life. I'm in your debt. But what happened to Krystyna and the others?"

"Gone. Your father will be better able to tell you what

happened. Come, let's go to him." Kaspar tugged eagerly on his sleeve.

A short while later, Andrzej stood outside the cottage door. Sebastjan and Kaspar remained at a distance out of respect for this first reunion between father and son. He raised his hand to knock. Then, he reconsidered and pushed it open.

"Kaspar, close the door. The draft." His father's voice spoke. He sounded weak, tired and querulous. He lay on a makeshift bed set by the hearth.

Wordlessly, Andrzej moved through the familiar darkness until he stood behind the bed. The chamber was stiflingly warm after the cool, fresh out-of-doors. The fire cast a flickering red glow on the scene. Roderyk didn't move from his reclined position.

Andrzej closed his eyes and took a deep breath. At last, he'd come home. For the first time in so long, he dared to hope. His father was alive. Maybe Krystyna…

"Kaspar, you tell me I need to rest then you continue to bother me by popping in and out. I cannot sleep with the door continually opening and closing."

As his father muttered his irritation, Andrzej moved to stand at his side. Roderyk's eyes remained closed, and shadows danced in his hollowed cheeks. He looked older, ages older than when Andrzej had last seen him. He took one frail, long fingered hand, and pressed it to his cheek. "Father… Father… It is I."

The lined lids didn't flicker. "Dreaming again, curse it!"

"Father, I've come home."

Roderyk's eyes fluttered opened. The claw-like fingers in Andrzej's grasp clutched desperately at his face. "My son! My son!" He struggled to sit up and embraced his son with all that remained of his once great strength.

Tears slid unashamedly down both faces.

"What a miracle, a blessing! You're alive! You cannot imagine the hell of not knowing, of fearing you were dead." He drew back enough to rest his palms on either side of Andrzej's face and studied the much-loved features. Peter chose that moment to hop up onto the bed. "And Peter, too. It's just my luck that this beast would survive a war." He chuckled through his tears.

"Where is Krystyna?"

"Krystyna isn't here."

Yet again, Andrzej experienced the cruel twist of terror in his innards. "Where is she? Is she…?"

"Russians came to Sweet Air. They were no regular unit, mostly mercenaries and scoundrels, and a beast named Bestuzhev led them. We, Krystyna, Matylda and I, hid when they took the house. I had already sent the servants away. I should have sent Krystyna, too, but she wouldn't leave me. I should have made her go, but I didn't know the Russians were so close. I'm sorry, my son. I've failed you in this. They captured Matylda and tortured her until she revealed our hiding place. They came for me there, but Krystyna wasn't with me. She'd gone for water and hadn't returned. I didn't know what happened to her until later. They took her. The Russian count, their leader, knew Krystyna before. He's the one who has been pursuing her these years. His name's Bestuzhev.

"They didn't bother killing me because they knew I'd not last much longer anyway. They left me lying in the mud like an animal to watch as my home burned down. And I would have died, but Kaspar found me." Having fought to get all of the words out, Roderyk began to cough. The force of the coughs wracked his frail body, and Andrzej held onto his father until the fit passed, and his breathing grew calmer.

He swallowed hard when he saw that the handkerchief his father pressed to his mouth was now spotted red with blood.

"Father, we must get a physician for you."

"I would be better served by a priest, Andrzej."

"Don't say that. We'll go after them."

"You'll take me nowhere, boy. I'll only slow you down. No, let me die here where I've lived my entire life. You go after Krystyna, and no matter what has happened to her, love her."

"I'll bring her back, Father, or die trying. Then, we'll all be together."

Roderyk cocked one thick, white eyebrow dubiously.

"Have you any horses?"

"They were all stolen. There's something else you should know. Brasinski led Bestuzhev and his men here."

"You saw him?"

"That coward didn't dare to show his face to me, but I heard my captors speak of him. When I think I invited that snake into my home…"

"Did you hear anything else?"

"They've gone to Russia, to Moscow."

"How long ago did they leave?"

"Five days ago. But they were in no hurry, and they would be traveling slowly, burdened as they are with ill-gotten gains."

"Five days," Andrzej echoed despairingly.

"Sleep a few hours. You'll be better for it. Your horse must rest as well. I've prayed to the Virgin Mother over these matters. Now, she has returned you to me. Soon Krystyna will be safe also. Then, I will be at peace."

CHAPTER 35

Andrzej and Sebastjan readied their horses the following day. Peter waited patiently by his master. Kaspar had provided them with food and other necessaries. With clean clothes and a full stomach, Andrzej felt more alert and ready than he had in weeks.

Saying goodbye to his father proved difficult. Roderyk had gripped him fiercely with his wasted arms. "Bring her back, Andrzej. She's the woman for you. Then, leave Poland. Don't come back here."

"Father, of course I'll return."

"Andrzej, there's nothing left for you here. I'm dying, and I'm sick and tired of fighting it. If I know you two are safe and well then, I can let go. Don't spoil the one joy left to me by coming back here."

"I can't just leave you."

"Wherever you go, son, I'll be with you. Across the ocean, there's a whole new land and room enough for a bold, enterprising young pair. Nothing will be the same here. We are now an occupied country… Do you see that coffer there?"

"This one?" Andrzej stepped over to a small, wooden chest set on the table by the bed.

"Look inside."

He opened it and sucked in a breath, viewing the bounty of jewelry inside. He picked up a garnet necklace. "It's the Morzinski jewels."

"I hid them out here months ago. They were sure to be stolen from the house. Now I want you to take them. Use them to fund your future."

"No, it would be wrong."

"Would you leave them here for Brasinski to steal along with the land? No, it's all yours and Krystyna's now. Take it to begin a new life."

In the end, Andrzej emptied the coffer into a soft, deerskin satchel he then secured under his saddlebags.

As he prepared to depart, he hadn't been ashamed of the tears that wet his cheeks. For he knew it was unlikely he'd ever see his father alive again, and there appeared to be little left for him here in the land of his forefathers.

Renard, his mount, snorted and tossed his head, clearly ready to be off.

"Shall we?" Sebastjan asked respectfully.

Andrzej nodded. "We ride east, toward Brasinski's estate. Someone will have seen this troop of Russians."

Krystyna lay atop the bed in the dingy chamber. Saddle sore, mentally exhausted and more than a little defeated, she hadn't been able to summon the energy or enthusiasm to eat. They'd been traveling for more than a week now. With each passing day, every passing hour, the odds of her rescue diminished. Pan Roderyk was likely dead. If, by some miracle, Andrzej lived and returned to Sweet Air, he would never guess what happened to her. He might even believe she'd run away and abandoned his father. After all, he'd doubted her before, after she left him in Vienna. She couldn't blame him if he thought the worst of her now, though she hoped and prayed that he wouldn't.

She was well and truly trapped. Shifting in her bed, she glanced around the room. The bed on which she lay was hard and lumpy, and probably infested with bed bugs, but the linens looked and smelled reasonably clean. In addition, a fire burned in the hearth and oilskins tightly covered the small windows, so the room was warm. She had stripped off her travel-stained clothing and crawled under the blankets in only her shift, but falling asleep proved impossible. Her fate was in her own hands, and she had to come up with an escape plan, but nothing plausible came to mind. Eventually, she dozed fitfully.

She awoke when a rough hand clamped across her mouth and a thick arm encircled her body. Instantly awake, she fought her attacker. The man reeked of rank sweat and foul body odor. He was much stronger than she, and he used his weight and his strength to bear her down into the bed. When Krystyna felt the blunt, cold jab of a pistol muzzle below her breast, she went still.

"Don't cry out, or I'll kill you now," Count Bestuzhev ground out, his breath rank with garlic and spirits.

In that instant, Krystyna realized she wanted to live, that despite everything, all that she'd already lost, she didn't intend to lose her life as well.

"You will be quiet?" He dug his pistol more painfully into her ribcage. Silently, she nodded.

"Brasinski's gone. There is no one for you to call. Understand?" Krystyna nodded again. Then, the smothering hand moved away from her mouth. Greedily, she sucked in air. The bed shifted, and she was free. Bestuzhev stood up, set his pistol carelessly down on a small, round bedside table, struck a flint and lit a candle. She measured the distance to the pistol and concluded there was no way she could get to it before he did. He had only to reach over.

Dragging over a wooden chair, he sank heavily into it. It creaked under the burden of his weight. His eyes were moist and heavy lidded while his pock marked skin was ruddy. He'd obviously been drinking heavily.

Acutely aware of her vulnerability in this situation, she shrank back into the shadows and adjusted the pile of bedding more securely over her body. She glanced over at the door. He sat between it and her, and if, by some miracle, she made it to the door, men were sure to be stationed in the hall and downstairs. Her wits were her only defense.

"At home, in Russia, my brother and I used to hunt wolves," Bestuzhev began. He stared at his hands as he stretched and flexed his blunt, thick fingers. His nails were dirty and ragged. "I remember one wolf, in particular. It was in January, and the snows were deep. This she-wolf had been preying on livestock, but no one had managed to catch her. She was too clever for any of the traps the serfs set. Then, one of them came to my father's house and told us of the beast.

"From the first, I knew that she-wolf was meant to be mine. I convinced Ivan that it would a great adventure to go after her. For more than two weeks in miserable weather, he and I tracked her. She was a lone creature, with no sign of pack or mate. To this day, I swear she knew we were after her. She played games with us, toyed with us. Eventually, Ivan grew tired of the hunt, of the conditions. We were low on supplies, sick and cold. He wanted to return home and argued that the she-wolf was now so far from our lands that it wouldn't matter if we didn't kill her.

"But I wouldn't give up. I knew we were embarked on more than a hunt, that she was no mere wolf. But Ivan didn't see it that way. We fought. He cursed me, said he wanted to leave. I told him I would kill him if he did.

"That very night, the she-wolf made a fatal mistake. In many ways, it was strange. She had avoided so many bait traps, but this one, she walked right up to it. She may have been starving, but wolves can last quite a while without food. She wasn't yet dead when I came upon her. I can still picture her, her body gray and black, her blood crimson against the whiteness of the snow. Her eyes shone golden and unblinking." He went silent for a moment, lost in his memory.

Krystyna couldn't resist asking, "Did you release her?"

He gaped at her then guffawed with laughter. "I shot the bitch right between the eyes."

Her heart pounded frantically now.

"What did you feel when you murdered my brother?"

Krystyna hesitated, completely unsure of how to respond.

"Why did you kill him? We had discussed everything, planned it all out. What went wrong? Ivan was handsome and charming. Women threw themselves at him. You adored him. I saw the way your eyes followed him when I visited your father's estate. I knew you two had worked out all sorts of stratagems to be alone together. He imagined himself in love with you."

"And yet I found him seducing one of the maids."

"Then you murdered him out of jealousy."

"I swear to you, I didn't murder Ivan. It was an accident. I told him I wouldn't marry him, and it seemed he accepted my decision. But one night, he broke into my bedroom and attacked me. When my parents rushed in, he swore I'd invited him there. Ivan thought my father would force me to marry him. But Papa didn't. He ordered Ivan from the house and forbade him to return. A few nights later, I found Ivan in the stable. He was drunk and attempting to steal my father's best breeding stallion. I should have gone for help, but I didn't. I just wanted to stop him. The stallion panicked. He reared up then fell. Ivan was crushed beneath him. It was an accident."

Lunging forward, Bestuzhev backhanded her across the face, driving her back onto the bed. He loomed over her, furious and immense, his breath unremittingly foul. “Lying bitch! You murdered him. I know what happened. There was a pitchfork driven through his heart. I heard it from a servant who saw his body.”

Krystyna felt his spittle on her face and resisted the urge to wipe it away. Bestuzhev would never believe her. His hate and anger had fueled him for three years. She ignored the coppery taste of blood in her mouth. “You mean to kill me.” It was a statement, not a question. “You would betray Brasinski?”

“He was useful, he brought me to you. And now that the hunt is over, I won’t allow him to cheat me of my just reward. Killing you is not enough. I want it all now, revenge and wealth, and you are the key to both. Why should I share anything with him?”

He leaned closer still. “Of course you will die.” Suddenly, he dug his fingers into her hair and yanked her upright and against him. “On the day Ivan died, your life was forfeited to me. You are mine, my possession.” Then, he ground his foul, meaty mouth against hers. His tongue thrust against her lips. At first, she resisted by turning her head from side to side. Then, she stopped and opened her teeth minutely. Again, his tongue sought entry, and she clamped down hard. As he reared back in pain, she smashed her knee into his groin. He howled in agony.

Leaping from the bed, she flew to the door and found it locked. Bestuzhev staggered to his feet. His eyes glazed with agony, and his expression was one of murderous intent.

There was nowhere for her to go, no one to call. Looking about desperately, she sought a weapon. He lunged, and she struck out wildly with both fists and feet as she felt his fingers close around her throat. The pressure was unbearable. She fought frantically, pulled at those iron hands that bore her unremittingly down.

Desperate for air, she scratched him and bit, but found her vision beginning to cloud, and her movements growing weaker.

Suddenly, a shot rang out. The unbearable pressure around

her throat abruptly ceased. She sucked in air, deeply and raggedly.

Bestuzhev's bulk collapsed forward onto her. She struggled to thrust the bleeding corpse from her. Then, hands helped her, drawing her up to a sitting position.

"You killed him." The observation emerged from her lips in a strangled sort of hiss.

CHAPTER 36

"Yes, but it was sooner than I'd intended," Viktor Brasinski agreed as he offered her a hand. Krystyna deliberately ignored his gesture. She raised herself up, staring in shock at Bestuzhev, the enemy who'd chased her across two countries for three years and irrevocably altered the fabric of her life. It was difficult to grasp that he was dead, when seconds before he'd been so close to killing her.

Brasinski's expression was sardonic and amused. "I suspected Grigori planned to break the terms of our agreement, but as a gentleman, I tried to adhere to them until I knew he would not. Thus, I gave him this time alone with you as a test." He prodded the body with a booted toe. "He failed. Grigori lacked vision. He was so set on revenge he couldn't see the true potential of the situation."

"He was mad."

"I quite agree."

Krystyna became aware of the Russian's blood covering the front of her shift. She shuddered as she drew one section of scarlet cloth away from where it adhered to her body.

"My dear, it appears that you owe me." He calmly stepped

over his fallen comrade's body. "Let's drink to celebrate the change in my fortunes. For, it appears I'm about to become a wealthy man." He opened the door and stepped into the hallway. "Vladimir," he called out. "Ah, there you are," he turned his back and gestured at Bestuzhev's body as the hooded figure of a man moved up behind him. "The Count underestimated the young lady and suffered an unfortunate accident. Please tend to this. We will be retiring to my rooms."

"I don't think so." The man drew back his hood. A draft caused the candle to flicker madly, and it was Andrzej Morzinski who stood on the threshold, a cocked pistol in his hand.

"Andrzej!" Krystyna stepped toward him.

"Morzinski!" Brasinski reacted immediately, lunging for Krystyna. In the wink of an eye, he had an arm about her neck and was pressing a vicious looking blade to her throat. "Put down your pistol. I'll kill her! Don't doubt me."

Andrzej squatted and carefully set the gun on the floor. He raised his hands in supplication. His eyes met Krystyna's, and he sought to reassure her with the look in his own. There was no point in endangering her through a direct attack. He needed time. "Viktor, there's no need to proceed with this. We've known each other our entire lives. We can work out a compromise here. I know you're a reasonable man."

"I'm amazed to see you still alive. This has been quite a night for surprises. I would never have expected you to be so resourceful. However did you get past my men?"

"It wasn't so difficult or heroic. I came up through the servants' entrance."

"I left Vasilii at that door."

Andrzej shrugged.

"Again, you surprise me. You were always so tender-hearted as a boy. You've changed."

"A war will do that. Viktor, let Krystyna go. There's no point in killing her. You've won. All of Sweet Air will soon be yours.

She's all I want. Let her go, and we'll be out of your life. You don't need her."

"Andrzej," Krystyna's voice was little more than a throaty whisper.

"Be still, woman!" Brasinski barked. The fierce grip by which he held her and her blood beading on the tip of the knife he pressed to her throat assured her of the deadly serious nature of his intent. "Morzinski, this girl is the key. The one who holds her stands to gain a fortune. I'm afraid I will require her for some time yet."

"Do you?" Andrzej countered calmly with one dark eyebrow cocked. "Sweet Air falls in that region of Poland which is sure to go to Russia. We both know the Tsarina will reward those loyal to her."

"The girl comes with me."

"I won't allow that. You've destroyed my home, abused my father, kidnapped my wife and dragged her almost to Russia. It's enough now. It's all over." Andrzej took a step closer.

"Stay where you are!" Brasinski shouted. Krystyna began to struggle. "Don't move, wench. I'll cut your throat. I will!"

"Krystyna," Andrzej cautioned with a raised hand.

She went still and swallowed hard. Her neck burned where the tip of the blade pressed in.

"Did you expect to simply come up here and spirit her away?" Brasinski demanded incredulously. "You are more of a fool than I thought. It's unfortunate you managed to survive the war, but I don't believe you will last long in a Russian prison. The Tsarina doesn't care for rabble rousers. You forget who holds the winning hand in this game. Aleksei! Dmitri! Vlad!"

A rumble of running footsteps pounded down the hallway, and Brasinski's henchmen burst through the door. "Take him," Brasinski directed. The large, thuggish men took in the scene, including Bestuzhev's body and then set upon Andrzej.

Two of them rushed him and were upon him before he

could grasp his pistol. After kicking a blade from one man's hand, Andrzej drew his own and thrust only to lose his weapon as the weight and momentum of an opponent's body carried him to the floor. He grappled furiously with another assailant, and by sheer strength managed to come out on top. As he was striving to wrest the knife from the man, a blow crashed down onto the back of his skull. The world went black.

He awoke in a gray haze. Struggling against the muddle of his vision and his mind, he glanced about the room. Krystyna now sat on the bed. She watched him with concern. Tear tracks streaked her cheeks, and her eyes remained suspiciously bright. He winked at her to indicate that he was all right, disregarding the throbbing pain in his head.

"You've returned to the world of the living," Brasinski announced cheerfully. He sat in a chair opposite him with Andrzej's pistol trained upon him. Brasinski's men remained in attendance. At his gesture, they heaved Andrzej upright with his arms pinned back. His legs wobbled and wouldn't support his weight, so two men held him up.

Brasinski stood up and stepped closer to him, tucking the pistol into his belt. Krystyna hadn't moved from her strangely stiff position. Andrzej saw that her hands and feet were bound.

"You always were an impetuous fool." Brasinski slammed his fist into Andrzej's stomach.

Krystyna cried out as he doubled over.

"Did it seem prudent to you to confront me alone? No doubt you thought to play the hero by coming here and carrying your bride away. At least now I can be sure she's a widow when we wed in Moscow. Krystyna and Sweet Air will both be mine. You've lost everything." Brasinski pounded his fists into Andrzej's midsection and sides. Then, he struck him with a forceful back handed blow across his face.

Andrzej's lip tore from impact with Brasinski's signet ring.

Puffing and reddening with his exertion, Brasinski brushed a long strand of hair back from his forehead.

"Stop! There's no reason to torture him. Please, I'll do what you want."

Bransinski turned to Krystyna, who now openly sobbed. "My lady, it's time to bid farewell to your husband."

Andrzej needed a few more minutes, and there was one sure way of obtaining them. He spit the blood pooling in his mouth onto the floor. "Brasinski, you've always been a coward, as well as a traitor and a thief." His words were thick, fuzzy and slow.

Predictably, the other man attacked him with renewed strength and fury. Andrzej sagged against the arms that held him.

When he'd vented his fury, Brasinski snarled into his ear. "Your priceless honor has earned you nothing but failure and death. Die knowing I have everything that you value." Brasinski pulled out the pistol and leveled it at him.

The door crashed open. A large, snarling wolf-like dog launched himself upon Brasinski. Andrzej glimpsed Sebastjan's pale face in the doorway before someone or something knocked over the candle. Now the only light in the chamber was the dull, reddish glow from the fire in the hearth. Suddenly, he was released. He heard Peter growling deep in his throat, footsteps running, furniture being knocked about. Blindly, he struck out, encountering yielding flesh more than once. He tripped over a flailing body but rose up swinging wildly.

He caught an uppercut on the side of his chin, but managed to stay on his feet, and delivered a series of blows to an opponent's stomach and chest. The man retreated. But Andrzej followed him, dispensing a punishing combination. Stepping over his now fallen foe, he waded further into the melee. He heard a dog growling furiously, muttered oaths and the sounds of blows landing as he lurched toward a struggling pair. One of the men turned and grabbed at him. They grappled.

The door swung wide again, casting more light on the

combatants. The man whom Andrzej was fighting suddenly collapsed to the ground. He glanced up to see Krystyna teetering precariously on her bound feet, a heavy candlestick dangling from her fettered hands. Brasinski struggled with Sebastjan by the bed. In the next moment, Andrzej was driven to his knees from behind. He fought to keep his assailant from getting a good grip on his neck. The man shifted off of him when Peter sank his teeth into the Russian's thigh.

He shrieked in pain and rolled about frantically, but the dog wouldn't release his hold. Andrzej dispatched the Russian with his own dagger.

Then, a shot reverberated in the small room. Everyone froze. Viktor Brasinski rose up slowly from the bed where Sebastjan still lay. Andrzej glimpsed the dark sheen of blood on the man's linen shirt and the projecting hilt of a knife before he crumpled to the floor.

Krystyna was suddenly on her knees beside him, kissing him, pressing herself against him.

He embraced her equally deliriously. "Krystyna! Krystyna. It's all right. It's over now," he murmured between kisses to her lips, her forehead and her nose. "You came for me!"

"Of course, I did. Thank God you're alive! Are you…well?" He searched her eyes, looking for some sign that her spirit hadn't been damaged by her ordeal.

"Yes, I am now. I love you."

"And I you, but we have to get out of here." He made quick work of untying her hands and feet and tenderly raised her up. Together, they turned to face Sebastjan who, curiously enough, still reclined upon the bed. "Sebastjan, what took you so long? I'd about given up hope," Andrzej teased.

Still, Sebastjan didn't move. "It took longer than I'd expected and more vodka than I'd planned to get that sleeping draft to take effect on those Russians downstairs. Fortunately, most of the troop was quartered in tents by the river. Still, it cost me a small fortune. My uncle would be appalled. I may have been late, Morzinski, but I didn't miss the action this time. I think I even managed to finish Brasinski off. Remarkable. It's such a simple thing, to kill a man."

Krystyna offered him a tremulous smile. "Dear Sebastjan. You came as well. What are you doing in Poland?"

"I should think that's obvious, rescuing a fair damsel."

"You are a good man, Sebastjan, and a true friend."

"Come, you two. Let's be on our way." Andrzej moved toward the door. "Where are the horses?"

"In the stable. I paid a lad to have them tacked up and ready to go. However, I'm afraid I won't be joining you," he continued, still not moving from his supine position.

CHAPTER 37

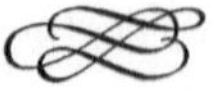

"You can't stay here. The Russians…"

"I don't believe they'll be a problem for me."

"You overestimate your social skills, deSzinay."

"It's not a question of whether I wish to join you, Morzinski. But I find myself unable to do so, despite my most fervent desire."

"What nonsense are you spouting?"

"Andrzej, look." Krystyna pointed to where a dark stain was spreading out beneath Sebastjan onto the bed linens.

Stepping closer, she could make out a powder stain and a darkened hole in the rich green material of Sebastjan's coat. She kneeled down by the bed.

"Let me see," Andrzej gruffly ordered. "These past few months, I've gained an unfortunate familiarity with wounds. "Krystyna, would you please get the lamp from the hall?"

She was back in a moment with it, and she set it on the table by the bed. Sebastjan didn't protest. He lay still and allowed the other man to open his garments. Andrzej's lips thinned with dismay. Krystyna saw it, but Sebastjan was oblivious.

He was staring up at her. "Would you take care of some matters for me?"

"Of course. But you will be better in a short while and able to manage them yourself."

"Hold still, this will not be comfortable." Andrzej rolled Sebastjan onto his side and applied pressure to the gushing exit wound.

Sebastjan struggled to maintain his composure. He bit his lip against the pain. "Please, Krystyna, hold my hand."

She took his outstretched hand. "Don't worry, Sebastjan. You'll be fine."

He grimaced. "There's no point in pretending. This isn't at all the end I or anyone else expected for me. Uncle Edward will be most surprised. That last night in Vienna," he shut his eyes against a new wave of pain.

Andrzej met Krystyna's glance. He shook his head, his expression grave. Carefully, he lay Sebastjan back down onto the bed. "Rest, deSzinay, and lie still."

It didn't appear the other man heard him for he continued on, "He berated me for wasting my life. He said I would probably die drunk and choking on my own vomit. You will tell him, won't you, about all of this? He said I was craven and worthless. He wasn't far wrong. He's one of the main reasons I returned to Poland. It sounds foolish, but I wanted to prove him wrong. It was my luck to arrive after the war was over."

"The war wasn't over for you or for me," Andrzej countered.

"You're no coward," Krystyna asserted. "You'll tell your uncle yourself about how you valiantly saved us all."

As she brushed the damp, blond locks from his forehead, Sebastjan's fine features relaxed. "I did, didn't I? I suppose that makes me a hero, of a sort. Morzinski, sorry I was late."

"Your timing was impeccable."

"I'm cold, very cold." He began to shake.

Andrzej gently laid the bed coverings across him. Then, Krystyna said, "We should stoke the fire."

"Don't leave me."

"But you're cold."

"Please stay, Krystyna, and hold my hand."

But she was already gripping his right hand, so she seized his left. "I'm here, Sebastjan."

"Krystyna?" His voice was fainter, tremulous. "You know I love you, that I always have, don't you? You'll remember me sometimes, won't you?"

"Of course, I care deeply for you, too."

"But you don't love me. Not in the way that I have loved you. It's only ever been Morzinski for you. But this makes me special, doesn't it?"

"Oh, Sebastjan." She pressed her forehead to his arm.

"The pendant…my mother's pendant." He let go of her to grasp weakly at his neck.

She reached out to pull the necklace from beneath his cravat, which she loosened.

"Will you take it as gift from me now, to remember me sometimes?"

"Sebastjan, don't…"

"I've never been very religious. I always thought I would have time enough to make up for it. You think they will let me in, to Heaven, I mean?" He paused and drew a gurgling breath. "I should pray now. Some prayer. I can't think… Our Father, who art in heaven."

Andrzej and Krystyna picked up the prayer when Sebastjan's voice tapered off. His hands had gone limp in Krystyna's.

CHAPTER 38

Dawn was breaking over the horizon as the two riders paused. A dog gamboled along before them. One of the horses snorted gray plumes into the chill air, and the other stamped its hoof. The pair faced east, surveying the burial mound and rough wooden cross that stood out blackly against the morning light.

Krystyna felt exhausted, ancient, as she surveyed the unhallowed ground where they'd laid Sebastjan to rest after Andrzej had carried him from the inn. She toyed with the pendant around her neck. She wasn't yet used to it. Then, feeling herself the object of scrutiny, she glanced up to find her husband's eyes upon her.

"He was a hero, and he died a hero's death. But we have to keep living to make his sacrifice meaningful."

She nodded slowly, now staring at the horizon. "Then, let's ride west. To Sweet Air."

"My father may not be there to welcome us. He was not long for this world when last I saw him. But let's go there to bid our farewells."

"Then, you mean for us to leave Sweet Air?" She stared at him.

"There's likely nothing left for us there. Next, we'll go on to Vienna," Andrzej paused, his eyes lingering on the mounded dirt over Sebastjan's grave. "From there, England, and then perhaps even further west. Thaddeus Kosciuszko often spoke of America. It's a whole new world, wide open, free. We could make of it whatever we wished."

"A whole new world." The words held sweet promise and hope.

"Yes," she spoke determinedly. "We ride west. To a new life."

The End

~

Don't miss out on your next favorite book!

Join the Satin Romance mailing list
www.satinromance.com/mail.html

GLOSSARY OF POLISH TERMS

Na Zdrowie—On health (A toast)

Pan—Gentleman, Mister, Sir, Squire, Lord, Master, Mr.

Pani—Lady, Mrs., Dame, Mum, Ma'am, Madam

Panienka—Girl, Lass, Miss, Damsel, Young Lady

Seym—This was the Polish legislative body of the time

Szlachta—Nobility, Gentry, Gentlefolks, Gentlefolk

All translations came from www.poltran.com.

THANK YOU FOR READING

~

Did you enjoy this book?

We invite you to leave a review at your favorite book site, such as Goodreads, Amazon, Barnes & Noble, etc.

DID YOU KNOW THAT LEAVING A REVIEW…

- Helps other readers find books they may enjoy.
- Gives you a chance to let your voice be heard.
- Gives authors recognition for their hard work.
- Doesn't have to be long. A sentence or two about why you liked the book will do.

ABOUT THE AUTHOR

Isabelle Kane believes that romance and love are among the most delightful aspects of the human experience. She seeks to provide her readers with rich tapestries of stories in which love is just one element of the forces that intertwine the lives of her protagonists. She believes every dreamer deserves the adventures and escape offered by an exciting novel. The greatest sources of joy and inspiration in Isabelle's life are her husband and their three children. Isabelle is a graduate of Bryn Mawr College and holds an MA in English from the University of Wisconsin-Eau Claire.

For updates on Isabelle's writing,
please visit her at
www.kaneandtremaine.com

She loves to hear from readers. You can email her at kane.
tremaine@gmail.com

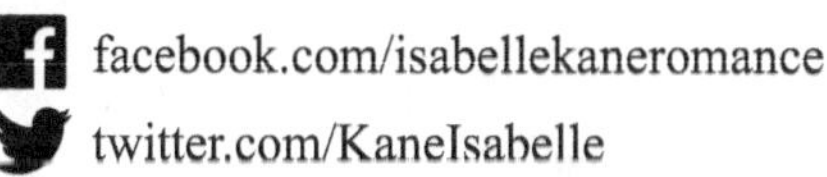

BOOKS BY ISABELLE KANE

One Last Farewell

Calypso's Secret

Eagle River

www.ingramcontent.com/pod-product-compliance
Lightning Source LLC
Chambersburg PA
CBHW050556260626
47157CB00002B/595

* 9 7 8 1 9 5 3 7 3 5 9 0 4 *